All That Mullarkey

All That Mullarkey

Sue Moorcroft

First published 2010 by Choc Lit Limited
Penrose House, Crawley Drive, Camberley, Surrey GU15 2AB
www.choclitpublishing.co.uk

A CIP catalogue record for this book is available
from the British Library

ISBN-978-1-906931-24-7

Mixed Sources
Product group from well-managed
forests and other controlled sources
FSC www.fsc.org Cert no.TT-COC-002063
© 1996 Forest Stewardship Council

Printed in the UK by CPI Cox & Wyman, Reading, RG1 8EX

To Paul
For being in the next room
writing songs that I'm the first to hear.
Love you, darling.

Acknowledgements

My thanks again to Det. Supt Mark Lacey for telling me about Friday nights at the nick, police procedure and how Crimestoppers works; Laura Longrigg; Mark West, who read the draft and had many perceptive remarks to make about Cleo. And to Roger, who read the script when I thought it was ready and pointed out a big hole in the plot.

Special thanks go to all those friends who shared their experiences of nuisance campaigns. Better if I don't name any names! Some of you have been so naughty.
To all at Choc Lit for supporting me with determination and enthusiasm, particularly Lyn, who understands the importance of chocolate and champagne, and Gill, copy editor extraordinaire.

And for all my friends in the Romantic Novelists' Association who made me see what is possible.

Prologue

Gav's key in the door. Cleo's heart skittered uneasily but she lifted her chin. All she had to do was tell him that she was going to the reunion.

All day she'd considered retreat; the easy option. The reunion would be full of her uni classmates of a decade ago, flashing their kids' photos, looking blank when she'd none to show in return, and babbling about the careers that their business studies degrees had earned them. She'd come home thinking, 'So what?' And Gav really, really didn't want her to go.

So why was she going?

Because Gav had told her she mustn't.

Now he stepped through the sitting-room door, tie untied and hanging, curls ruffled, jacket over his arm. Halted to take in her new jeans, shiny blue top and make-up, then slammed the door shut. 'So you're going to this piss-up, then? Even though you know how I feel about you hanging around with your ex?' He threw down his briefcase, yanked off his tie and flung it behind him.

Cleo kept her voice calm. 'You know I don't do as I'm told, Gav. Anyway, I'm not "hanging around with my ex" – I'm going to my course reunion. I'll have a few drinks with a few old mates, then come home.' She slipped into her jacket, flipping her hair clear of her collar. 'I don't know why you're so angry. Yes, I went out with someone on the same course and he might be there. Am I planning to jump his bones the instant we're in the same room? No. If you choose not to believe me –' She shrugged. 'It's you that's got the problem.'

A sudden crash made her jump. Before she could properly

take in the mark on the wall where Gav had kicked his briefcase against it, he was bawling in her face, eyes bulging. 'And I'm just supposed to sit home whilst you go out with your old boyfriend, am I? While you piss me about and make me look stupid?'

Furious colour scalded Cleo's cheeks but she stood her ground. 'I've never pissed you about! But if you don't trust me –!'

Gav's normally tidy hair hung into his eyes, sweat shone on his face. 'It simply isn't on!' he roared. 'You're supposed to be my wife!'

In her outrage, Cleo could hardly breathe. 'It was all over two years before I met you, just like it was all over between you and Stacey. You know that!' He didn't like talking about Stacey. Cleo knew how hurt he'd been when Stacey had ended things.

'I just don't want you to go!'

Cleo actually stamped in frustration. 'This stupid lack of trust is hardly any thanks for five years' loyalty, is it? Don't try to control me, because you can't!' Several heartbeats passed before she added, coldly, deliberately, 'And you never will.'

Gav halted. He gripped the back of the sofa, breathing hard, his face creased in disgust, as if he'd examined an apple and found a worm in it. 'Fuck you. If you go to the reunion, I won't be here when you come back. There will be no marriage.'

Fury blocked Cleo's throat. Black then red flickered across her vision and she trembled from her knees up. Over the clamour of her heart she forced out words to hang in the air between them. 'If that's how you feel, it's worthless anyway.'

Outside, her car key shook so much in her hand that it took three attempts to get it into the ignition. She ripped away from the kerb without looking, driving at a stupid speed out of the village, not noticing the ponies in the field or the nicest gardens or any of the things that made her love Middledip. She flew through Bettsbrough and into the traffic circulating Peterborough to find the big pub at Wansford, the venue for the reunion.

Half an hour later, her breathing had slowed. Reason prevailed. She slowed the car, indicated right at a roundabout and turned back.

However much she was not in the wrong, she felt sick to think of the way they'd screamed at each other. They'd suddenly found themselves careering down a slippery slope and she had to find a foothold. The sensible way would be to show Gav that their relationship was more important than some stupid reunion – even a stupid reunion she had every right to attend.

She'd sort things out. Discover why Gav was acting as if he were possessed by the insecurity demon.

They'd make up in bed. She presumed so, anyway. They'd never quarrelled like this.

Outside the house she drew up and saw that Gav's silver Focus was gone.

The front door was wide open. Cleo ran upstairs ... Gav's wardrobes and drawers stood open and ransacked.

And then. A moment of utter stillness and dislocation from the world, of horrified incomprehension, as she saw the message written large in thick, black marker pen on the bedroom wallpaper.

THIS MARRIAGE IS OVER. Love Gav.

Part 1

Cleo Callaway

Chapter One

Cleo's eyes burned with the effort of trying to pierce the ultraviolet glare of a nightclub that heaved with partying Friday-nighters, as she willed her sister's blonde head to bob into view. Liza had said she'd be here at Muggie's tonight.

Cleo needed Liza's sisterly arms around her, needed to rain foul insults on her absent husband (safe in the knowledge that, if Cleo forgave Gav, Liza would forget every word). And, as the bass and drums music thumped, Cleo had already texted her four times, without reply.

With a squeak of relief she glimpsed two golden heads and began wriggling her way towards them. 'Angie! Rochelle!' she gasped. Not Liza, but close. Angie and Rochelle, Liza's cronies and clones – hair up in a series of complicated plaits, necklines low and hems high – swung around and gave Cleo air-kissy little hugs. 'Cleo! *Hiya!*'

'Where's Liza?'

Angie, a starlet in scarlet, pouted heavily glossed lips as she raised her voice above the music. 'She's supposed to be here but we haven't seen her. Have you tried texting her? What you having?'

Cleo paused. She hadn't bothered with the bar yet but, actually, a drink would be perfect. Until Liza showed, Cleo could drink with Angie and Rochelle in this, the city centre's pick-up joint, simply because she knew how much Gav would hate it. If he was going to insult her with accusations of bad behaviour, she might as well behave badly. Alcohol would be a good starting point. She turned to the red leather and chrome bar and surveyed the bottles in the cold cabinet behind the scurrying black-clad bar staff. 'Lager, thanks.'

The pint of special brew Angie passed back to her wasn't quite the bottle of Becks she'd had in mind, but the big, fat, frosty glass felt satisfying. Gav hated her drinking pints.

She checked her mobile but found no texts and no voice messages. Aggravated that Gav wasn't even trying to get her – so that she could ignore him – she drank the pint down steadily and took her turn to buy a round, making her own another pint of special. Gav's giant strop had made her feel unsafe, unstable, as if she could combust at any moment. Fury clanked around inside her head. She needed Liza.

She kept one eye on the iron staircase that brought punters up into the club from the street below, hovering beside Angie and Rochelle as they quartered the room with beady eyes and heads on springs. 'There's Duncan, look, with Daniel. And Ross!' They waved across the room at men Cleo couldn't identify in the crowd.

Cleo couldn't even raise a smile, wishing deeply, dreadfully, that Liza would appear so that she could share her festering fury before she ripped someone's head off. She heaved a sigh.

'What's up wiv you?' Angie had recently affected an inability to pronounce certain words containing 'th'. 'You look like you're, like, spitting fevvers.'

'Nothing,' Cleo muttered. 'I just want to talk to Liza.'

Angie exchanged glances with Rochelle before asking, slyly, 'Your Gav not wiv you tonight?'

She shook her head, blinking back tears.

'Ah. Right.' Angie nodded, sagely.

Rochelle, eyes outlined startlingly in aquamarine, patted Cleo's arm. 'It'll be all right when you go home! He's probably waiting to make up.'

Cleo felt her eyes begin to melt. 'But he stormed off –'

Angie's attention was suddenly whipped away. 'Who's *that*?'

'Where?' Rochelle craned to follow her friend's gaze.

'There! Spiky hair, pointy face. Hot, or what?'

'Wow!' Rochelle's intake of breath was so deep her neckline almost gave way under the strain. 'He's looking! Make as if he knows us.'

Finger-twiddling waves in the direction of Spiky Hair ended in sighs of disappointment. Cleo glanced across as he threw back his head and laughed with two men wearing excruciatingly short platinum crops and wrap-around shades. Angie and Rochelle were probably missing the pulling power of Liza, tiny, fey, blonde man magnet. Cleo had long ago accepted philosophically that Liza was the one who turned heads. She didn't mind because Liza, her kid sister, heap of trouble, oddball, was one of Cleo's favourite people.

Cleo had what their mother (another tiny, fey, etc.) termed 'dark and uncommon attractions'. All, apparently, to do with Stanislaw, a Polish grandfather who bequeathed Cleo Slavic cheekbones, a kind of stocky sexiness and medium height to make her the tallest female in her family. Her eyes, her mother decreed, were her big asset. 'Dark and twinkly, turning down at the corners to meet your big smile turning up.'

'Crap,' Liza would mutter, 'your big assets are your boobs.'

Cleo rose onto her tiptoes to do a 360-degree scan of the room. Turning back, alerted by straightening of tiny skirts and hair flicking, she saw that, despite unpromising early indications, the laughing man with the spiky hair was on his way over. 'I saw him first!' hissed Angie.

'His call,' Rochelle growled, bolstering up the contents of her bra under her thin lace top.

Spiky arrived through the throng with a dazzling smile. 'Evening, ladies.'

'I'm Angie!'

'Rochelle!'

Cleo sank into the background, content to be the audience

for Angie and Rochelle's forthcoming boob-thrusting assault. But suddenly she found herself under the brown-golden gaze and it was like being fixed by the eyes of a leopard. His mouth curved. 'I'm Justin.'

Through her astonishment, Cleo heard dual sighs of disappointment.

'This is Cleo,' Angie snapped, turning away.

'Her husband's run off,' added Rochelle, meanly.

Cleo gazed uncertainly at Justin. His hair was cropped tightly at the sides, sharpening his features, and his smile seemed to poise him on the point of laughter. Somehow her eyes kept sliding down to his mouth – perhaps because he kept looking at hers.

Justin smiled. Centrefold material. 'Sorry to hear about the husband.' Cleo had never seen anyone look less sorry about anything. He cocked his head. 'So, what did you do?'

Cleo's stomach twisted on fresh indignation. 'He left *in case* I did something.'

Slowly, he grinned, teeth white and narrow. 'That's ... unreasonable. So. Option A or Option B?'

She blinked. 'Sorry?'

He edged nearer as people tried to push past him to the bar, dropping his head close to hers so that she could hear him over the clamouring music. Warm. He smelled of aftershave and beer. 'Option A is where I leave you to brood about your gitty husband. Option B is where I take you to dance to forget your gitty husband.' His eyes laughed, inviting her to join in.

'Gav isn't gitty,' she objected. Then added, honestly, 'Or not normally.' But she thought of *THIS MARRIAGE IS OVER. Love Gav*. Maybe he was gitty. A bit. A bit she hadn't noticed before.

Which was why she was there, on her own. Anger adrenaline combined headily with special brew, making her feel suddenly reckless. And free. Her head buzzed and she felt that delicious first slide into drunkenness, quarantining all common sense behind closed doors in the back of her mind. She drew in a deep breath. 'Option B!'

She might not be dressed to pull in a pelmet skirt and see-through top like Angie and Rochelle but, man, she was pissed off enough to dance with a stranger.

The dance floor was hot and crowded. Cleo was tingling-aware of Justin's hand in hers as he led her into the heart of it, alive and giddy with drink and naughtiness. This would show Gav. Mistrustful bastard. She'd give him something to mistrust.

She would treat herself to this naughty little step out of time, a wicked moment where there was no one to sit in judgement of her. Heedless and unbounded, she felt disconnected from her normal – married – self. No husband to guard her; no sister to make her feel safe. Cleo raised her arms and let her hair swish over her face and the beat move her, the flashing lights bathe her, the hot bodies around her give her their rhythm.

She did keep an eye out for Liza. But Liza never came.

Unbelievably, the music was winding down into the slow stuff already. She looked at her watch. One thirty!

Couples were drifting into each other's arms and the lights had become slow and purple. Angie and Rochelle were long gone.

The passing hours and several special brews had been softening the details of the row with Gav, but now it flooded back. Like a punch in the stomach. Cleo felt freshly adrift.

Justin took her hand. 'All right?' His smile faded at her silence. 'Or are you ready to select Option A?'

Her heart shrank. She'd drunk five times too much to drive home and she didn't want to face lonely, empty home anyway. When the club closed she'd get a taxi to – where?

Back to Liza's to sleep in the car in the hope that, sooner or later, she'd turn up?

She shuddered, forcing a smile. 'Still Option B.' On the crowded dance floor he scooped her into his arms and she allowed herself to enjoy the delicious heat of him. She heard his breath catch, felt his hands move to the small of her back to press her closer.

His head dipped, lips close to hers, waiting. Her heart galloped.

She shouldn't.

She absolutely shouldn't.

But, slowly, tentatively, shoving the thought of Gav away because he deserved it, she did. She lifted her face to Justin's and their lips brushed, soft as angel's wings. Cleo felt lust shiver up the back of her neck as he fleeted kisses along her jawbone, each a tiny starburst of heat.

Then he slid his hand under her hair and kissed her mouth.

Their dancing halted and her fingers clutched his shoulders. When he finally released her, the floor felt spongy under her feet.

'Wow!' he breathed.

She nodded as her heart drummed the air out of her lungs. Wow.

Outside, the night air was fresh enough to make the head spin, particularly when you'd drunk as much special as she had. Clinging to Justin's arm, she tried to marshal her thoughts through the after-loud-music ringing in her ears.

Justin kissed her temple. 'There are still some taxis.' He paused. 'Where ...?'

Abortively, she checked her mobile for messages from Liza, then heaved a mega-sigh as she fought the alcohol fumes for a half-sensible idea. 'I suppose I'd better go to my sister's and see if she turns up.'

He ducked his head to see into her face. 'Not home?'

THIS MARRIAGE IS OVER. Love Gav. 'Taxis won't go right out there at this time – I live in Middledip village. My car's at my sister's in Bretton. If she doesn't come home I'll sleep in it.' In the dark. In a cold inhospitable car.

Breath whistled between Justin's teeth and he slowly shook his head. Then, more rapidly, 'You can't do that. That's not safe.' He traced the side of her neck with his thumb. 'You'd better come home with me.'

Oh crap, she mustn't do that! That would be a desperate, awful thing, hurling her rather drunken self over a line that must not be crossed at any cost. She was married. Possibly. Probably.

He smiled, a huge, frank, sexy smile. 'Don't look so freaked, there's a spare room. OK?'

'Even so, I don't think that –' She was interrupted by the *dee-di-dee-dee* of her phone announcing a text message and scrabbled thankfully in her bag. 'Maybe this is my sister.'

But the name on the screen wasn't *Liza*. It was *Gav*. Cleo's shoulders sagged with relief. He'd be worried about her, apologising, offering to drive into Peterborough and pick her up –

The writings on the wall, the text said. She froze. He was reminding her! *THIS MARRIAGE IS OVER*. Fresh rage bubbled up inside her.

She snapped the phone shut and turned back to Justin. 'It does sound better than sleeping in the car.'

In the back of the taxi, Cleo closed her eyes and let Justin kiss her again, his hand on her waist. She ought to stop him. This wasn't fair to anybody. Ought to …

His flat was just like him, laid back and unfussy. Sexy dark greys, drab blues, one huge black sofa, a wiiiiide-screen TV, a big computer monitor beside an impressive stereo. He made her coffee and poured clear liquid from a chilled bottle into two shot glasses.

She watched him. 'What's that? Vodka?'

He took a sip, rolled it round his mouth. 'Aquavit. It's like medicine. Couple of nightcaps and no hangover tomorrow.'

She alternated the odd, stinging liquid with sips of coffee, a mixture that totally failed to sober her up.

Justin flung his down his throat in one, then watched her over the rim of his coffee mug. 'You're lovely,' he said.

She grinned. 'You're on the make.'

He shifted on the squashy sofa until his breath was gentle on the side of her face. She turned and regarded his lips, a finely chiselled bow. The night, at first so hideous, had become a kind of dream. And in dreams all kinds of weirdness went on. Giddily, she let the lips touch hers. He gave a long *mmm* of pleasure as his hand trickled behind her knees and hooked her legs over his.

His touch almost burned. As her breathing rate increased he planted hot kisses across her face, her neck, along her collarbone until it disappeared under the fabric of her top. And all she let herself think about was how good it felt.

His voice was husky. 'There is a spare bed. I promised you could have the spare bed if you wanted it ... You don't, do you?'

Justin's bedroom held a king-sized bed and a row of wardrobes. He fished out his mobile phone. 'Let's turn these off.'

'Good idea.' No more horrible texts from Gav. She located the off button and placed her phone neatly next to his on a chest of drawers. Her heart hammered. She was about to do something incredibly bad. Last chance to select Option A. Last chance to retreat to the spare room. Last chance to behave well, or at least no worse than she had already. She tried to summon up Gav and their marriage.

But, somehow, the image broke up because the desire in Justin's eyes went straight to her knees. And his hands sliding delicately up her back made her body jelly. And his tongue tip flicking across her earlobe shot spangles down her back.

Last chance, last chance … She slid her hand inside his shirt, skimmed the hot flesh across his ribs and felt him shiver. Desire welled and she knew she was going to do it.

His hands shook as he tackled the five big buttons at the front of her top. She arched her back to help him slide it off, tipping back her head to offer him her throat as he slid her bra straps from her shoulders and struggled to extricate her from her jeans.

And she gave herself up to his tingling hands, trailing fingertips, scalding kisses.

When he entered her in one aching movement, she bit his arm, making him gasp, swear, and leap deeper inside her. 'Cleo!'

Cleo drifted towards sleep.

Justin was already dozing. She shifted, peeling her back from his chest, the back of her legs from the front of his and he roused, pulling the quilt over them. His voice was already gravelly with sleep. 'I didn't ask you. Was it all right without?'

Her head was beginning to spin, making her feel queasy. She tried to concentrate. 'Without?'

'Without a condom.' He pulled her back against him.

Cleo's heart fell out of her chest. Shit. *Shit*! Appalled, her hand flew to her mouth. She shook her head.

'Not on the pill?'

'I've just changed to the diaphragm. But it's at home.'

'Oh,' he said. 'It's not all right.'

Chapter Two

He didn't feel that bad.

Not considering the excesses of the night before. Justin opened his eyes cautiously and let them ache gently in the light filtering into his bedroom.

He turned to look at the woman he'd pulled last night. Cleo, sleep tossing her dark hair across her face.

Funny, half-sad, half-angry Cleo, who'd looked frankly astounded when he'd turned away from her more obvious companions to her and her dark eyes. Cleo, who'd seemed grittily determined to act as if she were having a good time.

He eased onto his side to study her. Interesting face. High cheekbones, eyes that turned down at the corners, a wide, sexy mouth. A great body. He felt himself twitch.

She'd been lovely in bed; grave and thoughtful, seeming to enjoy him undressing her and exploring her body. Had made love with concentration, with sighs and gasps, arching towards him, enveloping him. He'd felt ready to explode.

He lifted his right arm and examined the purple mark where she'd bitten him. Really bitten! It had sent him crashing white-hot into the final fast and furious act when she'd yanked his head down to hers and they'd bruised each other's mouths. Lovely.

Cleo. She was ... catchy. Like a tune. Growing on him. He'd only anticipated a one-nighter, but she really could be fun.

Cleo woke to the smell of coffee and toast, pushing her hair from her eyes and focusing with difficulty on a man wearing only a pair of South Park boxers and sliding a tray onto the chest at the foot of the bed.

He looked up and smiled. 'Feeling human enough for coffee?'

Her thoughts circled, seeking sense, familiarity. The night before rushed back at her. She'd slept with this guy, Justin. She was in his bedroom. Bed. Because – unreal, this bit – Gav had left her. Left! Had bellowed and roared and left that raw, hateful message on the bedroom wall.

So she'd gone out, got drunk and got laid. Oh shit.

Automatically, she responded, 'Thanks. No sugar.'

Why was she so calm?

Where was the debilitating guilt, why wasn't she clutching her sides and weeping that she'd been unfaithful to Gav?

Because the powerful anger simmering on her back burner reminded her that he didn't deserve it. *THIS MARRIAGE IS OVER* ...

'Oops!' She almost spilt her coffee as Justin climbed back into bed.

Under the quilt his leg rested hairily on hers. 'Sleep OK? You looked as if you did.'

She found herself responding to his laugh. He was really nice. She smothered a yawn. 'I need a shower.'

His eyes slid down to her breasts. 'That'd be nice.'

'If you can spare the hot water.'

His eyes twinkled. 'There's really only enough for one good shower in the morning. But there's room for two people ...'

The steaming water stung her skin. She used his herby shampoo to cleanse the smell of booze from her hair.

She jumped as he helped her wash and her flesh gathered into a million goosebumps, her head resting against him whilst he soaped her in silence. His chin was level with the top of her head. Tipping her head back he kissed her, nipping her bottom lip. Her nipples bunched tightly as he caressed them, making her shiver. 'Are you busy for the rest of the day?'

She turned her face and shook her head as the water flew off her hair. What would she be doing, otherwise?

Leaving him shaving, Cleo located her phone in his bedroom and turned it on. Waited. No messages. No texts. She snapped shut the smart black handset, switched it off and tossed it back on the plain wooden surface.

She drifted through Justin's comfortable and functional sitting room, a grown-up room with no space wasted on anything that did nothing, no ornaments, no pictures. Justin obviously liked expensive but functional things: TV, DVD, computer, stereo. The big, squashy, leather sofa. In the kitchen, honey pine and shiny white tile, she filled the kettle, found bread and dropped it in the toaster. She made tea, buttered toast and perched on a red-topped stool to breakfast thoughtfully, staring through the window.

In the heat of the action when she'd been in Justin's hands, astride Justin's body, clutching, gasping when he nibbled at where her shoulder met her neck, only pleasure and satisfaction had been important. But now reality was rendering the tea tasteless – and the toast was in danger of reappearing.

Unprotected sex. Idiot. Moron. Irresponsible, careless slut. Unprotected sex. At her age! Talk about should have known better. She did know better. Knew every bird and bee there was, and what caused little birds and baby bees. And had avoided them like the plague!

How could she have been so stupid?

Hadn't she always sneered at women who didn't take care of contraception? For Cleo it had all been so straightforward till now. Married to the same man for five years, and on the pill until erratic blood pressure had made it inadvisable.

The doctor had recommended some new intrauterine device, but the idea of a piece of plastic lodged permanently in her body had made Cleo feel odd. The notion of an implant was just as creepy. So, for the last five weeks, she and Gav had been struggling to use the diaphragm.

And, as she only slept with one man, she was hardly going to troll it around in her handbag on an evening out, was she? Because she wasn't going to need it, was she?

Except ... she had.

And until Justin had asked – too late – she hadn't given contraception a single thought. At Muggie's there had been condoms in the machine in the ladies' toilets and she'd walked right by, as if they were just for other people.

She jumped when Justin sauntered into the kitchen, the fair tips of his hair glowing like a dandelion clock in the morning light that streamed through the window. 'The service in this hotel's rubbish,' he joked, kissing the top of her head.

His eyes were so bright that Cleo found herself smiling in reply. 'Sorry. I began without you.'

He slid more bread into the toaster slots, switched the kettle back on, staggering in mock exhaustion. 'I need to keep my strength up. You are such a horny lady.' And something in his languid movements and little jokes quietened the squirming worries in Cleo's tummy.

Over his fourth slice of toast, Justin suggested, 'By the way, there's a barbecue later, if you're up for it?'

She stared out of the window at more flats across a paved area punctuated by young copper beech trees shaking in the breeze, the sunshine filtering through their purple-gold leaves. Was she up for it? Or should she be going home, sorting out her marriage? Texting Gav and asking if he wanted to talk? That's what any sane woman would do when her husband began behaving like an alien – try and sort it out. But she remembered the hateful message on the wall and a hard splintery part of her refused to end this step out of time. 'Sure, where do we go?'

He was already reading the paper, pouring more tea and drifting towards the sofa. 'Out to the lakes,' he said, glancing at the clock on the DVD player. 'You've got about an hour. By the way, will your sister or anybody be wondering where you are?'

She thought of her phone with no texts and no voicemail. 'Doesn't look like it.'

Gav pulled up outside the house in Port Road. Cleo's sleek blue Audi TT wasn't there. Bollocks. Indoors, the sitting room looked as if nothing unusual had happened. No cataclysmic row, no hurting words, no stupid ultimatum. A newspaper was folded on the floor where Cleo must've discarded it half-read, a couple of apples in the willow-pattern bowl were wrinkling gently amongst the usual clutter of pens, bills and rubber bands.

He trailed upstairs to their bedroom, hoping it wouldn't be there, that it would all have been a horrible dream. Oh hell. He stared miserably at his horrible, disgusting, childish message, *THIS MARRIAGE IS OVER. Love Gav.* Groaned. 'Gav, Gav, what were you *doing*?'

Gently, precisely, he closed the wardrobe doors and pushed shut the drawers. He'd slept last night in his car and his clothes were still lying in the boot.

The bed was tidily made, undisturbed. The bed where they made love, cuddled up on cold nights or lounged with coffee and the Sunday morning papers.

So Cleo hadn't slept here.

Her mobile, uselessly, was switched off, and having a let's-make-up conversation with her voicemail didn't appeal.

He picked up the phone to call Liza, Cleo's number

one refuge. But all he got was Liza's annoying answering machine message, 'I'm just *never* in, am I?' He could drive over to Liza's flat ... but he didn't relish making his grovelling apologies under the beady eye of his sister-in-law. The pair of them were probably drowning Cleo's sorrows, which meant Liza would be an utter pissy bitch. Cleo's eyes would be red from crying, face white from not eating, agonising over why he, Gav, the love of her life, soulmate, darling (if he still had any claim to these titles) had acted like a prick.

And what could he tell her?

He made an inept and abortive attempt to wash the marker pen from the wall then trudged up the road to The Three Fishes, where they generally did a good lunch. Settling himself on a stool, he smiled at Janice behind the bar. 'Cheer me up – did Peterborough United win their friendly yesterday?'

A track curved from the main road between nettle banks to a clearing beside the water. According to a peeling sign, it was a lake unsuitable for water sport, but when Justin's car drew up behind the other vehicles, three jet-skis waited on trailers.

The barbecue sulked in a haze of blue, three men were unpacking beer and two women chatted over the bread rolls, sausages and chicken drumsticks.

The men waved beer cans. The women paused, drumsticks in hands, to stare at Cleo. She stared back. Justin's friends, after all, not hers. They could look all they liked; she wouldn't break.

Justin's introductions were brief. 'Gez and his girlfriend Jaz. Vicky.' Gez and Jaz grinned; Vicky didn't. Jaz was tall and had that no-nonsense look of being a girl who's one of the boys. Vicky was the pretty one – when she wasn't slinging sausages sourly onto the barbecue. Cleo guessed that Justin had been expected alone. Better check her food was cooked through before she ate it.

'Drew and Martin you might've seen at Muggie's.'

Drew and Martin were the platinum twins. They swiped off their shades and greeted Cleo with a friendly 'Hiya!', their wetsuits of peacock colours clashing with their blazing bleach-blond hair.

Flopping down onto a crusty Regatta jacket from Justin's boot, Cleo watched with interest as Drew and Martin manhandled two of the jet-skis into the water. Drew's was silver with red lightning flashes and Martin's navy, graffiti'd with neon orange and yellow. Standing beside the skis in the shallows, they fired the engines, holding tightly to the rear as the power growled through the machine.

Moving their grip to the handlebars, each executed a practised scoot and hop aboard and in an instant they were roaring across the khaki lake, on their feet like charioteers.

'Whoo!' Cleo watched as the jet-skis skimmed across the water with their rooster tails of spray behind them, impressed by the power and manoeuvrability. Out in the middle of the lake, Drew's jet-ski howled as he squirted on power and jumped Martin's frothy wake.

Gez began to untie the remaining jet-ski and Justin helped lift it into the water. If Drew's and Martin's jet-skis were chariots Gez's was a motorbike, with a big seat, one that would take rider and pillion passenger. Cleo had always liked motorbikes.

Gez zipped up his wetsuit. With his fluffy brown hair and the wetsuit clinging lovingly to his paunch, he reminded Cleo of a teddy bear.

'Are you going out there today?' he asked Justin.

Justin glanced at Drew and Martin carving up the lake and wriggled himself into a position where he could watch over Cleo's shoulder. Two people lying on one jacket meant close proximity. 'Probably later.'

Gez skimmed out to join the others. Cleo propped herself on her elbows and admired the patterns of spray hanging on the air in the sunlight. 'You haven't got one?'

He shook his head. 'I've got a share in Gez's. I'm not as into it as the others. Drew and Martin jet ski year round.'

Cleo's gaze moved on to Vicky, sulking over the sausages. Jaz was talking earnestly, her hand on Vicky's shoulder. Cleo felt sudden compunction. She coughed. 'I don't think Vicky's very pleased to see me.'

Justin glanced up, vaguely. 'No?' He turned back to the jet-skis, howling back towards the shore, three abreast.

'I think she expected you to be … available.'

Justin looked at Vicky again. 'Oh. I wondered what she was doing here. She's a friend of Jaz's. Jaz has this peculiarity that, although nice herself, she seems to attract high-maintenance friends.'

'Have you known the others long?' The skiers banked violently, several yards out, spewing spray rainbows to patter around Cleo and Justin and shiver on their hot skin.

Justin wiped a drop from Cleo's arm. 'Ages, since school.'

'So you were brought up locally?' It was odd, not knowing anything about his life previous to Friday evening.

'Yeah. I'm Mr Ordinary: ordinary parents who have cleared off to live in America, a sister to squabble with, a family dog. School, art and graphics course, job in graphics. Ordinary.'

She hadn't thought of him as 'ordinary', not with that face and its smile always ready to develop into a laugh, not the way people followed him with their eyes.

'You'll love it.' Justin patted the jet-ski invitingly and closed the neck of his wetsuit, black with lime piping. 'One of the girls will lend you a suit.'

Cleo looked at the jet-ski longingly.

Jaz smiled serenely from her position on a blanket, her head pillowed on Gez's big tummy. 'You could've borrowed mine, though it would swamp you. But I haven't brought it today, sorry.'

Vicky, like flotsam washed up on the corner of the blanket, gazed across the water. 'I don't think I want to lend mine. It's a bit ... personal, isn't it? Like lending your knickers to a stranger.' Then, insincerely, 'Sorry.'

'Don't worry.' Cleo rose and slipped off her shoes and socks. 'I don't need Neoprene.'

Justin stared. 'You're bonkers. You'll get saturated!'

Cleo opened her eyes very wide and waded into the lake up to her knees, wet jeans rasping her ankles. 'I'll dry, won't I?'

Justin shook his head, eyes laughing, and mounted the ski. Cleo clambered on behind him, locking her arms around his waist. His wetsuit felt warm and both smooth and rough. She was aware of his body beneath it.

The jet-ski bobbed, vibrating as the engine coughed. Justin shouted back above the raw sound, 'Hold tight! Lean when I do, don't try and sit me up. Away we go!'

The ski leapt and Cleo shrieked as she left her stomach behind, then whooped as they accelerated hard in a spout of freezing spray. Her jeans were soaked instantly, clinging and clammy as Justin slewed the jet-ski into a figure of eight, bouncing across the surface, the engine pounding woah-wow-woah.

'Yeah!' she yelled as Justin arced the ski into a wide turn, faster and faster, leaning further and further. She screamed as flying spray chilled her arms and plastered her hair across her eyes. 'More!' she yelped, against the wind. And, 'Wow! Whooo! This is great!' Faster and faster until it was all she could do to cling on, lacing her fingers together on the other side of Justin, her chest against his warm back, tensing her thighs against the sensation of falling, every inch of skin stung by cold water.

Justin raced around one final circuit of the lake, then let the ski idle back to shore. Cleo was laughing, gasping, as she splashed off the ski and through the shallows. 'That was fantastic, brilliant!'

The engine died and Justin jumped down and dragged the ski in. 'You're mad! Look at the state of you.'

Cleo laughed helplessly as she squelched onto the shore, pulling her T-shirt away from her breasts, her bra showing through the wet fabric. 'But it was fabulous!'

'Come here, you crazy, crazy woman.' Justin hauled her into a big hug and a breathless kiss. 'You're an absolute headcase! You make less noise having sex.' He didn't bother to lower his voice. 'We'd better get you into something dry.'

The men laughed and Jaz grinned; but Vicky glared as Cleo squeezed lake water from her hair.

As Cleo sat in the car, grinning through an adrenaline high, wrapped in the musty Regatta jacket, Justin gripped the steering wheel against the bumpy track and shook his head. 'Everyone thinks you're mad.' He flicked the indicator and joined the road. 'You'd better marry me, madwoman. Anyway, you might be pregnant.'

Cleo's heart stopped. Laughter evaporated. Throat shut. *Marry?*

The doors at the back of her mind burst open on an abrupt heave and common sense careered out to shake an image of Gav at her, screaming, 'You're already married!'

Oh ...

Chapter Three

… shit.

As she plummeted back into real life, hideous reality zoomed up to smash her in the face.

Her marriage was in bits.

Her husband had walked out.

She'd had unprotected sex with a stranger.

The righteous anger that had seethed in her – sustaining the sensation that she could do anything, get away with anything, it didn't matter and never would – gave one last growl and drained away.

Her breath caught in her throat so hard she almost gagged. She croaked, 'I'd better go home.'

Justin glanced at her, a frown beginning. 'We're going home … oh, your home?'

'Yes.'

'Not right now?'

'Yes.' She felt cold, exhausted and stupid. Why was she here, soaked with algae-fouled water? Why on earth had she embarked on this reckless fling? Which was over now.

Justin changed down for a turning, voice suddenly stiff. 'Have you left any gear at my place?'

'No, but you can drop me off and I'll get a taxi back to my car.'

'I'll drive you.' He lapsed into a silence that lasted for the whole of the twenty-minute drive.

Liza lived in some jaundice-yellow flats slung in lines of two storeys over carports, a bus ride from the city centre. Cleo's car was still parked under the flats in the space that car-less Liza never used.

Justin killed the engine. 'What changed?' All the laughter had gone from his voice. He was almost a stranger (again) without his semi-permanent grin.

She shook her head, choked by the enormity of everything she'd done.

He stared, mind obviously ticking. 'It's to do with "married". You're married.'

Her face felt as stiff as plastic. 'You knew that.'

'But you're separated!'

She looked away, clenching her hands in the folds of his jacket. 'Well ...'

'Aren't you? Did your husband leave?'

She sniffed and nodded. Her voice strained to work. 'He walked out on Friday.'

His voice was suddenly a bellow. '*Friday*! Yesterday? What happened?'

She avoided his eyes. 'We had a big row.'

'And he stormed out?'

Miserably, she nodded.

His voice dropped to a furious hiss. 'For fuck's sake! That's not what I call "separated". That's just a barney, an argument, a tiff! You scream at each other then you make up!' He hesitated. 'You spent the night with me ... to punish him?'

It was so close to the truth that her voice refused to let her deny it.

'So it wasn't an attraction, a wild thing, an affair – I was just *convenient*! You somehow fouled up meeting your sister and needed a place to stay!'

She winced.

Her eyes burned with tears as she scrabbled for the door handle and bolted, abandoning the warmth of both him and his smelly old jacket in the car.

Trembling with cold and nerves she drove home badly,

forgetting to use her mirrors, driving straight over at a crossroads, hearing a scream of brakes.

What had she done?

What about Gav? She felt sick. Clouds like battleships rolled up to obscure the sun; she turned her heaters up high, yet still shivered.

When she reached home and saw Gav's car drawn up outside, she seriously thought she'd faint.

Gav was back.

For what? For ever? For something he'd left? For another row?

Her brain began feverishly to concoct a plausible excuse for why she was soaked with lake water. Her guilty heart beat so hard that it seemed to rattle behind her eyes.

Relief though, he wasn't actually in the house. She called his name into the empty air, voice stretched to cracking in the answering silence. Gratefully, she hurled her sodden clothes into the washing machine and raced for the shower to scrub urgently at the lake water on her skin and hair with shower gel and shampoo, to obliterate the vegetable smell. As well as any traces of extra-marital sex.

In the bedroom the writing on the wall remained. *THIS MARRIAGE IS OVER. Love Gav.*

When Gav burst through the front door, pounding up the stairs – 'Cleo?' – she was standing looking at it, in her yellow towelling robe.

He skidded to a halt. Somehow he looked gaunt, as if he hadn't eaten for a week. They stared at each other. His voice was disbelieving and exultant. 'You're back!'

She nodded. Watched his eyes flick to the marker pen message and back to her, his face flush and then pale.

'Cleo …' His eyes were red at the lower rim. His Adam's apple bobbed. 'I am *so* sorry.' He walked slowly towards her, hands out, palms up, rushing his sentences, falling over his apologies. 'Can you forgive me? I don't deserve it, but when I came home and you'd gone …!' He bit his lip and shut his eyes for an instant. 'You must've thought I'd gone mad.'

Mad. She flinched. Crazy madwoman. Justin, laughing, hugging her tightly with delight. The smell of lake water, his hot mouth taking her cold lips. She pushed the image away.

Gav lowered his beseeching hands. 'I don't know what came over me, Cleo, I just went off on one.'

She studied his desperate face as if she'd never seen it: sandy eyebrows, fair skin lightly freckled, softly lined. Not a sunburst of laughter lines radiating white in a tanned skin, not a sharp nose above curving, laughing lips. As if in a visualisation exercise, she brought a picture of Justin deliberately into her mind's eye – and set a flame to it. Watched it catch, balloon, shrivel and collapse like a photograph in an ashtray. He must be gone.

Gav was her husband. Her guilt reared up like a serpent and speared her heart with its forked tongue. He was obviously waiting for a flurry of questions from poor wronged little wifey. She supposed that, if she wanted to save her marriage – she did, didn't she? – she must discover what had happened to make Gav 'go off on one'. And make certain that he never found out that she'd been off on one of her own.

Her anger, so sustaining till now, wouldn't creak into action. She pointed to THIS MARRIAGE IS OVER. Love Gav and her hand shook.

His eyes were huge. 'I don't know what happened.'

Her emotions seemed to have iced over. 'Something certainly wound you up. Something at work?'

His eyes flickered to hers. For a long moment it seemed as if he would deny it. Then his head dropped. 'I suppose that's it. There's been talk of redundancy and Bob Chester …'

Now that he'd decided to admit it, it was as if he couldn't wait to let it all out; he became almost eager. 'He told me, in front of everybody, that underperformers would be first to go.'

She stared. 'But you're not an underperformer.'

'He still said it! I suppose I've been stewing, not wanting to admit perhaps I'm not as good at my job as I thought. I got strung up and twitchy and I took it out on you. I'm ...' – he swayed forward on the balls of his feet, brushed the top of her head with his lips – '... ashamed.'

So Cleo got her first experience of her and Gav making up after a row; as the hot summer's day ended in a storm that crashed about outside the bedroom window, they made love to seal the rift. He was thoughtful, the act protracted. It must've been guilt that made her feel so numb and unresponsive. Or maybe shock. Or plain fatigue. When Gav arched his back and cried out she felt relief. And then guiltier than before.

And so weary. Utterly, deadly tired. Leaden, aching, exhausted. Probably nobody in the living history of mankind had ever been so tired. Ever.

But then, and for long into the night, she couldn't sleep. She closed her eyes and experienced flashbacks of being with Justin – sex with Justin. She'd been ... overt. No 'getting to know you'. No inhibitions.

In the morning she was suddenly yanked awake by a horrible realisation. 'I didn't put my cap in last night!'

Gav stretched and sighed. 'Don't you think things were much easier when you were on the pill?'

Cleo lay very still on her pillow. Oh crap, not again.

Chapter Four

Cleo tipped her handbag upside down and shook everything out. Where the hell was it? It was Monday and she needed her wretched mobile phone! When had she last had it? She flicked back through her memory.

And went cold. Deeply, horrifyingly cold.

Squeezing her eyes tight shut, she willed herself into positive thought. 'I have not left my mobile phone at Justin's flat!' But she had, of course she had. In her mind she could see it nestling alongside Justin's phone on the chest of drawers when –

As if things weren't bad enough.

She heard Gav's leaping footsteps and looked up to see him appear at the top of the stairs. 'All right?' He smiled, fresh and attractive in his grey shirt and blue tie, hair still damp from the shower.

'Fine, fine!' She scooped up her card wallet, purse, pen, comb. The weather had broken with Saturday night's storm. Rain still slanted across dull fields and over stoical sheep to whisper against the windows.

The bed gave as he sat behind her. 'Sure?'

''Course! Won't you be late?'

His sigh was hot on her neck as his arm slid around her. 'We could ring in sick.'

Fastening her bag, she eased away and reached for her jacket. 'Best to get back to normal. Just normal.'

His eyes were huge with guilt. 'Maybe you're right.' Above his head, a stripped patch in the wallpaper signposted where his message had been.

Normal used to be good and comfy. If only finding it

again was easy. If only Cleo didn't feel so betrayed by Gav's behaviour at the same time as being so guilty over her own.

She felt as if she'd been through some life-altering experience. Perhaps she had.

At coffee break she should have been mixing with a trainee sales team, as the whole focus of the day was on teamwork. She should be making herself the hub. Instead, she slipped along the corridors of the client's building to find a phone.

In an empty office, she dialled her own number. Five rings. Six. Then the line opened. She could hear the tinny buzz of background noise.

'It's Cleo,' she said.

A moment, then Justin responded. 'Hang on.' The squeak of a chair, footsteps, the tinny buzz fading, a door clicking. 'Yes?'

She took a deep breath. 'Obviously, I left my mobile with you.'

'Yes.'

She waited while he made no useful suggestions. Then she tried, 'Can I come and fetch it?'

A pause. A noise which might've been his fingers drumming. A quick intake of breath. 'The problem is, I'm in Ipswich. Until Friday.'

'Oh.' Her breath whisked out in a sigh of disappointment. She was in Northampton herself, there was evidently going to be no instant solution. 'You'll appreciate I need my phone back.'

'Oh yes.'

Another pause. 'Could I meet you in Ipswich and –'

He cut her off. 'I'm working.'

Sod him. 'Right. So can I call round for it on Friday?'

Another pause before, 'I'll meet you. Muggie's at nine.'

She groaned mentally. 'Does it have to be there?'

'That's where I'll be.'

Voices and footsteps passed in the corridor outside. She froze until they'd gone. Hissed, 'Do you have to be so unco-operative?'

He half laughed. 'Muggie's at nine.'

Next, she rang Gav.

His voice was happy, soppy, delighted to hear from her after three hours apart. 'Mmmm, my sexy, darling wife.'

She had to concentrate to achieve the breezy conversation she'd mentally rehearsed. 'Can't be long, I'm borrowing someone's phone. I just rang to tell you not to try me on my mobile, it's turned temperamental. Tom's got a mate who can sort it, so I've given it to him.'

Annoyingly, Gav immediately objected. 'You shouldn't give it to some amateur, it's an expensive phone, I'll take it back to the shop.'

Damn it to soddery, of course Gav had bought it for her. She tried to be dismissive. 'It's already out of guarantee, the shop would be mega-expensive. Yes … I love you, too.' She hoped. When the guilt and the anger were over, she was sure she'd find she still loved him.

Glancing at her watch, rapidly she dialled Liza at the treatment centre, who, bless her bless her bless her, wasn't engaged with a client's bare feet and was able to answer her phone. Cleo heaved a sigh of relief to hear her calm, 'Hiya!'

'Oh Liza!' Suddenly she wanted a huge, cleansing cry, had to dig her nails into her palms to stop herself from bursting into loud, sisterly boo-hoos. 'If anyone asks, *particularly* Gav, I spent Friday night with you, OK? I was upset and you spent the whole time getting me drunk and wiping my tears. Can you do that?'

'Of course,' Liza agreed promptly. 'But what's going on?'

Cleo checked her watch again. 'I'll ring you later to explain. And *definitely* don't try me on my mobile! And will you come with me this Friday evening to Muggie's?'

'What, Muggie's in Bridge Street? I go there all the time.'

Cleo fought down sobs again. 'Pity you weren't there last Friday. None of the horrible mess would've happened!'

'Ah.' Liza sounded satisfied. 'I met this farmer's son …'

Cleo broke in hastily. The client would be complaining to Nathan if she left her team much longer. 'Just come with me this Friday, OK? Promise?'

Liza promised. 'As long as you tell me then what's going on.'

The heavy hand on Justin's shoulder made him jog his drink. He flicked at the splashes on his jacket.

Martin grinned. 'Sorry, mate. New phone?'

Justin looked at the petite folding mobile phone in his hand. 'I'm just minding it for a bit.' While Martin caught the barman's eye and Drew pressed up beside them in the crush, hands jammed deep into the pockets of his drainpipe jeans, Justin slipped the phone into his pocket.

'Thanks.' He accepted the drink that Martin passed him.

Drew drank half his lager in one long slurp, then burped. 'On your own? No lady of the lake?'

Justin shook his head.

'Still seeing her?'

The cold beer was good, tightening his throat on the way down with its iciness. He shook his head again. 'There was the little matter of a husband.' He had to raise his voice; the pub was filling up.

Martin and Drew showed him matching surprised expressions. Drew's brows descended – 'Didn't she tell you?'

'Kind of. She said he'd cleared off. I didn't realise she meant the day before, until she went home to see if he'd turned up.' Justin wiped the bottom of his glass on the bar and remembered, belatedly, how, a couple of years ago, a girlfriend of Drew's had lied about her marital status. Drew had only discovered the truth when the husband had come after him with fists swinging. Drew had been hurt in more ways than one.

'Bad scene.' Drew's black look suggested that he was remembering, too. 'You don't need that kind of aggro. She should've told you. You liked her. She looked top in the wet T-shirt, by the way. Shame she had to be so troublesome.'

'Certainly is.' Justin thought of Cleo, ringing on her own phone, the one in his pocket. Wary, apologetic, worried. Defensive. If she and her old man had got it back together, she'd be mostly worried. He thought about her naked on his bed, in his arms. Taking the phone out again, he switched it off to preserve the battery. Friday would be interesting.

Cleo and Gavin had been invited to midweek supper at Keith and Dora's Tudor-look posh pad in a cul-de-sac of other posh pads in Orton Longueville. When they arrived, Rhianne and Ian were already settled with glasses of wine while Will and Roland, their overactive sons, raced circuits through doors and up and downstairs.

Cleo felt edgy and uneasy. She ought to be cheerful and relaxed, letting Dora, plump and smiling, take their jackets, Keith deliver glasses of wine held exaggeratedly high as he stepped over his kids, Meggie and Eddie. Roland and Will whizzed past again, flying two of Meggie's dolls alongside them, howling, 'Super-doll!' and 'Bat-doll!'

Probably it was the kids being so noisy that was winding her up. From the start, she and Gav had agreed not to have kids. All their friends had embraced the horrendous-sounding sacrifices of sleep, money and leisure and putting the children first.

For the first time, Cleo wondered why their close friends were people with families. Cleo and Gav were so determinedly childfree; it didn't make sense.

Meggie, poor soul, began tugging at Dora. 'Mummy ...' Pointing sorrowfully at her undignified dollies. Dora sighed and looked at Rhianne.

''S all right, Meggie,' Rhianne responded unhelpfully, 'it's only 'cos they're boys.'

Ian mumbled into his glass of red, 'Boy-devils.'

Keith, Gav and Ian began discussing Wimbledon.

Dora and Rhianne turned to their favourite topic – children. 'That little Davie boy's got worms, so I'm keeping Meggie off playgroup for a week. It was nits a fortnight ago.' They were an unlikely pairing: Rhianne so slender and invariably carefully painted before ever facing the outdoor world; Dora reminding Cleo irresistibly of a giant schoolgirl, fresh-faced and clumsy.

Cleo, pretending to listen, watched Gav. Smiling, talking, laughing, arguing. Sipping wine, nodding. Gav, apparently, had returned from whatever planet he'd been on.

The conversation moved on to money – Keith complaining about the pressures of earning loads, Ian bitter about the pressures of not earning enough.

As Roland and Will raced by once more with Meggie's favourite dolls, now naked and with their hair stuck together in clumps, Meggie tugged Dora's trouser leg, eyes melting with tears. 'Mummy ...!' Dora smiled uneasily and whispered about guests.

The little girl's shoulders drooped and Cleo wondered how Dora could bear to let her agonise like that over her much-loved dolls. As Roland and Will raced past on their fortieth irritating lap, she stuck out her arm. 'Give the dolls to Meggie, please,' she said, quietly.

Roland, after a stunned moment, gave Bat-doll back to an awed Meggie. But Will ran at Cleo and slapped her leg.

Unmoved, Cleo raised her eyebrows. '*Give* the doll to

Meggie, *please.*'

Will threw Super-doll sulkily in Meggie's direction.

Several seconds passed. Rhianne stared at Cleo as if correcting her boys' behaviour was a totally foreign concept. 'Never mind, boys, go and get Coke from the kitchen.'

Keith, no doubt thinking about his carpets, rose reluctantly. 'Best if I help them.'

Smiling sweetly, Cleo said, 'Yes, do hype them up with sugar. Lovely.'

Uncertainly, Rhianne tittered. 'Are you practising to be a parent or something?'

Chapter Five

'I want to try tantric sex. It's a deeply gratifying experience, apparently.' Rhianne had finished eating long before the others – if she was going to imbibe huge numbers of calories she generally drank them. She twirled her wine glass and looked around expectantly.

Ian was only halfway through his mound of pepperpot stew and talked through a mouthful. 'Very twentieth-century of you, darling! I suppose you've read an old magazine article in the hairdresser's and suddenly you're an expert. A three-day build-up to a bit of the other? Between Roland wetting the bed and Will getting up at half five to watch telly, I suppose?'

Rhianne admired her long, almond-shaped nails. Cleo knew Rhianne actually had a favourite nail, the most elegant and perfect. 'Who changes Roland's bed? And what do you know about Will getting up at dawn? You're still snoring.'

Cleo watched Roland and Will listen to their parents bicker, exchanging conspiratorial glances as their names came up. Now that Meggie and Eddie were in bed, the older boys had quietened enough to watch Cartoon Network eek-zing-pow-banging on the television.

Rhianne pursed perfectly orange lips unspoilt by contact with her wine glass, crinkling her full-face make-up. She lifted one long, thin, shiny-orange-nailed hand, palm up. 'We could make time.'

Ian smothered a belch. 'OK. You spend an hour stroking me. I'll watch Match of the Day.'

'The idea is to lavish attention on each other, Ian! We need an intimacy space to retire to where we can breathe each other's breath and harmonise –'

Cleo stared down at her plate. Must they keep talking about sex? All her problems were because of sex.

What was sex after all? An urge to be gratified? An expression of love and intimacy? Or a weapon?

'Your wife's asleep, Gav.'

She lifted her eyes to see all faces turned towards her. 'Sorry – did I miss something?'

Gav smiled at her. 'You OK?'

'Tired, that's all.' She managed a smile in return. Tired of listening to variations of the same old, same old, that was for sure. Ian complaining about Rhianne; Rhianne wanting something more than she had. Keith a world-weary wage slave; Dora a put-upon domestic slave.

Cleo wondered again why she and Gav were part of this group. In fact *Gav, Keith* and *Ian* were friends – Cleo, Dora and Rhianne were the women that they'd married. Expected to become part of a set that spent a significant portion of their time together because the men were friends.

And what happened when Cleo wanted to see her old college friends? Gav threw a wobbler and declared an end to the marriage.

Sometimes, it seemed as if there was only Liza there for Cleo. How had that happened?

Frustration swelled inside her and suddenly she experienced a fierce and unexpected longing to be like Liza. Answerable to no one.

Gav settled on his side under the crisp comfort of the duvet as Cleo climbed into bed in his favourite tumble-haired, unmade-up, clothes-discarded, bedtime state. He ran his thumb up the inside of her bare arm. 'Mmm, all that talk of sex …'

But there was no answering sexy smile or twinkling eye.

No dive into his arms, no delicious wriggle. Instead, she sighed her way under the duvet, well on her own side of the bed, and shut her eyes. 'I'm really tired.'

Gav laughed incredulously. 'For crying out loud, when have we ever been too tired for sex?' He ran his hand gently across her breasts.

She opened her eyes. 'I'm too tired for anything.' And shut them again.

'This isn't like you!' He shunted across the empty sheet between them, confident he could get her going. He nuzzled his face into her neck, kissing, nibbling, humming, 'Mmm-mmm!'

Instead of rolling back her head, arching her neck to his mouth, coming alive in his arms, Cleo twitched slightly. 'Not tonight, Gav.'

'Why not?' Not a very cool reaction but he was in uncharted territory. When had Cleo ever refused him?

Cleo sighed. 'Because I'm tired, OK? These few days have been exhausting. I've just got into bed and the last thing I need is to get out, mess about with the cap and the spermicide, then reverse the whole performance in the morning!' She rolled onto her side, her back to him.

A still moment before he slid away. 'I told you it was better when you were on the pill.'

'Pill or cap, you don't have to take responsibility, do you?'

He opened his mouth to demand whether she really wanted to try condoms, to him the armoury of the uncommitted, had a sudden nasty suspicion that she might suggest a vasectomy, which was unthinkable, and shut it again.

So. She was still angry. He'd thought they'd made up but she was obviously still punishing him in the peculiar woman-way of reacting to injuries at a later, unconnected date. He decided to be dead cool and understanding. He stroked her shoulder. 'You'll get used to the cap, and you won't feel so negative. I just wanted ...'

Cleo twitched from under his hand. 'I understand what you "just wanted"! But I don't happen to want the same. OK?'

Chapter Six

The lights were the same, and the music. Cleo clutched a single, cold, restrained bottle of Budweiser and watched the crowd. Liza hovered loyally beside her in a tiny gold dress with a broad black belt that sat just below her breasts, a glass of black absinthe over ice in her hand. The atmosphere in Muggie's was so hot and moist that even though she, too, wore a short strappy dress, Cleo felt cooked.

Last Friday she hadn't realised the place sprawled so far, rambling off between pillars and around corners. Or just how many people could cram into those spaces.

'Quarter past nine.' Cleo sighed. She was tired of gazing over the mass of heads for the giveaway spiky hair. 'Maybe he's not coming. Maybe I won't see him again. That'll be OK, that'll be fine. I can pretend the phone's lost and get another with a new number. I should've done that in the first place. Then I wouldn't have to be here.

'And I could've avoided another squabble with Gav this morning when I told him I was going straight to yours after work and would stay over until tomorrow.'

Liza, considering she'd never before displayed antipathy towards her brother-in-law, was unflatteringly fast with it, now. 'Gav's being an arse.' She thought for a moment and added, honestly, 'But, this Justin thing – it's so not like you, Cleo.'

Cleo tried to ignore the unpleasant creeping sensation of being in the wrong. 'I was so pissed off with Gav it was like I stepped off the real world and into a fantasy one where nothing – Gav, in particular – mattered. My head got really messy.'

Liza's mouth set in a way that was as close to disapproval of Cleo as she got. 'I can't believe it – you and Gav, you've been so perfect. But it's just a blip, hopefully? You'll be good as gold again in no time – oh, don't cry!' She flung anxious arms around her sister. 'It'll be OK. Get your phone back, forget it ever happened. It was a one-off. You've still got your old life.'

Cleo scrabbled for a tissue. 'Everything was great. Compared to our friends, our marriage was blissful. *Was.* But this "blip" has made me feel disorientated. It's as if I've woken up to all kinds of things I used to accept without thinking, like Gav asking where I'm going and who with. Suddenly it grates.'

Incomprehension widened Liza's eyes. 'Hello-o? That's just marriage, isn't it?'

'But now I've stepped outside the marriage. Even if I regret it,' – did she? – 'I feel … empowered. I did as I liked. I can do as I like, again.'

'Ah.' Liza sipped her absinthe. 'But if Gav finds out about Justin, your options will narrow dramatically. Won't they?'

Cleo wondered how she'd feel if that happened. 'If he doesn't show up I can forget him. And he can forget me.'

And then he was there. Strolling across the dance floor in a dull blue silk shirt. Grim and gorgeous.

Cleo felt shock waves ripple her spine. 'I didn't see you arrive!'

He flicked a nod towards the darker recesses of the club. 'I was over there. Let's go outside.'

Cleo didn't have much choice but to follow, turning over the thought that he'd apparently been in the club all along, watching her as she waited. Bastard. She'd retrieve her phone and be out of it.

It was a relief to leave the stifling club and step into the open air; she paused to savour a couple of clean lungfuls before realising that Justin was already striding away. Crossly, she hurried after, until he stopped in a deep recess formed by windows angling in towards a shop door, waving her past, into the shadow.

She turned, back against the bevelled glass of the door, her heart and breathing fluttering. She licked her lips and tried to smile, saying, lightly, 'Have you got my phone?'

He extracted it briefly from his trouser pocket, held it up then put it back, ignoring her outstretched hand. He didn't smile, although she felt she was grinning rather idiotically at him.

'I just want to clear a few things up first.' In the street light half his face was plainly lit, half in shadow.

He leaned one hand on the door above her shoulder. 'I'm curious about what exactly led up to you spending the night with me.'

She tried a theatrical groan. 'I've just done this routine with Liza!' He waited. She sighed and resigned herself to another airing of the edited highlights. Gav. Reunion. Craig. Gav storming out. Message on the wall. Trying to find Liza. Meeting Justin.

His gaze flicked between her lips and her eyes. 'So you did have sex with me to punish your husband?'

'No! I ... well, I just ... didn't feel any particular loyalty to him right then. I was angry. Not thinking straight.' She wished he'd step back; take the warmth of his disturbing body away.

'What about me? Was it fair to me?'

His aftershave seemed to envelop her, making breathing difficult, preventing her brain from wholly commanding her mouth.

The heat of his hand settling suddenly on her bare leg below her dress startled her into exaggerated recoil. She ought to push him off, slap him away, but her limbs seemed to have turned to rubber. Unchallenged, the hand slid higher up her thigh, stroking gently. 'If a bloke used a woman in the way you used me, you'd be calling him seven types of bastard, wouldn't you?' He began to lift the cotton fabric.

'I didn't use you!' Honesty made her add, 'I didn't mean to, anyway.' Her voice sounded squeaky and she was unable to concentrate on much but his scalding touch. If she objected, he'd stop. But her mouth wouldn't issue the objection.

His hand drifted higher, reached the soft line where her knickers began. 'You used me for sex. And to get back at your husband.' His fingers probed thoughtfully past the lace. 'Without worrying how I'd feel about it.'

Cleo gasped and clutched hopelessly at the smooth door behind her, her knees loose with desire. She seemed to have forgotten the mechanics of breathing, her chest moved unevenly, pumping air in haphazard chunks.

Yet he seemed perfectly controlled, his voice low and even. 'Do you want sex tonight?'

Clinging to the last remnants of sense, she managed a shake of her spinning head.

He whispered, 'It could be right here. Right now.'

She shook her head again. 'Don't, Justin!' She despised herself. The next word that came out of her mouth was going to be *yes*.

Slowly, slowly, he released her. And asked, casually, 'I suppose you took the morning-after pill?'

She stared at him, at his sharp nose and sensual lips. Slowly, she shook her head.

He remained calm. 'Why not?'

She dropped her eyes. 'I didn't think of it.'

He laughed, a sharp crack, without humour. 'You're brilliant, you are.' Taking her phone out of his pocket he lifted her left hand, stared for a moment at her wedding rings, and dropped the phone into her palm. 'And you've got bad fucking manners.' One step back and he no longer filled Cleo's vision. She could see Liza waiting, out of earshot. Another step back. 'I hope, at least, that everything was to your satisfaction.' He turned and stalked away.

Freed of his presence, suddenly infuriated at his snooty, wounded pride, she bawled after him, 'You got every bit as much sex as I did!'

A passing group of lads laughed and whooped and Cleo felt mortification curl her toes; that really improved the situation.

Justin turned back, made a pistol out of two fingers and a thumb and pointed it at her. 'It was ... fine. But let's just keep it between us two, shall we? As you're a married woman.'

Silently, Liza joined Cleo, watching Justin pass the other shops until he disappeared into the darkness and was gone. 'Phwoar!' She whistled. 'He's succulent. Have you got his number?'

Cleo shook with a sudden laugh, rubbing her arms as if to warm away goosebumps. 'I don't suppose it's easy to get Justin's number.'

Finally, when they were back at Liza's flat, in the familiar, tiny second bedroom with magnolia walls and no carpet, Cleo removed her make-up and undressed, waiting her turn for the bathroom.

And when Liza appeared, looking clean and miles younger than twenty-eight, Cleo blurted, 'What do you know about the morning-after pill?'

Liza halted abruptly. 'Oh shit! What have you done?'

Cleo looked down at her hands. 'I came off the pill. And forgot the cap. And didn't think about condoms because I'm just not in the habit any more.'

'*Cleo!*' Liza hissed. 'You've got to take it within three days of having unprotected sex. The sooner, the better.'

Cleo chewed her lip.

'Or you can have a coil fitted, within five days. When exactly did you ...?'

'Seven days.'

Liza closed despairing eyes. 'For fuck's sake, go and get some help. Ask for an emergency appointment in the morning. Honestly.' She shook her head. 'Cleo! Wake up! The real world's not as safe as a cosy marriage, you know! You'll have to go and get sorted, first thing.'

But, even earlier than first thing, at six in the morning, Gav phoned, fighting panic. 'My sister's just rung, Dad's in hospital. He's had a heart attack!'

Chapter Seven

Cleo dashed home, tormented by pictures of her father-in-law, George, helpless in a hospital bed, his normally ruddy complexion as grey as his toothbrush moustache, and jumped straight into Gav's car for the drive to Yorkshire. She was still struggling with her seat belt as Gav flung the car into Cross Street, left into Main Road, straight out of the village past slate and stone cottages and The Three Fishes. 'How is he?' she gasped.

Gav's knuckles were white on the steering wheel. 'Not good. More than just a warning, Mum said. He'd been having pains in his arm all evening, then in the early hours he began to feel as if his chest was being crushed.' Jerkily, he fed the car onto a large roundabout.

'Poor George.' Cleo liked both George and her mother-in-law, Pauline. A warm, twinkling Yorkshireman, George had returned to his county the minute retirement had let him; and Pauline didn't seem to mind where they lived, so long as they were together.

Their house, normally airy and tall, seemed to have shrunk at the advent of family with weekend cases and neighbours milling between the sitting room and the hall. Squeezing her way through the clutter, Cleo thought Pauline looked inundated even without Gav's sister, Yvonne, having arrived a minute before them, smothering her with a hug, sniffing, 'Allen has to work today, he'll phone this afternoon. How's Dad? How're you? Oops, I must sit down.' Yvonne was three months pregnant and spent most of her time feeling faint, her skin taking on an alarming pallor and her cloud of hair frizzing from the sweat on her forehead.

Gav kissed his mother's white cheek, letting Yvonne totter to the hall chair unaided. 'What's the news? Can we see him today?'

Although looking drawn and grey, Pauline managed a smile for her children. 'He's "resting comfortably, but not out of the woods". Which means they don't know what's going to happen, of course. I'm OK, a bit shell-shocked. I've got to ring after the doctor's rounds ... oh, can you answer the door, Gavin?'

Another neighbour had presented herself on the doorstep. 'Not to bother you, love, but I wondered if there was any news. Or if I could do anything to help?' Gav ushered her to join two other neighbours grave-faced in the sitting room. Yvonne bustled after, no doubt to regale them with accounts of her journey, her condition and how worried she was about her father. Pauline sat down suddenly at the bottom of the stairs.

Cleo crouched beside her and took her hands, chilly despite the summer's day. 'Haven't you slept?'

Bags hung under Pauline's eyes. 'Not a wink, darling. Everything's been so ... I haven't even said hello to you, Cleo.' Her bottom lip trembled.

'Doesn't matter.' Cleo piled the bags into the corner under the phone shelf and helped Pauline to her feet. 'Come sit in your rocking chair with a hot drink.' In minutes she had a steaming cup of tea at Pauline's elbow with two digestive biscuits in a saucer, then she loaded a tray for the sitting room, which Yvonne took over, as Cleo had known she would.

Stomach-growlingly aware of her own hunger, she returned to delve in the fridge for bacon.

Through the doorway she could hear the neighbours' voices dominating the sitting-room conversation, though Yvonne wasn't giving up the arena easily.

She half listened as she grilled bacon and kept an eye on her mother-in-law. Pauline's head had tipped back and her eyes closed, her half-drunk tea cooling on the table. It was the first time Cleo had seen Pauline grey and beleaguered, her face slack as she dozed. If ever someone needed a bit of peace!

Cleo gave the neighbours fifteen minutes to drink their tea then marched in, disrupting the debate about whether George had looked well recently. 'I've made bacon rolls for you, Gav and Yvonne. The rest of you will excuse us now, won't you? Everyone's upset, Pauline's asleep and we've had no time to eat.' The neighbours, after an instant's surprised silence, rose to their feet.

As Gav saw them out, Yvonne rushed into the kitchen after Cleo. 'I wish I could make direct requests like that! I'm afraid of upsetting people but you don't give a bugger, do you? I should be doing the breakfast! I just sat down for –'

Cleo, finger on lips, indicated Pauline. 'You're too upset. Don't worry. You guys look after George and I'll do the boring stuff, OK?'

So, for the next few days, Cleo took on the catering. Yvonne didn't really like not being Queen of the Kitchen but clung to her condition as an excuse to concede the throne. Pauline continued to look as if she'd been hit by a truck. Gav prowled restlessly, pouncing on any errand that would get him out of the house.

Cleo visited the hospital only once because she didn't think that her father-in-law needed to be tired by unnecessary visitors. Waxy and weary, George had been tied to his hospital bed by monitors and drips, looking calm but curiously loose and dishevelled. An oxygen mask was within his reach and the smell of sick people hung on the air.

Cleo hated the temporariness of camping in her parents-in-law's spare room. She had only the few clothes that Gav had thrown into a bag for her, and slept in pyjamas because she never knew who she'd meet on the way to the bathroom at night. But she had no real option other than to ring Ntrain on Monday morning and arrange to stay longer.

Nathan hummed as he consulted the bookings schedule. 'Let's see, let's see …' Cleo could imagine him wearing his telephone headset, scrolling across the on-screen roster. 'I can cover your work till Wednesday but is there any chance of you coming back for Thursday? You've got Interpersonal Skills at Rockley Image and I just haven't got another body to fill in. Rockley's a brand new client so I don't want to have to reschedule.'

The Interpersonal Skills Through Effective Communication seminar *for every communicator wanting to climb the ladder of success!* was a day of quirky exercises, discussion and group activities aimed at encouraging colleagues to communicate effectively with each other and with clients. It was popular with firms who wanted training short and easy on the budget. Their *newly aware* staff usually emerged chattering and joking, giving the impression that Ntrain had done a great job in helping them to *enjoy outstanding working relationships* and *become people masters* and making good the promo material's promise: *Employees will smile.*

Gav looked a bit stony when she told him that she had only three days' compassionate leave but, as George was making progress, he had no real grounds for objection. So, late on Wednesday evening, she cruised home, having agreed to return at the weekend.

Stretching blissfully in her own bed, she slept like a log away from the tensions of Gav squabbling with Yvonne and Pauline and George worrying about each other, overslept, and had to rush to get ready and reach her 'gig'.

Ntrain employees had a look – a glossy, groomed,

flight-attendant look of suits, sharp hairstyles and, for the women, expert make-up. After a lightning-quick shower and drying her hair whilst she ate her toast, Cleo whizzed through foundation and powder, a flick of bronzer on her cheekbones, copper eyeliner to catch the lights in her dark eyes, brown-black mascara, cinnamon lipstick – and it was time to go.

Rockley Image occupied a business park unit, comprising a large print works with a glossy reception in front and a floor of offices above. As was boringly common, she'd been allocated a staff room. It boasted grey tables, green chairs and armchairs and a little kitchen area. After setting up the portable screen and hooking up her laptop to the projector, she dragged a table and chair to the front for herself and arranged the others informally, facing her. The armchairs she demoted to the back of the room. She loved the familiar feeling of anticipation and excitement as she set the room up. Would today's group be bright, eager and productive? Sluggish and coy? Or, as occasionally happened, hostile and abrasive?

Nathan, bless him, had had someone prepare and drop off a bag of name tags, seventeen including her own, which she picked out and clipped to her jacket as the first Rockley Image staff sauntered in. As her mobile rang at that moment, she shoved the list of participants to one side and spread the name tags over her desk for everyone to find their own, while reassuring Nathan that, yes, she was at the venue with no problems, and yes, she'd be able to meet clients the next day to plan a Telephone Etiquette and Customer Communication seminar.

She clapped the phone shut and launched herself into being a training professional, making connection through a flurry of words that would quiet the muttering and shuffling as the members of her group settled themselves.

'*Right*, sorry about that, everyone got a seat? Badge? Great. Hi! Nice to meet you all, I'm Cleo Callaway.' She pointed to her badge. 'Together, today, we're going to look at how we need to excel at interpersonal communication in order to succeed, to cheat time and achieve results by effective, focused communication.' As she spoke she looked around the room, making eye contact, assessing her audience. They were youngish and dress code was casual, which made her, in black skirt and burnt-orange jacket, stand out.

Though she'd done her homework and knew what Rockley Image did, she liked to break the ice and get everyone vocal before they got used to being silent. 'Can you remind me what Rockley Image provides for its clients ... oh!' It was very nearly, 'Oh *shit*!' Because her visual check had progressed to the back row.

And the last person in the back row, slouched in the chair, polo shirt buttoned to the neck, deck shoes sticking out between the chairs in front, was Justin.

Horror swept the colour from her face.

By the delight in his eyes he'd been waiting to be noticed and was hugely amused now that he had been. With elaborate co-operation he answered, 'Corporate logos, stationery, leaflets, brochures ...'

Other voices contributed, '... product graphics, multi-media and web design ...'

'... posters, banners, design and print.'

'Great,' she said, weakly, trying to recapture her stride. 'You shouldn't have any trouble with the bit of drawing required for our first activity.' She swallowed and made an effort to put some beef back in her voice. She smiled determinedly at two people in the front of the group – the ones who risked sitting at the front weren't normally worried about being picked on. 'Could you be the first to come out here and help me? The challenge is for one person to describe a simple design of shapes and lines and the other to draw it from only the description.'

Cleo used this ice-breaker regularly; the sometimes outlandish results were always good for a laugh. Positioning a woman called Bernadette to face a gangly, thinning man named Ian, she outlined the rules. 'No peeking, no repetition and no gestures! If you're good at Pictionary – well, this is the reverse. You have two minutes.'

Bernadette flourished her thick black marker pen and started drawing eagerly the instant Ian began, 'Draw a circle, then a zig-zag ... oh, that should be coming from the bottom. Under them draw a triangle ...'

Bernadette looked crestfallen. 'I've run out of space.'

'You should've let me finish before you crashed on!' Ian slouched back to his seat as his co-workers grinned at his lack of success. Cleo broke through the sniggers to select Holly, a pretty, pink-faced girl from the centre at the back – it was always as well to involve those at the rear before they got the idea that they could get away without doing any work. 'Could you be our flip chart artist? I'll give each person a different diagram to describe in turn. You just do the drawing.' When Cleo turned back after passing out the papers, she realised that Holly was heavily pregnant.

She paused. Morning-after pills and intrauterine devices flashed into her mind. Sod it. Because of George's heart attack, she'd never made an appointment with her doctor. Her concentration was wavering enough with Justin smirking at her, and she felt hot and fatigued. She forced a smile. 'Are you OK to stand up and do this?'

'Yeah, yeah.' Holly rubbed her belly through her denim dress. 'Safe for a while yet.'

Ignoring the film of sweat that had burst out on her cheeks, Cleo turned back to the group. 'OK, we'll work to time limits to keep things moving. Could you begin?' She pointed at a thin, dark man. He began uneasily. 'Draw a circle ... no, no, wait, about halfway up the page! Draw three parallel lines ... oh, I meant vertical ...' By the time a few had taken their turn they were getting it, learning from the errors and inaccuracies of those who went before, making their instructions ever more precise. At the end, each would hold up his or her diagram to compare to Holly's interpretation while Cleo lobbed in light feedback. 'Bernadette, succinct and successful ... Philip, nearly there but I think you could save time if you spoke more clearly with fewer hesitations.'

Justin was last. He smiled at Holly. Holly stopped arguing with a truculent Phil and smiled back. 'Holly, in the centre of the page, draw a circle with a three-inch diameter.' The marker pen squeaked as Holly drew. Justin continued, 'Let that circle be a bucket seen from above. Equally spaced, and likewise seen from above – draw four Mexicans peeing in it.' A gale of laughter. Holly giggled, considered, then drew four more circles with dots in the middle to represent sombreros, joined to the original circle by short, straight lines.

Justin turned his page round to display exactly the same design.

Cleo had to raise her voice over the applause. 'Justin – unorthodox but effective!'

She found herself smiling into the laughter in his eyes. Oh no, that wouldn't do! She snapped her gaze away and moved quickly to the next segment, a presentation on her laptop.

Just before they broke for lunch she began her favourite routine, speaking rapidly, slapping written papers face down before each person, exam-style.

'Right. Must hurry! By now you should have assimilated sufficient strategies to race through this paper in the two minutes allowed. I don't expect any failures! Read the whole paper before you begin. Two minutes to do precisely what it says. Two minutes, don't let me down! Don't speak to each other. Begin.' Conspicuously, she checked her watch.

Pens were snatched up, first answers scribbled. And the second. They progressed to the section that required actions, jumping to their feet, counting backwards, 'Ten, nine, eight ...', sitting down, shouting out their middle names, 'Margaret, Edmund, John ...'

'One minute gone!' Cleo called.

With anxious glances at the clock, they folded over the top quarter of their pages, then wrote a large letter T on the backs of their hands. 'Forty seconds left.' Cleo let her voice rise on a warning note.

Two people did absolutely nothing other than read the paper. One of them was Justin.

And as the two-minute mark was reached, others began to clutch their heads and groan, 'Oh no!' Or laugh.

'Two minutes up.' Cleo beamed round. 'Nobody but Justin and Phil listened to my instructions. I said *read the whole paper first* – what does the final point, number twenty, say?'

She was answered by a sheepish chorus. '*Disregard points one to nineteen.*' More groans.

'So,' she grinned, 'that's reminded you to follow instructions even when you're under pressure!'

Lunchtime.

Cleo turned back to her laptop to cue up the next presentation; the staff filed out, still complaining at being caught out. Any chance Justin would suggest they lunch together? She hoped he wouldn't. No, she hoped he would. She glanced up.

He'd gone.

Cleo left only to buy a BLT on wholemeal from a little kiosk across the car park, then returned to help herself to a spoonful of the office coffee and ring Gav from her mobile. 'How's your dad?'

Gav exhaled loudly. 'Not bad. The doctors are saying he might be discharged on Monday.'

'What about your mum?'

'Coping.' She could picture Gav pacing to and fro as he talked into his phone. 'She'll be OK if I come home at the weekend. When's good for you?'

Because he hadn't tried to impose his own schedule Cleo felt generous. 'If I drive up Friday evening, we can come back Saturday or Sunday.'

'You're going to work to the end of the week, now?'

'I have to, really.'

He paused. Then, 'You've left your pyjamas here.'

They'd still be under the rose-splashed pillow and satin-quilted bedspread of George and Pauline's guest room. Cleo laughed. 'I didn't need them.'

Gav's voice dropped. 'They smell of you.'

'That's reasonable.'

'I like them. I was thinking ...' But he broke off without sharing his thought. 'You know I love you?'

'Mmm.' For a stinging moment, she actually felt sorry for Gav; for this new, uncertain Gav, anyway, trying to coax a loving reaction out of her. And failing. It was a new sensation. She hoped that this weirdness would fade soon and she'd go back to being glad to hear his voice and touch his skin. Approaching chatter in the corridor outside forewarned her that her time alone was up. 'The group's coming back. Must go.'

Justin was enjoying himself enormously, watching Cleo and how excruciatingly conscious she was of him. When he'd realised *Cleo* was 'the training woman' taking the seminar, a huge bubble of delight had lodged in his chest. And her expression when she'd noticed him! The shock-horror. Brilliant. A real 'Beam me up, Scotty' moment.

During the afternoon break, from his place in the coffee queue he watched her shunt armchairs into a circle at the back of the room before fetching one of the taller, straight-backed chairs and reserving it with her handbag. Her mobile, the one he'd carried around for almost a week, peeped out from a side pocket.

She raised her voice – 'Let's wind down in the comfy chairs' – and turned to accept the coffee that Bernadette – she would – had poured for her.

Justin took the seat dead opposite Cleo's.

Funny – and infuriating and frustrating – how he'd missed her. How could he miss someone after a mere fling? He couldn't. But he had. Tucking away the kitchen stool she'd used, snapping shut the lid on the shampoo she'd massaged through her hair, drying himself with the towel that had wrapped her body, her absence had been a palpable thing.

Discovering her mobile phone in his bedroom had temporarily broken his mood and he'd thrown his head back and laughed in gleeful anticipation of her efforts to retrieve it.

Later, he'd felt a deep, malicious satisfaction at giving her a right bollocking in that shop doorway. He had been *so* pissed off with the way she'd twisted the truth regarding her married status. He'd enjoyed turning his back on her; he wasn't accustomed to being used by women and it didn't sit well.

But he was also half regretful that she hadn't agreed to sex. He would've abandoned the Mr Angry stuff in a moment.

Cleo's voice cut into his thoughts. 'OK, if you'll all sit down ...' She was careful with her just-on-the-knee dress as she took the chair that gave her six inches of height above everyone else.

He looked at her legs.

She flicked a glance at him. 'We're all guilty, sometimes, of *not listening to each other*. We're busy. Our thoughts are elsewhere. We're not interested.'

She smiled around, engaging every member of the group. She was the moon and they were the waves, Justin thought: she could draw them along with her. 'A general understanding of co-workers promotes ease and helps dispel time-wasting antagonism. You don't have to like a colleague but you do have to communicate effectively with them to get your job done efficiently, and tolerance is part of team building. Harmony promotes respect. Not that I'm suggesting four-hour gossips on the firm's time, nor a barrage of deeply personal enquiries!'

Laughter, and Phil pointing accusingly at Holly.

Cleo grinned. 'It's a question of good business practice and achieving objectives, higher morale and increased levels of satisfaction. You spend too much time at work to make it miserable for yourself.

'And now we're going to explore how we feel giving a minute's thought to a colleague, to learn a little more about them than we already knew.'

She crossed her knees. He dropped his gaze back to her legs. She uncrossed them and colour touched her cheeks. But her eyes were amused. She turned to one of the web design girls, Fran. 'This concentrated exchange of information might feel a bit scary at the beginning – but it's a fun activity, honest.' Fran laughed and Cleo grinned back. 'Everyone will take their turn to ask someone a question, one to which you won't know the answer. The person who's answered will be next to ask. And I'll begin ... can you tell me about any part-time job you had as a teenager? Speak for about one minute.'

Fran pinkened, wriggled about and said 'um' five times

before faltering into an account of working in Woolworths as a Saturday girl, growing more articulate as she described the nylon overall, sadistic till rolls and stroppy customers. Two other women, alight with shared memories, exclaimed in recognition of the days they were Woolies Saturday girls, too.

Cleo moved the activity on. 'Brilliant! Your turn now, Fran. Choose somebody, then ask them a question. Try to be specific.'

After a moment's thought, Fran addressed Phil. 'Can you remember something that made you sad when you were twenty-one?'

Phil clutched his chest theatrically. 'She was twenty-three, blonde, sexy and beautiful – and going out with my brother. When I asked her out, she laughed. I was so heartbroken I almost joined the Foreign Legion.' He was greeted with laughter from the men, *aaah*'s from the women.

As the chain progressed, Phil asked Bernadette what she expected to be doing when she reached forty. Bernadette asked Holly how her family had reacted to news of her pregnancy.

Every time Justin looked at Cleo, she was listening intently. Encouraging a few more words if an answer came up short, nodding at exclamations of experiences in common, neatly curtailing responses that threatened to ramble. Cool, quietly authoritative. Good at doing her thing.

Then it was Holly's turn. 'Justin. What do you do in your spare time? Keep it clean!'

Lovely. Good old Holly, he couldn't have scripted a better question. 'I've got a part share in a jet-ski. Me and my mates go out to a lake.' He described the speed, the plumes of spray, the carving of patterns in the surface, the noise, how it felt to be carrying a passenger, warm arms around his waist like a seat belt. He smiled at Cleo, who was looking down at her notes, cheeks pink. 'My question isn't it?'

She nodded.

'Cleo.' Her head jerked up, eyes horrified. 'Cleo, tell us about the last time you got drunk and regretted it.' He grinned. Couldn't help it. Her flush became a scald and a sheen broke out below her eyes and his grin stretched until he must look like The Joker.

She attempted a shaky laugh. 'Oh, I regret it *every* time I get drunk!' As if in the throes of a hangover, she clutched her head.

But the group waited expectantly, gazes fixed on her. And Justin added calmly, 'Come on. Be honest.'

Chapter Eight

She bit her lip and shot him a glance. The expectant silence dragged on. She squared her shoulders. 'OK. A couple of weekends ago I was upset and came into Peterborough to find my sister, to cry on her shoulder.' Her voice was thin, tight, artificially casual, a verbal shrug as if to make the story unimportant. 'I couldn't find my sister –' She looked at him again. And this time he read her eyes.

Betrayed. Reproachful.

He cut across her. 'I'm sorry, I was supposed to be asking another staff member, wasn't I? Ian, when did *you* last get drunk and regret it?'

Ian groaned. 'Yesterday! Regretted it this morning when the alarm went off. Don't you just hate alarms? *Yeep, yeep, yeep*! I couldn't face breakfast –' Laughing heads turned Ian's way. But Justin looked at Cleo and saw that her eyes were swimming. She rifled through her handbag, found a tissue and shook her hair forward whilst she blew her nose.

Balls, balls, *balls*.

They filed out at the end of the day, chattering, stowing pens, calling cheerio, fishing out car keys. Cleo responded brightly, flashing her best smile. 'Thanks for attending! I hope you enjoyed your day.' Collapsing her flip chart, binning pages covered with coloured headings and emphatic arrows.

At last the door shut and she halted, sagging against a table. Her professional smile flicked off. Slowly, she rubbed her temples. Bastard Justin. Backing her so publicly into a corner, making her heart pump as she broke out into a sickening all-over sweat. Bastard.

'It was meant to be funny. And then I realised it wasn't.' His voice, from the doorway, startled her upright.

She wanted to turn to him coolly, arch an eyebrow and say, 'Oh *that*? Don't worry, I can handle your pranks.' But a ball had jumped into her throat and her eyes burned. She pushed her finger and thumb against her eyelids to stop the tears from spilling over.

His footsteps rustled over the nylon carpet tiles. The table moved as he perched beside her, his arm sliding around her shoulders. 'Sorry.' One arm became both and he pulled her against him, his cheek hot against her hair.

And when her breathing evened, when she had fought the silly tears and won, he tightened the hug momentarily, kissed the top of her head, and left.

The motorway was Friday-evening hell. Lorries and coaches lumbered nose to tail in the inner lanes and the outside lane was infested with headlight-flashing maniacs. By the time she reached her in-laws' pebble-dashed home, Cleo had developed a pounding headache.

It went with the pain in the neck when Yvonne opened the door, beaming. 'Hello – I'm just leaving!'

Cleo waited for her sister-in-law to step back and allow her into the house. 'Not just because I'm here, I hope?'

Giggle. ''Course not! Oh, I'm stopping you getting in, aren't I?' Giggle. 'Gav and Mum are at the hospital. I'll get you a cup of tea before I go.' Yvonne checked her watch.

'No thanks, it'll hold you up.'

'Won't take a minute.'

Yvonne could never resist trying to make Cleo the guest. She bustled importantly towards the kitchen. Instead of following, Cleo strode upstairs, calling, 'I'll make one when I'm ready.'

The guest room was scattered with Gav's stuff. Shirts

on hangers hung from the picture rail; his bag stood on the dressing table with jogging pants hanging half out – probably Pauline would allow no one else in the world to stand a sports bag on that beautifully polished surface – and an electric razor sat on top of a Bernard Cornwell paperback on the bedside table.

Cleo stepped out of her skirt, shrugged off her jacket and slotted the hanger into the otherwise empty wardrobe, balling her blouse back into the bag for washing. A bath would be nice but other people's hot water arrangements were delicate; one unscheduled bath might sabotage the household routine. Maybe she'd wait and ask Pauline. She sure as hell wasn't going to ask Yvonne, who'd find a way to say no, subjecting her to an earnest, apologetic explanation of the timer and the cylinder capacity.

It would've been far better, she realised belatedly, if she'd showered and changed at home rather than coming straight from the office. Gav and Pauline would have been home and Yvonne wouldn't.

But a wash and a change of knickers would have to do for the moment.

'Here's your tea … Oops!'

'Don't bother to knock.' Cleo, knickers in hand, raised both eyebrows at Yvonne with her best 'You're a total arse' look.

Blushing, Yvonne cast about for somewhere to deposit the steaming mug. 'But I did shout!' she protested. 'Your tea was getting cold.'

'And now my bum is.' Cleo stepped into clean undies and unfolded her jeans.

'Anyway' – Yvonne studied the doorknob as Cleo dressed – 'I don't know what's the matter with Gav.'

Armed with a clean T-shirt and her sponge bag, Cleo waited.

Yvonne shot her a look from under her eyelashes. 'He's been really funny. Even Mum's noticed how moody he is, always wanting to be on his own. Half the time he doesn't answer when I speak to him.'

Not everybody did want to hang on Yvonne's words, of course, and particularly not Gav, who still had a very adolescent relationship with his sister. 'Maybe it's his time of the month,' Cleo cracked. Oh yes, her own period was due. That probably explained her headache. And she'd brought nothing with her. Shit. Hopefully it would hold off until tomorrow when she could shop. And then, seeing her sister-in-law's uncertain frown, 'It was a *joke*, Yvonne! I know Gav doesn't really have periods.'

Yvonne's face cleared. She giggled.

Despite the fact that he'd been commissioned to fetch a takeaway, Gav stretched on the silky quilt and watched Cleo brush her hair. 'How about going home tomorrow?'

'Fine. Are you going to fetch the food soon? My head aches.'

Gav didn't move. 'Mum says she'll be OK. Dad's coming home on Monday. Best to leave them alone.'

'Maybe we could do them a big shop before we go.' Lunch was ages ago. Visions of prawns in black bean sauce were making her salivate. Her headache was worsening as her stomach felt more and more hollow.

With the toe of one foot, Gav prised his trainer off the other. It clonked onto the rose-splashed carpet.

Cleo trod into her own shoes and picked up her keys. 'I'll go for the food.'

With a sigh, Gav rolled to his feet and retrieved his shoe. 'OK, OK, I get the message! Heaven forbid I should chill for a minute.' Dull colour heated his face.

Cleo jingled her keys. 'The only message is that I'm very

hungry. I'm quite happy to go. Chill as long as you want.'

'I said I'll *go*!' He brushed past her, shaking his head.

Down in the kitchen, when Cleo clattered in and slid plates into the oven to warm, Pauline roused herself from sitting in the rocking chair and stared gently at nothing. 'Was that Gavin going? I'm sorry I didn't have a meal ready for you, Cleo. Whatever must you think?'

Cleo studied the lines of anxiety and fatigue on Pauline's face. 'Don't worry. You're shattered. Let's just be glad George is on the mend.'

Pauline knocked hastily on wood. 'Thankfully. I'll be OK when he's home and all the toing and froing is over. It took poor Gavin forty-five minutes to drive the thirteen miles today. What with the lights and the ring road.'

Cleo wiped the table and went to the cutlery drawer. 'We're thinking about going home tomorrow, leaving you in peace. Or do you want us to stay to drive you to hospital?'

'I'm quite happy to go at my own pace and bring George home on Monday. You get off, it's probably best. I think Gavin's had enough of us. He's been a bit ...' Pauline ended with a vague wave of her hand. Her hair was flattened at the back and Cleo missed her mother-in-law's usual combed and lipsticked smartness.

She hunted for the salt and pepper. 'I thought we could do a big shop, before we leave. One less thing for you to worry over.' She tracked the condiments down to a narrow cupboard, on a plate to collect spills. Probably a spot of Yvonne reorganisation; only Yvonne would reorganise someone else's kitchen.

Pauline heaved herself up and slid an affectionate arm around Cleo. 'You spoil me. Thank you, darling. And I haven't even asked how you are or if the motorway was awful.'

'I'm fine.' Her headache would go when she'd eaten. Or

when her period began.

Pauline dropped her cheek onto Cleo's shoulder for a weary moment. 'I'm just desperate for everything to be normal again. It doesn't seem much to ask.'

But sometimes too much. 'I know what you mean.'

The night was close and Cleo woke up clammy, Gav's arm hot, heavy and trapping her, his body touching hers all the way up. She tried to ease away but found herself already at the edge of the bed. Gav inched closer, mumbling sleep language, his breath scalding her neck.

She tried to remember the dream that had just broken. Skidding images of holding something and being frightened it would be seen but not knowing how to conceal it. And a feeling of being trapped.

'Give me a bit of space, Gav,' she whispered.

Chapter Nine

Usually Gav liked the friendliness of his parents' street, but the neighbours had driven him nuts with their constant demands for up-to-the-minute George-bulletins. And he'd been stuck with his mother's claustrophobic half-a-car, little heap of shit.

Still, his dad seemed to be on the mend, that was the main thing. He was grateful.

And he was free to come back to work. He locked his Focus and glanced up at the endless windows of the Clyde, Rhode & Owen offices. Standing in the car park in the sweet unidentifiable smell of the CR&O flavourings plant, he shrugged into his jacket. But, instead of heading straight for the office, he wandered towards the brook that idled at the edge of the industrial estate past their building. Climbing over the two-bar fence, he pushed through the cool fronds of a willow tree and joined the dog-walking track beside the water.

The sun dappled through the elders and a lacy edging of cow parsley almost made the olive water pretty. He kicked stones into it as he walked. Birds, seemingly uncaring that their home was only an overgrown patch no one else wanted, sang liquid songs to the pale-blue sky. A cloud of gnats danced infuriatingly around his face and he swatted at them futilely.

He dropped sticks into the water to see how fast they left him, watched leaves dance with the sunlight, nodded at two dog walkers and let time go by.

What was he going to do about Cleo?

Her picture slid easily into his mind. Dark hair thick to

her shoulders, a long and wispy fringe sweeping above her beautiful eyes, the generous mouth he'd possessed a million times. Her curvy body. The body he'd held, stroked and loved, been faithful to for so long. His playground.

Fear was a monster in his guts. Bad things were happening and, even whilst he hid them from her, Cleo's apparent inability to see them was making him unreasonably angry with her.

Things were tense at home, but he didn't want to go to work. Lillian would be back. With Lillian's holiday and his hurriedly taken week in Yorkshire, he'd avoided her for a fortnight. But now she'd be back with her cocky one-upmanship. The fear monster stirred. Sometimes he hated Lillian and could envisage changing jobs to get away from her sharply styled hair of red and blonde streaks, her tight skirts.

But sometimes he fancied her absolutely dead rotten, despite loving Cleo. And that made him feel guilty. Which made him mad at Lillian. And, improbably, again at Cleo.

He turned for the office, feeling no better about his life for having taken ten minutes to reflect on it.

Crossing the marble foyer floor, he swiped his security pass to open the lift door, forcing encouraging and motivating phrases into his mind to reassure himself that Lillian was no better than him. 'We're the same grade, both tens.' Ten. A junior management grade. Gav a 10A and there weren't too many people who merited an A. And only one who merited an A (Special). 'Bloody Lillian. Same grade, same sodding grade, I do my work just as well, she isn't actually my senior. Only a "special", not Superwoman. Lillian is *not* Superwoman. Lillian is dangerous.'

His section was at the far end of a floor so enormous that some of the young headcases brought micro scooters to whiz up and down on. Often, members of a section had no idea about the function of other sections. The flavourings industry was secretive about what it did and how it did it and the hierarchy of privileges and passwords would do MI5 proud.

His quadrants were sketchily separated from the others with wood-edged screens. His section had grey desks and blue trays; Lillian's section black desktops and red trays. The section members got mid-backed chairs; section leaders high-backed chairs with arms. And larger computer monitors. The trappings of success.

Lillian filled her corner with a huge, frothing asparagus fern. Gav had a wooden tidy with little compartments for paper clips and staples.

Gav was on time; Lillian looked as if she'd been at her desk for hours. He nodded as he passed on to his own section of twelve women and four men, all with groovy names like Daryl, Rowan and Erin, scrolling through their call lists and unwinding headsets.

It took three passwords – the company's, his section's and his own – before he could access his emails. Last week's figures waited at the top of his inbox and he scrolled through them. They were OK. Next section meeting he'd tell his team that OK was *not* OK. Outstanding was OK. And the first person to make excuses about the credit crunch would be put on a warning.

Lillian swayed up to his desk, tight little arse in her tight little skirt close to his arm, perfume cooking nicely on her pulse spot. 'How's your father?'

He thought about saying, 'Nice offer, but do you think howsyerfather is appropriate to the office?' But he was always a model of office courtesy. 'On the mend, but he's got to be careful for a while. Thanks.'

She nodded and began to wiggle away.

And then it just came out without warning, bleh, his voice

working independently. 'I need to speak to you.'

Her finely marked eyebrows lifted slightly over cool grey eyes. A fall of hair slid slowly, silkily from behind her ear, a curtain across her cheekbone.

'Later,' he added.

She nodded and swayed back to her seat. Gav made himself not watch. Wished he could take back his words. The less he had to do with Lillian, the better.

Definitely. Less, the better. He checked his BlackBerry for the time of his meeting with his line manager, Bob Chester, then set an alert to phone his mother later to see if his dad was home safely.

Hopefully, by the time Gav and Cleo paid a follow-up visit Dad would've got his stuffing back after the brutal conflict with his own body, and begun to care again whether his hair stood on end or his face was unwashed and unshaven. For now, Gav could forget the desperate prospect of his father's death.

During the whole panic, Cleo had been great. Unflappable, helpful, thoughtful, seeing what had to be done and doing it. A better wife than he currently deserved.

Cleo. He conjured up an image of his wife. Things weren't warm between them. Not since ... He tried to push the memory away but it came sneaking back. Maybe on Saturday they could go shopping for new wallpaper and, without the stripped patch above the bed reminding them both of the stupid words he'd scrawled there, they could forget the amazing rage that had frightened even him.

He tried to recall Cleo's schedule. He thought she was taking a training day somewhere. He'd text her and she could read the message at her next break.

He began a new text message. Inviting others 4 meal 2nite will cook spag bol love G.

Then there was just time to visit the Gents before

presenting himself in Bob's office.

An hour later, when he emerged, Lillian was loitering in the corridor reading a noticeboard. He jumped.

She smiled slightly. 'Well? What?'

He screwed up his face and rubbed his forehead. 'What was it, now?' A short, embarrassed laugh. 'It's gone. Completely slipped my mind. Sorry.'

He didn't want to talk to her after all.

Gav's text message made Cleo sigh. 'Now, do I really feel like an evening passing the wine, listening to everyone complain about their kids and about each other? No, I don't, actually.' Gav was a pain, not bothering to consult her before he invited guests. What if she'd wanted a quiet night in or a loud night out? Maybe she should go out with Liza and send Gav a little message about that? Sorry. Made other arrangements.

But when she texted her sister, Liza returned: Soz. On a date 2nite.

So Cleo made herself available to Nathan for a planning meeting and encouraged him into discussing strategies for getting established staff with entrenched ideas to accept current trends, thus ensuring that she'd arrive in Middledip later than her guests.

'Sorry,' she breezed in, 'heavy, heavy day.' Dropping her jacket on the sofa, she flopped onto the only vacant dining chair, helped herself to white wine and beamed around at Dora looking cheerful, Keith's dark brow knitting into his habitual slight frown, Ian's hooded gaze and Rhianne's full-face make-up. 'Hello, everyone!

Gav glanced at the clock. 'We thought you'd got lost.'

She took four swallows from her glass. The wine was a little fruity for her taste and yellower than white wine had a right to be. She turned the bottle to read the label. 'I had a

71

planning meeting.'

'You never said.'

'No. When are we eating?'

'There's just the pasta to drain.' Gav stayed in his seat, twirling his wine glass on the pearl-grey tablecloth – the best linen one that was hell to launder.

Cleo finished her wine and poured another with a sigh of relish. 'That's better. Who needs a top-up? Rhianne, you're looking healthy. Been soaking up the rays?' She focused on Rhianne's skin, as smooth and matte as a brown egg, as if genuinely unaware that Gav was waiting for her to execute a lightning clear-up in the kitchen, find the napkins, drain the pasta and serve the meal. 'I'm starving.'

Several beats passed before Gav got to his feet. 'How hot does the oven need to be for garlic bread?'

'Whatever it says on the packet. How's business, Keith? How are the kids, Dora? That shirt really suits you.'

Dora flushed. 'I'm down to a size *fourteen*! I've been such a good girl!'

Rhianne raised her glass. 'Give Ian the diet sheet, quick!'

Ian decided to take the joke. 'My chest measurement's already less than Dora's.'

Cleo lit some candles and chose a bottle of red from the wine rack. Through the doorway she could see Gav struggling in the kitchen, tutting when he couldn't find the oven gloves, turning the bread into rips and crumbs through using the wrong knife. How agreeable to loll back and await her meal. She must do it more often.

She let the conversation buzz round her. Dora really did look great. She seemed less clumsy and mumsy and what Gav had dubbed 'A-Dora-ble'. Being a few pounds lighter suited her and the buttercup-coloured shirt brought brightness to her fair hair. Or maybe she'd had her hair highlighted.

Keith seemed quiet. But then Keith specialised in being

saturnine and silent. He liked to give the impression that he knew things that others didn't.

'Grub's up.' Awkwardly, Gav carried in two big bowls. The spaghetti was watery and overcooked but nobody complained as they splashed the bolognese sauce over it. Cleo tried not to look at the red freckles appearing on the tablecloth.

Once the garlic bread and parmesan had made the rounds, Gav turned to Rhianne. 'Got any more tips on tantric sex?'

The corners of Rhianne's lips quirked, her thick lipstick magically unsullied by the act of eating. 'Think I've told you all I know. It's all to do with intensity, quality rather than quantity. Building up slowly, taking time to attune to each other's bodies.'

Gav smiled down the table at Cleo. 'Maybe we ought to try it?' His hair looked amber in the candlelight and a little quiff curled up over his forehead.

Cleo felt her eyebrows lift. Since the make-up sex when she came home fresh from the time with Justin, she and Gav hadn't made love. She hadn't wanted to. Guilt must be interfering with her libido. Or maybe it was that, until the memory of Justin's hands and lips had faded, she didn't trust herself.

Not that Gav seemed to notice. George's illness had upset normality, of course, with its rush, panic and fear. She rubbed her head above her ear where there was a small pain and wished her period would arrive to drain her tension headaches away. Maybe she'd stop feeling so perverse and in a constant state of mild aggravation, too.

Gav was still smiling at her through the yellow candlelight. 'How about coffee, now?'

She stretched and yawned. 'Lovely, bring lots or I'll fall asleep.'

A hesitation, then he climbed to his feet. 'How much do I

put in the machine?'

'It's on the *packet*.'

'Let's try it.'

Cleo collapsed slowly into the welcoming bedclothes like a deflating balloon; avoiding all the chores that evening had been almost as wearing as doing them and she was exhausted. She'd had to field a whole list of peevish questions: 'Can this go in the dishwasher? God, look at the state of the tablecloth, will that wash out? This dish won't come clean. Well, I didn't know it ought to have been soaking all evening!'

Cleo had let him do the lot. After all, he'd issued the invitations. She'd flopped down on the sofa and offered advice until the jobs were done and they could come to bed.

Bed. Bliss. She closed her eyes, let her lungs gently empty, then took a deep, calming breath. 'Try what?'

'Tantric sex. Or something like it.' He landed heavily on his side of the bed and her eyes reopened.

Gav was wearing summer pyjamas, matching shorts and T-shirt. New. Unaccountably, he held a pair of her pyjamas, shell pink and shiny. His eyes were bright. He let the pyjamas unfold and ran them up Cleo's arm. 'But I have my own interpretation. How about covering up for a while to whet our appetites? Then, after a week or two, sex will be really intense.'

Since when had Gav needed his appetite whetting? Cleo groaned and shut her eyes again. 'I can't be bothered with pyjamas. I'm *tired*.'

'Come on, let's try it.' And laughing, coaxing, he actually began to hook the pyjama trousers over her feet. Grumpily, she lifted her behind to allow him to pull them up. Silent and unco-operative as he awkwardly fought the top on, one arm, rolling her over the bunched material, two arms, fumbling with the buttons. By the time it was done, Gav was panting and Cleo felt like a badly wrapped parcel.

'There,' he said. 'What do you think?'

Cleo snapped, 'That it's a stupid idea!' Then, noticing the bulge in the front of his smart new jammies, 'We're not going to take them all off again now are we? I'm so *tired*!'

Yet when she could have slept, when Gav was breathing loudly beside her, she lay awake and brooded, feeling uncomfortably restricted. Pyjamas! Deliberately depriving themselves of sex? Gav and Cleo Callaway? Not the pre-That Weekend Gav and Cleo, anyway. Very strange. If it hadn't been for the bulgy shorts she would have suspected Gav of trying to hide a problem.

But, whatever his motives were for taking a sexual holiday, it was funny that she didn't mind.

She nudged her breast with her forearm. Uncomfortably tender. She wished her period would hurry up. Used to the regime of the pill, erratic periods were something she'd forgotten about.

The doctor had said that she might be irregular when she came off the pill. That's all it was, the feeling that she'd boil into a temper any moment, the tenderness and loss of libido. Coming off the pill could do funny things to a woman. Well-known fact.

But she would be glad when her period arrived.

Chapter Ten

Four weeks later, Cleo's hands, as she paid at the unfamiliar pharmacy counter on the outskirts of Leicester, felt clammy. Her period never had arrived and she was finding it harder and harder to believe it was because of post-pill ovulation eccentricity.

Clamping the bag to her side she stole out, past the incontinence aids, past the perfumes and make-up, past the photo booth and into the tree-lined, paved street. She paused, fumbling as she tried to tuck the long, flat package into her handbag.

But it seemed gigantic. She felt as if it might spring to life and leap from her bag, gleefully accosting passers-by: 'Look at me, I'm a pregnancy testing kit! Cleo's period's really late. She's afraid she's pregnant and isn't sure of the father. She picked a man up at a club! What use is the diaphragm at home in the box? There were condoms – yes, right there in the room – if only she'd thought about them in time. And then when she went home to Gav she did exactly the same thing. Absent-minded, or *what*? No morning-after pill either. Isn't she useless? I say, did *you* know Cleo's period's late? What will Gav say? Who do you vote for? Let's flip – heads for Gav and tails for Justin.'

All through the afternoon's Dealing with Difficult People workshop Cleo kept checking her bag was fastened so no one should catch a glimpse of the evidence of her guilt and laxity. Oh, to be home! Do the test. And know.

She'd hoped for a miracle for long enough.

The afternoon ended eventually and as her group clattered off she sighed with relief, bundling laptop and screen, flip chart and bag of pens into the back of her car. It seemed to take forever to negotiate Leicester's one-way system, fight her way along the A47 and circle the Peterborough parkways until she could peel off for Middledip. She reached home taut and edgy.

But, 'Damn!' There was Dora, waiting on the pavement, Eddie asleep in his buggy, Meggie hunting ladybirds on the shrubs leaning over the wall.

Dora looked great in black trousers and a square-necked top. She beamed as Cleo climbed from her car. 'We're surprise visitors. I thought it would be nice to walk around your village rather than the city. Meggie would like a go on the swings behind the village hall.'

Cleo blinked. Dora lived right on the edge of all the miles and miles of footpaths and playgrounds around Ferry Meadows' lakes.

'Lovely,' she lied. 'Come in and give Meggie a drink – hello Meggie – while I change.' And, casually, 'No Keith?'

Dora busied herself manoeuvring Eddie and Meggie over the doorstep and through into the kitchen. 'Keith's doing his own thing.'

'Doesn't look like Gav's home yet, either.' Was that a slight feeling of relief? 'Orange juice OK, Meggie?'

The stolid little girl nodded, bunches jiggling. ''S please.' Mousy strands of hair stuck to her forehead and cheeks. Her sandals made a sucking noise on the tiles as she hovered foot to foot.

'And some biscuits?'

''S please.'

'I'll just pop up and change.' She leapt up the stairs, tugging at the zip of her handbag and jamming it on the paper bag inside, before wrenching out the box and tucking it at the back of her knickers drawer. Later, have to be later. Or did the test only work in the mornings? Bugger Dora, why did she have to turn up tonight, just when she'd psyched herself up to learn the worst?

They stepped outside into the lavender light of a heavy English August evening.

Cleo tried gently to move Dora along. 'Shall we call on Rhianne?' Rhianne and Ian lived in the new part of the village, Bankside, where the houses were of pink or yellow brick.

Dora wrinkled her nose. 'I'd rather not, to be honest.'

'We'll go straight to the village hall then.' The muggy air smelled of cut grass as they took the path to the hall to the swish of the chubby rubber wheels on Eddie's buggy. Meggie scampered straight off to the swing.

Dora got her going in smooth arcs then beckoned Cleo out of earshot.

Cleo sighed. This was what the 'walk in the country' was about, obviously. Dora had something to tell her.

Unusually flushed and bright-eyed, guarding her mouth with her fingertips as if afraid someone might lip-read, Dora cleared her throat. 'Cleo, do you remember Keith and me going through that sticky patch? Before Eddie came along?'

'Of course.' Cleo had no trouble remembering that draggy period of Gav and Keith vanishing for long man-to-man talks. Dora had been silent and tense and merely shrugged whenever Cleo had asked if she could help.

Dora looked suddenly desolate. 'Keith had an affair.'

Cleo bit her lip. Had Gav known? 'That's so …! I did wonder. Is it over?'

'It was over before I found out. But when I did find out – bloody credit card receipts, would you believe, for hotels on weekends I thought he was at seminars; he was so careless it was insulting – I couldn't get over it. I couldn't forgive him for doing … that, with someone else.'

'Yes. I mean no. Right.' Guilt made Cleo suddenly hot. Dora's eyes were shining with tears and Cleo didn't want to think about Gav feeling like that. Please, the great god of mistakes, he wouldn't have to. As long as she wasn't pregnant.

With a baby that could be his.

Or could be Justin's.

'Mummy! Mummy! Push!'

Dora nipped over to Meggie's slowing swing, dragged it back and let it go, 'Wheee! OK, darling?' before scurrying back to Cleo. She was smiling, now. A smile touched with triumph. 'But this time, the boot's on the other foot!'

Cleo's brows shot up. 'Dora! You? Who?'

Dora's face softened. 'He's Meggie's swimming instructor. Sean. I've known him for months through taking Meggie for her lessons. But I met him in Bettsbrough by accident. The car had broken down. The kids were so tired and miserable that I felt like having a good cry – and he rang a garage and took us all into his house. We had coffee and he fed the children ... oh, Cleo, I can just *talk* to him for hours! Hours and hours. And he listens. He doesn't go behind his paper and answer, "Mmm?" He doesn't watch other girls when he's with me. He doesn't "just mention" that I've gone up two dress sizes since having the children. He's kind and generous and funny. And he *likes* me.'

She nipped back to tend Meggie's swing once more. 'Aren't you going high, sweetheart?' Eddie's wispy-haired little head tocked from side to side as he watched his sister from the buggy.

Cleo realised that as well as Dora's hair colour being lifted, she looked as if she was trying to grow her nails. And she was wearing perfume. Cleo felt an uncomfortable sense of impending change. 'This is serious stuff, isn't it? Have you ...?'

Dora's eyes danced. 'Have we ever!' She gripped Cleo's forearm, her words tumbling over one another. 'On the mornings when Sean's not teaching until the afternoon session, I take Meggie to preschool then rush to his flat and get into bed with him. I put Eddie on the floor in his car seat and give him a biscuit when he wakes up. I'm so wicked! But I've never felt like this about anyone. Cleo, I finally understand how you and Gav feel about each other. Nobody else matters.'

'Oh,' said Cleo, thinking that maybe things weren't as bad as she imagined if people still thought that. 'So, what do you think's happening? Is it a fling?'

Dora checked again that Meggie couldn't hear. 'Better!' she beamed.

Hesitation. 'An affair?'

'Better. It's … *it*!'

Eddie began to grizzle and Meggie, slowing, shouted, 'Mummy! Off now.' They trailed back to 11 Port Road to find Gav's car parked outside. 'I won't disturb Gav just now.' Dora hurriedly settled a squalling Eddie in his car seat as if frightened Cleo might frogmarch her in and force her to face Keith's best friend.

Meggie, drooping, began to whinge. 'Mummy, Mummy …'

'When I've strapped Eddie in,' Dora soothed.

On impulse, Cleo lifted Meggie up on her hip and felt the girl's tired head nestle gratefully into her shoulder. Hot, moist arms looped Cleo's neck and sandalled feet tapped her thigh. Meggie smelled of Milky Bars. Cleo found herself rocking gently as she wondered what kind of enormous changes were on their way into the child's little life.

Dora looked up, having finally succeeded in bending Eddie in the middle so that his straps could be fastened. 'Now there's something you don't see every day. Cleo Callaway being maternal.'

Cleo's face caught fire. 'She looked tired out.' Was guilt written across her face like graffiti? *Cleo might be up the duff. Justin + Gav were 'ere.*

Dora moved closer and Meggie instantly shifted her weight towards her mother's waiting arms. Cleo's side felt cool as Dora took Meggie up.

Dropping a kiss on her daughter's hair, Dora's eyes flickered across Cleo's face. 'You don't have to sound apologetic. It's not a crime to feel affection for a child.'

A child. A child? *A child.* Impulsively, Cleo asked, 'How did it feel to be pregnant?' And instantly wished she hadn't.

But Dora didn't seem to see anything odd in the question. She hugged Meggie. 'For me it was lovely. I'd been aching for a baby. My boobs got bigger, then my stomach. I used to love to feel the baby kicking, as if I was hugging a secret. When Meggie was born I actually missed the constant movement inside. But that's just me – I've heard others say they felt invaded, couldn't wait for it to be over, were sick for the entire nine months, got greasy hair and spots.' She slid Meggie onto her booster seat and fastened the belt, stroking the little girl's damp fringe where it hung over heavy eyes. 'Pregnancy changes your life completely.'

'Yes. I can see how that works.'

As Cleo stood on the pavement and waved Dora off, Gav bounded from the house behind her. He kissed her lips, hard and briefly. 'Hello and goodbye, I'm playing seven-a-side. Unless you want to come?'

'I haven't eaten or anything.' She pressed an answering kiss to the corner of his mouth and stepped out from his arm. 'Hope you score.'

He slammed the tailgate of his car and looked at her oddly. 'Not very likely, is it? As I'm goalie now?'

She shook back her hair. How could she have forgotten?

81

Gav downshifting to goalie had been a big enough deal at the time. He'd slowed up, he'd been told, and would no longer be picked as a forward. She'd lost count of the number of times she'd heard the word 'gutted'. 'I hope nobody from the other team scores, then.' Just go. Drive away. I need to be alone.

A final blown kiss and he slid into the car.

Her legs, as she trod up the stairs to their bedroom, vibrated very slightly. Surely they couldn't be *shaking*? Maybe she was just tired.

The box. Blue and white. Cellophane. Instructions. She stared at the wand for a long time. Read about the ludicrous procedure of peeing on it and waiting to see how many blue lines appeared in the square window. The test could be done at any time of day.

She was sure they knew what they were talking about, but maybe she'd do it in the morning. She was so tired now, weighed down by Dora's confessions; too tired to face up to things.

Carefully, she tucked the box back in the drawer.

In the shower, she soaped. Her breasts felt funny. She cupped them – was there an unusual weightiness? They ached. Could be premenstrual, she suffered that way occasionally. And her stomach, surely, was rounder? But if she was pregnant shouldn't she be feeling sick? Immediately, she did feel sick, nauseated at what she might have to deal with. She thought of Yvonne's fainting fits. Was that why her own legs felt like jelly?

She held her stomach, pressing hard as if she could squeeze a period out. Surely *she* couldn't be pregnant. It couldn't be *her* checking her pants every time she went to the loo. Going more often than usual – and hell, that was another sign, wasn't it? She didn't want children. Gav didn't.

She couldn't begin to guess how Justin would feel about it.

Chapter Eleven

'Gav's really odd.' Cleo pulled her jacket more tightly around her and sipped her wine. If only the sun would come out and breathe a bit of colour into the summer flowers in the pub garden by the river, a little warmth into the air. 'Ever since, y'know, he's been strange.'

Liza, the non-driver, drank deeply and topped her wine up generously. 'In what way? He hasn't taken up gardening has he?'

Cleo glared. 'I'm talking about this pyjama thing. Have you ever heard of couples voluntarily depriving themselves of sexual contact to enhance a "big bang" at some future date?'

Liza's busy eyes followed four men cycling past in black and rainbow lycra. 'Yup. Channel 4 documentary. Men with impotence problems.'

Cleo felt the urge to grasp her sister's elfin face by the nose and yank her around to pay proper attention. 'But if that's his problem, why the big bulge in the pyjamas? All he ever wants is passionate hugs and intense kisses. But anyway, sod him, I don't like pyjamas and I've gone back to sleeping in the nud. He can please himself.'

The cyclists out of sight, Liza turned blue eyes on Cleo. 'So you're not having sex?'

Cleo shook her head and shivered, wondering if she could persuade Liza to move indoors where it was warmer. The scenery in there was inarguably duller – Liza's eyes had flicked now to two red kayaks skimming up the river towards them, powered by broad shoulders and flashing paddles.

'Don't you mind? *No* sex?'

Cleo shrugged. 'Guilt over Justin's still interfering with my appetite, probably, and I've had other things to worry about.' Like a pregnancy test that had somehow achieved bogeyman status, so scary that she'd mustered a string of excuses to avoid taking it. Because if she knew she was pregnant, then she'd have to face the tricky paternity question –

Was becoming a total wuss a symptom of pregnancy? She sighed, blowing someone's discarded paper napkin off the wooden table.

Liza's contemplative gaze swivelled her way. 'I suppose you're sure, by now, that you're not going to be a mummy?'

Cleo deliberately assumed her most withering expression. 'Liza! I'm old enough to cope with life, you know.'

So why hadn't she taken the pregnancy test?

Why was she doing nothing while her husband acted like a prat and her marriage became a shell? Why was she avoiding contact with the couples she'd long considered her friends? Why wasn't she even confiding properly in Liza, Liza, with whom no subject had ever been sacred? Why wasn't she sharing her fears with someone. Anyone?

Perhaps with one of the men responsible, if a baby was on the cards?

Stupid expression, 'on the cards', as if an embryo was balanced on a pack of Waddington's. No, it'd be growing inside her body. Part of her. Taking sustenance, developing, moving. Inside her body. She cupped her hand furtively to her stomach. It was rounder, she was sure. She felt dull with fear and dumb with misery.

Gav made the phone call. He'd put it off for too long. He found the number in the phone book and dialled it with the rubbery phone buttons. Something had to be done about him and Cleo. He listened to the automated instructions coming through the telephone, and sighed as he made arrangements. None of it seemed real. This couldn't be happening to him, to them.

He dialled again, a familiar number this time. 'Keith, fancy a drink, mate? I could do with a chat.'

'I'm drooling over the one with the blue eyes and the bouncy chest,' Drew decided, chin on hand, eyes, behind the stare-disguising shades, fixed on a tableful of females.

Martin rubbed his chin while he deliberated. 'OK, I'll settle for the freckly one with the shiny green top. That leaves Justin with the curly one. All right, mate?'

'What?' Justin checked out the table of three girls that Martin and Drew had in their sights. It was a familiar enough scene, hitting on pretty women. But tonight it seemed an effort. He couldn't even be bothered to go over and kiss a cheek or shake a hand. The last woman he'd kissed had been Cleo.

The last woman in his bed. The last to lay her pretty hands on his body.

He just didn't feel like the chatting up, the drink buying and the bullshit. He stood up. 'Sorry. I'm feeling a bit rough, I'd better have an early night.'

Drew and Martin sent him astonished looks over their shades. 'That married woman's really fucked you up,' observed Drew.

Instead of going home, Justin drove to the lake and sat in his car, watching the water in the twilight; the evenings were getting shorter already. Where the moorhens bobbed now, he could see Cleo climbing on the jet-ski fully clothed, hear her whooping and squealing at the power and the freezing spray. Wading from the lake, picking bits of weed from her saturated clothes. Laughing herself breathless.

Madwoman.

Where was she now? He glanced at his watch. At home, with her husband? In bed? Maybe an early night? He imagined them turning gently to familiar exploration of the body next to them.

Balls. His problem was that he hadn't had time to get tired of her. She'd landed in his life and then whizzed off, taking him by surprise. That was it. She'd taken him by surprise.

Any time now he'd get over it.

He took his mobile from his pocket, pressed *phone book* and 'C'. *Cleo 077* ... His thumb hovered over the green button. All he had to do. Press the button and she might answer. He thought of her voice.

Then he thought about her in bed with her husband. He sighed.

He ought to be glad that nothing he'd done had screwed up her marriage. He should respect her feelings more.

He put the phone away and drove home.

Chapter Twelve

'One moment, she's here now.' Francesca, a recent addition to the staff of Ntrain, waved her telephone handset as Cleo walked back to her desk. 'Rockley Image for you, Cleo, can I put them through?'

Cleo, fresh from yet another fruitless trip to the Ladies in search of her missing period and wishing she'd had the courage to take the pregnancy test already, hoped her nod was casual. Sliding into her chair, she grabbed a pen with suddenly slippery fingers and picked up the ringing phone. 'Cleo Callaway.'

During the two seconds' silence at the other end before he spoke, she knew it was Justin. She had a sudden, blinding vision of that smile. 'Are you free to talk?'

She wrote *Rockley Image* on her pad, kept her voice carefully professional. 'How can I help?'

'I want to talk to you.'

'Yes, go ahead.'

A sigh. 'Perhaps a drink after work?'

She drew a box around *Rockley Image*, super-aware of Nathan, at his desk, watching her through his red-framed glasses and listening. 'I haven't got the information with me, can I ring you back?'

He laughed shortly. 'What, to have another irritating half-conversation like this? Can you meet me at six thirty tonight? At The Almshouses?'

She hesitated. Then, 'I can do that. 'Bye.' She scribbled down the time, tore the page from her pad and stuffed it in her pocket, returning to studying the big sheet of paper where she'd been roughing a presentation plan about measuring team performance. She paused, waiting for the pulse pounding in her temples to steady. Waiting for Nathan, always alert for further business or even, God forbid, complaints, to speak.

'What's up with Rockley, Cleo?'

She made as if dragging her attention away from opening a new PowerPoint presentation on her computer. 'It was just one of their staff. When I did the gig there we got talking over coffee about scuba diving. I said friends had taken a holiday with tuition, he's asking if I could get the name of the tour operator.'

'Yeah?' Nathan picked up his headset, uninterested if the query wasn't work-related.

Francesca brought round coffee, never – bless her brown doe eyes – seeming to mind the chore. Cleo took the first hot and heady sips with her eyes closed against the steam. Heaven. Bliss. Opened her eyes. Of course, caffeine was definitely on the no-no list for mums-to-be. A booklet she'd picked up in Boots told her about following a healthy lifestyle before as well as during. She'd been flabbergasted to learn that the father should be prepared to contribute healthy sperm by eating a balanced diet, stopping smoking and cutting down on alcohol for three months before conception

Who wrote that stuff?

What planet were they on?

Maybe it was sound advice for earnest couples pragmatically plotting an immense change in their lives, exchanging meaningful glances over the lettuce leaves and decaff. But for her? Too late, irrelevant and hugely annoying. Then she grinned, reluctantly, at the thought of what state of inebriation Justin's 'guys' must've been in. Any baby produced would probably be born with a hangover. Unless the Aquavit had got that far.

Justin was watching for her from a seat in the corner, facing the door. His black shirt was open at the neck.

On her way over, Cleo bought a bottle of water from the bar. Once settled across the table from him, she raised her eyebrows, her voice tight. 'So? What's the problem?' Dark strands of her hair fell across her eyes.

'No problem. I just wanted to talk to you.'

The water bottle chilled her fingers. She was aware of her own breathing, rapid, uneven. All day apprehension had pinched her belly with mean fingers. Don't let this be more trouble! She had enough already.

He smiled suddenly, lighting his golden eyes. 'I didn't want to leave things as they were. This is a sorry. Sorry I was foul to you outside Muggie's, sorry I wound you up at the seminar. I'm a bit of a git sometimes.' His smile looked like the Cheshire Cat's. Wide, drawn into sharp points at the corners. For a bright instant she let herself wish that they were meeting as lovers. And that she was free to.

Little muscles tugged at her top lip, drawing her mouth into a reluctant, answering grin.

He touched her hand lightly. 'Let's forget all the crap, it's a shame if that's all that's left from that weekend. Although I *was* really pissed at you.'

'I noticed.' She swallowed some of her drink.

He slouched, extending his legs until she felt them brush hers. 'Can you blame me?'

'Not entirely.' A sudden, vivid memory of the shop doorway; the liquid sensation of reaching out for more.

'But it's all behind us, we're just two friends having a few drinks.' He raised his glass to her.

Heartbeat calming, she returned the salute. Everything was going to be fine. She glanced at her watch. 'But I can't stop long.' It had been worth keeping the date now that she'd discovered everything was going to be OK; but Gav would be wondering where she was.

'Oh, come on. It's just a drink! I want it to be all right when we see each other.' He folded his arms on the table, leaning towards her. 'I like you, Cleo. I'm sorry I was an arse. You've obviously had your problems. Whatever happened between you and your old man was bad enough to send you my way. I shouldn't have let pique get the better of me. I want to be on good terms.'

It was ridiculous that his words should bring sudden tears stinging to her eyes. He wanted her company! She felt inexplicably touched. 'But I'm still married,' she pointed out. 'There's still Gav.'

For the first time, he looked impatient. 'And he dictates your every move, does he?'

She flushed. 'Of course not!' It would sound wimpish and under the thumb to admit that Gav would absolutely hate her to have a male friend.

'If I was a woman there wouldn't be a problem. I'd say, "Have another drink, Cleo," and you'd say, "Lovely, Justine!" Right? But just because I'm a bloke ... Can't you trust yourself that we'll act like two civilised people? Or doesn't your old man trust you?'

She wanted to cry, 'Both! Both!' But instead she met his gaze coolly. 'Fine. We're out for a drink.'

And as they talked, she emotionally repositioned herself, consigning him to the past as a lover. They compared films, countries they'd visited, favourite music, like two civilised people. He made her laugh.

When her mobile bleated to signal an incoming text message, she was amazed to realise it was almost ten thirty. She read the screen. R u ok? Gav. She hesitated, locked eyes with Justin, and rang home. She imagined Gav stretched on the sofa as she heard his habitual, 'Hello?'

She cleared her throat. 'Hi, I'm fine. Just having an after-work drink. I'll be home soon.'

And she was fine. They were talking. That was all.

Justin walked her back to her car. ''Bye, then,' he called, moving on as she slid into the driver's seat. The door was still half open when he swung back.

'Oh yeah.' He crouched beside the car and laid one hand on her knee, a knee that jumped as if someone had done a reflex test on her. He lowered his voice. 'I suppose by now you know that you're not pregnant?'

The heat from his hand beat through the fabric of her trousers. She succeeded, second go, in starting the car. His eyes were on her face in the evening shadows and she willed her features into nonchalance. 'You're not still panicking about that, are you?' She smiled her most brilliant smile, then ended, teasingly, 'Clear off. Time I was going.'

When Cleo got home, Gav was lying full length on the sofa just as she'd imagined. He folded the paper onto the floor. 'OK?'

'Yes, of course.'

'What happened?' Hands linked behind his head, he watched her.

'What?' She shrugged out of her jacket, smothering a yawn. Suddenly she was shattered.

'The football. I thought you were coming to watch?'

Oops.

'Rhianne and Dora were there.'

Her life had been happening, she hadn't had time to think about his. 'Had I promised to be there? Somebody suggested a drink, so I went.' She hung her jacket up, kicked off her shoes and dropped into an armchair.

'I just thought you'd be there.'

'You could have asked me. Instead of just thinking.' She hadn't meant to be confrontational but he made her feel so defensive. So she added, lightly, 'Sorry if you were disappointed.' Slowly, still yawning, she walked upstairs.

The package was still hidden in her knickers drawer under tossed cotton, lace and satin; white mainly, some black. Three pairs of French she didn't like much, but Gav did, sundry sexy wisps, two pairs of iron knickers for tight dresses. And for trousers that showed visible pantie line, thongs. Gav liked those, too. But Gav would never look in her knickers drawer; only knickers there, not very neat, and her mobile phone charger.

And this, her secret. She slipped the package out. Reread the instructions, tapping her thumbnail against her teeth, her stomach see-sawing.

Then, suddenly, Gav was in the doorway. 'Are you sure you're OK?'

Shoving the package away, she pounced on the tangled charger flex and began to wind the wire neatly. 'You made me jump!'

'So who was it tonight, did you go somewhere nice?'

She pushed aside the fact that she knew he'd object if he knew that her companion had been a man, and focused instead on her growing irritation. 'Why are my movements an issue now? Why are you keeping an eye on me? This never used to happen.'

Gav began to tug off his clothes, movements sharp. 'Maybe you were less secretive then.'

'Maybe I felt less patrolled!'

His eyes narrowed and he sat on the end of the bed. 'It shouldn't matter.'

'You should trust me.'

Into bed, in silence. Cleo switched out the light. They lay, side by side but not touching. Eventually Gav said, 'O-kay. It's the semi-finals tomorrow night. If you'd like to come?'

Her voice was tired in the darkness. 'Thanks. I'd like that.' No she wouldn't, not particularly. But she ought to go.

Chapter Thirteen

At the edge of the spectators' balcony above the sports hall, on the wooden rail that was just right to lean on, Cleo, Keith, Dora, Ian and Rhianne lined up their forearms next to Gav's. Kids screamed in a netted-off crèche, where poor overworked nursery nurses tried to prevent them from maiming each other with enormous sponge shapes. Eddie, in his buggy on the other side of Gav, mumbled at a rusk. Messily. Gruesomely. Long trails of beige slobber festooned his chin and cobwebbed from his pudgy, starfish hands. Hastily, Gav looked away.

Already in the neat royal blue of the Bettsbrough players, who were to meet The King's Arms All Stars after Brecks United had slugged out the present match with the Air Training Cadets, Gav flexed his fingers and studied the opposition. Brecks were OK, a team from a local haulage concern. Big blokes, but at least halfway sensible. But the ATC? He groaned. 'If we get through to the final, I hope the ATC don't. They're all so young and up for it, they just crash into every tackle as if they're made of rubber.'

Cleo's answering, 'Really?' suggested a degree of detachment.

Gav sighed, newly dejected that he was no longer selected to play forward. He'd slowed behind the pace of the ball, found the incessant beating up and down the pitch too much. There were twenty-year-olds to take his place. But his height and reach gave him good coverage of the goal, particularly with the seven-a-side, scaled-down goal.

He sipped orange juice and gloomily watched the ATC beat Brecks 2-1, no matter how loudly he roared on Brecks.

'Bollocks,' he sighed again, before trotting down to join his team in the warm-up.

Breathing in the rubbery smell of the sports hall, jogging floppily on the spot before the goal, he glanced up at the gallery. Instead of watching, Cleo was talking to Dora, chin on hand. About him? Last night's squabble? Was Cleo sighing, 'I can't imagine what's up with him these days'? He punched a flying ball away. What could he try next? The keeping-off-sex device was patently failing to convince. Every night, Cleo stared uncomprehendingly at his pyjamas as she climbed into bed gloriously naked and tempting.

All he could do was hug and kiss and hope desperately he could do more soon. At least she seemed prepared to accede to his temporary sex ban and didn't initiate sex herself.

He bounced on his toes as the ref blew the whistle and The King's Arms fell on the ball like dogs.

He thrust his palms out hopefully as the ball hurtled towards him, successfully deflecting it to one of his own players, who sent it soaring up the pitch. Bouncing on his toes, he clapped his gloved hands together gently to ease the stinging.

As soon as Gav went down to play his match, Dora sidled up and whispered to Cleo, 'I've decided to leave Keith. Or almost decided. It's just too good, the thing between Sean and me. I can't ignore it. It's shown up all the craters in my marriage.'

Cleo checked that Keith, several feet away, was deep in the football match, leaning over the rail and roaring Bettsbrough on. She muttered back, 'But what about the kids?'

Dora turned a set face. 'They stay with me.'

'Aren't they just as much Keith's as yours?' A vision of the package in her knickers drawer flashed across her mind. The father was important. Wasn't he?

The spectators yelled as Bettsbrough fluked a goal. Dora and Cleo cried, 'Yeah!' exchanging obligatory triumphant grins with Ian and Keith. Rhianne was at the crèche, confronting the nursery nurse in charge, hands on skinny hips, head tossing. The nursery nurse had Roland and Will by their hands, patently wishing to pass them back. Rhianne's body language suggested no desire to take them.

When Keith's attention was safely back on the game, Dora growled, 'You don't know about motherhood! I'm the one programmed to look after the kids and I've always done it. Keith will be able to see them when he wants. And they'll have Sean.'

Cleo tried to sound sympathetic. 'But will Keith's love for his kids just conveniently dry up and the kids transfer their affections to the incoming male? And do you tell Keith he's got to leave the posh pad he's slaved for, so you can move your boyfriend in? Or take the kids to live in Sean's flat in the city centre where there's no garden, no space and you'll have to dry the washing on the banisters? Do you think Keith will be OK with that?'

A great groan went up as Gav let in the equaliser, retrieving the ball from the net with resigned sheepishness. King's supporters cheered madly.

Dora massaged her temples. 'I'm entitled to half of everything,' she muttered uncertainly, 'and because of the kids I think I can force Keith to move out. But it'll be fairer if we sell the house and buy separate places.'

Cleo nodded. 'But I'm afraid you've got an awful lot of shit to get through first. To front up Keith and his grief and anger.' She felt Dora flinch. Keith had a temper and was known to clamour like a gorilla when enraged. 'To face his pain over the children, his fury at being effectively chucked out of his home. Fight any action he brings against you –'

Dora flung herself away. 'Oh shut up, Cleo! You don't

know a bloody thing about it.'

Cleo watched Dora stalk over to the crèche to check on Meggie. Maybe Dora was right, she didn't know much about children and broken marriages. Though she felt she was beginning to get some idea, she thought, as everyone craned over the balcony to watch another attack on Bettsbrough's goal, which Gav halted by catching the ball hard against his stomach and cuddling it protectively.

Cleo began to relax as they filed into the familiar brass-and-beam interior of The Three Fishes, with its ripple of conversation. She blessed Rhianne's kind mum who had offered to have the kids for a couple of hours so the adults could have a drink and relax.

Bettsbrough had beaten The King's Arms 3-1 and Gav seemed almost his ordinary self, easy and familiar as they ordered drinks. Cleo had just taken her Budweiser bottle from her lips to laugh at Gav's pained recap of deflecting the ball with the 'midriff method', when she heard her name.

'Hello, Cleo! I didn't know you came in here.'

Her heart did a vertical take-off before nose diving into the pit of her stomach.

She turned slowly, aware that sentences had been suspended as everyone looked, half smiling in case it was someone they might know too.

'Hi.' Her mouth was dry. Her next gulp lodged as if solid in her throat. 'I've never seen you in here before, either.'

Justin grimaced. 'Bloody car's broken down along the road. My mate, Pete, looks after it, I'm waiting for him to turn up with his magic spanners.' He glanced at his watch. 'Shouldn't be long, I left a message with his wife.' He smiled and Cleo's friends smiled back, nodded sympathetically. Then glanced at Cleo expectantly.

She took a deep breath. 'Right ... well ... this is my

husband, Gav, and Keith and Dora, Rhianne and Ian.' Oh shit, shit, look at them shaking hands, nodding, murmuring. She rushed on, waving casually towards Justin. 'I met Justin at a workshop.'

Justin, apparently blissfully at ease, leaned on a convenient wooden pillar, one of those that looked as if it'd had an axe taken to the corners. 'Cleo put us all through hoops for a day. We thought we could communicate adequately until then – very switched-on lady.'

Rhianne gave him a coquettish smile. 'Cleo's very focused on her job. I'm sure you do more interesting things, outside of work. Sit down and tell us.'

'Thanks.' Justin dragged up a worn brown stool. 'I do a bit of jet skiing. You ought to try it sometime, you'd love it. You need a wetsuit though. No good turning up in jeans or anything.' He blinked innocently at Cleo.

She tried to make her eyes flinty but Justin looked supremely unmoved.

Ian butted in. 'Can you imagine letting our two terrors lose on jet-skis? God save us.'

'Perhaps not for young families,' cooed Rhianne. 'You married, Justin? Got any kids?'

Justin shook his head. 'Haven't tried it yet.'

Cleo, in the time it took to get her breath and steady her heart, decided that, if Justin was playing some sodding silly game of his own devising, she would play, too. And laughed. 'Married? Well, no ... Justin's *gay*.' She smiled her sweetest smile. 'Where's your partner tonight? Tucked up at home with a cookery book?'

She registered reactions around the table. Curiosity. Surprise. Justin turned to face her very slowly, eyes narrowed. Then his face grew sombre and he sighed. Massaging his temples above suddenly sorrowful eyes, he swallowed. 'To be honest ... there's a problem. He suddenly ran out on me in favour of a previous relationship. It's very difficult ... oh, where's the Gents?' Head down, fingers splayed dramatically across his eyes, Justin dashed through the nearby door with a brass outline of a little man on it.

Cleo watched him go, remembering to close her mouth after a second.

A long moment of stillness, then everyone began to speak at once. 'You said the wrong thing there, Cleo!' Dora sounded quite censorious.

'Is he really *gay*? What a loss to womankind.' Rhianne clucked.

And Gav, 'How does that come out in seminar?'

Cleo shrugged. Swallowed. 'He's quite open about it. "Out", as they say.'

When Justin finally reappeared, he seemed subdued but recovered and everyone avoided any mention of his missing partner. Rhianne bickered as usual with Ian, while Keith and Dora listened, hardly a word to exchange of their own.

Cleo's phone gave the tone that heralded a text message. She read expressionlessly then snapped her phone shut. Catching Gav's enquiring expression, she remarked, 'Liza wants to know if I'm going out on Friday.'

He looked dismayed. 'Hang on, Friday's the footie final!'

Cleo finished her drink. 'I'll tell her that then, won't I?'

All the light seemed to fade from Gav's face. 'Yes, you'll have to.'

Her cheeks burned and she couldn't seem to stop herself musing, '*Have* to?'

Several dangerous seconds of silence as they exchanged stares, Justin, between them, glancing from one to the other.

'You said you'd come –'

'But I don't *have* to. I choose to.'

These little, strained exchanges were becoming drearily commonplace. But better they squabble over Cleo's social life than Gav should read the real text message: U look delicious 2night. Reminds me of the taste of u. J. Obviously, whatever game she tried to play, he could play harder.

So he was a great hit, Justin. Interested in everyone. Telling Gav that Cleo was great, that Gav was a lucky man. Was sorry with apparent sincerity that Keith, Dora, Ian and Rhianne had to leave to reclaim their children. Tried again to get his mate on the mobile, shook his head and said, 'Still nothing doing.'

Gav was just offering to give him a ride home so that he could arrange for his car to be collected the next day, when his own mobile rang. 'What – now?' he exclaimed into the instrument. 'Won't it wait? OK. All right. I will.' Cleo took the opportunity to shoot a fierce glare at Justin, who blew her a tiny kiss in return.

Gav sighed as he ended the call. 'Got to go into work.'

'Now?' Cleo flicked an incredulous glance at her watch. Gav never had to work unsociable hours.

He was already standing, slapping his pockets to check for his wallet, fishing out car keys, looking away. 'Intruders have been in the building, I've got to check my section with the police and report on anything damaged or missing. You know what security's like.' He dropped a kiss on Cleo's hair. 'Be home later – will you be OK?'

'Yes –' And he was gone. Everyone was.

Apart from Cleo. And Justin.

As soon as the heavy door swung behind Gav, she whipped round on Justin. 'Just what the fuck are you doing? You nearly gave me a heart attack!'

He grinned, jiggling his car keys. 'My car won't work.'

She snorted her disbelief. 'Right, and which wire did you yank to stop it working?'

He laughed, eyes dancing, mouth wide and delighted. 'You've got a nasty suspicious mind. We'll go and try it, if you like? Or how about I walk you home while I wait for my mate to ring?'

'*If* he rings. And I don't need walking home in Middledip.'

'Famous last words.' He rose, whisked her jacket from the back of her chair and walked out.

Chapter Fourteen

So, of course, she had no choice but to follow. In the road outside he was walking backwards, waiting for her. His car was slewed on the verge a few yards up the road. Nothing for it but to catch up, snatch her jacket and shrug into it. 'You're a bastard, Justin.'

'I'm only walking you home.'

Cleo snorted at his mock hurt and led the way, by habit, the quickest way – the footpath around the playing fields and behind the village hall. She sniffed. 'I thought you'd forgiven me?'

He linked his arm with hers. 'I have.'

'So why turn up when I'm with Gav?' She stumbled into a pothole behind the goal posts stark in the moonlight.

His arm steadied her. 'You don't need to worry about introducing some gay bloke you met at a workshop to your husband. And I was right by the way, he is gitty.'

'He's *not* ... Or he didn't used to be.' When she looked up he was watching. His lips looked very smooth, the lines gentle.

They set off again, strolling instead of the earlier irritated march. His voice was kinder. 'How long have things been bloody?'

They paced slowly in step in the balmy, breezy night, and Cleo heaved a gusty sigh. 'It's all quite recent. Since he stormed out.' Since Cleo had allowed her wounded rage to lead her into rash behaviour and rebellion against the growing sensation of being trapped in the paraphernalia and responsibilities of a shared life.

She slowed. They were standing behind the village hall,

invisible in a lonely place on a dark night. 'We never used to bicker like we do. He's just ... *different* these days.' She found herself spilling her confusion about her marriage, to Justin. And she even told him about the pyjama thing. And that was disloyal.

Justin snorted. 'What's his problem?'

'I don't know, and don't understand. He's acting very oddly. Maybe he's going through some crisis. Perhaps I should be more understanding.'

Spikes of Justin's hair trembled in the breeze and moonlight caught his cheekbone, accentuating the angles of his nose and jaw. 'He must be mad. You deserve better.'

Her reply came out flat and scornful. 'You hardly know me.'

'Probably more than you think.' In the darkness he lifted his hands until his fingertips encountered her face. 'Eyes, twinkle when you smile, dark and sad if you're worried. Tiny, tiny lines at the side. I guess you're what – thirty?' His fingertips barely touched her incipient crows' feet.

It made her shiver. She hoped he hadn't felt it. She ought to move away, laugh it off. Instead, she answered, 'Thirty-one,' her voice husky.

He traced above her eyes. 'You don't pluck your eyebrows,'

'Much,' she amended. She really should shove his hands away. But his fingertips felt so good on her skin.

He laughed under his breath, his thumbs sliding down her cheeks. 'Lovely skin. No freckles. Happy, smiling mouth.' He brushed her lips before he moved on to her hair. 'Dark, straight, shiny hair. Flicks around when you move your head. Pretty ears, earrings.' He touched them; then his hands drifted back across her face, making her shiver again, down to stroke her collarbones, further down to outline her breasts.

Her breath stopped. His touch was light, hands cupping,

smoothing. Tender, gentle. Almost unbearable. Her entire body rose in gooseflesh and her nipples gathered to press against her clothes. His fingers slid between two shirt buttons. 'Your skin is *so* exciting.' The fingers trickled like the wings of a dancing butterfly across her breasts where they swelled above her bra.

It was several heart thuds before he sighed and slid his arms around her, pulling her lightly against him. 'At Muggie's, that first night, you wore a raunchy smack-over-the-head perfume. At the seminar it was lighter, flowery, pleasant but inexpensive. And the same at The Almshouses.' He inhaled. 'Tonight, I can only smell shampoo. Clean and sexy.' His mouth was suddenly right against her ear, lifting the hairs on her neck with his breath. 'When I kiss your ears, you shudder.' On cue, at the tickle of his breath, a shiver of pleasure shook through her. 'I know the feel of you, the taste. The way you look naked.

'I know you're a live wire, bright, good at your job. I recognise the craziness in you, the moments of recklessness.' His eyes glittered in the darkness. 'OK, so I don't know how many A levels you got, when you lost your virginity or who was your first boyfriend. And I'm not as predictable, nice, or sensible as your husband. But I know something about Cleo Callaway that seems to be passing him by – I know that you're not happy. And that's a dangerous thing for me to know.'

The spell broke.

Her hands seemed to spring up under their own power to thrust him away. Bones grew again in her legs and muscles pulled themselves together. Her heart slowed and clarity and reason flooded her mind. 'So you must know that I'm not up for this.' She heard her voice, calm and cool. 'I'm not available, I'm committed elsewhere.'

He was very still.

'Justin, this has to stop. I can't cope with you. We had a fabulous night. You're an exciting man. In other circumstances ... But I'm a married woman. And I'm not going to ignore that – again.'

The rest of the way home he stalked beside her in silence. She stopped where Port Road met Ladies Lane, short of her house. 'What now? Will you phone your mate again? Or call a cab?' She was reluctant to offer to drive him home. To be in the intimate space of the car. To return to his flat.

'I'll go wait.' He hesitated. 'I'm not sorry that my car broke down tonight. It gave me a clearer idea of things.'

Cleo sat on the toilet, sobbing. Heaving, gasping, with fury at her own incompetence and the futile way she spent her emotions. The empty packaging from the test kit lay on the floor between her feet.

After Justin had gone she'd flown upstairs, filled with the compulsion to know, to be sure, to be free of the uncertainty. To face what was coming and deal with it. Not knowing suddenly seemed insupportable. Why on earth had she made excuses for so long? She scrambled at the back of her knickers drawer, thrusting aside the satin and lace, snatched out the packet and fought the cellophane with shaking hands.

She checked the instructions one final time – as if she didn't know them by heart!

And dropped the wand straight down the fucking toilet. Where it lay, useless, unused, in the water which was automatically and hygienically bleached with every flush.

Her shoulders heaved.

Tomorrow, she'd buy another one.

Chapter Fifteen

Cleo felt like drumming her heels in frustration. Nathan had scheduled her to take a Professional Voice Over the Phone workshop *again*! Was the services world really running on multi-choice telephone systems and operators equipped only to deal with standard queries from customers they never met?

She parked. Withdrew her mobile from its pocket. It grew warm in her hand as she gazed through the windscreen. Then, in a moment's resolution, she selected last night's message from Justin and pressed *reply*. Prefer not 2 meet again. Can't hack yr games. Got enough 2 worry about. C

There. Done. Over. She ought to feel better. Soon. Soon she'd get peace of mind, having done something positive to save her marriage, salve her guilt.

She retrieved his reply at morning break, reading as she blew gently across the surface of her coffee. Most of the members of her group were occupied with texts of their own. None of them over twenty-five, they were firmly of the constant communication generation.

Don't b a wimp. Only playing. Wouldn't hurt u. What r u worried about?

She made herself carry on brightly with the session, although it felt like wading through treacle. 'OK, I'm Ms Grumpy coming through on the line of ... Amanda! Amanda, Ms Grumpy says to you: "Your company's crap, your company is! You've had my cash for two weeks and the bike I ordered hasn't left your effing, beeping warehouse yet! Do you know what the effing, beeping interest is on £109.99? Eh? No, you don't, do you? Eff, beep, eff, beep!"

Right Amanda, what's your response?'

Amanda, blonde and fluffy and not long enough out of the classroom to mind courses, looked gobsmacked. 'Shit,' she quavered.

Cleo grinned without betraying a trace of irritation that kids were apparently being stuck on customer services hotlines without even basic training in telephonic interaction. 'Any better suggestions? Bad idea to swear back. Better to remain calm and impeccably mannered, always. The ruder Ms Grumpy gets, the politer you become. Try again, Amanda?'

Amanda put her hand to her head. 'Umm ... I'll get my manager?'

'Maybe, not yet, not yet. Anyone else? Jason?'

Jason adjusted his tie. Coughed. Looked desperately around the room for inspiration. 'Can I have your postcode, please?' The others tittered.

'Eventually. Something else, first. Cathy?'

Cathy gulped audibly. 'Don't swear at me?' Everyone tittered again.

Cleo managed not to sigh. Barely versed in their basic script, these kids disintegrated in the face of trouble and were totally blank where initiative was concerned. 'We'll come back to that.' She held up one finger. 'First, your first and most important response – "*I'll certainly try to sort this out for you, Ms Grumpy.*"' Everyone sighed in relief at learning the answer and nodded. 'Defuse the situation, reassure your caller you're on their side. Be aware of your tone of voice – only twenty per cent of the message is received through the words. Remain polite, your tone conciliatory.' More sage nods.

'Then?' She cast about for someone brave enough to voice an opinion. Phew, the temperature was high in this place. Slipping out of her jacket, she eased the high neck of her silk top, evidently too hot for energy-efficient office blocks in summer. She was forced to supply the answer again. 'Then – *tell them what you intend to do*. "Ms Grumpy, if you'll bear with me while I take the details, I'll be able to look into your problem and see what I can do to solve it." *Then* you ask for the postcode or customer number and go into the right screen for the account? OK?'

Murmuring, nods, 'Oh yes, 'course.'

A final point to clear up before she took them through the whole caboodle again to see if any of it had lodged in the vacant little brains. 'Cathy didn't want to be sworn at. Good. Reasonable. But it happens, and it happens all the time, swearing is becoming casual in situations where it used to be inappropriate. So when is it time to react? Does your company have a policy on swearing?' For a strangled moment she couldn't even remember the company name.

She gazed encouragingly round the clutch of teenagers and twenty-somethings. They all gazed back, waiting for her to give them the answer.

The blonde-streaked fluffy girl, Amanda, tried, 'The CEO seems to like it. Particularly on a bad day.'

Cleo moved on through the laughter, intent on retaining the collective attention. 'No one know? Some firms used to have a policy of passing the call on immediately to a supervisor or manager who would politely ask the customer not to swear before dealing with the enquiry him- or herself. But it's become the norm to simply ignore it. OK? Don't rise to it, don't comment on it. For goodness' sake don't repeat it!' Delighted laughter. 'I'll grab your human resources manager at lunch and talk to him.'

She looked at the clock and sent them all off to lunch. 'Five minutes early because you're all working so hard. I'll see if I can get you a policy decision on the swearing.' They all responded to her wide, professional smile as they filed out. Cleo switched on her mobile phone as the last of them left.

Just 4get it. Gr8 at time but over now.

With little appetite for lunch, she made do with a couple of digestives. Another pregnancy symptom? She hadn't been nauseous but Rhianne said she never had a moment's sickness with her first pregnancy.

Outside, she discovered that the only local retail outlets were a burger bar and a sandwich trolley; but she felt better in the fresh air, the silky top less cloying. She bought iced Perrier from the sandwich trolley and sank down on a sunny bench, just as Justin's next message came through.

What r u worried about? Have u email addy I can msg or can I ring? Sorry if u r upset.

Her response was curt.

Not appropriate.

Received back:

What worry? What worry? What worry???

Glancing at her watch, she stabbed at the stupid, unco-operative, titchy buttons, making mistakes and having to work backwards and forwards.

Worry whether u will drop me in shit. Please piss off.

She checked her watch and hurried up to the human resources manager's office.

After a weary afternoon of being the irate customer in endless role-playing situations, she flopped back into her car and switched her phone back on. It beeped immediately.

Sorry. Accept u r married 1. I withdraw! xxx

She smiled, although her vision was swimming. Replied, Thx. Did she feel better now? She ought to.

It took a couple of minutes to delete all Justin's messages; then she rang Liza. 'How are you fixed for a drink and a moan tonight? I can't come out with you Friday because I've promised to watch Gav playing football.'

'Had we arranged something for Friday?'

'If Gav asks, yes.'

Liza giggled. 'Cleo, I rather like the unruly you. Do you want to meet me at the flat now, or come back later?'

She thought of the clingy top and hot, window-window-window room she'd been slaving away in all day, and knew she needed a shower. She was glad she had all planning and client account work for the rest of the week. 'Later, OK?'

And she had to brave the pharmacy. But Bettsbrough, when she hit it, was a mass of roadworks and dust hanging in hot still air, with home-time drivers looking murderous.

'One more day won't matter,' she persuaded her rear-view-mirror self.

'What's up?' Gav zipped the pizza into sections with the stainless-steel cutting-wheel.

Cleo pulled a face. 'It's too hot.'

'Rain's forecast for tomorrow.'

She watched him polish off four slices of pizza, spooning coleslaw onto each before he folded it up and ate it. Yuk. She swallowed. Was she feeling pregnancy nausea? To divert her mind she told him, 'I'm going out with Liza tonight. I can eat then.'

'Again?' He put his pizza down, wedge five out of eight, one bite taken. 'I never seem to see you.'

'I came to the footie last night,' she pointed out reasonably. 'And I'm coming again tomorrow night.'

'Don't do me any favours.' He picked up the pizza and took a massive unattractive mouthful.

Silence. Cleo rubbed her temples. How had her marriage suddenly become like everyone else's? What could she do to eradicate the memory of Gav's ugly anger? To forget her own conduct and the guilty memory of Justin?

And find some way of fancying Gav again.

The thought kapowed through her brain – *she didn't fancy Gav*. And perhaps he no longer fancied her, judging by the way he avoided contact.

Tormented by the questions she'd asked herself a hundred times already, she went up for a shower. She hardly even remembered that she'd left Gav downstairs in a big black sulk.

When Cleo stooped to kiss him goodbye, Gav pointedly proffered his cheek. He felt her hesitate. Withdraw and spin on her heel. Heard the rapid thuds of her footsteps returning upstairs, a pause of several minutes, then her footsteps clattered down again. The bag over her shoulder said more than she did. 'I'll stay at Liza's tonight, it's handy for work in the morning. Be back in time for the footie tomorrow night.'

He kept his eyes on the television.

The front door closed and she was gone. Gav clasped his head. 'Gav Callaway, you handled that just perfectly. Why did you try to contain her when you know it's the very thing she objects to?' Maybe so he'd have some head space to psych himself up for tomorrow ...

A tomorrow of appointments he didn't fancy. Not least a possible meeting with willowy, scornful Lillian.

He fetched beer from the fridge and armed himself with the phone. 'Keith, you're not free to pop over for a pint, are you?'

'No, I'm flaming not because flaming Dora's out some-bloody-where, Meggie wants her mum and Eddie wants his supper!' snapped Keith, raising his voice over the terrible cacophony.

'I'll ring back later,' Gav said hastily. He didn't want Keith to suggest that he should go and help with the kids.

'Strikes me,' observed Liza, wriggling up onto a black bar stool and swigging her drink, 'that things ain't what they used to be. Ooh, see that bloke with the dark hair? That's Angie's latest.'

'Yeah?' Cleo sucked down sweet, cooling mouthfuls of her wine and pushed aside worries about possible effects on the possible foetus.

Liza caught the eye of the dark man and waved before giving her attention to her sister. 'So, what's the matter? Gav's pyjamas? Bodice-bustin' Justin?'

Cleo laughed. Thank God for Liza, Liza she could tell anything and everything to. Nearly.

She began, 'I'm trusting you not to pass any of this on to Mum and Dad – I don't need them poking their noses in as well as everything else. But things are a bit strained at the moment.'

Liza propped her cheek on her hand and studied her sister. 'Know what?' she offered, draining the last drips from the bottle into her glass and upending the empty over Cleo's, as if that made it equal. 'Mum and Dad would only say what I'm going to say – I think your marriage has had it.'

Chapter Sixteen

Maybe it was the memory of Liza putting her worries into words, but Cleo had a funny, eerie feeling, as if she was close to the edge.

To the edge of what, she wasn't certain. But the sensation had been strong all day of something that was fermenting, building, gathering to tip her over into some new place.

It was a stupid, unsubstantiated feeling, but she found herself being wary, watchful, so that when the edge appeared she'd be ready for it. Especially when she stepped back inside her home that night, mindful of the foul mood Gav had been in when she'd left the evening before. She paused. Listened.

Gav was singing!

He swooped down on her, beaming. ''Evening, sweetheart! Dinner's nearly ready. I'm sorting my footie kit out.' He surprised her with an abrupt, intense kiss. 'We don't seem to be spending much time together, lately. What d'you say we pop off somewhere tomorrow? Throw some stuff in an overnight bag, find a hotel in the Dales for a couple of days of decadence? Steak dinners, a four-poster ... a little champagne? Fancy that?' He dropped a kiss on the end of her nose, whispered, 'Bring an end to the celibacy?' And stroked her bottom.

It sounded as if he were making a lot of effort. She smiled and said lightly, 'Sounds great.' Maybe a few romantic trimmings were all they needed to find each other again, exorcise the memory of the recent tension. Perhaps she'd learn to melt again when Gav touched her, to feel her heart trot at the base of her throat. Maybe. And as she shrugged into her jacket she felt a little lift in her heart, as if the edge had receded a bit.

At the sports hall, the spectators' balcony was thronged. Scores of teenagers in RAF-blue uniforms seemed intent on being the loudest supporters and Bettsbrough was thinly supported in comparison. Cleo had no trouble finding her friends where they'd staked a claim at the railing. 'Hi!'

Dora looked as if she might've been crying; Keith was white and tight-lipped.

Rhianne, in contrast, was bubbling with joy, couldn't wait to spill her can brimful with golden beans. 'Cleo! Ian's got a brilliant new promotion. Brilliant! The salary's miles higher – isn't it, Ian? Miles!' She clenched joyful fists and bounced on the spot. Her pale-blue shiny pumps matched her pale-blue perfectly pressed trousers. 'Isn't he clever? Aren't you, Ian? Haven't I always said so?' Rhianne linked happy arms with her husband.

'Not all the time,' Ian answered dryly. But he gave her his lop-sided smile and accepted Cleo's congratulatory hug.

'And a company car,' squeaked Rhianne. 'And performance bonuses!'

'Supposing I perform.'

''Course you'll perform.' Nothing was going to damp Rhianne's bliss. 'I'll buy you a congratulatory coffee! Coming, Cleo? Dora?' Even in the queue she could barely stand still, jiggling and grinning, squeezing arms. 'I'm glad I stayed with him, now.'

Cleo stared. 'Why? Were you ever leaving?'

Rhianne reddened, eyes flickering to a point past Cleo's head. 'Well ... well, yes, we were talking about a trial separation. Last summer. But we stuck it out, so –'

Cleo slid a sympathetic arm along Rhianne's slender shoulders. 'I'm sorry, Rhianne, I'd no idea. It must've been dreadful, keeping it to yourself. I'm glad things worked out. How awful to go through something so crappy without anyone knowing.'

Then she caught it. The glance lancing between Rhianne and Dora. The penny dropped. She withdrew her arm and turned to Dora. 'You knew!' Dora blushed and studied the floor.

The queue shuffled up. Rhianne bit her lip. 'Sorry. It was just too ...' But they'd reached the head of the queue. As Rhianne didn't seem about to, Cleo paid with angry little movements, snatched up the tray of drinks and headed for Keith and Ian. Gav was already downstairs warming up, the clatter and slap of the ball echoing up to the gallery.

Rhianne's hand on her arm meant she had to stop or risk shooting five cups of coffee across the room. Rhianne's lipsticked mouth had stopped smiling and her artistically made-up eyes were apologetic. 'I just couldn't admit it to you, Mrs Perfectmarriage, that my relationship was in the shit. Sorry, but that's how it was.'

Cleo managed a frosted smile. 'OK. Your call.' She made herself a place at the railing, cheering Gav on, joining in every burst of applause or groan, glued to the match, agonising when full time saw the score at 2-2, the same at the end of extra time. And then the match must be decided by penalties.

'How bloody for Gav,' Ian groaned, 'I can't watch.'

But if Cleo didn't watch, she'd have to face Rhianne's apologetic eyes once more. The ATC began lining up behind the ball as Gav crouched grimly in front of his net. And she'd have to pretend that she didn't mind that she'd been excluded. When she did.

There were photos and a proper prize ceremony. A trophy that looked ridiculously small in the hands of the team captain; Gav bouncing with joy to be the 'keeper who let in only two penalties and saved the match. The rubber ATC players accepted their even tinier trophy and joked that at least they didn't have to buy the drinks.

Gav rushed up and, in front of everyone, took a deep, jubilant kiss from Cleo before plunging into an animated ball-by-ball analysis with Keith and Ian. Dora and Rhianne were in a huddle over by the crèche, casting uneasy glances at Cleo.

'Suppose that means it's my round.' But Cleo smiled as she went to join the queue. Their group had never been one to keep score. Well, all right, there was a tiny bias – and it was in favour of Rhianne and Ian, which was OK because Cleo and Gav had two incomes and no kids and Keith and Dora had Keith's mega-salary. She ordered red wine for the women and pints of lager for the men. Their crowd had been together for ages; it'd be a pity to spoil that over inconsequential matters like whose round it was. Or who'd been kept in the dark.

So she smiled reassuringly at Rhianne and Dora when she proffered red wine that looked like cough mixture and forgave them their secrets. 'I'll just take the men their drinks, OK?'

The tray was heavy. Because of her route via Rhianne and Dora, she approached the backs of Gav, Ian and Keith. She'd actually begun to say, 'Beer's here!' But her words were drowned out by the post-match hubbub.

And coincided with Keith turning to Gav and asking, 'So where did you go? GP or GUM?'

Cleo's words stuck to her lips. GP or GUM? For a moment the only amplifications she could think of for those abbreviations were General Practitioner and Genito-urinary Medicine.

She opened her mouth to ask what Keith meant, but Gav's undervoice reply halted her. 'GP. I put off going for too long, but there was a chance I'd passed something on to Cleo. Bad enough having to get the todger out to show my own doctor but it'd be worse at the clinic. All those strangers and sad bastards with false names, suppurating with VD and ...'

GP and GUM stood for precisely what they'd always stood for.

She felt the strength wash from her arms and the three glasses fell to the floor to explode in a shock of glass and foam and interrupted voices.

The edge had turned out to be an overheard snatch of conversation. And she'd stepped off so unexpectedly.

Chapter Seventeen

In brittle silence, they drove home, sleepwalking through the routines of parking, unlocking the house, stepping into their own sitting room. Then they faced each other.

Gav had never experienced panic attacks but surely he must be having one now? Blood pounded in his ears and his palms sweated whilst his thoughts fled in all directions, his justification and explanation refusing to be marshalled. And Cleo was perfectly silent, perfectly still, her face perfectly white.

He wished she'd cry! Then he'd feel it was OK to slide his arms around her. It was a jolt to realise that he dare not touch his own wife.

He forced himself to meet the shock in her eyes. 'Aren't you taking your jacket off?'

A headshake.

'Do you want to sit down?'

Another headshake.

He sank to the sofa and took a steadying breath. 'Everything's been so shitty and just when I thought I'd got it sorted, this happens.' He flicked his eyes to Cleo's. 'You've obviously twigged – I thought I had something. The clap.' He wished she'd speak. Her still eyes seemed as black and expressionless as a shark's. 'But the good news is' – what an excruciatingly *stupid* thing to say – 'that it's only psoriasis. Psoriasis! The doctor's given me some cream.'

He gripped his hands together. This was not going well. All those weeks on tenterhooks since the red, scaly, itchy patch appeared, searching silently for information on the Internet. The swing between pessimism and optimism –

the patch looked exactly like an illustration in one of the booklets. He must have a venereal disease. But – yesssss, pain-free peeing, it *couldn't* be! And no discharge, there you are, see.

So what was the red, scaly, itchy patch ...?

Finally screwing up his courage and seeing his GP. 'No discharge, no pain on urination, it looks exactly like psoriasis,' Dr Tancred had said, wonderful, educated man that he was. 'Could be stress.'

'So ...' Cleo's voice was no more than a croak. 'How did you think you'd caught it?'

Gav found himself spewing all the clichés of the unfaithful. 'It was just once, it's so unfair! It didn't mean anything. She came on to me, you know how she is! We were at the sales conference and we'd drunk too much, I swear it meant nothing. But she did the most amazing thing. We were listening to all the boring speeches and laughing in the right places and she took my hand under the table and put it on her ...! And she had on this non-existent skirt, you know the sort of cock-tease stuff she wears. Cleo, I'm sorry.'

Cleo's lips opened just enough to allow out one word, filled with disbelief. '*Lillian?*'

His head drooped. 'Afterwards, I was dead with shame, disgusted with myself. Our marriage was, is, everything to me – but I got drunk and she turned me on.'

Offended comprehension had replaced Cleo's blank expression. He found his hand extending to her, entreating, begging her to reach back. But she withheld her touch.

He finished his explanation in an irritable rush. 'So when I got this red patch, I thought it might be the clap – well, I don't know, do I? I haven't had it before. Which is why I came up with this pyjama game shit to try and hide it from you, and why, once I'd got the all-clear from the doctor today, I suggested the romantic weekend away.' It didn't seem the time to explain how he was desperate for a shag, tortured during his self-imposed celibacy, watching, wanting. Knowing he was getting nasty, snapping like a hungry dog chained out of reach of a delicious steak.

He slumped back on the sofa, tilted his head and shut his eyes. 'It's why I've been in such a bad temper. Originally, I just felt like a shit for sleeping with Lillian and then I got the rash and was scared to death that I had the clap. I thought I might have given it to you when we had make-up sex after that first big row. I was in agony. I knew that the rows were hurting you but they gave me the excuse to avoid sex. I could have kissed the doctor, today, when he told me that there wasn't anything for me to give. And that's about it, really. The whole sordid, sorry, shitty mess.'

When her knees were on the point of buckling she moved to the armchair furthest from him. 'Maybe alcohol ought to be registered as a date-rape drug. It seems to remove all resistance.' Her temples throbbed as she mulled over his confession.

Gav's erratic behaviour, the pyjama game, all explained, all perfectly obvious. She blew out a sigh. 'What a *relief*.'

Gav's eyes brightened. 'I really am relieved that I can't have given you anything –'

'Not that! I'm just relieved that we can finally deal with what's happening. It's extraordinary that this marriage, which we and everyone else thought such a roaring success, should be brought down so easily. Despite all our boasts over the years about the depth of our commitment, isn't it frightening how little we actually committed, with our rented house and lack of children? Realistically, we could divide everything and be out of here in an hour. Don't you think we've made ourselves look stupid?'

'I don't understand.' Blinking in shock, Gav hitched

forward until he was balanced on the edge of the sofa. 'We can get over this. Everyone hits bad patches, don't talk about dividing up our things ... *We can get over this*!' Stumbling to his feet he stepped clumsily over the coffee table, barking his shins, before blundering to his knees in front of her, his breath coming hard.

Cleo gazed into his face and wondered whether she would have forgiven him if his infidelity had been the only issue. 'So far we've only talked about you.' She forced herself to look into the eyes of the man she'd thought would wake up beside her forever. 'We've both done it.'

Emotions flickered across his face as he tried to compute her words, came up with the obvious conclusion, denied it, came back to it. 'I don't understand.'

'You're not the only one to get drunk and ... be unfaithful.'

Slowly, slowly, Gav pushed himself away until he could use the table for a seat, making it teeter. 'No! You? No. No! Cleo, you're just ... you're hurt and you're trying to hurt me back. You haven't had an affair. When? Who with? You haven't, you haven't, *you haven't*. Have you?'

Her heart gave a great squeeze of compassion. 'I'm sorry. I'm really sorry, Gav.' Even as she confessed, part of her mind worked independently. And it produced a staggering thought.

She was free.

Gav's fist crashed down on the table, making her jump. 'But *who*? Who is he?' The pain in his eyes was awful.

Cleo had to swallow sudden wretched tears to reply. She wanted everything to be out in the open but she hated seeing his pain. 'Justin.'

'Justin?' He shook his head in incomprehension.

'The guy with the broken-down car at The Three Fishes.'

His features hung in the slack lines of denial. 'That Justin? He's not gay?'

'Of course he's not.' She jerked to her feet. 'I'm going to spend the weekend at Liza's. I want to think.'

Gav's breath seemed to come in chunks, a tearless sobbing. 'You've got to stay! We've got to talk. We have to get over this. Cleo, for God's sake.' He lunged to his feet, grabbing for her, scratching her arm, digging his fingers into her wrist. 'You can't just pretend it isn't happening, we've got to find ways to forgive each other.'

Suddenly sorry, suddenly frightened at the hugeness of what was facing them, tears spilled from Cleo's eyes even as, instinctively, she twisted her wrist from his grasp. And stepped back. 'Don't you see? It's over! We each wanted someone else and had them. We're a sham.'

The sound of the door clicking hung in the air behind her. If he could only instil the strength in his legs, he could walk to the window and look down, watch her sliding a case into her car. And leaving him.

For months he'd balanced perilously on a tightrope of lies, inching his way along. Any time, he'd thought, he'd wobble and fall. But he'd made it as far as the final step and even had the remembered feel of firm ground beneath one foot, when the rope had snapped in spectacular fashion.

Cleo had gone.

And where he wanted to shut himself away with her, repossess her, try and overlay what had just happened with what would happen next, she wanted to get away from him.

But, surely – she'd come back?

Chapter Eighteen

Gav waited in Bob Chester's office on Monday morning and wished he could ring Cleo. Wished he knew where she was. That she'd come home tonight.

As shitty days at work went, this one was a real public toilet – and he would handle it better with a little of her good sense to calm the churning anxiety in his guts. But Cleo hadn't come home and her phone had been off all weekend.

On a chair as far across the room as possible, Lillian held an ice pack to her visibly swelling eye.

Bitch. Bet she'd find some way to make everything sound worse than it was. He realised he was tapping his right foot in a staccato beat. Stopped.

'Right.' Bob's grave voice cut into a silence that had been perfect since he'd ushered them into his office. 'Obviously an incident has occurred between you today, which has to be investigated. As your department head I will be the investigating officer.' He stroked his hair back, the bit at the front that was greasiest and slithered forward all the time. 'I'm sending you both home for the rest of today to cool down. Tomorrow I'll need you here to make statements. If you're in a union you may be accompanied by your rep, if not you can choose a third party from within the company – if it would make you feel more comfortable.'

He harrumphed awkwardly. 'As for now, you'll be escorted separately from the premises.'

'Holy shit,' breathed Gav.

Even Lillian looked shocked. Her good eye flickered for a moment towards Gav.

The human resources manager walked Gav out, across an

unnaturally silent set of sections, into the lift, out through the foyer and right to his car, standing there, watching as Gav strapped himself into his Focus and tried to get himself together. Tomorrow he'd have to tell his story. As evenly and unemotionally as possible, lay it out about the sales conference and the one-night stand with Lillian. The love-hate stuff, the fancying her rotten – plenty of men in the company probably fancied her rotten. A beauty queen who dressed like a whore. He'd have to lay his cards on the table.

His limbs trembled as he drove slowly towards a home that would be empty and silent, to wait out the hours until tomorrow's meeting. To try and still his trembling he visualised himself at tomorrow's investigation, suited and brushed, quiet and thoughtful, saying gravely, 'Although my wife expressed no animosity towards Lillian, I felt it was only fair to warn her that our past relationship had been discovered.' He'd explain how he'd stopped by Lillian's desk on some pretext, pushing the tickly fronds of her fern aside to bend close and murmur, 'Can we have a few words in private?'

She'd followed him to the photocopying room, smirking like a cat. She was dazzling. Smart and sexy and cool, skirt too short and eyes just daring anyone to look. And *he'd* ... He battered down the small, inappropriate surge of triumph. She halted just inside the door. 'Can you remember what you want to say this time? Or is the old memory playing tricks again?'

Last time, of course, he'd been going to complain that he'd contracted a sexually transmitted disease from her. Good job he'd bottled out, in view of the eventual diagnosis.

He cleared his throat. 'I'm, er, sorry, Lillian. I just thought I ought to warn ... well, there's a possibility that Cleo might ring you. She knows.'

'She *knows*?' Lillian exploded, not quite so gorgeous as

her complexion drained in panic. '*You moronic bastard.* Couldn't you keep my name out of it? I hope you don't expect me to pull your nuts out of the fire and tell her it was all my idea, do you? That I tempted you, and you were merely weak?'

Merely weak. He blinked. 'No, I hadn't thought that, but ... it's true, isn't it?'

'Don't be such a jellyfish.' Lillian swung her back to him, tapping her thumbnail rapidly against her teeth as she huddled in thought. Then, 'Who else knows?'

'Nobody. Unless Cleo –'

'I suppose she's running round bleating to everyone that some bitch in her husband's office gave him one.'

Gav's temper whizzed around the dial and straight into the red zone. 'You did give me one and you are a bitch, a calculating bitch who doesn't mind borrowing someone else's husband but doesn't want to know when he's caught out!'

That's when he'd flung the door open, he'd explain to Bob, and stormed into the corridor. And Lillian had flown after him, discarding discretion in her fury. '*I am not a bitch*!' From behind she'd grabbed at his shoulder, long nails scraping on the fabric of his suit, attempting to force him around to face her.

But he'd flung up his arm to shake her off –

'So,' he would conclude sombrely, contrite and aiming to look shocked. 'That's how I hurt her. I threw my arm up to get her off and I suppose she must've still been coming forward. My elbow hit her in the face. Hard, I suppose. I'm sorry – but it was an accident.' And he'd clear his throat, ask, 'How is she?' Hopefully Bob wouldn't realise that Gav didn't care if he'd knocked her head off.

The benefits of visualisation techniques were something Cleo put a lot of faith in; and he did acknowledge that, although he wasn't completely confident that his subconscious would help him to control the situation as he'd visualised, he did feel less scared.

Bloody, bloody, bitching Lillian. Over the past few days realisation had slammed into him, in many degrees of pain, that – because of Lillian – Cleo seemed to be considering opting out of their marriage. His Cleo! Bright, larky Cleo, who he had thought he'd have for always. Exchanged for Lillian Trent, worthless, shallow cock tease. And only one night with her, at that.

Bad bargain.

As he pulled up in Port Road, Gavin's heart gave a great bounce. Cleo's car was parked outside. A fumble for the front-door key and he burst into the house and into the sitting room, praying. Was she home to stay? Or at least to talk? Surely they could talk? And he could persuade her, he was sure. His Cleo, she would surely listen.

'Cleo!' She was standing at the far end of the room by the kitchen door, looking white and shocked, dark hair shining. He sidled nearer and she didn't back off. So he slid his arms around her, her emerald green jacket, and she didn't flinch. His heart settled into a hopeful waltz.

She was looking up at him with huge eyes. Her voice was unsteady. 'I'm sorry, Gav. Yvonne's just rung ... there's some awful news about your mother.'

Awful, awful, terrible, dreadful, horrible, heartbreaking news.

They made another unscheduled drive up the M1. But there was no urgency this time, no dread of what they'd find. No worst to fear, because the worst had happened when Pauline died that afternoon in a twist of metal on a road a minute from her home.

Gav's parents' house, when they reached it, was heart-wrenchingly unchanged. Pauline's slippers stood at the foot of the stairs, her jacket hung on a peg near the door.

George had taken to his armchair. 'We'd just lit the fire for the first time,' he kept repeating, grey, old and disbelieving. 'It was such a nippy day for September and we lit the fire. We'd got cold.' Yvonne had arrived before them again and was patting her dad's hand, tears flooding her face.

George turned to Gav. 'She only went out to buy her magazines to read in front of the fire. Then she didn't come back. I thought she'd be chatting, though it seemed ages. But the police came. It was this lorry – well, she's only got a tiddly little car, hasn't she? Probably didn't see her.

'There's got to be a post-mortem. Things to arrange with the undertaker.' He gazed at Cleo. 'The fire's gone out now, see, I forgot to feed it, with Pauline and everything. And the police took me to look, y'know. At her.'

George's eyes were empty. The tremor in his hands was reflected by the quaver in his voice. Cleo patted his shaky hand. It was icy. 'Shall I light it again?'

George considered. 'It won't make any difference now, will it?'

'It might warm you up.'

George, Yvonne and Gav watched in silence as she screwed up newspaper over the ashes, laid the sticks, the split log, and struck a match.

'Thanks,' George said mechanically.

They went on in distant voices chewing over unacceptable things: the funeral, the post-mortem, searching each other's shocked expressions for answers. Yvonne kept bursting into noisy tears then sniffing, 'I'm sorry, I'm sorry!' George seemed too moribund with grief to comfort her. Gav patted his sister's arm awkwardly. His eyes kept shifting away from the pudding tummy under her dress.

Cleo made cups of tea that were only half drunk and sandwiches nobody ate. Slipping outside into George's row-on-row vegetable garden, grown weedy the last few weeks since his heart attack, she rang Nathan from her mobile to explain. Next, she rang her mother and Liza.

And then, in the bright, damp chill, she was struck by the urge to ring Justin's mobile.

His message service cut in, she listened to his recorded voice: '*Justin's phone.*' But she hung up without speaking anyway, breathed in the scent of wet soil and cabbages, and went back indoors.

George's GP came, his side parting and freckles giving him the odd air of a solemn, middle-aged kid. He perched on George's footstool, took his pulse and looked into his bewildered face. His voice was low and sympathetic. 'You know you're going to have to be careful, don't you?'

George said, 'I don't care, now.'

'She would've wanted you to care. She tried hard to make you well.'

'I don't care. Not now.'

'You owe it to yourself. Your kids.'

George gently freed his wrist and glanced over at Yvonne, Gav and Cleo perched on the sofa. 'I'm that tired.'

'It's to be expected.'

George remained in his chair as everyone else filed out after the doctor and gathered in the square at the bottom of the stairs.

Unsmiling, the doctor gave them what advice he could. 'See if you can keep him resting. Make sure he's taking his medication.' He glanced down at Yvonne's expectant belly. 'And how are you? Looking after yourself?'

'I'm OK.' Yvonne voice was as small and dull as her father's.

'Get plenty of rest. Don't overdo.' He turned to Gav. 'There will be arrangements. Best if you can take as much as possible off your dad.'

Gav nodded and fumbled for Cleo's hand. His was hot and sliding with sweat and she squeezed it quickly before freeing herself. She sensed his disappointment.

'I'll make hot chocolate,' she said. Once again, the only thing she could usefully do was to organise the family nourishment. She had to do something because she felt a fraud just being there. Though no one could've been so harsh as to let Gav face this alone.

The cracks around the curtains were barely showing light and the house was entirely still, when Cleo woke to the instant realisation that everything was wrong.

She turned and tried to settle again. Last night Gav had cried, and she'd put comforting arms around him. He'd tried to make love to her and she'd withdrawn, pushing him gently back into his own space. 'No, don't, Gav,' she'd muttered, feeling a totally wicked witch.

The memory wouldn't let her slither back into oblivion. Gav. Lillian. Justin. Poor Pauline. They whirled about in her restless mind. It was unbearable lying there, miserably watching the minutes tick by on the clock. She was bored silly but a gripping paperback hadn't been top of her list when she'd flung their things in bags. Downstairs, she knew, George kept a collection of war stories and crime novels.

She eased herself out of bed and into her robe, visualising a fat mug of hot tea to blow on while she browsed the bookcase. Maybe there would be a Ruth Rendell she hadn't read, or a Patricia Cornwell.

Kitchen, the door squeaked. Kettle, the water rushed as loud as a waterfall in the early quiet. A sudden sob from the corner made her jump.

Dropping the kettle with a clatter, she twitched around. 'Yvonne!'

Yvonne was huddled in her mother's rocking chair, face blotched and swollen with tears. Automatically, Cleo rescued the kettle and abandoned thoughts of the bookcase. When the tea was made, she carried a steaming cup to Yvonne, hesitating as Yvonne stared listlessly out of fat rubber eyes.

'Would you rather be alone? Or shall I stay with you?'

Yvonne's voice emerged shakily. 'I'm so …' Another sob, a rattled, jerky breath. 'I'm so *frightened*.'

Not even the hardest-hearted sister-in-law could ignore such misery. Cleo dragged up a wooden kitchen chair. 'It's an awful time. But you mustn't be frightened of life without your mum, she wouldn't want that.'

Yvonne's eyes fixed on her. 'But she was going to be *with* me! Allen isn't any good with hospitals. He faints if he hears the theme music from *Casualty*. I'm …' Her sobs burst out again. 'I'm going to give birth alone! It's so selfish but I'm frightened. I want my mum.'

Cleo had absolutely no idea what to say, so she simply patted Yvonne's hand and sat with her while she drank her tea. And thought about the prospect of giving birth alone.

Chapter Nineteen

Cleo folded the last of her clothes back into her weekend case.

She felt mean and low and flattened by guilt.

Still, she'd better get used it, the guilt and the packing. More of both lay ahead. Much more. She felt like crap about deserting Gav at his lowest; but his announcement last night that he'd be staying in Yorkshire another week had prompted her into action.

The taxi was booked to the coach station. She'd be back in Middledip in a few hours.

Gav stepped warily around the bedroom door, closing it behind him, speaking softly so that his father and Yvonne wouldn't hear. 'I can't believe you're leaving me now. With Mum only just buried and all this trouble at work.'

She shut her case, zipping it around, feeling tears start. 'I'm sorry. My first instinct was to hang on for a better moment – but then I realised that I had no idea when that would be. Best if I just go, get it over with.'

In two strides he was around the bed and yanking her into his arms, pressing his mouth against her hair, his voice raw. 'Cleo don't, don't! Wait for me at home and let's talk. Please? We can get over this. Please! I love you.' And then, voice breaking, 'We need each other.'

She allowed his arms to remain around her, helplessly hating herself. But she'd gone over this a hundred times in the long nights as he'd alternately slept or sighed wakefully beside her.

There was no good time to leave. She could hurt him more by hanging around sheepishly, waiting for him to seem well enough to be left.

She crooked her head back to look into his distressed eyes, asking gently, 'Would it truly be any better if I stayed for a few months because now is a painful time for you? Knowing I'd be going? Living apart in the same house? After what we used to have, Gav? Be honest. Is it what you want?'

His arms tightened. '*Of course it's not what I want.* I want us to forgive each other and get back what we had.'

She squeezed his arm. 'I'm sorry. But it won't come back. Not for me.'

'It will for me!' The cry hung in the air.

'I'm so sorry.' Gently, she released herself, watching his arms drop hopelessly to his sides. 'I'm really sorry. And there's ... can we sit down?' She drew him to the bedroom chair, perched herself on the corner of the bed.

Deep breath. This was going to be incredibly hard, making a bad situation truly dreadful. 'There's another reason we can't go on – you're so definite about not wanting kids.'

His eyes were guarded. 'And you want them, suddenly? Out of the blue?'

It seemed late in the proceedings to be owning up to her knickers drawer secret, but she owed him a bit of honesty, here, at least, in the dying moments of the relationship. She shifted uncomfortably. 'I ... probably am pregnant. I haven't done a test – but,' she shrugged. 'Every day that passes ... well, I must be.'

Slowly, the light died in his eyes. His hands clenched. 'It's not mine.'

'It could be. That time we made up –'

But his head was shaking exaggeratedly, wearily, his hair sliding over his eyes. Eyes that looked so hopelessly into hers it almost split her chest with guilt.

'No. Not mine. I'm infertile. I've known for years.'

Years ... The word shot into her brain, lighting the

touchpapers of incredulity and shock to rocket around inside her head. Her voice rose. 'What are you talking about?'

He bowed his head. 'Years ago, when I lived with my ex, Stacey, we tried for a family. It didn't work so we went for tests. It was me. Firing blanks. I produce no sperm, there's a name for the condition – Klinefelter's. The fluid's there and everything when I … anyway, it's untreatable.' The words almost choked him. 'It's why Stace left. I couldn't give her babies.'

Funny, Cleo didn't feel like crying. She just felt very, very sick at the many ways in which they'd betrayed one another. Hurt one another. 'Oh, Gav,' she whispered. 'No wonder you've never liked talking about Stacey! But making out you're so anti-children to protect yourself from reality, marrying me without telling me your condition – so many lies! How can you say you love me?'

His face crumpled. 'You agreed you didn't want children! And, after Stacey, I couldn't risk admitting the truth.'

She stared at him, bitter over this betrayal as she never had been over Lillian. 'And that makes it OK? What if I'd changed my mind?'

Gav dropped his face into his hands.

Cleo raked her hair back from her eyes. 'This marriage has been phoney, the whole thing. Empty, pointless and fabricated on a huge lie.'

A tear tipped itself over the rim of Gav's eye and slid down his cheek. 'It's not. I love you. You didn't *want* children.'

Cleo's voice emerged around the ache in her throat. 'But you prevented me from having a choice. You've let me take the pill for years, then struggle with the diaphragm, all to protect yourself from having to own up. What kind of love do you call that?'

Gav made himself stand at the window and watch the

black cab leave, Cleo's rigidly held head visible through the rear screen. 'She's leaving me,' he whispered. He wanted to thunder his fists on the bedroom window till they went right through, scream that it was unfair to blame him. She should've understood; he needed understanding.

If she'd stayed, if she'd tried, they could've sorted everything out. Almost.

If she was pregnant, it could be tricky. Bastard, bastard Klinefelter's.

The coach was held up by glinting lines of traffic stretching away up the motorway. Other passengers tutted and fidgeted, checked their watches every five minutes and explained to their seat-neighbours about connections they were going to miss or people who would be waiting.

Cleo didn't care.

It was as if she was encased in an icy bubble, which separated her from her sighing fellow passengers, whether the coach was whistling along in the middle lane or inching up a queue. Her thoughts were all about how the solid ground on which she'd thought her marriage was built could have trembled and so easily cracked. How rapidly it had exploded into a shower of wounding stones and bitter-tasting dirt.

She wiped her eyes; they kept refilling. She thought of the cemetery in which they'd laid Pauline, her favourite in-law. Lilies, chrysanthemums. White, cream, sherbet lemon and baby pink. 'She would've loved the flowers,' George had said.

Yvonne had wept fresh tears. 'What use are flowers?' Her husband, Allen, stolid in a dark grey suit and black tie, had rocked her and stroked her hair and not minded the mascara on his lapel.

By leaving, Cleo was isolating herself from people she'd

considered family. Running out on them when they were in trouble, which went against her grain. She just couldn't see how it was better – or even possible, in view of her missing periods and Gav's confessed infertility – to perpetuate the illusion that their marriage was OK.

Her heart shrank to remember Gav's face when she'd finally kissed him goodbye. A gentle peck on the cheek that mocked all the hot, full-on tongue-thrusters they'd shared. Their future together had gone west, and, horribly, so had their past.

What was life going to be like without him? Too big a thought.

Funny how still the house seemed when she let herself in: empty, although she hadn't yet removed a thing.

Throwing open the windows, she stood in the bedroom to gaze out over the familiar view, the fields, many ploughed under now after the harvest. Shivered. Chilly for September. Down to the kitchen, she tried to organise her whirring brain. She needed to move out of this house. She needed to pack. But she needed somewhere to go. Maybe Liza ...? She shoved the thought away. Surely she was too grown up now to cram all her possessions into the miniature spare room belonging to her kid sister.

There was lemon pepper chicken in the freezer; she slid one portion – one portion! – into the oven, stirred pasta into sauce.

One of Gav's favourites. There was half a jar of sauce left. *Oh, wouldn't it be simple to stay, to give in to the enormous compassion she felt for him?* Easy to make things easy for the man she'd once loved, who'd been perfidious in so many, fundamental ways.

The time had come for her to think of herself as single. Possibly a single parent – which would be tough.

Chapter Twenty

In the morning, over breakfast – biscuits dunked in black coffee because she'd had to bin the bread, milk and fruit they'd left behind – Cleo tried to identify a starting point. In order to pack her things, she needed boxes and bin bags. And she could do with somewhere to go.

Pausing at the front window overlooking Port Road she was struck by a sudden unhappy thought – there probably wasn't much property to rent in Middledip. Her heart sank at the thought of leaving the village. She needed to do some research.

Cleo began at the village shop at the Cross. But Mrs Crowther, in her neat grey overall, couldn't be much help. 'Sorry, duck, the remainder of yesterday's evening papers went back when the morning papers came. But, as it's Saturday, today's will be in about lunchtime. I'll save you one if you want to call back for it?'

Cleo nodded gloomily and paid for a bar of wicked, dark Bournville, along with rolls of bin bags. 'Thanks. I suppose the property supplement was in Friday's?'

Gwen Crowther nodded. 'Moving, then?' She was famed for keeping customers talking while she wheedled out their news, casually squaring up her display of Polos or Fisherman's Friends. 'There's plenty for sale up the new village.'

'I was thinking more of renting. But I suppose rentals are few and far between in Middledip.'

Moving on to tidy the Tic-Tacs, Mrs Crowther tipped back her head to look through the correct part of her bifocals. 'Have you tried Ratty?'

Intrigued, Cleo returned to the counter. 'Have I tried what?'

Mrs Crowther nodded in the direction of the shop door. 'Have you tried asking Ratty, at the garage? He's got a few places hereabouts.'

Cleo's spirits stirred slightly. She knew the men at the garage to nod to in the pub. 'To rent?'

'Yes, duck. One of his tenants has just left, I believe, and I don't know as anyone else took the house.' Cleo shoved the chocolate into her pocket and, clutching the four empty brown boxes that Mrs. Crowther had kindly slotted inside one another, made the shop bell clank as she barged awkwardly through the door.

On the garage forecourt across the road, five small old sports cars lined up as if on the front of a Brands Hatch grid. Cleo knew the business dealt mainly in classic cars. The garage doors were folded back to show an interior of tool chests and a ramp, a man bent over a beautifully kept, but ancient, yellow saloon and two others welding in masks under an equally elderly sports car on the ramp behind.

Yellow-car man looked up through black curls as Cleo stepped into the oil-scented interior.

'I'm looking for someone called Ratty?'

'Yep. That's me.' He shook his hair out of his eyes and stretched deeper under the bonnet, craning under an inspection lamp and fiddling with a wrench. His voice came back hollowly. 'What can I do for you?'

She moved round to the side of the vehicle so that she could see his face. 'Mrs Crowther at the shop said you rent out some property in the village.'

She hopped out of the way as he backed out, grasped the front of the car and began to rock it. When he'd inched it forward he tucked himself back under the bonnet again, made an adjustment with a screwdriver and straightened up.

'I do, but I've nothing vacant. Sorry.' He wiped his hands on a well-used rag.

Cleo's hopes settled back towards her boots. She sighed and shifted the boxes uncomfortably in her arms. Even though they were empty, the rigid edges dug into the crooks of her elbows. 'Mrs Crowther thought one of your tenants had just left.'

He nodded. 'Cleared off owing rent and left a disgusting mess behind, presumably the result of a party and several people being very poorly. The key money didn't even cover the cleaning company costs. So I've pretty much decided to sell.'

'Right. I see.' She bit her bottom lip hard to stop her disappointment showing. She could've used a bit of luck. Her voice sounded thin as she said thanks and goodbye.

She was walking away when she heard him call after her, 'Got a problem?'

She turned back. He was in the driver's seat now, looking at her through the windscreen. She trailed back to stand in the open doorway. 'A bit. I need somewhere to go, quick, and I want to stay in Middledip.' The engine coughed into life. The car vibrated then settled down.

Ratty's eyes stayed on her face, although his tilted head suggested he was listening to the engine note. 'Live up Port Road, don't you?'

She nodded, swallowing the lump in her throat.

'But you're moving on?'

She nodded again. 'This week, preferably.'

He switched the ignition off and on again, listening. 'Just you?'

It seemed a kind way of asking if she was leaving her husband. ''Fraid so. Well …' She hesitated, felt a sudden scalding of her face. 'There might be a child. In a while.'

He raised his eyebrows. Easing out of the car, he tore blue

paper towel from a roll on a wooden shelf, wiped his hands then rolled down his sleeves over tattooed forearms. 'OK, you can have a look at the house.' He called towards the rear of the garage, 'Back in ten minutes.'

Two muffled voices shouted, 'OK!' from behind welding masks.

He strode off across the Cross and up Port Road.

Cleo beetled along beside him, wrestling with the light but cumbersome boxes, which the wind kept trying to snatch – until he took them off her. It was easier to talk, then. 'Where is the house?'

'Ladies Lane, just round the corner from where you are now. Will being that close cause trouble?'

'Don't think so.' They crossed Church Close, passed 11 Port Road without comment and cornered into Ladies Lane. A real lane with no kerbs, just narrow unedged tarmac between hawthorn hedges and overgrown verges that would froth with cow parsley, come spring, but were now just dandelion and nettle.

Three ironstone long houses spaced themselves out along the left-hand side, facing a hedge and a ploughed field on the right, and Ratty made for the third. Two black gates, one wide for cars, and one narrow for pedestrians, fastened together. He unlatched the narrow side and Cleo followed him to the front door.

He dropped the boxes on the path and put an iron bootscraper inside to keep them from blowing away. 'This is it.' Two steps and they were under the porch and into a tiny hall with the stairs straight ahead. He opened the right-hand door. 'Kitchen with cooker, sink, cupboards, washing machine.'

Cleo stepped in behind him, taking in plain wooden doors and drawers. The kitchen had a window at each end, the one at the back tiny. He rattled a locked door in the side wall. 'That takes you through to the barn.' Cleo opened cupboards and gazed at the kitchen table and two chairs. The floor was laid with lovely uneven quarry tiles; the walls were cream, the ceiling white and the beams black. The windowsills were broad enough to sit on.

The sitting room, the other door from the titchy hall, had the same two-window arrangement. The walls were pale pink. 'Not my idea,' Ratty observed. 'Blame the last tenant.' A cottage suite stood beside a small table and a tall lamp. A black wood-burning stove squatted in the centre of the long wall on a stone platform topped with a granite flag.

'I've never used a wood stove.'

'It's easy.'

Upstairs, the bedroom was above the sitting room with a double bed, two wardrobes, a mirror, and a chest of drawers. 'You'd need all your own linens, including bedclothes.'

'Right.' Excitement was beginning to rise. She liked 3 Ladies Lane. And surely somewhere in the last few minutes, even if he hadn't put it into so many words, Ratty had decided to let the house to her?

They moved across the landing. 'Bathroom.' he pushed the door and let her step in.

'Wow! It's nice in here.'

For the first time he smiled, as if he'd been reserving it until he decided whether he liked her. 'Not bad, is it? I liked it, when I lived here.' The glossy white of the big shower cubicle and the bath contrasted with the black tiles. Cleo admired the mirrors, heated towel rail and thick blue carpet.

Outside, he showed her the garage doors in the end of the single-storey part of the building. 'This bit would've been for the animals, originally.' They stepped inside. A pile of logs huddled in one corner of the oil-stained floor. 'I used to keep a couple of cars here. You can use it for storage, garage, or both.'

Cleo walked out into the garden and frowned. 'I suppose the tenant's responsible for the upkeep of this?'

'That's about it. Of course, the tenant can keep on the lad the landlord presently pays to do it for three hours a week.' When he smiled it was as if the sun came from behind a cloud. He showed her a bench made of split logs, twisted with age, where they could sit.

'OK. If you want this place I'll rent it to you. It's a small house and it comes with the furniture as is, it's got no gas and the heating's oil, which is a pain if you don't remember to order it on time.' He suggested a monthly rental that was less than Cleo and Gav were paying for the house in Port Road. But of course she'd be paying this one alone. He looked very directly at her. 'Before I sign anything I need to hear you say you can pay the rent and bills and you can keep the house nice. I'm responsible for any maintenance and repair, but the dust and fingerprints are all yours.'

She felt a sudden billow of happiness. She'd like to live in Ladies Lane, facing the flat fields. 'I can pay that. And keep the place nice.'

'And there won't be any bother from your ex-significant other?'

She shook her head, her smile fading at the thought of poor old Gav. 'He's not like that.' Or not often. She thought of the writing on the bedroom wall.

'When do you want to move in?'

'Straight away? I can transfer the first month's rent and the key money to your account today.'

His blue eyes rested on her for several moments. 'Fair enough – I'll run an Agreement off on the computer.' He offered her an oily hand and she shook it. She got the impression that the handshake meant more to him than the written Agreement would.

He dropped the keys into her hand. 'Be happy.'

She sat on the twisted bench and watched him leave. Then she looked up at the house. She could be sleeping in her new bedroom tonight!

'Well you'd better shape yourself,' she said, aloud. 'There's a shitload of stuff to move and, from today, you're officially single.'

In view of the pathetic state of her food supplies, she took herself off for lunch at The Three Fishes. With her boxes tucked under the table, she munched her way through a substantial Ploughman's, mentally cruising through the rooms of what used to be her home to decide what to take.

Must be fair to Gav and leave the place reasonable for him. Newly bereaved, it would be horrible for him to come back to a home stripped of all the best kit. It wasn't going to be very nice in any case. She shivered. He might remain at 11 Port Road, they might be near neighbours, and she didn't want him howling round the corner to claim custody of the teapot.

Breaking up a home was a big job and had to be thought hard about. But first …

… knickers drawer. She gathered up her boxes and made for home, where she fished out the flat blue box of the pregnancy testing kit and took it into the bathroom, tearing at the polythene with her teeth.

Chapter Twenty-One

There were two blue lines.

Positively positive. She was pregnant.

Even though it was what she was expecting, she trembled as she went slowly down and made coffee, sitting very still on the sofa, blowing and sipping, and thinking.

It was an hour before she stopped feeling sorry for herself and blotted up the tears tipping from her lashes.

She was too busy to sit around bawling; she had to move out. Boxes, bags, TV, stereo. In the car, round the corner, out of the car, into the new house. Back to the old house, begin again.

By evening everything was moved, somehow, anyhow, but the worst job was still hanging over her. Reluctantly, she picked up her mobile phone and sent a text to Justin.

Would like 2 talk. Could we meet? Suggest Fri night at Muggies. Cleo

Friday night at Muggie's. Having spent half the week chewing it over, Cleo decided to go to Muggie's alone.

Much to Liza's disgust. 'I won't be in the way! C'mon Cleo, you don't want to meet him on your own, he turned awkward last time.' Her delicately arched eyebrows lifted in entreaty.

Cleo thought of the doorway, the shadows, Justin, his anger pinning her to the door while ... She shivered. 'I'd rather be alone this time, Lize. OK?'

'It's not OK, really. You need a bit of backup.' Liza pretended to pout, but Cleo could read the concern in her sister's eyes.

'Not this time.' Cleo gave her sister a quick, guilty hug. Thing was that, in all the soul-baring about her marriage, her affair, Gav's affair, Gav's infertility and consequent cover-up, Cleo hadn't quite got around to telling her sister that she was pregnant. In fact, she had an old-fashioned idea about telling the father first; and it would be appropriate on a Friday night at noisy old Muggie's, where it had all begun.

Cleo got herself a glass of fizzy water and hovered, watching the stairs. She waited. And waited. By ten o'clock she was uneasy. Justin hadn't shown. She combed every section of the throbbing nightclub, peeping around every nook and nib and onto the dance floor.

Gradually, her heart turned to lead. He wasn't coming. She tipped back her head and drained her drink, letting the ice chink-plop into her mouth. Last look round, big sigh, no Justin. Just when she'd been daring to let herself think of him, of his smile, daring to think, 'I'm separated now. There's nothing to stop me and Justin ...'

Her palms got hot at the thought.

And then her heart jumped. There, at least, were the two platinum blonds Justin hung out with, slouching about in the no-man's-land between the stairs and the bar. Relief! She wriggled her way between backs and shoulders, brushing shirts and catching handbags, trying to keep her eyes on the blond heads before they could move away. Maybe they'd have a message, maybe Justin had been held up.

She grabbed the forearm of the one she reached first. 'Hi!'

He nodded, without showing enthusiasm at seeing her.

'Martin, isn't it?'

He nodded again. 'And you're the woman from the lake. Wet T-shirt.'

'The married one,' the other one, Drew, added.

She flicked her hair out of her eyes and tried her best, wide, smile, the one she used to begin her workshops, the one that made people she'd never met before smile back. 'Do you know where Justin is?'

'He's –'

Drew butted in. 'Justin who?'

Cleo stared, and they faced her, gazing back, hands in pockets, shoulders rounded. She opened her mouth and then closed it.

Surely she must know Justin's surname? Of course she did! Didn't she? She pummelled her memory. A hot, dark flush swelled up her neck. 'Justin,' she repeated, weakly.

Drew and Martin shrugged at each other, looked back at Cleo, carefully blank.

'You *know*,' she stammered. '*Justin.*'

'Justin?' They shrugged elaborately at each other again. 'Justin?'

Theatrically, Martin clapped his hand to his head. 'I know who she means – Just-in time!'

With a laugh, Drew fished theatrically in his back pocket and held up a condom packet. 'Or, Just-in case?'

Martin produced his wallet. 'Just-in it for the money.'

Drew gave Martin a mock shove. 'Just-in the way!'

Martin stuck his finger in Drew's ear. 'Just-in 'ere.'

Drew crowed with helpless laughter. 'Just-in the USA, not available in England. And all that mullarkey!' So side-splittingly funny they were, they had to prop one another up.

Cleo shrank with humiliation, watching the blond bombshells shuffling off to the bar, still giggling. 'Gits!' She sent burning thoughts of revenge after them as she turned hollowly to the stairs. Might as well go home.

It had been a funny week. Cleo cleared her desk, dropping files and pads into drawers. She'd had to inform Nathan of her change of address, flushing at the palpable surprise flitting from face to face around the office. Worse, on Monday morning, taking a deep breath, she'd had to ring Gav at his dad's house and give him the same information. That had been *horrible*.

The pause on the other end of the phone had been accusing. 'You didn't waste much time.'

'Sorry.' Why did she apologise? 'I didn't want you to come home and find out the hard way.'

The silence was longer and more despondent. The sigh before he spoke was huge. 'Aren't you being hasty? We both had affairs, they can be forgiven, it happens.' Cleo heard the catch in Gav's voice. 'And I think that if you put yourself in my place about the Klinefelter's and had any, any ... *compassion* you'd understand why I hid it. Can you imagine how it was for me? Chatting a girl up, taking her out, to bed, falling in love, wanting to marry ... just where do you interpose, "by the way, I have no sperm"?'

Cleo sighed back. 'Immensely difficult, I agree – but you should've found a way. It was just dishonest. Infertility is a joint problem. I can't accept that you decided on behalf of both of us that we'd live a lie. That was worse than the Lillian thing.'

He moved away from the subject of his infertility. 'I've phoned Bob Chester and arranged to make my statement. Lillian has already made hers and, in my absence, been allowed back to work. I get to see a copy of her statement after I've made mine. So I'm coming home tomorrow, seeing Bob on Wednesday.' He stumbled over the word 'home'.

Cleo searched for something that might make his homecoming easier for him, trying feebly, 'I could buy milk and bread to leave in your ... the kitchen, if you like?'

His breath hissed. 'I fucking don't like! You won't forgive me, you won't stay – but you'll do me a bit of shopping? Big deal. Haven't you got any feelings left for me at all?'

Her side of the conversation could be heard by the whole office; so she didn't point out that she no longer loved him and was definitely carrying another man's child.

'Sorry,' she said again. Why hadn't she simply bought the few essentials and left them in the kitchen? Putting the idea into words had rubbed his nose in the crappy situation. What a mess, what a jumble of guilt and regret. But the relief was there. The relief at being free topped everything.

On Tuesday, as she was staring blindly at her screen and wondering whether Gav had set off, Nathan came to her desk. 'Tom's taking a team-building workshop at an insurance company but he's developed one of his killer migraines. You'll have to rescue the poor bloke, Cleo. He's got a plan so you should be able to pick up where he leaves off.'

'Give me the address.' She was quite pleased. A workshop would distract her; stop her mind whirring about Gav, infidelity and infertility. Relieved, she grabbed her briefcase and rushed to the rescue.

Tom, white and disorientated, glasses in his top pocket, was pathetically grateful to see her, as much as he could see anything for double vision and flashes of colour. 'Thanks, Cleo, I've had to leave the room twice to barf.' He flipped his notes open. 'They're in four groups, each comprising three decision makers and an observer. This is the problem outline they've been given.' He tapped the page. Sweat glistened suddenly on his upper lip. 'Gotta go!'

Cleo watched Tom dash off, wrinkling her nose in sympathy, then turned back to her getting-restless group, junior management, eight men and four women, wearing suits and banging their ankles on each other's briefcases. 'Right,' she began with a wide smile. 'I'm Cleo Callaway, sorry to barge in on your party! We'll start this activity while poor Tom suffers.' They looked at her expectantly. 'I'll just plunge in as best I can, because you're probably woefully behind schedule anyway. Can the observer in each group please identify themselves? Right, thank you.

'What I'd like everyone to do is listen to the scenario I outline, then the decision makers in each group must confer and come up with the best solution they feel that the circumstances allow. OK?' She helped herself to a plastic cup of mineral water from the nearby stand.

'Here's the outline: we have twelve people in a boat on a high sea.' She mimed waves with her hands. 'Far away from land.' She shaded her eyes and pretended to peer into the distance. 'Twelve, OK? These twelve are …' Everyone snatched up their pens to jot down what they obviously recognised as the meat of the problem. '… A priest, a timber worker and his pregnant wife, a nuclear physicist, an SAS soldier and his wife who is not pregnant, a ferry boat captain, a rocket scientist, two miners, an engineer, and a carpenter. OK, everyone got that?' A few moments while the slower people finished scribbling, then she continued, 'Of these twelve, only seven can reach the faraway desert island and begin a new community.'

A dark man in a grey suit and crimson tie raised his pen. 'What happens to the other five?'

Cleo spread her hands. 'The surviving seven have to eat.' Everyone laughed, a couple of women wrinkled fastidious noses.

'So you have forty minutes to discuss, in your groups, which seven are going to survive – and be prepared to substantiate your decisions.

'Observers, your purpose is to observe and formulate conclusions as to whether your group functions, or not, and why. Be prepared to make suggestions at the end, but please don't make any during the exercise. Go!'

The designated observers turned to fresh sheets in their A4

pads and prepared to listen earnestly as the decision makers blew out their cheeks, tapped their pens and searched for obvious sacrificial lambs. Cleo walked very slowly around the groups, listening, watching.

Experience told her they'd make a complete arse of their early attempts. The assertive would dominate, the quiet give up, the exercise culminate in disagreement and disarray.

But this lot weren't too bad. Enough of them had suffered such workshops before to appoint a timekeeper to keep them on schedule or maybe a chairperson to make sure everyone got their say. But one group – there was almost always one – were falling out big style over the pregnant woman. Sonia, a woman with a no-nonsense manner and a navy suit, felt it non-negotiable that the unit of pregnant woman and timber worker should survive.

'It's *obvious*,' she snapped, glaring tight-lipped at her colleague, Frankie. 'They're an embryonic family unit. His timber-working skills will be important for building shelter.'

Frankie glared back. 'The carpenter's skills are *more* appropriate to building shelter.'

'What about the pregnant woman?'

'We take her, too.'

'But she's married to the timber worker. Why separate baby and father?'

Cleo watched Frankie's dark eyes light up. 'Nobody said the timber worker is the father. His wife is pregnant but how do you know that the baby his?'

Sonia tutted. 'Do you disagree with me on principle?'

'My point's just as valid as yours. Suppose it's not the husband's? Is there hostility between him and his wife? It's a very small community for them to hate one another. *And*,' Frankie persisted as Sonia opened her mouth once more, 'the pregnant woman might even be a liability because her history is uncertain.'

And, in spite of her trained neutrality, Cleo found herself offering, 'But isn't new life paramount?'

The group paused in their glaring at each other to stare at Cleo. A blush crept out from her collar. She would normally never dream of interfering like that. She had new life on her mind – and in her abdomen, apparently. Although she still had trouble believing that.

Gav was wearing the expensive russet sweatshirt that Cleo had bought him last year, the one that she'd said made his hair glint red.

She'd asked to come and see him! He had an hour before she was due. Let her come back! Let her stay!

Steaming round with the Pledge in one hand and the vacuum cleaner in the other, shoving frozen lasagnes in the oven, setting the table, he found he also had to set up the mini system from the study because Cleo had taken the other stereo. There. Now: Cleo's favourites. Elton John? Sting? Nope, of course, she'd taken 'her' discs. Have to make do with his collection. Starting nervously as the doorknocker clattered, he shoved on Celine Dion and hoped for the best.

'Hi!' He flung open the door. They looked at each other. Gav wanted to kiss her. Christ, he really, desperately wanted to kiss her, to clutch her against his chest and let all the despair wash away as he took possession of her mouth. Instead he stepped back with what he hoped was a friendly grin. 'I was just fancying a beer, can I get you one?'

'I'll just have water,' she said, following where he led, like a guest.

Lasagne, golden and bubbling, was ready in the oven, and they sat down at the table. He was glad that he'd decided against lighting candles. He could see now that she would be wary of a wooing-back scene. He plonked the margarine tub on the table between them with the hot, crusty bread, tipped the lasagne onto plates and began to eat as if he had a normal appetite; as if the oily fringe where the cheese met the sauce wasn't churning his stomach.

Perhaps if he got the good news out first, it would pre-empt all the painful explanations that he didn't want to hear, about her salary being paid into a shiny new bank account in her sole name, what her new phone number was and what she'd told her mum? Gulping his first mouthful he blurted, 'I've got my job back, anyway.'

'Already? Brilliant! How was it sorted so quickly?' Her eyes rested on his without any discernible awkwardness, whereas his were flicking tensely between her and his meal.

'I met Bob for my interview and he was all grave and officious. Then I made my statement and he read it. Then he asked me if I wanted to hang around while it was discussed with the HR manager. Said Lillian was in the building, so we could read each other's statements, blah, blah. So I spent half the day in his office like some rep, drinking coffee and staring out of the window, reading a paper Bob borrowed for me and being ignored.' Nervously, he'd spread margarine on four chunks of hot French bread as he talked. He stopped suddenly. What the hell was he going to do with four? Feeling foolish, he offered her the plate as if that had been his intention the whole time. Watched her take one chunk.

'Then suddenly I was in with Bob and the HRM, they said Lillian had read my statement and had agreed that it *could* all have been an accident. I think she realised that she actually laid her hands on me first. So.' He smiled.

Cleo's eyes were bright with pleasure. 'I'm glad. You don't deserve any more trouble.'

Gav laid down his fork. His voice came out in a back-of-the-throat growl. 'How are you?' Clumsily, as if he'd never done it before, he took her hand. 'Are you OK on your own?' He thought he saw a softening in her expression and suddenly, desperately, he was pleading, 'Cleo, it's not going to stay like this, is it? I know I was wrong not to tell you about ...' Sod, he was spewing up his spinning thoughts just the burbling way he'd promised himself he wouldn't. He halted, finished lamely, 'But if it had been you, wouldn't you have been tempted to pretend so everything would come right?'

Her eyes were especially dark when they were overlaid with sympathetic tears. She sniffed. 'If I'm honest, yes, I might've done something like creating a pretence to cover up the problem. But,' she withdrew her hand again, 'then *you* wouldn't have been able to forgive *me*. Would you?'

His stomach contracted. 'Why not? We've been together for five years –'

She laid down her fork. 'It's stopped mattering. All this has simply opened my eyes – I don't want to be married any more.' A large tear slid down each of her cheeks. 'I'm sorry, Gav, because I used to think we had something extraordinary, better than anyone. And all the time we had nothing. And ... and I'm really sorry to have to tell you this, Gav, but I am pregnant. I've done the test.'

He dropped his face into his hands. That rather made redundant suggestions of talking and forgiving.

So, though he had resisted it, they did end up talking about separate bank accounts, the barely tasted remains of the lasagne congealing between them, and Gav managed somehow to keep up his end in the conversation.

But all the time he could almost see the foetus like a black tumour growing in the body of his Cleo.

Tapping downstairs from the office after work on Thursday, Cleo's mind was full of her pregnancy, which still seemed unreal. Surely she should be feeling something by now? Some big clue about what was going on? She swung out of the front door and onto the broad pavement. And skidded to a halt face to face with Justin.

After a long moment, he smiled. 'I hear you wanted to see me?'

Swallowing, heart pattering, Cleo jerked her head to indicate he should walk along with her, away from the ears of passing colleagues. 'It's a bit late – that was last Friday.' Her voice was sharp; but the memory of hanging around on her own at Muggie's, the butt of his friends' impenetrable jokes, was fresh enough to sting. It had put her on her guard.

He lounged beside her as she rounded the corner into Ntrain's tiny car park. She paused by her car and checked her watch, conscious of Tom and Francesca throwing her curious glances as they went to their cars.

Justin leaned his elbow on her car roof and lifted his eyebrows. 'So, what was it you were after?' His sharp features were tanned, making his laughter lines into white creases. He grinned, a slow, teasing, mischievous grin. 'My body? A bed for the weekend? I'm afraid I was otherwise engaged.'

Nettled by the thought that he'd been too 'otherwise engaged' to even reply to her text and save her dangling around, she flushed. He'd probably thought it funny. 'Nothing. Doesn't matter.' Rapidly, she hopped into her car. The parking space behind had become free and she was able to back up and tootle off without any inept shunting.

She got a good look at his surprised expression as she whipped past and out into the street.

At home, she told herself that being alone had a lot of advantages. Cleo no longer had to negotiate over television programmes, or worry about Gav trying to sleep when she wanted to read in bed. Nobody else's tastes had to be considered at mealtimes. Shopping, meals and laundry were easy and, when she decided to go to bed all evening with the papers, no one bugged her to watch a football match instead.

Solitude was comfortable.

And, she supposed, tugging the quilt up to her shoulders as she chucked the sports sections on the floor and turned to the fashion pages, she should make the most of it. The peace. The quiet. When Junior made his or her appearance on the scene ... well, she had the impression that peace would be a thing of the past.

'So-o-o,' said Liza, a couple of Sundays later, screwing up her face in concentration as she applied a tiny transfer of red stars to her pinky nail on her right hand, cross-legged like a little pixie in Cleo's armchair. 'Guess who was looking for you at Muggie's, Friday night?' Cleo could invite Liza over to paint nails and watch *EastEnders* now, without anticipating that Gav would get restless and sarky at feeling excluded and Liza wouldn't be able to resist winding him up.

Cleo took her eyes away from the doings in Albert Square. 'No. Really? Was he?'

'Very casually, you know. As if it didn't really matter. But he looked pretty disgruntled when I told him that you were probably safely tucked up at home.'

'Oh.' Thoughtfully, Cleo began to apply a second coat of sparkling top coat to her nails. 'Did he say what he wanted?'

Liza shook her head. 'Nope. You don't think I'd give him the satisfaction of asking, do you? Have you got *Hollyoaks* recorded, too?'

Later in the afternoon, when Liza had been picked up and whizzed off in Angie's car, Cleo gazed at her mobile phone and felt herself weakening. After more than a week, her pique had subsided and she had returned to thinking sensibly.

She must speak to Justin. Tell him how things had changed

... and that he would soon be a father.

Picking up her phone, she set her thumb to moving rapidly over the keys. I hear u wanted 2 c me?

Wanted 2 tell u something, he returned.

That made two of them, then. She went to his name in her phone book and pressed *call*.

'Hello.' His voice was like melting brown sugar.

'So what was it?' she asked, smiling. Knowing he'd be able to detect the smile in her voice.

'When you texted me before, I was in America and had forgotten my charger. That's why I didn't meet you at Muggie's. I didn't get the text until too late.'

Something in her neck relaxed. 'Oh. Right. OK.' She pondered. 'Look, any chance you could meet for a drink and a chat?'

His voice warmed. 'That would be good. Where? The Three Fishes in Middledip?' He laughed. Obviously he'd expect Cleo to recoil as if stung.

But, 'OK,' she agreed brightly, enjoying his instant of surprised silence. 'If you don't mind driving to Middledip.'

Anticipation prickled up her back as she closed her phone. He'd sounded friendly, practically pricking up his ears at the prospect of seeing her.

Maybe everything was going to turn out right, maybe everything was going to be OK-hey-hey!

Chapter Twenty-Two

Sundays weren't meant to be busy nights at The Three Fishes. A few locals in corners, a couple of logs dancing with flames in the wide fireplace. The barman ambling between customers and the barmaid rolling cutlery into paper napkins.

But Cleo arrived twenty minutes early to secure a nook facing the room, only to find a raucous darts match in full swing and the smell of spilt beer strong on the air, rather than woodsmoke. Dismayed to find not a single empty table, she took a stool at the bar.

Justin breezed in a few minutes after eight, slid his phone and keys onto the counter, bought himself a beer and hoiked a leg over a stool to pull it underneath himself. He'd changed his clothes and he smelt of shaving foam. It was a languid, earthy smell.

Cleo felt somehow touched that he'd bothered. 'So, how was America?' She raised her voice over a great, 'YESSSSS!' from around the dartboard.

His eyes gleamed. 'Great, I love it. I stayed with my parents in Massachusetts. Then we all drove up to a log cabin in the woods – supposedly for the walking and the fishing, but actually to eat steaks and drink beer on the porch while we watched the leaves changing. The colours are amazing at this time of year.'

Cleo watched his hands moving as he spoke, his eyes shining as he described brunches and lunches, hire cars, trains, autumn leaves and historic ports. He was drinking Budweiser, she noticed, as he launched into a lengthy description of American hotels, road systems and shops.

His voice began to blend with the background racket as a leg of the darts tournament reached an apparently thrilling crescendo. Her thoughts wandered over the knotty problem of how in hell she was going tell him she was pregnant, with constant cries of, 'He only needs the double!' and 'Wrong side of the wire. Hard luck, mate,' crashing over their conversation.

The pub had obviously been a bad idea. So … maybe over coffee at her new house? There was such a lot to explain about Gav and the separation, about the baby. Heavy stuff. This was just not the place.

Of course, she didn't *expect* anything from him, she'd make that clear. But he ought at least to be privy to the information that there was to be a child. His child.

She started from her thoughts. He was waiting. Had obviously just asked something. She found herself smiling suddenly. 'How about a coffee? My place?'

Slowly, he put down his Budweiser. 'If that's … feasible.' And he smiled.

Cleo licked her lips, swallowed. 'It'll be just us.'

'If you're certain.'

His black BMW was tucked round the side of the pub. She waited at the passenger door, which, although it unlocked with the central locking system, for some reason wouldn't budge.

'Bugger, hang on.' He ran round the car and pointed out a small vertical crease in the door panel. 'Someone's bumped it in the airport car park, it's awkward to open.' Grasping the handle, he tugged, bracing a hand against the car beside Cleo, brushing her shoulder. The door groaned and gave way.

Cleo looked up to find him looking down. Suddenly she felt as if she was experiencing a souped-up hayfever attack, making her throat close and her eyes burn.

Slowly, tentatively, he lowered his head until their lips brushed. Cleo closed her hot eyes and let her lips part under his, let their quivering tongue tips meet and felt her hands creep onto his chest. His weight settled comfortably against her, the small questing kiss became a hot, deep kiss and his hand stroking her breast under her jacket. His breath was hot in her ear. 'Are you sure it'll be OK at your place? We could go to mine.'

'No, mine, please.' She couldn't blurt out further explanations in the car park. When she told him about her separation and about her pregnancy she wanted to be calm and look him in the eyes. He might be delighted. It might be a beginning. But he might want to put his running shoes on. She wanted him to be free to leave.

At Ladies Lane the front-door lock stuck, or maybe her fingers fumbled. He hooked her hair aside and brushed a kiss onto her nape as she struggled. Finally indoors, he peered through to the sitting room where the flame of the wood stove flickered and murmured 'Firelight – mmm, inviting. But I'm sure we'd be more comfortable if we were at my flat.' But then he turned and kissed her again, properly. And then improperly, which was delicious.

Meaningful conversation might've been first on her agenda, but Justin seemed to have interpreted the invitation to her home in his own way. She let him kiss her again, feeling her scalp prickle with excitement and she settled her body to his as if she'd done it a thousand times.

Justin's voice was rough in her ear. 'I keep wanting you!'

'Justin, I –' But his mouth took hers, his hands sliding under her T-shirt. Her breath caught as his fingertips glided up her sides. Her back prickled as if gangs of hedgehogs were tobogganing down it and she let her head fall back, groaning when his teeth grazed her throat. So dizzy with joy and ready for him it was obscene and –

And something began banging, right behind her.

'There's someone at your front door. Is this bad news?' Justin tensed. The doorknocker rattled again, harder.

Planting a 'till later' kiss beside his mouth, Cleo smoothed down her hair and her T-shirt. If it was that bloody woman collecting charity envelopes she'd swing for her. She snatched open the front door.

'Sur-*pri*-hise!'

'Oh hell!' Too stunned to stop them, Cleo fell back as Liza, Angie and Rochelle surged in, wine bottles waving. Liza, obviously pissed, staggered, eyes over-bright, hands gesticulating, feet dancing. On spotting Justin, shirt untucked, she cackled with glee. 'Oh, look, boddice-bustin' Justin! I wondered whose that car was outside, Cleo. Naughty girl! Naughty sister! We've come all this way to help you drown your sorrows, and you ain't sorrowful. You're busy doin' Justin.'

Rochelle and Angie, having the advantage of not being plastered, hovered at the sitting-room door and giggled uneasily.

Liza, perhaps becoming aware of an awkward atmosphere, grew rattled in the louder, graceless, cringeworthy way of the drunk. She wavered her bottles onto the low table, giggling unconvincingly and taking all her steps twice. 'I'll plonk the plonk on there and leave you to it. You're not letting the grass grow, eh?' A lopsided, backwards conga took her to the door and then cannoned her back to clutch Cleo's arms. She cleared her throat theatrically and began to sing. 'Out with the *old* and in with the *new*! Out with the *old* and in with the *new*!'

'Shut up, Liza.' Cleo's stomach clenched. She herded her sister to the door, trying to cover her embarrassment and increased heart rate with reproving clucks. 'Do you have to be permanently pissed? Are you driving, Angie, you're not over the limit, are you?' She hid behind an expression of concern although she wasn't far from wishing the dippy crowd in the nearest ditch. 'Do you need coffee before you go?' Appropriately, she sounded like a mother.

'What did she mean?' snapped Justin.

She swung back to the sitting room, pausing in the act of closing the door behind her sister. Liza had slapped the lights on as she fell in and his expression was painfully clear. Teeth gritted. Arms folded.

This wasn't going to plan. She cleared her throat. 'I've left Gav.'

'And this is how you decided I should find out?'

'That's what I wanted to tell you. When you were in America.'

'I've been back two weeks.' Then Justin's blazing gaze moved from Cleo to the doorway. And back.

Slowly, Cleo turned. And there, right where she absolutely didn't want him, stood Gav, in the open doorway, glaring at Justin.

'What's he doing here?' Gav demanded.

'Almost making a big mistake!' Justin's voice splintered with rage. Reaching for his jacket, he yanked it on in angry jerks.

Cleo managed, 'Wait a min—'

And suddenly he was roaring, 'Wait for what? You're full of shit! You always manage to piss me off, Cleo! When I'm with you I think you're fantastic, I want you like crazy. Then you always do something to show me how wrong for me you really are. I swore to myself I'd leave you alone as you asked, then you come looking for me and I rush to your side like a spaniel. Despite all my promises to myself, I can't resist getting you back in the sack. So I push your husband to the back of my mind, tell myself it's his lookout if he can't keep you happy, your business if you're looking outside the marriage. It's better than nothing.'

He stamped his feet into his shoes. 'But it's not. It doesn't appear to me that you're very clear about whether your marriage is over.' He pushed past her. 'And I thought blokes were meant to be the bastards.'

'But –' Cleo protested.

He span back, making Cleo leap with apprehension. 'Do me a favour? Next time you think about contacting me – *don't*. I can't think of any circumstance under which I'd want to hear from you.'

Trembling, she listened to the crash as he threw back the gate, the protest from his car engine as he screeched back into the lane.

Shaking, she pushed her hair out of her eyes.

'Dear, dear,' said Gav.

Part 2

Cleo Reece

Chapter Twenty-Three

Cleo dashed up Dora's garden path, out of breath. Today's Powerful Listening seminar had flown by, the young and enthusiastic group becoming caught up in role playing as energetic as any drama workshop, sweeping her along with their verve. Her heart had thudded when she suddenly noticed that the clock said five thirty.

She'd rounded up with a rushed, 'Great workshop, hope you'll be able to use what we've done today!' as she reached for her bag and snatched her name tag from her lapel. The traffic up Soke Parkway had been diabolical and, at nearly six thirty, she was definitely late.

'Sorry,' she gasped, as Dora opened the door. 'Time management failure.'

Dora grinned. 'Don't worry – come in.' Cleo followed a rear view of stretch jeans far smaller than in the days when Dora had been married to Keith, into the long, two-rooms-knocked-into-one lounge. Here, Sean was frowning at the *Daily Express* while Meggie read aloud and Eddie clonked a racket from a multicoloured xylophone. Shona, who Dora childminded, danced to Eddie's tune with froggy little leaps and pushed-out lips.

When she spotted Cleo, her face split into a huge, sunny grin and she broke into an inexpert, one-year-old's run, most of her energy bouncing her upwards rather than sending her along. Both small hands reached, curling and uncurling, as she squealed, 'Mummee!'

Cleo dropped to her knees to let Shona run into her arms, clasping the hot little body to her in a fierce burst of love. 'Hiya, baby! Home time then, here's your coat. Quick kiss now for Auntie Dora, wave to Sean, bye-bye. Let's go find the car ...' For all Dora's understanding, Cleo always felt horribly guilty when she arrived late to find Dora's cooking smells at the mouth-watering stage – and Dora's family famished and waiting politely for Cleo to get her daughter out of the way so that they could eat. Dora did feed Shona sometimes, if Cleo's work schedule really dictated it; but Cleo was intent on cooking for her own child whenever possible and seeing that they sat down to eat together at the end of each day.

Shona, strapped into her chunky red car seat, looked cocooned and cosy in the headlight-lit winter evening. 'Mummee!' she shouted twice.

Cleo answered, 'Yes, baby?' but the conversation went no further, like so many of Shona's conversations. Her current favourite gambit was to point at someone – often, mortifyingly, some complete stranger – and explode 'HA!' at the top of her healthy lungs.

'Mummee, HA! Mum! HA!' she shouted now, lips pursed in concentration.

Cleo grinned into the rear-view mirror. 'And ha to you, too. Have you had a good day?'

'HA!'

As long as Shona was occupied with 'HA!' at least she wasn't crying for supper. Cleo's nippy little TT was a thing of the past, now that she needed more space in the back, so she ran around in a Civic. Eight minutes was the record journey time from Dora and Sean's tall old-fashioned terraced house in Bettsbrough to Ladies Lane, without necks being risked, and it was often a fraught journey.

In fact the whole single-parent thing was fraught. Cleo seemed to spend a fair amount of her time agonising over it. Did Shona see enough of her? Was the village the best place for them to live? If Dora was to continue to be Shona's childminder – and there was nobody to whom Cleo would rather entrust her precious daughter – Shona would have to attend playgroup in Bettsbrough when the time came, because Dora couldn't be ping-ponging between Bettsbrough and the playgroup in Middledip village hall. So how would Shona make friends in the village? Rhianne's moving away with Ian's latest promotion meant that Shona didn't even have a friend in the third child, Emily, that Rhianne and Ian had produced. Cleo didn't want to think about what would happen when Shona started school.

She swung the car into the drive and fished Shona out of her car seat. The instant they stepped through the front door, Shona began to shriek with hunger; the smell of dinner cooking was a harsh reminder of how growlingly empty she was, judging by the way she pawed her round little tummy.

During the final ten-second wait before Cleo could share out the contents of the slow cooker, Shona began to throw herself back and forth in Cleo's arms until their heads banged painfully together, making Cleo wince and Shona scream louder.

'Your head's like concrete,' Cleo grumbled. 'Only a minute now. Arms up, coat off.' Shona continued to fling herself around in a sheer unadulterated agony of hunger. In the seven months since Cleo's maternity leave had ended, always these coming-home minutes were the hellish ones.

Cleo posted her protesting daughter expertly into the high chair and clicked the straps. 'Thank goodness for slow cookers.' On week nights they always ate stews and casseroles that could be prepared in the morning and left to cook all day in the slow cooking pot.

Taking down a big plate from the cupboard, she ladled chicken casserole across the chill surface.

'Nearly done, nearly done.' She grimaced at her daughter's red and angry face, the real tears, the runny nose. 'I know what Shona wants.'

Shona geared her fuss down to listen.

'Juice! Nice, cold juice.' Shona resumed her wailing but reached a clenching hand towards the fridge. Cleo passed over a two-handled, lidded beaker with just an inch of apple juice and water. Something else prepared ahead, in a morning that began at five thirty or six to stretch the day so that it would accommodate everything.

The plate of food had stopped steaming; Cleo scraped it swiftly into Shona's bowl, blue plastic with a circular sucker on the bottom, perched on a chair and began to spoon-feed gravy, crooning, comforting, as her daughter gradually calmed. By the time the gravy had been spooned into her mouth, the edge was off Shona's furious appetite and she was willing to dig pudgy fingers into the slices of potato and carrot, pick out her favourite cubes of chicken and root delicately for peas. She even began to smile her three-toothed smile.

And there was peace.

Cleo ladled out her own portion of casserole and sat down companionably in a kitchen chair. It was an odd echo of when she and Gav had wound down over the exchange of the day's news at the meal table.

'So how was your day at the office?' she asked Shona, grinning into the sparky brown-gold eyes.

Shona shouted, 'HA!' and pointed at the fridge.

'You can have yoghurt afterwards.'

Shona nodded exaggeratedly and turned back to the carrots. 'Mmm-mmm-mmm'.

This evening was much like every evening. After the casserole, Shona got her yoghurt. They had a spoon each and Cleo ended up with yoghurt in her hair. Shona suggested, 'Gink?' and Cleo gave her another mug of juice. Then Shona got down and played, banging toys on the fireguard or posting the dog figure down the chimney of the Fisher Price house, while Cleo cleared up. Then they shared a bath, splashing with Shona's water toys and singing.

A fragrant Shona was bundled into pyjamas to sit in the armchair with Cleo and a book. One last drink of warm milk and she was ready for carrying through the stair gate and up to her pine cot in the corner of Cleo's room.

"Night.' Cleo paused at the door after setting the cot mobile playing 'It's a Small World', half relieved, half reluctant to see her daughter settle, wondering where the last few hours had gone.

'Yite,' Shona responded, still chewing the lid of her empty mug.

But thank the lucky stars, thank the patron saint of Mummees, Shona was a brilliant sleeper. It took only three minutes before the fans of her eyelashes were resting on her soft cheeks. It was only then that Cleo had time for herself, a leisurely dessert, a read of the daily paper and the day's post.

Pulling back the fireguard she opened the stove, added two logs, and sat cross-legged on the floor, so that the kind offers of credit cards or laser eye surgery could be chucked straight into the flames. She glanced at the electricity bill, read a notice from her bank about how her savings account – a slender thing these days – was changing, and then turned over and over an envelope addressed in Gav's writing.

'Now what does he want?' She shut the stove and hooked the fireguard into place. Carrying the envelope with her she made, as a treat, a cafetière of coffee, Costa Rican. She had no concerns about strong coffee making her wakeful; she generally had to force herself to stay awake until eleven, then fell into bed and slept like a Shona for six and a half hours before she needed to drag herself up to do it all again.

Saturday and Sunday mornings were just bliss; then she didn't rouse until seven when Shona's cheerful squeals of

'Mummee!' and 'HA!' would scrape open her eyes.

Mooching back to the sitting room with her coffee cup, she nestled into the armchair, selected a TV drama for company and slit the envelope. Poor Gav. After Pauline, and the sad end of their marriage, Gav had given in his resignation at Clyde, Rhode & Owen – hurled it in, he said – and gone to live just north of Doncaster, near his dad.

'I need to get away,' he'd explained, earnestly, as if she'd been begging him to stay; whereas, in fact, she hadn't even wanted to look at him and the sad looseness of his body language. 'Dad could do with company. I don't think I can hack it at CR&O, I've been cleared of woman beating but they all know I'm an unfaithful bastard.'

'I shouldn't think you're alone,' she'd reassured him, unthinkingly.

He'd glared. 'Hardly, eh, Swelly Belly?' And then, sarcastically, 'Is Justin likely to be around for the birth?' He knew that Cleo and Justin were absolutely not in contact, but seemed to enjoy reminding her of the fact.

'No,' she answered calmly, patting her stomach. 'It's just me and the baby.'

Cleo and Shona. Shona and Cleo. A package. At the birth, at that final heave with the midwife coaxing, 'You're doing beautifully, well done,' and Liza marvelling, 'Oh. My. *God!*' Cleo had yelled out, just once, on a peak of pain, '*Justin!*'

The echoes of his name had died in the bright, hot delivery room and everyone had tactfully pretended to be deaf.

Then Cleo and Liza were laughing and crying together at the feebly waving bundle that blinked as she was placed in her mother's arms.

'You're a mum!' Liza had accused, wiping her eyes with the backs of her hands. 'Cleo, she's so … *amazing*. Isn't she amazing? Isn't the whole thing amazing?' Then Liza dashed out because she'd been dying to pee for hours – and probably wanted a crafty fag as well, because she only pretended to have given up.

The midwives went quietly about, clearing up the yucky stuff.

The baby blinked, dark hair plastered above a puzzled forehead. Fists of unimagined delicacy trembled and clutched at nothings.

And Cleo suddenly realised where the saying had come from: 'left holding the baby'.

Her back was tucked up with a dragging ache. She was so thirsty after the endless sucking on the gas-and-air that she thought her throat would zip up and dry out. She held on to her daughter tightly, scared her arms would go nerveless and let the baby plummet to the floor. A nerve at the base of her neck ticked. And she longed, for a frantic, frightened moment, for a man beside her to relieve her tired arms.

But there was no man.

No man beside her, no man on his way, no man waiting outside for news. Cleo's arms found strength.

When Shona was five days old, Cleo rang Rockley Image and asked for Justin, receiving the slightly evasive response, 'I'll put you through to the studio.'

The voice at the studio sounded surprised. 'Sorry,' it said, 'Justin doesn't work here, now.'

The magnitude of the task of formulating a reply defeated Cleo and she replaced the phone silently.

So it had definitely been just Cleo and Shona.

Pushing those thoughts aside, quickly she ripped open the letter, trying not to wonder whether Gav was pleased that once upon a time Cleo had had two men but now she had none.

Dear Cleo,
She skimmed the 'hope you're OK' and Gav and George were.

I'm going to be back in your neighbourhood for a couple of days. Could we get together for a chat? I've something particular I'd like to discuss. I don't know where I'll stay, Keith is doing the love-nest thing with his latest woman – God knows how he gets them (which made two of them) *but I don't want to be a hairy gooseberry.*

Believe it or not, I'm being headhunted by a firm I used to deal with when I worked at CR&O and I've got a couple of days of interviews. They haven't offered to pay my hotel bill so I suppose I'll have to find somewhere reasonable. Unless I could crash on your couch? I'd be no trouble, honest!

Cleo glanced over at the sofa, a two-seater with runged wooden arms. Gav would be dead comfy on that! She pulled the phone towards her, yawning.

She opened with, 'My couch is only a two-seater. You'd hang over at each end.'

Gav laughed, sounding drowsy as if he'd been snoozing in front of the telly, which he probably had. 'OK. Well ... OK, no sweat. I'll find a hotel.' He sounded flat and disappointed.

She let him sigh over this setback before saying thoughtfully, 'I have got an air bed, of course. And a sleeping bag. If you don't mind dossing on the sitting-room floor?'

'Brilliant!' It pleased him, she could tell by the sudden lightness in his voice. She hoped she was doing the right thing. But it might be nice to have another adult to talk to, someone she didn't have to go through the fag of getting to know.

Sometimes, although she had her work and Liza – however much anyone had Liza – Cleo was very alone. The only contact she had with her parents was in the form of disapproving, monthly, duty phone calls.

In fact she'd suffered one only the evening before. Her

mother had trotted out one of her favourite digs, 'Gavin must've been mortified about that baby. No one could blame him for leaving.'

Cleo snorted. 'I won't bother repeating the chronology of what led up to me leaving Gav, Mum. You've heard it all before and you obviously choose not to listen.'

There were never any of the traditional grannie questions about Shona's teeth or vocabulary, there was never a home-knit cardigan sent or a voucher for a new toy. Cleo's parents had only once undertaken the hour-long journey to see their grandchild, when she was a fortnight old; a censorious duty – so far as Cleo, half dead with shocked fatigue, had been able to tell.

And Cleo hadn't embarked on the reciprocal journey at all.

Chapter Twenty-Four

Justin stretched the small amount that was possible in the ridiculously small space allowed by economy air travel, and longed to be home in his flat.

The past eighteen months had been great, an experience he'd never forget or regret and just what he'd needed, but now he was ready for home. He was sick of snow and bitter, biting cold that had made wearing great fat coats and fleecy hats and gloves a necessity during the iron winter.

Heathrow was below; home was only a couple of hours from there, no doubt in the grip of typically British drizzle – but home.

Funny: cramped in his aircraft seat he'd dreamt of Cleo, presumably because he had had his mind fixed on home. He'd dreamt of her living alone in the little house in Middledip.

Unlikely! He grinned, glad he could remember her now without rancour. Cleo was quite a girl; if she'd given her husband the heave-ho she would've found other entertainment. What a prat he'd been over her, storming out in a huff, yelling all that crap about her getting to him and him minding. Inwardly, he groaned. Must've had a rush of blood. Must've mistaken lust for 'lurve' or something. Blimey.

But, considering he'd been curled uncomfortably onto his meal tray with his back bent and his toes bent and his arms bent, what a dream it'd been. A dream of dissolving clothes and hot hands. He'd woken up abashed, his erection making him feel still more crowded. Not that anybody would've noticed, all barricaded in by their own seat backs and chair arms.

Better when he was back in his own bed, his own flat. Maybe, in a few days, he'd even look Cleo up and make peace. Be the nice guy, now she was no longer important and out of his system. She was a loose end and he kind of liked loose ends tied out of the way.

Finally, after the long descent and the endless burdens of disembarkation and homeward travel, Justin barged through the door of his flat, keys swinging from his teeth because his hands were full of cases.

He was stunned to find a man and a woman there, eating a Saturday lunchtime takeaway on trays in front of the television. A dopey couple: the girl peering from between peroxide hair curtains, the lad sticking his chin out.

They all gazed at one another for several silent moments.

Then Justin dropped his cases and keys and groaned. They must be his tenants, the ones that the agent assured him would be out ten days ago. 'There must've been some slip-up,' he began, tolerantly enough. 'The agent said your tenancy ended last week.'

'We-ell ...' The couple exchanged glances. The girl smirked. 'But we never had nowhere lined up. He never gave us time.'

Justin tried to shake his head clear of jet lag. 'And the agent let you stay?'

The girl shrugged. 'We had a spare key cut. We come back.' She shrugged again, grinning now, triumphant.

The man stood up to demonstrate his size. 'Yeah, we come back, 'cos the agent won't give us back our key money so we paid another month here, really, ent we? We only need a few weeks to find somewhere else. Best if you find a couch to kip on for a bit, eh?' He grinned, obviously well impressed with their cleverness. Justin's heart sank. Bastards! Nasty, spiteful, parasitical bastards. They were expecting him to either get upset and bluster, so they could shout him down, or threaten legal action, which they knew would take forever.

Instead, he picked up his cases. 'Fuck you, I've got to crash.' Strolling to his bedroom, he found it heaped with faded, grubby bed linen and discarded clothes. When he'd kicked the door shut behind him and wedged it shut with a folded newspaper, he snatched out his phone. 'Drew? Yeah, I've just got in. Listen, you've still got a spare key to my place, haven't you? I need a *huge* favour ...'

While he waited, he unpopped the cheap and grubby duvet cover and stuffed into it the contents of the wardrobe, along with every other item strewn about the room. Someone tried the bedroom door handle and banged on the door. He ignored them, opened the window and heaved the bundle out, after checking there was nobody below. Various holdalls and carrier bags followed.

As he waited, he searched out correspondence from his agent and reminded himself of the names of his tenants – now squatters – Jason and Stephanie Blumfield. Far from model tenants, they'd been erratic with their rent and had had to sacrifice their deposit when the agent had inspected the flat and found it necessary to call in cleaning professionals.

A tense thirty minutes later, alerted by raised voices, he kicked the wedge out from under the door and burst back into the sitting room. Jason Blumfield rounded on him indignantly. 'These bastards are changing the lock!' Gez was already on his knees at the front door, toolbox open beside him. Drew and Martin stood in the sitting room between Jason and Gez, arms folded.

'And I've just called the police,' Justin lied casually. 'I've also chucked your clothes out of the window, you've got five minutes to gather anything else that's yours and *piss off*!'

'Our *clothes*? *Outside*? Oh right, that's really nice, you bastard.' Stephanie Blumfield shuffled into her shoes and out of the front door at an anxious trot.

A very tense silence followed while Justin, Drew and Martin stared at Jason. Then Jason began snatching up coats, stray shoes, videos, his fags and lighter, and followed his wife, snarling at Justin, 'I'll getchoo! Bastard! Fucking *getchoo*! You fucking wait. I won't half fucking getchoo!' On the way out, he booted the door out of Gez's hands as a final act of defiance.

Justin heaved a great sigh of relief. 'Cheers, boys. Wait till I get my hands on that bloody agent. Look at this shit hole! Fag burns, takeaway cartons – it looks like a squat in here.'

Drew grinned. 'I thought it looked quite homey.'

They set about the business of making the flat habitable again. When Justin finally threw clean bedclothes on the bed and crashed down onto them it was hours, hours and *hours* later. Further clearing up, the agent, Cleo and the whole rest of the world would have to wait until he'd had some *sleep*.

Gav stared up Ladies Lane, jingled his change, turned, measured ten paces up the drive, paused, turned again on one heel and one toe, and paced ten back. Stared up the empty lane again.

What should he do? He'd arrived ten minutes after Cleo had said she'd be home, had waited twenty minutes and still she hadn't arrived. He could call her mobile but if she was driving she wouldn't answer. Presumably, she would have called if she'd broken down. He took ten paces up the drive again, adjusting his glasses, the glasses he'd recently had to begin wearing, to his chagrin. Turning, he paced back down.

Wait. Surely it was only nine steps that time? He must be taking longer strides … 'For fuck's sake!' he exploded into the chilling, dark, evening air. 'Stop being such a sad bastard.' He strode out of the gate, up the lane, across the lush green playing fields to the beery warmth of The Three Fishes and ordered a big, fat, cold pint. Three-quarters of it disappeared in one prolonged glug. There. Much better. What was he doing, counting his strides in Cleo's front garden while she took her own sweet time getting home? Probably she'd accepted some last-minute task at work; she did that when she wasn't keen on what was waiting for her at home. He was familiar with her methods.

He should have booked a hotel. He still could, then he could go out for the evening, the pubs, maybe the clubs, see if he could pull. He finished the lager. Three or four men wandered in for a quick half on their way home from work and all nodded to him.

Another pint, just the job. Cold, misted glass, brilliant amber liquid. He wiped the bottom of the glass on a beer mat and dived in. Smacked his lips.

Oh, whoops.

Two pints. He'd drunk two pints. He couldn't drive into Peterborough now in search of a hotel. Dear, dear. Nothing for it but to wander back, more relaxed now, and see if Cleo had arrived.

And, look at that, she had. Her car was pulled up in the space where he'd been pacing. Weird, knocking on the door to Cleo's home; Cleo's home, after all, used to be shared with him. He shivered. She wasn't going to open the door, he was going to freeze to death with his shoulders hunched and his hands in his pockets. Ought to have gone to a hotel –

But then the door burst open and Cleo appeared briefly. Her hair hung as heavy and straight to her shoulders as it always had, her eyes twinkled darkly, her wide mouth smiled and, he thought sadly, the only real change was the baby on her hip. 'Sorry, stupid traffic, did you wait long? Got to get Shona's meal or she'll go mental. Come in.'

From Cleo's arms, complacent in her rightful spot, Shona gazed at him. Shona. Cleo's *daughter*.

He followed slowly into a kitchen that was warm, steamy

and smelling of chicken, feeling an awkward intruder in someone else's cosy domesticity. The little girl pointed at him and shouted, 'HA!'

'Yes, all right,' Cleo soothed, sliding her into her high chair. 'It's only Gav, don't get excited.'

Shona looked up at Cleo. Her mother. 'Gink?' She pointed at the fridge.

'Drink in a minute. Gav, do you mind eating straight away? Only Shona's starving.'

He seemed planted on the quarry tiles. 'No. Yes. Whatever.' He must be simple, really simple; all this time he'd known Cleo had a daughter but hadn't acknowledged the reality. He'd somehow thought he and she might go out to eat, that Shona might have dematerialised or be with a babysitter or a grannie. That Cleo would be unaltered, unfettered, dashing in from work and out with him.

Not tied, not mumsy, not putting Shona first.

She was looking at him, exasperated, hooking her hair behind her ears and trying to get past. 'Sit down. Shona's hungry, aren't you, baby?'

He sat. Shona watched him and pointed silently. He smiled and wondered if it looked as unconvincing as it felt. 'She's very pretty,' he managed in the end, wishing Shona would turn her stare elsewhere.

'Yeah, gorgeous aren't you, Shona?' Cleo rattled cutlery in the drawer and fished out a big steel ladle.

The whole meal came out of one big brown pot, which plugged into the mains. What the hell was that? Chicken fillets were arranged on top of new potatoes with carrots underneath, everything bubbling with gravy. Cleo tried to arrange it separately on the plates but it all ended up a bit jumbled and brown. Then she stuck the two big plates in the oven while she chopped up the baby's meal. Shona began to whinge, sucking one hand.

'Half a minute,' Cleo promised. 'Just hang on.' Once Shona had fallen on her food, Cleo retrieved theirs.

Picking up his knife and fork, Gav was glad he'd left the wine in the car. It would've looked ridiculous at a table with no cloth, no flowers, and no best cutlery. Cleo wasn't making any effort. She seemed more interested in Shona in the high chair than any conversation with Gav. 'This tastes nice,' he tried.

'You sound surprised.'

'It's just I've never seen … What's that thing?'

'A slow cooker. Invaluable aid to people who aren't home to cook. In the morning chuck everything in, in the evening slop everything out.'

It certainly seemed effective. The chicken fell apart; the potatoes could be cut with a fork and the gravy soaked everything. 'Very good. I like it.'

'Good.'

'Good.'

He tried to get a conversation going over Shona 'Mmm-mmm-mmm'ing to herself.

'HA!' she shouted, cutting across Gav as if he hadn't been speaking.

'Ha what?' asked Cleo, beaming.

Slowly, Shona picked up a piece of carrot and threw it on the floor.

Cleo put the dropped carrot in the bin and, bitterly, Shona began to cry, peeping at her mother through spiky lashes.

Gamely, Gav tried. 'I stayed a weekend with Ian and Rhianne after Christmas. They're back at each other's throats. Will and Roland are more monsterish than ever, little Emily's a tyrant. Me and Ian went out and he got extremely pissed. You wouldn't believe him, trying to get off with some woman while her husband sat next to her.'

Deliberately, Shona dropped another piece of carrot. 'No,

no!' she appealed as Cleo threw it, too, away.

'You don't want that, Shona! It's all dirty, yuk!'

Shona slapped her head into her fat little hands and began to grieve for the lost carrot.

'Right there next to her,' Gav repeated, raising his voice slightly. 'Her husband. Glowering at Ian and clenching his fists –'

'Don't cry like that,' Cleo remonstrated. 'Because you're not impressing me. Do you want a piece of my carrot?'

'Ian finally noticed the husband and suggested three-in-a-bed sex. I thought we'd both end up in casualty but the husband decided Ian was just a sad old drunk,' Gav persisted.

Shona flung the new carrot on the floor.

'As you like,' said Cleo serenely. 'But that's going in the bin as well.' Shona slapped her hands on her high-chair tray in rage and then held up the red palms to show her mother how she hurt.

'Don't do it, then,' Cleo suggested. 'Do you want cake? We've got cake tonight because Gav's here. Look, you can get all squashy and messy.'

Gav propped his face on his palm and watched Cleo turn her back as she wiped Shona's stubby fingers. He sighed. 'So the woman turned into an alien with eight breasts and Ian, being a breast man, was in heaven. She ate her husband, rather gruesomely, with lemon curd and ketchup, she and Ian have emigrated to the moon and I'm visiting them on Moon Day which is in September, this year.'

'Got room for cake?' Cleo asked him.

At least while they washed up Shona went to rattle toy cars across the fireguard and he finally had Cleo's attention for ten minutes while she asked about his new job prospects. But it felt most peculiar when Cleo and Shona disappeared into the bathroom behind a locked door for forty minutes, leaving him downstairs with the brandy and the telly remote. Thinking of Cleo in the bath, rosy-breasted from the hot water, he broke into a sudden sweat. Once, the door wouldn't have been locked and he would have wandered in and perched on the steamy bath side to chat. Touched her body through the bubbles. Those were the days.

On coming downstairs, Cleo read a story. Shona pointed to the pictures, pausing occasionally to give Gav the 'Ha!' treatment.

Gav was becoming very bored with Shona's 'HA!', particularly the pointing finger, and wondered how Cleo stood it. It wasn't as if 'ha' was a word. Just a noise. In fact he'd only heard Shona say about four words. 'Gink' for drink, 'ta' and 'no' – pretty popular, that one. And 'Mummee'. Then just as she was being carried off to bed she pointed at him and said, 'Gog!'

He heard Cleo's reply, drifting down the stairwell. 'He's not a dog. He's a man and his name's Gav.'

His nails curled into his palms. He wanted to shout, 'I'm not just some man called Gav! I'm your husband. You're my wife.'

And when Cleo finally came back downstairs he couldn't help sniping, 'Blissful silence. Alone at last.'

He could almost see Cleo's back go up. Her reply was careful and strained, reminding him how she got when she was annoyed. 'So sorry. Shona's a bit young to understand the concept of considering one's guest. If she wants to shout, she shouts. If the guest doesn't care for it, tough.'

To contrive a pause while he formulated something more conciliatory, he poured Cleo a brandy. 'I'm not used to it. I don't suppose she's any noisier than any other kid her age.'

'It's not something I gauge. This is Shona's home, she doesn't have to be quiet.'

'Of course not.'

'Of *course* not.'

He reached over to clink glasses but she kept hers stubbornly tucked against her chest, so he ended up ridiculous, stretching, silly. 'She takes all your time up,' he observed in what he thought was a neutral tone.

'She has a right to.'

This wasn't the way he'd run this conversation in his head as he drove down the motorway. Why was he allowing Shona the centre stage? He decided to cut straight to his subject. 'Um, Cleo,' he began, moving over to sit beside her on the floor before the fire. 'We're not divorced yet.'

Her eyes were wary and flat. 'Don't worry, it'll come.'

He flushed and a tight ball of annoyance formed in the centre of his forehead. He moved back to the chair and stared down at her, fresh after her bath, neat in softly faded old jeans, the way he'd seen her a million times.

He obviously wasn't going to engage Cleo in the nostalgic conversation he wanted, paving the way to *why did we ever split up?* Disappointment and rising anger made him ask, 'Where's Shona's father these days?' He saw her flinch.

'Haven't the foggiest. Me and Shona don't need anyone. I thought you realised.'

Conversation was strained for the rest of the evening. Cleo looked tired. At ten thirty she fetched him an air bed, foot pump, sleeping bag and pillow. 'You'll be cosy enough in here. The stove will stay warm till morning.'

He looked down at the bed things, sad and flat, and tried to lighten the air. 'Delightful, thank you. A do-it-yourself bed.' He'd meant to sound wry and instead he sounded whiny.

She pressed her hand into the small of her back, causing her chest to jut out interestingly. 'Maybe you should've brought your visit to Ian and the eight-breasted man-munching alien forward. The moon's probably lovely at this time of year.'

Chapter Twenty-Five

The second and third days were no better than the first. The atmosphere became less strained and there were no more heavy references to the divorce; but by Saturday afternoon Cleo was still glad that Gav was preparing to leave. She'd made his breakfast, she'd made his lunch, ignoring his, 'Funny when you think how we used to do all the domestic stuff together.'

He hadn't caught on to the sarcasm in her answering, 'I don't remember that.' Meaning she did remember doing the majority alone.

Then came his hints that he'd prefer lunch out. 'Perhaps Liza would have Shona for a couple of hours? Or we can take her over to your mum's and find somewhere to eat around Leicester? I know it's a bit of a trek from here but –'

She'd shaken her head without bothering to go into the impossibility of Liza being free on a Saturday unless booked a century in advance, nor how unlikely a babysitter her mother made. 'Nice of you to offer, but as I work long hours my time with Shona's limited so I don't want to farm her out.' She didn't know how to make it any plainer that Gav was no longer number one in her life.

She had love to spare and just now there was a vacancy. But the vacancy wasn't Gav-shaped.

He assumed a wounded silence. She prepared a cheerful cheese salad with all sorts of raw vegetables cut into chunks and soft brown finger rolls because Shona liked that.

Then Gav tentatively produced a bottle of wine from his car. 'I don't think so,' Cleo protested. 'You've got to drive and I can't fall into a post-lunch stupor with Shona to look after.'

''Course not!' He slapped the bottle of wine on the kitchen table. Loudly. Another wounded silence.

But now that he'd got as far as the doorstep on his way out, his hair lifting gently in the breeze, he seemed to have recovered his temper. 'I'll let you know how I did at the interviews.'

Cleo joggled Shona on her hip, enjoying a little weak sunshine filtering through the clouds. Another few weeks and they would see the first signs of spring. 'Will you take the job, if they offer it?'

'Think so. I miss Peterborough. And Middledip.'

'Would you come back here, actually to Middledip?' The surprise in her voice was too obvious for good manners.

His lips tightened. 'No law against it, is there? You don't own the whole village?'

Oh dear, she shouldn't have sounded so … well, horrified. She shifted Shona who kept leaning over to watch something in the lane. 'I didn't mean to sound unwelcoming. I hope you get the job if you want it, and somewhere nice to live.'

Gav took a breath as if screwing himself up to speak. Shona flung herself sideways again, Gav's eyes dropped to her and the breath puffed out.

He'd just picked up his holdall and begun, 'Well, it's been –' when Shona craned round Cleo's shoulder again and beamed, 'Huhyo!'

Instantly, Cleo's attention was on her, beaming as she exclaimed, 'Wow, a new word! She's never said "hello" before.' Then she saw the fury and repugnance on Gav's face as he gazed at whoever Shona had spoken to.

And there, in the gateway, was Justin, staring at Shona. His answering 'Hello' dropped into a crystal silence.

Afterwards, Cleo couldn't remember Gav's actual departure. She had to concentrate just to stay on her feet as the world around her receded and returned sharply and her inner voice hissed, 'It's *Justin.*' Justin, staring white-faced at Shona; Cleo staring at him and at his car pulled up beside the hedge.

She could remember walking back indoors and putting Shona down in the kitchen because her arms were shaking. Plumping down on a wooden kitchen chair, because so were her legs. Aware of Justin sinking onto the other kitchen chair and croaking, 'Fuck …' Then eyeing Shona and managing to turn it to 'F'crying out loud.'

Justin's eyes were fixed on Shona, so amazed, so staggered that it was almost comical.

Shona stretched out her fingers. 'Gink! Gink!'

Cleo's voice emerged high and thin. 'Your drink's in the fridge, Shona. Apple juice, OK?' She managed the simple task of making Shona a drink with juice and water and secured the beaker lid. Shona found the spout with her lips, regarding Justin over the top of the cup. He bent forward and held out his hand.

For a moment, a still, poignant moment, their fingers touched. Linked.

Then Shona discarded her cup into his palm, grabbed a chunky plastic car from her toybox and beetled off into the sitting room.

Justin's eyes swivelled to Cleo.

She gulped. 'I was going to tell you. That night – I'd asked to see you so that I could tell you about leaving Gav, about the baby. But then we … And Liza showed up. Then Gav.'

Aghast eyes remained glued to hers. He nodded. 'I stormed out.'

'And you didn't want to hear from me again.' She nodded back, until they were nodding earnestly at each other. She made herself stop. 'When Shona was born … I thought you had the right to know. I rang Rockley.'

'I'd already gone?'

'When she was about five months old, before I went back to work, I drove round and was sure I'd found your flat but someone else was living there.'

'I've been working in Boston. I let the flat out.'

'Boston? Can't you commute from Peterborough to Boston?'

He smiled for the first time since she'd seen him in the garden and instantly came into focus, became familiar, the real Justin. 'Boston, Massachusetts, not Boston, Lincolnshire. Where my parents live. It's colder.' He rubbed his forehead and screwed up his eyes. 'This is incredible.'

Cleo sipped her drink and watched him gaze into space. His hair was shorter. Laugh lines still lifted the corners of his eyes, the same gold-brown eyes as Shona's, full of light. His lips were still ... She looked away.

'You picked a beautiful name.' He tried it out. 'Shona.' Dragging himself from his contemplation of the doorway, he folded his arms on the wooden table and gave her his attention. 'What's her other name? Is mine on the birth certificate?'

'If only it had been that easy!' Cleo patted his arm. A friendly gesture, an excuse to touch him. Then she laughed, a sudden excited bubble that slipped out and burst on the air. 'Since I don't know what your surname is.' She went on to tell him about Martin and Drew at Muggie's, about the 'Just-in time' crap.

'Justin Mullarkey', he said, impatiently. 'You must've known, when you did the workshop at Rockley Image –'

He paused, because she was laughing again. Snorting with dawning pleasure that he was there. 'If that doesn't just suit you! Justin Mullarkey. That little sod Drew said something about "all that mullarkey".' As she crowed for breath, she suspected his stern frown was intended to disguise the light in his eyes. But she felt like laughing forever, enjoying the fizzing inside that might just be happy anticipation.

She wiped her eyes, steadied herself to be sensible. 'Her name's Shona Reece. I've gone back to my maiden name. I didn't want either of us to be Callaway. And can you imagine the insult to Gav?'

'Aren't you together? He was here – glaring at me.' He glanced round as if Gav might be lurking.

Gav. Justin. Shona. She had a sudden desperate need for caffeine. She carried the kettle to the sink. 'I don't suppose he feels particularly fond of you. But we separated and soon we'll be divorced.' She explained about Gav's interviews, about the air bed, about Gav's tentative overtures, which, she had a horrible feeling, were an attempt to resume their relationship.

'Didn't he ever assume Shona was his?'

She shook her head, her smile sliding smartly off at the reminder. 'Gav's infertile.'

The eyebrows lifted again. 'Sorry – I didn't know.'

'Don't apologise, neither did I.'

Coffee ready, she returned to her seat. Colour had returned to Justin's face and with his golden spikes of hair he looked heart-stopping.

Maybe his initial roller coaster of shock was slowing, because suddenly Cleo had to field a stream of questions. 'When's her birthday? Is she healthy? Do you work? At the same place? Who has her then? Were you alone at the birth? What do your parents think? What did Gav say …?'

Among the questions and interruptions, she felt her heart settle for the first time since its sudden mad spinning at Justin's appearance.

She tucked in a question of her own. 'How did you know she's yours? Most people would've assumed Shona was Gav's.'

He drained his coffee. 'She looks exactly like my kid sister did.' He leapt to his feet, eyes hunted, patting his jacket pocket for his keys. 'This has turned everything upside down. I've got to get my head round it. But I want –' He ran his fingers through his hair. 'I want to know her. Yes?'

She'd barely time to nod before he was heading for the door, throwing over his shoulder, 'We must talk but I need a while. I'll ring tonight.'

Through the window Cleo watched him hurry to his car. Her heart did a triple jump at the thought of him ringing later.

Maybe if she took Shona to the swings now she'd get tired and go to bed early.

It was the most irritating thing in the world. Any other Saturday night the phone would be silent, Shona would go to bed and the only sounds would be from the television. But tonight her phone had rung three times and not once had it been Justin.

Shona was long ago tucked in and the cottage seemed particularly empty. If she tidied out Shona's toybox – hated job – she wouldn't be able to reach the phone until about the eighth ring and he'd have time to wonder if she was there. Good.

But there, done already, the rainbow of plastic cars and chunky animals tidy, and no call. She even did the sad thing of checking the phone was working, which made her annoyed with herself. So. He wasn't going to ring. He wasn't going to ring because he'd turned up out of the blue and discovered he was a father. And though she hadn't asked for a *thing*, not money, not time, not babysitting, not support, the whole huge responsibility thing had rolled over and squashed him, and he'd hidden away.

He was probably back on a plane for America. Maybe California this time, warmer than Boston. Or he was at

Muggie's with Drew and Martin, pissed probably, to blot out the horrible truth.

What an arse.

She felt tremors begin to ripple through her. How dare he blot out his daughter? It wasn't as if Cleo had jumped into a short spangly dress and raced off partying while he did the parenting for a change. Bastard, irresponsible bastard.

The doorknocker rattled.

She snatched open the door. '*Yes*? Oh.'

'Is this a good time? I've been waiting for her to go to bed so we could talk. But then I realised the phone might wake her, so I drove over.' He was actually whispering.

Cleo grinned. 'An RAF bomber squadron could do a fly-past and Shona wouldn't stir.' She stood back.

He took a matching step backwards. 'I don't want to keep you.' As if she was rushing out. 'Can we talk tomorrow? Perhaps lunch?'

'Fine. Shona normally naps after lunch so we'll have a bit of peace. There's a family pub in Bettsbrough called The Cricket, I'll meet you there at twelve.' She added, deliberately, to give him an idea of what lunch out with a toddler involved, 'There's a toddlers' play area and Shona likes their fish fingers.'

She shut the door as he hurried off down the path. Why couldn't he talk now, where was he going next? Party? Club? Pub? His bed? Someone else's?

Nice to have the freedom.

All right for some.

Outside, in his car, in the lane, in the dark, he sat looking at the upstairs windows. Which was his daughter's room?

Her image was pin-sharp in his memory. The curls at the base of her neck, the soft cheeks, the tiny, feathery eyebrows above the eyes with the same golden flecks as his. The imperious little hands.

He had a child. A child! He'd dismissed the possibility. After the unprotected sex with Cleo it had occurred to him, of course. And he'd had slight stirrings of doubt – of doubt? Something, anyway – when Cleo had never actually said she wasn't pregnant. But he'd allowed it to fade, because she'd never said she was.

And he had been so angry at that last meeting, when everything was going his way, when he'd wanted her so urgently that he'd been prepared to forget his best resolutions and her marriage. Until bloody Liza had staggered in, giggling, making stupid jokes. He could hear her now, 'Out with the old and in with the new.'

His temper had boiled over. It did that. And he'd stamped out in fury.

Pity, because if his temper hadn't erupted he would have discovered that Cleo was pregnant and everything would have changed. The pregnancy, the birth. He wouldn't have taken the job in Boston on a spontaneous urge to reinvent himself.

He might even have been with Cleo all this time.

All this time.

Chapter Twenty-Six

From her post by the ball pond she'd watched Justin stroll in, scanning the noisy room for her. Together they watched Shona wallowing around in blue and yellow balls, wrinkling her bobble nose and hooting.

Then, at the table, Shona in a high chair, they talked about Boston, the day-after-day snow ploughed to the roadsides, the skiing, the ice storms. 'It was fun, then less so, then it was time to come home. My work permit was nearly up anyway. I would've had to go through the months and months it takes to apply for a green card. All that shit. So.' He shrugged.

'You'll find another job?'

He reached for a buttered roll, offered the basket to Cleo. Shona immediately discarded her chips and reached out a straining hand.

He hesitated.

Cleo nodded, and watched him cut a finger from the softest side of the bread and pass it to Shona. 'Mmm-mmm-*mmm*.' Shona smiled a chewed-bread smile at Justin and offered him the blob of butter on her hand.

'No thanks, sweetheart.' He pulled a face, making Shona laugh. He returned to Cleo. 'Rockley kept an opening for me. Our CEO is a director of the firm in the States. His idea was that I bring all the experience back with me. I did think of trying the magazines and I've got a mate who draws concept bikes for Honda, he's got a lot of contacts … But Rockley would be a safe bet.'

Cleo widened her eyes. 'Do you worry about "safe"?'

After a moment he replied, 'Sometimes I have to.'

Lunch over, Shona became abruptly niggly, rubbing her ears and eyes and whining.

'She needs her nap.' Cleo tried not to sound pleased. 'Shall we have coffee at my place?' Her heart skipped.

'Fine,' he replied, evenly.

They settled either side of the fire, their daughter asleep upstairs. Cleo felt buzzy inside with anticipation, but Justin seemed quite solemn. Enough to make her buzz fade a bit.

He began, 'Right,' but broke off and gazed at the stove, which Cleo had laid ready that morning and set a match to when they arrived. It was still chill enough for fires. 'Right,' he started again, clearing his throat. 'I've got to try and get myself up to speed with what's happened. Obviously, Shona's been a shock. If things had been different ...' He tailed off and gazed back at the fire. 'If I'd known, I wouldn't have gone away.'

Cleo watched his face and wondered what significance she could attach to 'wouldn't have gone away'. Was it time to welcome the happy buzz back?

His eyes met hers. 'I'm sorry she's been just your responsibility. You've done a brilliant job, she's just ... lovely.'

The buzz swelled a little. She'd taken more time over Shona than herself that morning. Baby shampoo and conditioner, a twinkly hair slide, Shona's best embroidered-denim dress to swing sassily above her ankles and a trendy pink-patterned hat. Cleo felt ridiculously pleased that he appreciated their daughter, even if he seemed scarcely to have glanced at her own smart grey trousers and soft, pale-blue cotton jumper which she knew, absolutely *knew*, clung in the places most calculated to please.

Justin fidgeted in his chair. 'I don't want to be a stranger. I want to be involved. Not just financially, either, I want to be ... her father.' He hesitated. 'Is that on?'

The buzz grew louder and she clutched the sofa arm.

'Of course.'

He leaned forwards. 'It'll give you more freedom. I can help.' His eyes lit up. 'It was like being touched with a cattle prod when I met her yesterday. I connected with her instantly. I just fell in love. Do you feel like that about her?'

Cleo almost nodded herself dizzy. 'Of course!'

He moved to sit beside her on the sofa. The buzz built, she was super-aware of every movement of his body, the lovely warm man-smell of him. He touched her shoulder. 'We could be together with her, sometimes, so she gets both parents at once?'

The buzz rose to a slight, all-over vibration and she couldn't stop beaming. 'Brilliant!'

Justin smiled, a wide, relieved grin, and visibly relaxed against the cushions. 'That's great.' He sighed. 'Obviously, there'll never be a *relationship* between you and me. That muddy water has flowed under the bridge, hasn't it? I don't suppose either of us would ever trust the other and we shouldn't begin a relationship in the middle just because there's a child. But if we can just be parents –'

The buzz died.

'Heavy stuff.' Drew shook his head in wonder.

Martin sagged against the bar. 'And you're sure the kid's yours?'

Justin nodded, clutching his drink – grateful to be back with English beer. 'I only had to look at her.'

'I'd still take a test.' Drew was ever belligerent and suspicious. 'This Cleo woman's not famed for being straight with you.'

Martin grimaced. 'Yeah, she could be looking for money.'

Justin shrugged. 'She hasn't asked.'

'Or someone to look after the kid.'

'She hasn't asked.'

Martin and Drew considered, eyes performing their habitual study of the talent in the room. Drew came up with the next minus. 'Somewhere to live?'

'She's got somewhere.'

Martin tried his best, most rehearsed smile at two girls in an alcove seat. 'Maybe she wants you to marry her.'

Justin snapped, 'She's already married! Or, at least, not divorced. Anyway, we agree there's nothing like that. It didn't work out before, and it won't now.' A sudden, vivid memory hit him – of the sex and fun before Cleo had suddenly remembered the little matter of her marriage. That had been such a knee in the nuts; it mustn't happen again.

He straightened. 'You just going to smirk at those girls all night, Martin? Or shall we try for some action?'

It wasn't until much later – when they'd seen the girls to their own vehicle after rounds of drinks and a Chinese meal, when he'd kissed all the lipstick off a woman called Anita and taken her phone number and they'd all piled into Drew's car – that Martin asked, 'So what's she like, your kid?'

Justin rubbed some feeling back into his legs where Anita had been sitting on his lap. 'Cute. Fair hair with a row of curls at the back. Light-brown eyes, like mine. She was wearing a denim dress as big as a parachute and a hat like a knitted biscuit tin.'

'Right,' Drew said politely.

Martin grinned from the driver's seat. 'And what about the mother? How's she looking?'

'Oh ...' Justin expelled a long breath and thought, with a sudden lift in his groin, of Cleo's stroke-me jumper and her peachy little behind rolling under the fabric of her trousers. 'Pretty good.'

Chapter Twenty-Seven

'This is going to be weird.' Cleo lifted Shona's buggy from the boot of the car where they'd parked behind the funfair.

Justin had been back in her life for three months now – or rather in Shona's life. Shona was the focus of his attention whenever Cleo saw him. But it had been Justin's idea to go on a 'family outing' to Hunstanton. 'It'll be a nice day. We can show Shona the sea, take her paddling, give her a taste of the great British seaside.' He joggled Shona in his arms and she turned her face into the breeze, screwing up her nose.

It would have been smart to wear a swimming costume beneath her clothes but Cleo hadn't thought of it. So she was left struggling uncomfortably behind a towel. And Justin – who had worn his trunks under his jeans, of course – held Shona's hand whilst Shona touched seashells with her toes.

'Damn!' Cleo tutted as she fumbled her knickers onto the sand.

Justin grinned. 'You drop your knickers too easily.'

Almost losing her towel as she hoiked her costume up to her waist. 'Actually, it's been over two years ...' She stopped. Bugger, damn, blast, if only she could bite that back! The silence seemed to hang her last words in the air in big black letters.

Arms shoved through straps under T-shirt, T-shirt snatched over her head, she aimed for composure and turned to her daughter. 'Let's paddle.'

She took Shona's other hand and they strolled down to where the wavelets were frilly. Mr and Mrs Average and their child, enjoying a day on the sand.

As the first cold water reached Shona's rounded feet she yipped and went sharply into reverse, then changed her mind and followed the wave out again. Cleo smiled as Shona laughed at the waves, stiffening as each ran further up her legs. 'Col'!'

'Cold,' Cleo agreed. 'But nice?' Shona's expression suggested it wasn't *that* nice and the tugging to free her hands declared that she'd ventured deep enough. Cleo stayed with her while Justin waded in to porpoise through the sparkling waves, resurfacing further and further out.

The breeze whisked Cleo's hair in front of her eyes as, not for the first time, she adjusted herself to a new responsibility. It was her job to keep Shona safe. The sea on the east coast could be treacherous and undercurrents had been known to snaffle children from right beneath parents' noses.

Still. It was difficult to conceive of an undertow that would drag Shona under in these six inches of salty froth. She risked a glance in Justin's direction, allowing herself to watch the water run off his back as he waited for a wave. To notice – she could hardly help noticing – the way his swimming shorts clung now they were wet and ...

She whipped around at the splash beside her as Shona tripped and executed a fine belly flop. 'Oh, whoops, up you jump!' Guiltily, Cleo hauled Shona to her feet. 'Did that taste nasty? What a sad face. Never mind, let's find your bucket and spade.'

Spurts of sand were soon flying though the air to shower Cleo's hair and eyes, as Shona added a sandy layer to a liberal coating of factor 25. They were both laughing at her fat, sandy legs when Justin returned.

How could Cleo not be aware of him drying his back, his arms, head, leaving his hair in spikes. He dropped down beside her and raised his eyebrows. 'Two years?'

Very interesting, watching Shona. Cleo couldn't unglue

her eyes. 'Mmm?' she answered vaguely. Then, 'Shona, look at these shells. Black, look, see?'

'B'ack,' Shona nodded.

'Really, two years?'

Picking up a little blue plastic mould, Cleo packed it with damp sand and tipped it over to make the shape of a sea horse. 'Sea horse, Shona!' Shona reached out a small, plump hand and tried to pick the sea horse up.

''Gain!' she demanded, when it was reduced to a pat of sand between her fingers.

Cleo made another. Another and another and another for Shona to destroy with a quick grab and a huge chuckle. Another so that Justin would keep answering Shona's chuckles with his own, another so that he'd lose the thread of his thoughts.

If only.

'You're kidding about the two years, right?' he persisted, when Shona had become fed up with sea horses and was engrossed in the sensation of pushing her toes through dry sand.

Cleo began filling the castle-shaped bucket so as not to have to look at him. 'Celibacy's very "in".'

He made a disbelieving noise.

She turned the bucket upside down and smacked it with the pink spade. Shona immediately grabbed the spade and began beating the bucket's bottom with grim concentration. 'Ban-ban-ban-ban-*bang*!'

He was still waiting, Cleo could tell without looking. Oh, what did it matter? What harm could she possibly do her image, maimed and bandaged already in his eyes? She lifted the bucket from a perfect sandcastle and watched as Shona pushed it slowly over with her feet. 'First I was pregnant and newly separated – not pulling points.' She laughed to prove she wasn't whingeing. 'Then I was a single mum, too busy, babysitters too few and far between. I'll get around to it, when the time's right.'

Another sandcastle, another Shona bulldozing job. The sun went in and Cleo slipped Shona back into her dress. Even when the sun was shining, the breeze was still enough to raise goosebumps and Cleo was glad to wriggle into her own T-shirt and jeans, conscious of the gritty layer on her skin.

'Gink!' demanded Shona, losing interest in sea, beach and candy-pink bucket.

'Here's your cup – let's get you back in your buggy while I clean you up.' Cleo brushed sand from Shona's feet while Justin repacked a backpack of mountaineer's proportions – proving that, thankfully, he wasn't a man who would hover helplessly.

They found a pub garden with a lawn and seats in the shape of wooden animals and ate seaside fish and chips for lunch, with mugs of tea and thick slices of buttered bread.

'Good to give this a go,' said Justin. 'Spending a day together for Shona's sake.'

Licking salty fingers, Cleo shrugged. 'I'm glad you can give up the time.'

He grimaced. 'It's nice to get away from the flat, to be honest. My old tenants, the Blumfields, seem to be playing juvenile revenge games because I hoofed them out when I got back to England. You know the kind of thing – insurance men arriving for mythical appointments, the police screeching up because they'd had a report of a woman screaming in my flat, that kind of prank stuff.'

'Was there one?'

'What? A woman?' He grinned. 'I'm seeing someone called Anita so she's been there. But not screaming. Now they've started putting disgusting things through the letter box, dog-do and a dead rabbit's head.'

'Sounds as if it's getting beyond a joke.' Trying not to

think about a woman called Anita in his flat, Cleo snapped off the delicious battery tail of her fish and ate it with her fingers.

Justin frowned. 'I'm hoping they'll get tired of all these pranks very soon. But I think the scumbags have moved into another flat nearby, because lately I've seen them about a lot. The bloke always shouts, "Fucking getchoo!" at me, so I'm pretty sure that he hasn't forgiven me for wanting my flat back.'

After, they pushed Shona's buggy past the bandstand and up the hill towards Old Hunstanton. Cars whizzed past on one side and gardens blazing with marigolds gazed out to sea on the other.

Justin took over pushing the buggy up the hill. 'Why did you and your husband split up?'

She felt a big, silent sigh heave her chest. 'He slept with someone else.' All this soul-baring was supposed to be behind her.

He snorted. 'So did you.'

She made herself face his mocking eyes and the eyebrows raised over them. 'So it wasn't much of a marriage any more, was it? He had a ding-dong with Lillian, a sex bomb he worked with and professed to dislike, then had to avoid sex with me because he thought he'd caught something nasty. Just when he thought he was safe with a clean bill of health, he got careless. I overheard him talking. All the ugly truths.

'Then his mother died in an accident and Gav had to cope with the grieving of his dad and pregnant sister, and a wife who wouldn't stay.'

They approached the top of the hill. After a moment Justin said, 'Poor bastard.'

'That's how I felt. But when I admitted I'd also slept with someone and was almost sure I was pregnant, that's when he told me he'd known for years he was infertile.'

She felt Justin turn sharply. 'And you really didn't know?'

She shook her head. 'I thought we'd just decided against kids. He was always vehemently anti-children but it was just a cover.' She paused to get her breath, gazing out at a white-tipped sea where a dozen tiny sailing dinghies rounded a buoy, her hair blowing around her head. 'End of marriage. I moved out. Despite Shona, he didn't want me to go.' She paused, staring out at the wind-ruffled waves. 'He's been living near his dad for a while but now he's thinking about coming back.'

'To live with you and Shona?' Apprehension threaded his voice.

Oh. Cleo felt fresh realisation and obligation settle around her. She'd assumed there was no one to be affected by her decisions, once she and Gav split. But there was. There was. If she wanted anyone to come and live with her, it could affect Justin's relationship with Shona.

She turned away from the eye-aching brightness of the sea's glitter.

Chapter Twenty-Eight

Cleo leaned back and let the wine float her mind. It was quite a novelty, these days, the chill of the wine glass in her hand and Liza perched on the seat of the wine bar beside her. The decor of antiqued gold and grass green made Cleo think of warm sunny evenings, relaxing and secure.

Contentedly, she mused, 'The more I drink, the more desirable and interesting I become.' She sloshed her glass in a gesture at the busy bar. 'Bet I could pull any man in this room.'

Liza blew a raspberry. 'Bollocks. You get horny when you're drunk and *think* you're desirable and blah-blah.'

Cleo sighed so hard that a nearby couple glanced up. 'I suppose that's true.'

'And I would've thought you'd learnt your lesson about drink and your love life.' Liza drained her glass. 'How *is* Justin?'

Just as unsettling as ever. 'OK, I suppose.'

Liza pushed her empty glass away. 'And he's really babysitting Shona at your place?'

Cleo nodded, then stopped, because it made the room tip.

It had felt extremely odd leaving Justin in her house. For the fortieth time she checked her mobile in case he'd been trying to contact her. 'He doesn't want her in his place just now because he's being hassled by his old tenants – prank phone calls and putting dead stuff through the letter box.'

'*Yurrr!*' Liza mimed the action of vomiting. 'Gross! What do the Old Bill say?'

Cleo shrugged. 'They spoke to the ex-tenants who, predictably, denied all knowledge.'

'They would, wouldn't they? Christ, let's go get coffee. My eyes are crossing.'

They wandered, reasonably steadily, into the red-vinyl aromatic warmth of the coffee bar across the road. It was busy but they found one of the tall tables free, in a corner. 'Short skirts, high heels, high stools – definitely a challenge!' Liza gave a whoop and hopped onto a stool, tossing back her hair.

As she struggled to slide up onto her stool in more cautious style, Cleo's giggle became a squawk of horror. 'Change places with me quickly! There's someone I don't want to see.' She pushed at Liza's shoulder.

Liza clung onto the table. 'Must be kidding, I've only just hoisted myself up here. Who, anyway? Ah, the blond twins. They're not bad, are they?'

Despite having been in a relationship for six months – an all-time record – with Lovely Bloke Adam, Liza couldn't break the habit of running her inbuilt desire-o-meter over men. But latte arriving in huge thick red cups, delicious and aromatic, distracted them both from Drew and Martin, who weren't looking over to their corner in any case.

'So,' Liza said, touching her impeccably made-up lips minutely to the too-hot surface of the coffee. 'Tell me about the trip to the seaside. Can't imagine Justin playing Daddies. Did he buy Shona candyfloss and toffee apple, then give her promptly to you when she honked?'

Cleo struggled to get a grip of her giant cup. 'Actually he's fine with Shona and adapts to her limitations. And incredibly,' she glanced at Drew and Martin, then lowered her voice, 'he seems besotted with her. Something I hadn't anticipated. My life's getting way too complex. With work and Shona I scarcely have time to meet anyone else, particularly someone cool about me being a single parent. And now I've realised I kind of need Justin's approval.'

Liza snorted. 'What for?'

Cleo groaned. 'Because whoever I'm close to will be close to Shona. It's not fair for that to be somebody Justin doesn't like.'

''Course it is, it's your life.'

'But Shona's life isn't mine. She's shared.'

Clattering her cup to its saucer, Liza snapped, 'I think you'll find, in law, Justin has no rights except to stump up for Shona's keep.'

'But there's honour and integrity, apart from law.'

Liza slapped her hand theatrically on the table. 'Crap! Bullshit. A crock of ... Ooh look, here's my Adam!'

'Oh ... hi Adam.' Cleo suppressed a sigh. Adam. Gangly, tawny, besotted Adam, love of Liza's life, was currently folding himself around Liza with relish and satisfaction. Brilliant. Probably adoring old Adam had searched them out so he could spend the night with Liza. Cleo was supposed to be sleeping in Liza's spare room and would end up trying not to listen through the wall. Oh, what fun.

Chapter Twenty-Nine

Although he was about to slide into the sleeping-bag bed, Justin went up and peeped into Shona's pine cot for one last time, to reassure himself that she was breathing.

He touched the back of his hand to the moist warmth of her cheek. This was his daughter. An unbreakable tie to Cleo, madwoman Cleo, the woman he'd least intended to be tied to, the one who'd been bad for him and who he'd decided to forget. His child: asleep in a cot in Cleo's comfortable room of natural earthy colours and sexy satin textures. He'd never been in Cleo's bedroom before, although he'd entered her body and maybe even some way into her mind. Intimate and yet distant. If he were to crawl under her quilt now, lay his head on her pillow, she'd never know ... He shook himself. Sad. He'd have to watch it.

He thought of her changing on the beach, not wanting him to hold the towel. From behind his sunglasses he'd pretended not to watch her, but wondered about her body post-childbirth.

Pity if it had suffered. Not that there was much sign, in a swimsuit it all looked pretty tidy. He had a sudden, freshened memory of her. Her skin against his, hair slithering, mouth ...

One last look at Shona and he backed from the room.

Clambering through the stair gate, a stride and a half from the front door, he froze. A scratchy scraping told him that somebody was trying to get in. The hairs on the back of his neck lifted. The knob turned suddenly and the door shot open.

And, surprise, surprise, in tottered Cleo.

She leapt like a guilty kitten. 'Oh *shit*!' she yelped, clutching her heart. 'You stupid arse, what are you lurking about in your boxers for? I nearly had a heart attack.' She leaned her back against the doorframe and her knees buckled gently until she knelt inelegantly on the floor.

He gazed down sternly, biting back a smile. 'No wonder you get into scrapes. Drunk on the floor, skirt up to your knickers –'

She gathered her legs beneath her. 'I'm not *drunk*. I just decided not to stay at Liza's. We met Adam, and Liza wanted him to go back to her flat, so I decided to get a taxi – at *huge* expense ... Who the fuck d'you think you are, you disapproving arse? My mother?'

Justin laughed. 'Yeah, right, I did sound like someone's mother. Give me your hand. Ready? Hup!' Co-operatively, she thrust herself to her feet and nearly toppled him onto the stairs. He had to grab the handrail to stop them both falling, her breasts pressing for an instant against his bare chest.

He freed himself. 'Go and sit in the kitchen, I'll make coffee.' He nipped into the sitting room to where his sleeping bag lay over the air bed and pulled on a T-shirt.

In the kitchen Cleo had pillowed her head on the table and closed her eyes. 'I was OK till I got in the taxi. But now I feel a little bit ... whizzy.'

'Whizzy. Right, I'll get you some sparkling water and paracetamol.' He also made black coffee – if it was an old wives' tale that it would help her, he'd chance it – and took the opposite chair. She drank the water, took the tablets and blew on the coffee. Hair tumbled and face flushed, Cleo's half-shut eyes glittered like marcasite.

Halfway down the coffee, her eyes opened fully. 'You'd been upstairs. Did Shona wake?'

He rubbed his nose. 'No, I've been up every five minutes to look in on her – remember, I'm a novice.'

'Novice at all this mullarkey?' She laughed. 'Were you checking she's still breathing? I do that. To reassure myself

I'm doing OK.' She folded her arms on the table. It pushed her breasts up.

No stretch marks there, so far as he could see.

'It's just her and me, what if I do it wrong? There's no one to ask whether she's too hot or too cold. I read about meningitis or sudden infant death and I panic.' Cleo shuddered, making her breasts shake.

He made himself look down into his coffee. 'Cheerful, aren't we? Let's talk about something else ... Cleo?' He looked up to see that tears were sliding slowly down her cheeks. 'What's the matter?' A truly dreadful thought hit him. 'Shona hasn't got something you haven't told me about, has she?'

Forlornly, Cleo shook her head.

Sighing in relief, Justin hitched his chair closer, hesitantly sliding his arm around her shoulders. The bareness of his arm connected warmly with the flesh at the top of her spine that was exposed by her scooped-neck top. 'Tell me what's the matter.'

Her breath wavered. 'It's just that, that, sometimes ... I get so frigh-frigh-frightened! Shona's only got me, what if I do something wrong? When she was tiny I used to feel sure I was doing something stupid, there never seemed enough information. The doctors, midwives and health visitors, they so obviously know what they're doing. They're *trained*.'

He let his arm tighten, smothering a smile. 'Did you think someone ought to have sent you on a course? Don't Ntrain do a seminar? "Powerful Supermothers" or "Mother-well"?'

For a moment she teetered on the edge of sobs – until a giggle bubbled out. She rolled her head onto his shoulder and he felt the wetness of her tears against his neck. 'But it was hard being pregnant, alone. Liza didn't really understand; one of my friends was ending her marriage and the other moving house. Mum and Dad were disapproving. So it was just me and the baby. There were no problems, I didn't get particularly big, didn't even see a doctor until I was over five months. But I felt anxious.'

He patted her back. 'But you've done a brilliant job. You're so in charge. I'm the total dunce, stumbling about, hoping I get it right, while you sail along.'

Another hiccup shook her. 'Thanks,' she whispered. Then began to disentangle herself stickily from his shoulder. 'I've probably cried my make-up all over your T-shirt.'

'Doesn't matter. Look – ' He hesitated, awkwardly. 'I'll still stay, if that's OK, you might not feel up to looking after Shona.'

She clambered unsteadily to her feet. 'Incapable, you mean. I'd better get to bed.'

'I'll give you a hand with the stairs.'

'You're such a hero.'

Oh God.

Cleo lifted a clammy hand to an aching head. Oh G-o-d.

She covered her face against the daylight glaring in through open curtains. Then she snatched her hands away and sat up.

The cot was empty.

For a moment she thought she'd be sick – and then she heard Shona's happy shout downstairs, the deep up-and-down of Justin's voice in reply, and remembered.

She rolled back down to the cool sheet. Now she need only feel hungover. And disadvantaged that Justin, coming in to fetch Shona, would have seen her asleep, perhaps mouth open, snoring. She cringed. Must have a shower. Must have fluids.

She scrubbed off the make-up, which should've been carefully wiped away last night. Last night. There was something bad about last night.

Oh, no – she'd cried. She made an appalled face at herself in the bathroom mirror.

Fantastic. She'd bawled all over Justin for no proper reason, been a maudlin silly drunk. He'd heaved her up to bed. She groaned as she dried herself, dragged on her comforting towelling robe, yanked up the hood over her damp hair and tramped down to grapple with the intricacies of the stair gate.

Shona clarioned her arrival – 'Mummee! Mum!' – accomplishing one of her knees-in runs, beaming, arms up, confident of her welcome.

Cleo automatically went into the corresponding delighted mum routine. 'Hello, baby! Were you a good girl for Justin? Mmm, what lovely kisses.' Fib. They were slobbery and rather full of Weetabix. She gulped hard.

Fully dressed, fresh, backside on one chair and feet on another, Justin lounged in the kitchen. Cereal bowls stood in the sink. He grinned. 'And how are we this morning?'

Cleo shuffled to the fridge, bending awkwardly with Shona happily astride her hip. 'You look OK, I feel like hell.' She poured orange juice, sploshing messily.

'Gink!' Shona threw herself forwards, fingers grasping air near the glass as she launched into rising, howling pleas.

Cleo put her down; the racket in her ear was pretty near unbearable. 'Where's your cup? Wait … let me put the lid on … there. Thank you.'

''K'you,' Shona repeated round the thick spout of the beaker. She suddenly caught Justin's eyes on her and burst into a rich baby chuckle before turning and trotting off into the sitting room. 'Bah-bye!'

'Bah-bye,' Justin called after her.

Cleo forced herself to drink orange juice, coffee and Alka Seltzer-Extra-Strong-For-Morons-Like-You, then dropped a single slice of bread in the toaster.

'That's no breakfast,' Justin chided. 'Sit down, I'll fry you some runny eggs.'

She turned throbbing eyes on him. 'Have pity.' Yanking the chair from under his feet, she sank down to nibble distastefully at lightly browned toast.

He stretched, looking great in a navy sweatshirt that said *University of Boston, Mass* up the outside of one arm. 'Apart from hungover, how are you?'

Under his gold-sprinkled gaze, she flushed. 'Look, you were great but don't take any notice of that stupid blubbing. Occasionally I get what my mum calls "gin-drunk" – weeping and wailing over absolutely nothing. You must've hated every second.'

She managed a corner of the toast. Yuk. Sipped her coffee. Urrgh. Orange juice. Yuk-urrgh. She closed her eyes for a long minute. When she opened them, he was still watching. She pulled a face. 'I've just remembered Gav's supposed to be calling this afternoon.' Gav had got the job he wanted, lucky old Gav, and was house hunting.

He smiled. 'A walk should clear your head ready for the fray. Shona's been telling me about the swings behind the village hall and how much she fancies a little go on them this morning.'

As the only vocabulary Shona possessed to support such a conversation was 'Zwing' and 'high', Cleo grinned and then grimaced. 'If I live that long.'

Justin rose. 'Get dressed, you'll feel better in the fresh air. Wrap up warm.'

Maybe she did feel a tiny bit better for a tramp around the village, showing Shona the waddling ducks at the ford, stopping for a newspaper. By the time they reached the swings she felt half human. A woman with two small children called 'Hello!' as she left. Her blonde hair was in a roll on the back of her head.

Cleo waited until the woman was out of earshot to say,

'I think she's married to someone who works with my landlord. I'm going to have to speak to him about the house. I'm either going to have to move, or buy it from him and extend upstairs over the barn-garage.'

Justin kept his head down, struggling to coax Shona's legs under the safety rail. 'Why? Fancy being nearer Liza?'

She pulled a face. 'No, I love Middledip, but I desperately need another bedroom. Shona can't share with me forever. And I've got to be mega-careful with my funds. My rent's reasonable at the moment. If I buy the house, it'll destroy my savings before I even begin to extend. And I might not get permission, because the cottage is so old. I could look for somewhere bigger to buy, but would it be in Middledip? It could end up a costly second bedroom.'

Justin paused in his swing-pushing. 'Find somewhere three-bedroomed and we could house-share.'

She felt her shoulders begin to hunch. 'House-share?'

'People do it. Room each, share the living accommodation, share the bills. The bonus, for us, is that Shona would have both her parents living with her.'

Cleo's back tensed so abruptly that it actually caused her pain. 'How lovely, I'd get the chance to vet your sleeping partners. Meet them on the landing in the middle of the night or hear bedroom noises. And how would you introduce me over breakfast? "Oh, this is Cleo, I accidentally got her pregnant once and we house-share because it's expedient." Piss off, Justin, it's a ridiculous idea.'

Justin fumbled for his mobile, which had begun playing the theme tune from *The Simpsons*. 'I'll take that as a "no", shall I? Hello? Yes, yes it is. *What*? You have to be *joking* …! I'm on my way.' He thrust the phone away and began back-pedalling rapidly in the direction of Ladies Lane, eyes wide and furious. 'That was my neighbour, Christ, can you believe it?'

He turned and began to run. 'My *flat's on fire!*'

Chapter Thirty

'What's this?' Cleo stared at a cheque, payable to C. Reece, in the sum of seven thousand, one hundred pounds, thirty-two pence. She had the sensation that her eyes were twice their proper size and her eyebrows lodged in her hairline. She moistened her lips.

Gav smiled, pushing up his trendy specs. 'I sold those shares. Remember that know-all financial whizz friend of Keith's who advised us to buy shares in some communications company we'd never heard of? X something Communications?'

Cleo nodded slowly.

'Apparently they've been bought by one of the dot.com giants – so I sold. Then I realised they'd been overlooked when we divided up our assets. I'd forgotten them.'

'So had I.'

'Celebration!' Gav fished in his jacket pockets and produced two individual bottles of Moët, the kind Cleo saw at the supermarket and wondered who bought such meagre portions.

She stared once more at the cheque. 'This is amazing. You could've kept all the money and I'd never have known.'

'It crossed my mind,' he admitted cheerfully. 'Glasses?'

Cleo pulled glasses from the cupboard, causing one of those difficult moments when they used something of hers that used to be theirs, but the popping corks got them over it. Cleo spluttered, taking too big a slug of new and lively bubbles. 'You don't know what a difference this will make. I was afraid it was going to be something to do with your mum's will, and then I wouldn't have been able to accept.'

'Oh that,' he grinned, the light glinting off his specs. 'She did leave me a handy sort of million quid, but I'm not sharing.'

'Fair enough.' She beamed, clinking his glass with hers. 'I'll be able to move house now. You're a star, Gav.'

Gav inclined his head modestly. 'A star back in your area – I've begun work at Hillson's as manager of Team Cardboard Box Sellers.' Hillson's was a huge packaging operation.

'So you've found somewhere to live?'

Gav's glass was empty and he hunted around for the bottle. 'With Keith, for now.'

Cleo raised her eyebrows, thinking of Keith's Posh Pad that he'd clung on to by remortgaging in order to pay Dora off. 'How's that working out?'

'Wicked.' Gav grinned conspiratorially, though 'wicked' didn't sound right on his lips. 'He's a right old stoat these days. Virtually always stray women about the house.'

The doorknocker rattled and Cleo rose.

'But if you need a housemate when you move, I could make myself available,' Gav tossed after her.

Just what she didn't need; Cleo shook her head and opened the old wooden door. Then sighed with relief. 'Justin, you're OK! I've been trying your mobile *all* day.' By the time she'd halted the swing and unfastened Shona's obstinate little fingers from the chains and followed him from the park, his car had gone.

Justin stood on the doorstep, grim-faced, eyes reddened and rimmed black. 'It's out of charge. Can I come in? Cleo, I'm in such shit, those stupid bastards poured petrol through my door and set light – oh.'

'Oh,' echoed Gav.

Justin hesitated. 'I'd better go.'

Cleo shut the door behind him and leaned on it. 'Don't be stupid, you're obviously in trouble. Just sit down –' Grizzles from the baby listener interrupted her. 'There's Shona. I'll have to get her, she goes mental if I leave her once she's awake.' The deep silence between the two men seemed solid enough to fill the space behind her as she ran upstairs.

Shona, nap-dazed, whined and clung hotly as Cleo carted her downstairs. In the sitting room Gav and Justin were waiting, unspeaking.

Shona peeped at Gav and clung harder.

'Hang on, I'll get you a drink.' She prised off Shona's limpet arms and swung her onto Justin's lap. Shona checked out the owner of the lap and accepted the change of venue.

'Hey, baby,' he said, softly.

When Cleo returned with orange juice, Shona had cheered up enough to let Justin show her one of the books that seemed to live permanently on the floor. Shona plugged the beaker spout into her mouth.

Gav launched to his feet. 'I'll see you another time, Cleo.'

Cleo trailed him to the door. 'Thanks for the –' But Gav was gone, snapping the door shut on her words.

'Sorry,' Justin offered. Gav had avoided his gaze, other than one, telling, filthy look; but, judging from the Moët bottles, he'd broken up a party and Gav could hardly be blamed for his antagonism.

Justin had impregnated Gav's wife and was instrumental in breaking up Gav's marriage. Yes, Gav had reasons not to like Justin. But, still, there had been hatred in that look.

Cleo shook her head. 'Doesn't matter. What the hell's been happening?' She poured him a glass of champagne.

It was probably Gav's champagne but he couldn't resist it and it was great. Dry enough to make his eyes prickle but warm his heart. He took two more gulps. 'Presumably it's the couple who lived in my flat while I was away, I can't imagine anyone else doing all this disgusting stuff with shite

211

and dead animals. But this time they meant business. The fire brigade think rags soaked in petrol were fed through the letter box, then set alight.'

Cleo put her hand to her mouth. 'During the night?'

'About five this morning.' He got up to pace about, stomach churning. 'The smoke was so thick and black that the neighbours woke up. I've been with the police and the fire brigade, looking at the damage and getting the door fixed temporarily. I'll have to find somewhere to stay. Everything stinks of smoke, the whole flat is covered in thick, black, greasy grime.' Shakily, he laughed. 'I don't think I'd be very well if I'd been inside.'

Chapter Thirty-One

As with most of her moments of madness, Cleo felt quite calm as she said, 'You can carry on using the air bed in the sitting room, if that's any good.'

He was silent, staring at her, before accepting gruffly. 'If I won't be too much in the way. The police say it'll be about a month before I can move back into the flat. It's mainly smoke damage.' His eyes were haunted. 'You realise that if I'd been looking after Shona there, instead of here –'

Nauseating fear shuddered through her. 'Let's view it as a horrible warning.'

Over the weeks, Cleo became used to adult company in the evenings and a dining companion who didn't fling carrots on the floor. Justin was such a good guest, with his sunny moods and jokey conversation, that she concluded that offering him a place to crash hadn't been a mad decision at all. For one thing, he didn't mind taking a turn at putting Shona to bed, which was especially useful if, like now, Cleo had work to do.

Planning a workshop on a big pad at the kitchen table, she listened to splashes and giggles from the bathroom above, aware of the rumble of his voice and the creak and bump of his footsteps. When he trod quietly back down the stairs, she lifted her head. 'Has she gone off?'

'Zonked. That girl can sleep.' He crossed the room to study Cleo's session plan over her shoulder. 'What's the "Three things you never knew about me" game?' He tapped the page where Cleo's slanting writing ran under the *Time, Module, Description, Goal, Learning Objective* headings.

'Just a common ice-breaking device. I sometimes use it at the beginning of a workshop. Each person has to make three statements, two of which are false, and the others have to try to spot the true one. People are so often stunned at which statement turns out to be true that it's also a useful exercise about assumption making.'

Justin grinned as he dragged out the other chair and picked up the paper. 'OK. then. I'm scared of dogs, I have a dagger tattoo on my bum, I believe in life on other planets.'

'You believe in life on other planets,' Cleo selected promptly, clicking her pen.

'Smart arse.'

'Well, I've never seen you flinch at dogs, you didn't have a tattoo two years ago – and you're daft enough to believe in any old crap.' Thoughtfully, she tapped her pen against her teeth. 'I once was arrested, I've blown some of my savings on a dress I can't wear, I can speak Czechoslovakian.'

Justin turned to the inside page. 'You can speak Czechoslovakian, I've heard you on the phone.'

'Wrong!' Cleo beamed in triumph. 'That was Polish, you ignoramus, and I don't speak it very well. My mother speaks it properly.'

He turned a page. 'So when were you arrested?'

'That's one particular adventure I've escaped so far – no, I've bought a new dress. One I don't need, can't wear and ought to take back to the shop. It was a stupid impulse buy and far too expensive.' With plenty of work clothes, jeans and tops, she ought to have been satisfied. Shona needed new clothes and shoes because she was growing like a runner bean and there were house-moving expenses anticipated as well as the permanent burden of household bills. Cleo scarcely led a wild life; definitely no new dress required.

But, oh, it had just called to her! All she'd done was cast a glance through the open shop door and there it was, its hanger hooked over a mannequin's hand. Even the mannequin's eyes had been fixed on it yearningly.

At half price it was still a hundred and sixty quid. Much too expensive and it wasn't even as if Cleo had somewhere to wear it … But she'd tried it on. And been seduced. It felt so good, hung so well and she did have that lovely money from the sale of the shares. But she wouldn't have it much longer if she blew it on extravagancies.

She pushed her fringe out of her eyes and turned back to her work, quickly becoming absorbed in constructing an evaluation chart. The boiler ticked from its place on the wall, the pages of the newspaper rustled and Cleo sucked the end of her pen.

Justin cleared his throat. 'I have three ears, I'm nine feet tall, I want to take a look at your expensive dress.'

She laughed, without looking up. 'It won't fit you.'

'Come on. I'm curious about how wonderful a dress has to be to make you part with your hoarded dosh.'

She shrugged and went up to retrieve the rustling bag from her wardrobe. The dress almost slunk out of the bag the fabric was so fluid, Ferrari red with a dull sheen. A short, hip-skimming sheath, it was sleeveless and slit from the high neck down to where broad black ribbon formed a belt just below the breasts. The dress draped like a dream, so lovely she could have kissed it.

Removing his gaze from the movie page, Justin's expressive eyes lit up. 'Now that's a dress! It deserves to be worn.'

She folded it carefully back into its bag. 'You're right. It's going back. Someone else will give it the glamorous life it deserves.' She hung the bag on the hook on the back of the kitchen door, so that she'd remember to take it with her in the morning.

Justin watched her. 'You know I'll have Shona.'

She dropped back into her seat and took up her pen. 'I

don't go out that much. Most available men avoid mumsy women. They have their own kids, they're agonised by separation from them, and they're terrified they'll create a one-his-one-hers-and-one-theirs family, only for that to break up too. And Liza's chosen just now to be involved with Adam, for the one and only time in her life she doesn't want to go out on the pull.

'And anyway, do I really want to put myself round the nightclubs? I've done that and regretted –' Her voice dried. She bit her lip. Flicked him a glance.

He twisted a grin. 'I remember.'

On her way to Dora's in the morning, Shona ya-la-ing happily from the back of the car, Cleo felt depressed. No, she shouldn't say depressed, depression was a proper, serious illness. She was just a bit low. Down. Blue.

She tried to count her blessings. She had a secure home – small, but safe and comfy. And if the only house she liked for sale in Middledip at the moment was too big and expensive, well, she'd have to wait, or look in Bettsbrough.

She had a reliable car; she had a good job with a fair income. And, thank every star in the sky, her darling daughter was happy and healthy.

And that was all that was important, her and Shona.

With Justin going home in the next few days, being alone with Shona was going to seem strange; but it wasn't fair to get used to him being around, to having someone to share the cooking and play Scrabble with, someone who let Cleo get an uninterrupted night's sleep when Shona had been up every night with spiky gums. Even if Cleo was getting accustomed to a sitting room strewn with the air bed and his clothes, Justin had his own life to live.

He was going home to his clean and decorated flat with a wardrobe and a proper bed. He must be delighted at the prospect of having his seclusion and space back. Anita, the woman he was seeing, could ring and he wouldn't have to go outside to talk to her. He wouldn't have to make do with Anita's shared flat when they wanted sex; his flat would give them privacy. They could bonk in bedroom, bath or hall.

She felt a sudden, tear-pricking, bile-tasting jealousy of Anita and Justin's healthy sex life. And of pigs. She'd read recently that a pig's orgasm lasts thirty minutes. That was simply unreasonable.

Three nights later, she arrived home to find him packing. 'My place is habitable again. I thought that, if I got most of my stuff there tonight, I'd have the weekend to buy whatever needs replacing.'

'Right. Good idea. I can't help until Shona's had something to eat –'

'It's OK.' He didn't look up from zipping up a big red bag. 'I'll get my stuff out of your garage and then Gez is coming with a van. Anita's waiting at the other end to help unpack. We'll get a takeaway.'

'So, you're all organised,' she said, brightly. She and Shona ate their meal and then they waved from the doorway as Justin left.

After that, even with Shona banging wooden pegs through a wooden frame, even with the radio on, it was really, really quiet. Cleo put the sleeping bag through the washing machine and dryer, did a blitzy polish round with lemon Pledge and sprayed the kitchen with anti-bacterial stuff.

She played for a while with Shona, putting the right animals in the right holes of a puzzle, bathed with Shona and went though Shona's bedtime routine.

And it got even quieter.

The flowers that arrived the next day were gorgeous. The

card read: *I'm ballooning, I'm training a dinosaur, I'm grateful you took me in. Thanks. Justin.*

She responded by text: You're dodgy, you're welcome, you're missed. Cleo.

Chapter Thirty-Two

Late on Sunday evening, Justin knocked at Cleo's door, wondering whether he was doing the right thing.

Suddenly, she was framed in the doorway, grinning, in a pair of cut-off jeans and a long pink T-shirt. 'You don't live here any more, remember?'

From Cleo's hip, Shona held out her arms and squeaked, 'Jussin!'

He swooped her up and she slid her tiny arm around his neck and beamed into his face. 'Hi-yah!'

'Hiya!' He plopped a kiss onto the end of her nose. Then, to Cleo, 'I've brought back your key.'

She stood back invitingly. 'If you had a key you should've used it.'

He stepped in. 'I didn't want to intrude.'

'Yeah, right, make me sound like I might be doing something interesting. Are you just passing? Or staying for a proper visit?'

He dropped right back into the routine, sharing a meal and bathing Shona. Warm water, suds, bath toys, Shona's dimpled, pudgy limbs glistening and hair like a shampoo punk rocker. Her robust protests at the intolerable process of hair washing, 'Nah-nah-nooooh!'

Sleeves rolled up, he crouched beside the bath, captivated by her pearly-toothed smiles.

It had been great, staying with Cleo. Apart from getting along so well with Cleo without sex to complicate things, he'd lived with his daughter. The thought of no longer doing so created a grey ache. Living alone this weekend had been odd, even with Anita around quite a lot of – too much of –

the time. Sleeping in a new bed, his flat smelling of cleaning fluids and paint, instead of squirming into the sleeping bag and flopping down on the air bed by the wood stove.

He sighed and reached for Shona's yellow duck towel, the one that folded into a hat at the corner, complete with beak. Trapping and wrapping her, he threw her over his shoulder, making her simultaneously squeal with delight and break wind with gusto.

Later, once Shona was snuggled up in bed, he settled himself in the chair he'd used when he'd lived there, while Cleo flipped through TV channels.

'Taken that expensive dress back?'

She pulled a guilty face. 'Tomorrow.'

He made an effort to sound casual. 'I was hoping you'd fancy giving it an airing and come out with me on Saturday night.'

Pleasure flitted across her face, then doubt. 'Where?'

'It's a work thing. Dinner with the bosses and a few bottles of bubbly dished out for achievement. It's also supposed to be an exercise in mixing up the three cliquey parts of the firm – studio, office and print works.'

He watched a frown form above eyes so clear he could almost see her brain activity. 'What about Anita?'

He blew out his cheeks. 'Anita wouldn't actually be much of an asset. We studio oiks are perceived as elitist bastards and we've been told we have to mix – Anita is a poor mixer.' Cleo's doubtful expression made him add, honestly, 'Also, she's getting a bit … serious. She wants to be full on and I'm not up for it. I'm cooling things. You'd be doing me a favour, really.'

Cleo pulled a face. 'You have to resort to taking me to ditch her? Sorry, no babysitter.' She slapped her empty coffee mug onto the table.

He did his wounded look. 'You're not a last resort. I'm

inviting you because you put me up for weeks when I didn't have anywhere to crash.' Except with Drew, Martin, Gez, his sister ... 'And because you'll be great at mingling, you have *aplomb*. Liza says she'll babysit.'

She stared at him. 'Do you usually organise babysitters for your dates?'

Impatiently, he rose. 'OK, forget it, you've got more excuses than a guilty schoolboy. I'll tell Liza no thanks.' He located his keys. 'I'll be in touch about seeing Shona.'

Her voice halted him as he opened the front door. 'Dinner will be lovely. But don't organise my babysitter!'

He reversed the car out of her drive. So, he'd asked her out, kind of. Which was bad. But he'd seen how lonely it was for her to be bright and together and professional all day amongst strangers, then to go home and spend her evening in isolation with Shona. He'd decided to do something about it. Which was good. Kind, thoughtful, all that stuff.

He hoped he wouldn't regret it.

Cleo rang Liza before the sound of Justin's car had faded. 'Has Justin asked you to babysit on Saturday?'

Liza giggled. 'That's right. You know I'm mad about Shona so it's no problem.'

Cleo waited for inquisitive questions or accusations of rude behaviour. They didn't come. 'I know how much you like to play the cool auntie. But you're actually free on a Saturday?'

'As it happens.'

'He's invited me to some works do. I don't know whether I ought to go.'

The theme tune of an American sitcom blared behind Liza's voice. 'It's up to you. Aren't you keen?'

She was, too keen probably, that was the issue. Reluctantly, though, she could see all kinds of obstacles. 'It would cost me about forty-five quid in taxi fares from Peterborough to Middledip after midnight on a Saturday. And the same if you want to go home, because you don't drive – or, if you stay here, there's only the air bed – so maybe it would be more sensible to forget it.' Her heart settled heavily.

'I'll sleep over at your place, you can sleep at mine. Easy. Don't fret.'

Chapter Thirty-Three

The following Saturday morning, Cleo drove Shona to Ferry Meadows to feed the waterfowl. The sunshine bounced off the three lakes and swarms of kids clambered about the playgrounds, or yelled their way between dog walkers and cyclists along the footpaths that circled each stretch of water.

Shona always adored a ride in the trucks behind the tiny train or a boat trip up the river past the golf course. Cleo preferred drinking cappuccino and watching the windsurfers skimming and slicing over the dancing water.

But today, she had to meet Gav.

Drag. She hadn't heard from him since the day of Justin's fire, so the phone call yesterday had been a surprise. And an inconvenience. Hardly in the door, Shona tired, famished and screaming for the food she could smell cooking, it hadn't been the best time for her phone to ring.

He'd been abrupt. 'Can we meet up?'

'Or I could ring you later.' Cleo tried to joggle Shona soothingly. Shona's rising wails indicated that joggling was not, in fact, all that soothing.

'I'd rather it was face to face.'

'As long as I can feed Shona first. Want to come round later?'

Gav sounded almost disgusted. 'No I don't! When we meet tomorrow, can you leave Shona with … someone?'

Tartly, she'd reminded him, 'We come as a package, Shona and me.'

Ferry Meadows had seemed a good meeting point, close to Keith's Posh Pad so Gav need only walk up Ham Lane. Cleo and Shona were crouching on the path, feeding the ducks, when he arrived, his hair lifting in the lake breeze.

Cleo took in his lowered brows and turned-down mouth. 'You look cheerful – not.'

He attempted a smile. 'So – you couldn't leave her?'

Cleo threw bread to the shiny-green-capped mallards over the heads of the thuggish white geese, making her tone neutral. 'People who leave tiny kiddies home alone get in big trouble.'

'What about ... her father?'

'What about him?'

The geese swayed and bobbed in unison on rubbery, webbed feet, all eyes fixed on the bread bag until it was empty. Then they all swung back toward the water. The mallards hung around for another few minutes, like visitors too polite to leave the moment they'd eaten.

'Fancy a walk round the lake?' suggested Gav.

'OK. Buggy, Shona?' It was a mistake to suggest that she had a choice, because Shona's emphatic headshake meant that Cleo was lumbered with pushing the buggy with one hand and hanging on to Shona with the other. Gav offered no help. Justin would've automatically taken either buggy or child and she'd obviously become too used to it, Cleo reflected.

She had better get unused to it again, hadn't she?

To add to her distractions, Shona launched loudly into her latest conversational gambit of exclaiming, '*Yook!*' and pointing dramatically at whatever she wanted admired. As she could cry, 'Yook!' every two seconds, it got a bit wearing. So Cleo probably sounded irritated when she asked, 'What's up?'

'Did you know he'd set the police on me?'

'Yook!' marvelled Shona, pointing theatrically at a fisherman.

'Yes, he's fishing,' Cleo responded dutifully, before turning back to Gav. 'What are you on about?'

Because he wasn't wearing his glasses Gav looked more his old self, except for what seemed like fresh frown lines. 'The police rang me at work – at my new job! – wanting to see me about that bloody flat. Did I know Mr Mullarkey, they said. 'Course I said I didn't. It was only when they said Justin ...'

Shona swung round. 'Jussin?'

Realising that she needed to concentrate, Cleo swept Shona into her bright-blue buggy, quashing her protests by peeling a satsuma and handing down segments as they strolled around the lake. The grass, rippled by the breeze, grew long either side of the path. Cleo frowned. 'What's Justin's flat got to do with you?'

'Abso-fucking-lutely nothing.'

She stiffened. 'Would you mind not swearing around Shona? I detest hearing those kids who say effing-this and effing-that. Obviously, they pick it up from adults.'

'Sorree!' Gav snapped. He jammed his hands in his pockets. Then snatched them out and folded his arms. Walking with him was about as restful as watching a wrestling match. 'I'm just angry. I was able to satisfy the police I knew nothing about it. But when I realised you were living with him ...! I just thought you ought to know what kind of a vindictive bast— bloke he is.'

She snorted, knowing that dismissiveness would get up Gav's nose. 'I'm not living with him. He stayed on the air bed for a few weeks, that's all.'

'He tipped off the police that I might have torched his flat. As if I'd even dream of it – although nobody would blame me if I had burnt his bloody – *blooming* – flat down and him in it. Which he wasn't. I've a perfect right to feel pi— peeved that he slept with *my wife*.'

A family walking the other way looked fascinated. Cleo

gritted her teeth. 'Make up your mind – either you wouldn't dream of burning down his home or no one could blame you.'

'Nobody could.'

'So why are you surprised your name came up?'

Gav stared stiffly ahead.

In the silence, Shona exclaimed, 'Yook, duck!'

'Mmm, a duck with a green head.'

'Yook, duck!' She pointed at a different duck.

'The brown one is the lady duck.' And to forestall the possibility that Shona might point singly at each of about fifty ducks in eyeshot, 'There are lots of ducks.'

'Don't you get sick of baby gabble?' Gav rolled his eyes.

Of course she did, but he was the last person she'd admit it to. 'Kids don't learn if they're ignored.'

Several minutes of silence. Even Shona gave 'Yook!' a rest. They'd reached the second lake before Gav emerged from his sulk. 'So you're not living with him?'

Cleo blew out an irritated breath. 'He's gone back to his own place, as was always intended.'

Gav stopped suddenly, reaching out and halting the buggy. 'I really miss you, Cleo.'

Oh n-o-o ...

'I haven't put in for the divorce, you know.'

Dismay shivered in the pit of her belly. 'I did suspect.'

'I kept hoping that we'd sort ourselves out, forget our bad patch and get back together. We were great.' He fixed his eyes on her with scary hunger. His voice dropped, striking chords in her memory. But then she'd found it thrilling, not cloying. 'Don't you remember our marriage that everyone envied? Keith says he used to love coming into our house, our sane world where bickering didn't seem to exist.'

Cleo tried to swallow down her heart, which had thumped and jumped into the base of her throat.

She tried to make her voice kind. 'But our sane, adult world was a lie and we each turned to someone else. Our aims weren't shared at all. The great time was based on a false premise and it ended.'

He hunched his shoulders. 'We could put it behind us! I was happy. It's miserable not coming home to you, I've been miserable every day since you left. Cleo ...?'

She hated to see him this way, misery graven in every line of his waxy white cheeks. 'I'm sorry,' she said, gently. 'There's nothing left of "us". We can't change history. I can't forget you lied rather than tell me you couldn't have children.

'And you'll never forgive what I did – look, here's a living reminder. My daughter. And you don't even like her.'

They cut between the lakes to a wooden playground. Gav made a clumsily obvious effort with Shona, pushing her on a swing and clapping when she shot down the shiny metal slide like a little ball. But she ducked away and climbed onto a wooden rabbit to glare. Cleo watched the light die again from Gav's eyes and sighed.

She tackled Justin the moment he arrived to pick her up, ignoring his dry, 'Great dress, is it new?'

She turned in the seat to face him. 'Did you tell the police Gav torched your flat?' Though her eyes were fixed on his, she was aware of his dark grey suit and cobalt-blue shirt, of the quills of hair hanging over his eyes.

He grinned. 'Has he been telling tales?'

'Did you?'

The grin faded. 'Not by choice. The Blumfields had alibis, friends who say they were with them in Brighton. The police asked me the direct question, "Anyone else with a grudge against you?" I said, "Not one who'd do this," and that was enough, they leapt in saying there was obviously something

227

I wasn't letting on, they were used to dealing with delicate matters, etc. I knew Gav's name and where he worked.' He shrugged. 'Couldn't be avoided.'

They looked at each other. She reached for the seat belt. 'Shall we go?'

The function room was unimaginative with red velvet curtains, white tablecloths and way too much brass and copper. Their places were at what was evidently the singles' table as no one but Justin had brought a partner. Her red place card was inked 'Cleo Reece' in gold pen, whereas the rest were properly printed. She even caught a hissed, 'Who's she?' It couldn't be more obvious that she was a late addition to the guest list.

She watched Justin from under her lashes and wondered why he'd really invited her. Her being a good mixer seemed a bit lame. And if it really was to thank her for putting him up for a few weeks ... hmm. Not much better. She sighed and admitted to herself that she was here because he felt sorry for her, with her nice new dress and nowhere to wear it. She shrank inside. She was a pity date.

He'd hardly want her glued to his side, in that case, so she'd better make a damned good job of 'mingling'. Brightest smile firmly in place, she said, 'Introduce me to everybody, then.'

There were ten others on their table, four from the studio, two girls from the office, Elizabeth and Zoë, and four men from the print works. Of these, three were machine assistants and one was a printer – Brad, tall and hunky with dark shoulder-length hair. He wore a seventies two-tone suit as if for a joke, collar undone, tie knot four inches too low, jacket straining over his shoulders. His avid brown eyes were trained on the sleek fabric of Cleo's dress where it draped and gathered around her breasts.

'Hello,' Cleo tried. 'I'm up here.'

With a blink, Brad snapped his gaze up to meet hers. 'You certainly are. Where has Justin been hiding you? Justin, swap seats – I gotta sit next to her.'

Justin examined the menu card. 'As if.'

Cleo couldn't resist giving Brad a second look. Whatever reason, she was here, and if Brad's attention was as obvious as the beam from a lighthouse, well, fine, it had been too long since anyone had offered such balm to her ego. Time was, of course, that Justin had gazed at her with identical wolfish intent and how had they ended up ...? Well, she was wiser now.

As a cheesy appetiser of scallop shells filled with prawns and piped potato was served, Justin lifted his wine and chinked glasses with her. 'Thanks again for taking me in. It must have been a pain.'

'No problem. The house seems very quiet and tidy without you, now. Poor Shona still bursts into the sitting room expectantly in the mornings.'

He smiled a crooked smile, forking potato around without eating. 'I so enjoyed being with her. I might be biased but I think she's a pretty fantastic kid. It all worked out OK, didn't it?'

'Fine.' Cautiously, she took a mouthful of soft prawn and dry potato. It didn't taste a lot better than it looked.

Slowly, Justin laid down his fork. 'I got to spend time with her, you got to share the load. To return to the conversation that was interrupted when I got the call to say my flat was on fire – that house on Main Road, nearly opposite the pub, the one you like but that you said was too big and expensive for you – we could share the deposit, share the mortgage, and all live there together. You, me, Shona. I could have my room, you have yours. Shona would have both of us.'

For an instant, Cleo had the dizzying sensation that her heart had just done a handstand. Was it with longing?

For company, for some of the responsibility to slide onto someone else's shoulders? Almost definitely its acrobatics were based on hope that eventually Justin would feel again something of what he seemed to feel for her in the beginning. And they'd be happy and it would be glorious and they'd be a family and have fun and –

Stop it!

These were stupid, impossible, impractical dreams based on ridiculous, unfounded optimism and almost bound to bring woe. Her heart flounced right side up again and began to sulk.

Discarding her fork, she snatched up her glass. 'I thought we'd already agreed that it's a ludicrous idea. Think of how sniffy Anita was when you were living at my place. And you didn't even bring her to spend the night. You'll regret it the moment that you begin seeing someone again.'

His eyes were calm. 'Let me worry about my own love life.'

She leaned towards him so that her lips were close to his ear. 'OK, let's worry about mine. I *have* no love life. Geddit? There's been no one since I left Gav – and, bluntly, moving in with you isn't going to improve my prospects.'

Around them, conversation swelled loud and raucous; but Cleo and Justin worked their way almost silently through the courses. In fact, Cleo didn't eat much. She turned politely when Rockley's head honcho took the stage to spout about the firm's good year and dish out booze as prizes for various achievements, and applauded with the polite glaze of a guest. Justin received a bottle of Armagnac for the Ashton Campaign, whatever that was, and she managed a stiff, 'Well done.'

On the closing round of applause, lilac and yellow discs of light began to race one another across the ceiling, and the base line of the DJ's opening number eased from enormous speakers at the corners of the dance floor as his deep voice rumbled out, 'Well, hello Rockley Image! Who's gonna be first on the dance floor tooooo-*night*?'

'Me!' Brad's big warm hand closed firmly on Cleo's wrist and suddenly she was arriving at the centre of the floor with Robbie Williams' invitation, 'Let Meeee-eeee EnterTAIN YOU', crashing round the room.

'Fancy a dance?' Brad's invitation, though belated, was delivered with a scorching smile. After a moment, Cleo laughed and settled her feet into the rhythm. The dance floor filled up, encouraging Brad in his apparent aim to dance with her as close as humanly possible, sliding behind her to move in tightly and follow the movement of her hips with his. She had to corkscrew her neck to try and get a glimpse of him.

The crowd thickened, everyone bumping into one another to gusts of laughter.

'This is terrible, I can't talk to you,' bellowed Brad. 'Let's get a drink.'

Cleo nodded and let Brad haul her behind him to the bar. She hung back while he procured her a cold Budweiser then fanned himself emphatically. 'Let's move closer to the door for a breath of fresh air.'

There was a bit of relief from the bass thump near the doorway, as well as the promised airflow. Brad moved in close, as if still struggling against the crowd. 'Love your dress,' he said. 'Fantastic. You look amazing.'

As they exchanged the obligatory, feeling-the-way information about work, films and music, one of the machine assistants came over with two more bottles of Bud. Pretty neat idea to arrange that, she acknowledged, as it meant Brad neither had to leave her unattended nor plunge back into the bar melee.

'So,' he murmured, one hand on the wall above her, eyes

flicking between her face and the slit at the neck of her dress. 'You're not heavily committed to Justin or anything?'

'Not even lightly,' she agreed. 'I did him a favour and he brought me here as a thanks.'

'Great.' He ran the back of his hand up and down her arm. It tickled, pleasurably. 'And you know he comes with mega-baggage? He's got a baby with some tart he had a one-nighter with.'

Cleo nodded, laughter putting a tuck in her stomach. 'That would be me.'

Brad's mouth dropped open for a horror-struck moment; but then his arm darted opportunistically round her shoulders. 'I'm so sorry! I didn't mean *tart*, oh wow! I'm really, really sorry ...'

His horrified remorse just made her laugh harder. She knew she ought to be drawing herself up in wounded resentment, but for several moments she even held onto him, wiping her eyes inelegantly on the backs of her hands. The whole situation was just so ludicrous. 'Forget it. Shall we dance again?' It was just slightly boring, standing on the edge of things while Brad tried too hard to rivet her with his conversation. Dancing would be better.

And it was. This was where Brad's talents lay; he ought to stick to simply being a hunk. Squashed by dancers on all sides, his arms slid around her to shield her from the worst of the jostling and, experimentally, Cleo let her flesh go fluid and reform against his hot body.

Instantly, his mouth dropped over hers like a hoover, making her freeze in surprise, and she clung to his shoulders, feeling his chest muscled and firm through his shirt. It was, after all, difficult to keep her balance with her face stuck to his.

Chapter Thirty-Four

It was definitely out of order, Cleo and Brad sucking the faces off one another on the dance floor like that. Justin felt the molten anger of the justifiably pissed off.

And with Brad's oversized hands cupping Cleo's round buttocks and all that stupid long hair sweeping down to brush her face, people were beginning to look.

Worse, some of them were then looking at him. And smirking.

He sighed and began to push towards the oblivious couple, dumping his jacket and tie en route. Bloody woman; bloody overgrown, oversexed man.

Threading between the dancers, he made a point of greeting people, hoping Cleo would hear and come up for air. Sure enough, her startled dark eyes soon met his. He ignored Brad. 'I thought I might have a couple of dances with my guest?'

Cleo nodded slowly. 'OK.' She smiled apologetically at Brad. 'Catch up with you later?'

Then it was Brad's turn to look very pissed off. Shame.

Justin slid his hands onto Cleo's waist, light, friendly, dancing – not getting-it-on. 'Sorry I upset you with the house thing. You know what it's like when you're convinced how great an idea is – you don't want to accept others might not see it the same way.'

Her hands, casual as his, rested on his shoulders. 'Forget it.'

Blithely, he prepared to upset her again. 'You and Brad are getting affectionate.'

Her eyes, nearly black in the low lights, moved to his face. 'So?'

They jogged in a gentle rhythm. Back, forward. Forward, back. As the music slowed down the crowds jostled them more closely together. He let his hands slide round to the small of her back and link up. 'It looked like an instant improvement in your love life.' He studied her expression. 'I'd imagine Brad thinks he'll get you into bed tonight.'

Her nod was slow and thoughtful. 'Probably he does.' Then she beamed suddenly, conspiratorially, eyes lighting up with mischief. And his heart sank. The madwoman was emerging.

A couple trying to push past jarred against her. He pulled her closer to speak into her ear. 'But you're not going to?'

'Why not?'

He swore under his breath. She was going to bonk Brad. He could imagine Brad fetching her jacket and they'd leave together, exchanging significant smiles, holding hands.

He made his voice testy. 'Chrissake, Cleo, how's it going to make me look if *my guest* leaves with Brad? I mean – Brad, testosterone man! I'm not sure I could survive it.'

For a second her eyes blazed in fury. Then her features stilled, became blank, and relaxed into acceptance. The swaying that had passed for dancing, halted. 'Right. You're right. I hadn't thought of you. It's not on.'

Another track began. They started to dance again, in silence. He gazed over her head and felt like eight kinds of git. She'd made it no secret that she was, bluntly, not getting any. The idea of two years – *two years!* – of celibacy was unimaginable. And Justin had scotched her chances with stupid macho pride, hating the way Brad had sniffed out the opportunity like the wolf he was.

'Justin!' The whisper whisked him from his thoughts. 'I'm not a complete sex-starved tart, but could you stop the up-for-it act? You're making me … uncomfortable.'

Her meaning struck him like a slap.

As the crowds had pressed he'd pulled her closer and, wrestling with the tricky Brad situation, his arms had tightened in aggravation. Just look at them – his leg between hers and hers between his; wrapped around each other so tightly that he could feel her heartbeat.

Fantastic. As well as a selfish git he was an insensitive bastard. For an instant he was super-aware of her flesh pressed to his flesh, her perfume warmed by the heat of her.

'If you intend to have sex tonight, isn't it better the devil you know?' They gazed at each other, the shock he felt at having voiced the thought mirrored on her face.

But she didn't pretend to misunderstand. Her reply came on a gurgle of incredulous laughter. 'But you've been pretty clear that the time for us to have anything between us has long gone!'

'And would there be "anything between" you and Brad? Or are we talking about just sex?'

Still now. Dead still in the circle of his arms, her brows straight thoughtful lines, eyes fixed on his. After a moment, she shrugged. 'Just sex, I suppose.'

'Well,' he drawled. 'I could certainly rise to the occasion.' He must be crazy even to think about this.

He watched her eyes crinkle up in a silent laugh. She was seriously attractive when she did that. 'You'll regret it.'

He felt the corners of his mouth tug upwards in reply. 'That'll be my problem.'

'You'll feel awkward tomorrow.'

'As if! We're grown-ups.'

She shook her head. 'I shouldn't even consider it. It's madness, it's asking for trouble.' He felt a very slight shudder run through her. 'But, if you're sure ...'

No, but how could he resist her laughing eyes and her hot body pressed gently against his? 'I'll get our jackets.' His heart bounced.

The flat was dark but for a glow of amber lamplight from the street. The smell of fresh paint reminded her that there had been a fire. The flat was too hot, or she was, and her heart hammered so hard that she thought it might be visible in a pounding heart-shaped lump, like in *Tom and Jerry*.

Justin's hands settled on her shoulders. Light. Comforting. Friendly. His voice was low, vibrating with tension. 'Sure about this?'

Hers was ragged and squeaky. 'If you are.'

And then his hands were moving, sliding her jacket down her arms and to the floor. He captured her as they drifted up the hall, easing down her zip, hands stroking through the fabric, breasts, stomach, buttocks, making every part of her crackle. Moving faster, breathing unevenly, Justin shrugging off his jacket as they cannoned gently into the bedroom, Cleo's fingers trembling over his shirt buttons. Cool air as he slipped her dress from her shoulders.

Sudden urgency as he yanked her against him, his mouth on hers. Stripping himself rapidly and pulling her onto the bed. Her small yelp of shock as her hot flesh touched the coolness of the sheet.

And then it was all about her and what Justin could do for her.

She should be ... But she couldn't co-ordinate, he was stroking, kissing, licking, nipping, his flesh sliding across hers, hands caressing, mouth exciting. Bringing her, in a shamefully short time, to a pitch where she was actually whimpering, 'Quickly, quickly!'

But he slowed, his tongue making moist trails across her breasts to cool and pucker into tingling goosebumps, his hand slipping between her legs.

And who groaned loudest when he touched her? She was getting pretty loud, maybe she'd sweep him along with her – but, no, he only chuckled when she half shouted, 'Come *on*!'

Desperate, she was desperate to reach the end of the ride, even though the trip itself was so exciting and particularly sweet.

When he finally slid inside her he refused to rush, holding on, building her up to bring her properly in on the crest of the biggest wave. She closed her teeth gently on his neck and tasted the salt of his skin. Or maybe her tears.

Afterwards, it felt as if there was only them, cut off from the rest of the world in a rainbow-strewn bubble of contentment. Delicious. Damp bodies stuck together, the sheet clinging around their legs.

'Fuck it.'

Cleo lifted her head with an effort, blowing hair out of her eyes. 'What?'

'It's broken.'

Her heart lurched. 'Not the condom?'

''Fraid so.'

Cleo let her head fall back to the pillow and groaned.

It was bright daylight when she thought about it again and decided that, leaving that little disaster aside, her favourite had definitely been the first time – when she lost sight of everything except satisfying herself and he'd been so brilliant, expecting nothing and giving everything.

Or maybe the second time, when it had been more leisurely, exploring each other in an exchange of information and remembering.

Then again … she stretched and sighed. This morning had been pretty sensational as well, waking up to the realisation that this was no erotic dream but real hands were cupping her breasts and a real erection was hot against her back.

'I may be out of practice,' she murmured, rotating her bottom gently in his lap. 'But that was outrageously good sex.'

He trailed an idle fingertip in and out of her belly button. 'Mmmm. The best.'

A fresh rash of goosebumps fled across her. 'And however special celibacy is meant to be, I find it vastly overrated.'

He laughed, his breath brushing her shoulder. 'Maybe it suits some better than others.'

It certainly didn't suit her. Being sex-starved had its advantages because whenever he'd touched her she'd felt the earth move, seen flames and fireworks. Next time she read in a magazine that women deprived of sex ceased to want it, she'd write and complain.

He pushed still closer. She sighed, drowsily.

He lifted his head from the pillow. 'That's not your mobile ringing, is it?'

'This early?' Cleo dragged herself up onto wobbly legs and over to where she'd abandoned her bag halfway up the hall to extract her phone. And the bubble burst.

She hurtled back into the bedroom to where he still lay curled in the duvet. 'Have you seen the *time*? Liza's going bananas, she's supposed to be with Adam's family for Sunday dinner. And I haven't even given Shona a thought. Where's my dress?' Into the bathroom to clean her teeth with his toothpaste and her finger, then she raced back out. 'Can you zip me up?' She halted. Justin looked ... tense.

After a struggle she managed the zip herself. 'Um, I've left my car at my sister's flat ...'

He lay perfectly still for several moments before unfolding himself with a sigh of resignation. 'Cleo, this gives me the most fucking appalling feeling of déjà vu.'

He pulled up behind Cleo's car, outside her sister's flat. She'd been clock-watching all the way, jiggling in her seat, worrying aloud that Liza would be frantically furious and Shona would feel abandoned, and scrabbled for the door handle the instant they arrived.

Brilliant.

But then she paused and turned, clasping his forearm with both her hands. She sucked in a deep breath. 'Thanks. Thanks for taking me out.' Her eyes crinkled. 'Thanks for the sackful of sex.' Her smile faded. 'And don't worry, I do know the score.'

He lifted his eyebrows.

Holding his gaze she said, carefully, 'Like you said, it was just sex. I'm not expecting anything. Nothing's altered since you said all that stuff – you don't trust me, you think I behaved unforgivably. Don't feel you have to go through some charade of "cooling it" with me now. We're adults. You don't have to wish you hadn't done it. It was just once.' She brushed his lips with hers and touched his cheek with her fingertips.

Then she was gone.

He drove home in a black cloud. One-night stands were a bad idea, sometimes. Full of misunderstandings and crap. And crap. Crap!

He slammed into his flat.

If that was 'just' sex, he'd never had sex before. And if it *was* just sex, it was just the best sex. It should've been on the ten o'clock news. Eleven out of ten, six gold stars, top of the premier league.

It had to be more than sex.

He couldn't get her out of his mind; her warmth, her, um, active participation – OK, she'd been as horny as a cat – and ... just everything.

The phone rang, and he snatched it up. 'Hello?' But the caller replaced the receiver without speaking. 'Oh piss off, you saddo.' He got really tired of this nuisance campaign.

Adam had whisked away a Liza in a whirl of self-righteous

indignation that she hadn't been the unreliable, unpunctual one for a change. Shona was already down for her post-lunch nap.

Cleo flopped into her chair with an icy beer and the end of the *EastEnders* omnibus.

She was beginning to realise she shouldn't have done it.

Bad, bad idea. B-a-d. Why had Justin made such a preposterous suggestion and why, why, *why* had she agreed?

And why did it have to be so great? She closed her eyes against a heavily significant conversation across the bar of The Queen Vic and remembered Justin's mouth. His hands. His body. She shuddered. Must be chemistry. Or sorcery.

Chapter Thirty-Five

'If you're pregnant this time, we get married!' Justin paced over the quarry-tiled floor.

Cleo kept calm, because one of them had to. 'For all the wrong reasons?'

'You wouldn't know the right reasons if they sprang up and bit your behind.'

Cleo counted to ten as she sliced the crusts off Shona's sandwich. An hour, one poxy, measly, tiny hour since Liza had leapt into Adam's car – and now Justin was here shouting the odds, making her regret over the night deepen with every step he took around the kitchen.

'We'd better talk about that condom, Cleo.'

Slowly, she shut her eyes.

He slapped his hands on the table. 'You would've thought we'd learnt our lesson. Neither of us is safe to be let out!'

... eight, nine, ten. She settled Shona into her high chair and began more sandwiches for herself. 'I'll get the morning-after pill.' Counting slices of ham, she decided she had plenty. 'Hungry? I can make you ...'

The ham packet shot out of her hand and across the worktop and she almost suffered whiplash as Justin swung her around to face him.

'Those pills don't always work. Stop dodging the issue – if you're pregnant this time, we get married. Right?'

She pulled free, pointedly smoothing back her hair. What an idea! Life would never be the same. 'All that shotgun stuff went out decades ago.'

For a brief moment she was scorched by his glare. Then he turned away and began to make tea, silently dropping tea bags into cups, slopping in the milk. He refilled Shona's drink and sat down at the kitchen table. It was almost as if they were back in those weeks when he'd lived there, when they'd readied meals together and eaten them together with Shona yelling and singing from her chair.

He remained silent while Cleo and Shona ate, while Cleo cleaned up Shona's sticky fingers, unclipped her plastic bib and set her free. But she was aware of his gaze and that he hadn't finished yet.

He waited until she settled down to her cooling drink, Shona playing with a wooden spoon and a brown paper bag on the floor. 'Are your parents together?'

Cleo sipped, nodded. She couldn't imagine them, rigid and conformist as they were, doing anything but staying completely married.

'Mine, too.' He'd finished his tea. His eyes were steady now, and calm. 'And that's what I want for my kids. A traditional family, mother and father living together, married if possible.'

'Not everyone does that any more.' But what a wonderful antidote to her loneliness. She flicked her hair out of her eyes. 'And, anyway, your argument's illogical. Why get married if I'm pregnant? We have a child, we aren't married.'

'You're right.' He nodded slowly. 'You'd better marry me anyway.'

She stood suddenly, clattering the plates together and whisking them into the sink. 'Such a romantic, old-fashioned proposal! But no thanks. You don't marry for expediency in this day and age, Justin, you marry for love and togetherness. When nobody else will do.' Steam rose as she ran water into the sink, making her eyes smart.

His voice was just behind her. 'Aren't you tempted? Someone to come home to, to share worries with, a proper sex life ...'

She swung on him suddenly, voice brutal with anger, eyes boiling. 'Don't make me sound like a lonely, desperate old slapper! I'm not needy and I'm not pitiful. I'm fine alone.'

Stoically, he stood his ground. 'I said that very badly.'

She forced out a laugh, raucous and artificial. 'Have you ever thought how many people used to be trapped in loveless, pointless marriages, because they married to legitimise children?'

He relapsed into silence.

Later, when he was leaving, she muttered, 'And anyway, what about when one of us meets the Nobody-Else-Will-Do person? The expedient marriage would dissolve faster than Oxo.'

He stared into the garden, at the enormous feathers of pampas grass nodding and lifting in afternoon light that brightened and faded as thin clouds raced across the sun. 'Possibly. In a marriage of only expediency. Probably. Yes.'

She wasn't pregnant. Her period arrived even before she could see a doctor on Monday morning and she told Justin when he came to visit Shona. 'You're off the hook, scare over,' she breezed. 'I'll be at The Three Fishes if you want me, I'm meeting Dora.' Then to Shona, 'Be a good girl for Justin,' kiss, kiss, 'I'll be home soon.' Back to Justin, 'So that's great, isn't it?'

He accepted the pink and blue sock Shona had just pulled off to deposit in his hand. 'Lovely.'

Chapter Thirty-Six

Muggie's was jumping, as it did every Friday night. Not that Justin was particularly in a nightclub frame of mind. He was annoyed to catch himself scanning the crowd in case Cleo was there with her dippy sister; but there was no sign of her glossy dark hair in the crush. She was probably sitting at home alone while Shona slept upstairs. He tried to push the image away.

He felt as if he was going through the motions: drinking, talent spotting with Martin and Drew. As he didn't feel drawn to any of the talent, he was glad of the distraction when Gez and Jaz turned up. 'Hey! Nice to see you. Gez, you've become a bit of a pipe-and-slippers man since Jaz moved in.'

Jaz laughed. 'Don't wind him up, you know he'll only try and keep up with the big boys.' She was drinking a pint, golden in the lights. It made Justin think of Cleo.

'He'll be fine.'

'Two hours,' predicted Jaz, pragmatically. And, sure enough, Gez insisted on matching Martin and Drew drink for drink and swamped his personal alcohol limit just about in line with her prediction. Jaz dragged him into a taxi and set off home, which left Justin adrift; Martin and Drew had already homed in on the women they'd selected as their targets for the night, not betraying how much they'd drunk by so much as a wobble. Justin, head spinning, envied them their capacity and decided to go and take a leak and then make for the taxi rank and home.

But his dad had always warned him that it was dangerous to be drunk and on your own.

One moment Justin was weaving out of the Gents,

pleasantly hazy. The next, he felt as if a charging buffalo had slammed him against the wall and was stamping on his ribs and stomach with well-placed hooves, each blow crashing into him with such force that he could utter no more than 'Whoof!' as he bounced off the wall.

Doubled over and crowing for breath, he was vaguely aware that the buffalo had vanished. Then some other bloke, large and loud, dragged him to his feet, whisked him round and slammed his arms behind his back. 'Steady on, mate. Had one too many, have we?'

Another, equally large, crowded against him. 'Calm down, calm down. There's no need for that – animal!'

Before he could crow sufficient air into his lungs to demand to know what the hell they were talking about, the bouncers arrived, resplendent in dinner jackets. They hustled him into a back room, along with the two gorillas who had 'restrained' him.

'Just hang about to tell the police what happened,' said the biggest bouncer to the two gorillas. 'And you, mate, you were the one involved, were you?' He was addressing a wiry man with a geometric goatee and a brown jacket. This, by elimination, should be the buffalo.

Justin blinked. No, that couldn't be right. Him? He was just some ordinary geezer, not tall, not broad, not muscly. Surely he hadn't inflicted the stabbing pain in Justin's ribcage and made his stomach feel as if it might heave out its contents at any minute?

Dizzily, he shook his head as he was hustled into a dusty little office and his arms released. He tried to frame truculent challenges. 'What's going on? Are you on something, mate?' But his lips felt like rubber, refusing to form the words, and his brain kept telling his body that he was falling violently sideways, making him stagger.

The police response time was impressive. They were two

well-built, close-cropped men who seemed as if Friday night aggro was all too familiar to them. The instant they rolled in, the buffalo sprang up, clamouring, 'Look at my arm! This bloody animal just went for me, he had a little knife. Like a razor it is.' He was clutching his forearm and blood was oozing through the brown jacket and between his fingers.

Justin wished he could sober up. Then he'd be able to sort out whatever was going on. But he was beginning to feel real alarm. He'd never carried a knife in his life. He tried to snort, 'As if!' It came out as 'Zff!'

Then the gorillas began their support act. 'We had to pull him off. He's obviously rat-arsed.'

And, 'It took two of us to calm him down. "Calm down, mate", I said. But it still took two of us.'

Justin tried to organise his mouth to exclaim just as emphatically that he hadn't even swung a blow. But with the buffalo maintaining, 'He's some piss-head, look what he's done to my arm! Search him, he's got a blade', the officers had to search him. And, sure enough. Would you look at that? A small, red-handled craft knife had appeared in Justin's side jacket pocket.

He was promptly nicked and escorted to a police car with his hands cuffed in front of him, just like in an episode of *The Bill*, and driven through the night-time streets under sodium-orange lights before turning into a gated yard behind the police station. From there he was taken to a holding area, the benches already populated by other arresting officers and Friday night naughty boys and girls.

'I wasn't doing anything!' he protested. But it was a waste of breath insisting that he had only been indulging in the innocent pastime of getting pleasantly pissed with his mates at a nightclub. Most of the other clientele seemed fuelled by alcohol or worse; and it was obviously all in a night's work for the arresting officers, whose navy-blue presence contrasted stolidly with the colourful, often raucous, sometimes nervous, occasionally nauseous miscreants.

'Bit of a queue,' Justin's arresting officer observed, philosophically. 'We'll get you through as soon as possible, mate.' As if he was in any particular hurry to explore the rest of the police station. Though he would have liked to be rid of the handcuffs with the bloody uncomfortable flat hinge between his wrists. The officer joined a discussion on the other side of him as to whether Man United's dominance could last forever and kept trying to draw Justin in. Justin wished he and the constant crackle of police radios would just shut up.

By the time it was Justin's turn before the custody sergeant, speech of a sort was returning. He was booked in as if in some kind of outlandish hotel, read his rights and offered a phone call. He had to empty his pockets and then they took his watch, ring and tie. As if he was going to hang himself. 'I'm not suicidal,' he protested angrily.

The custody sergeant was unmoved. 'Just procedure, mate. You'll get it all back.'

A custody assistant escorted him to a big cupboard where he was handed a bright blue vinyl mattress to cart under his arm through a grey metal door.

He was left alone to gaze at his claustrophobic cell of white tiled walls, a bed, a door with a sliding aperture, a steel toilet and a horrid tracing-paper loo roll balanced on the dwarf wall alongside it.

Sobriety was dawning, with panic chasing. This was all too scarily real. No one had charged in to rescue him or roared with laughter at the joke.

This was him. Justin Mullarkey. Sitting alone in a locked police cell on a Friday night, repelled by the pong of body odour, vomit and disinfectant, the constant racket of shouting against a background of unlikely piped music.

Chapter Thirty-Seven

'Sorry mate, there's no taxi expected at this address.' Justin slammed down the handset of the entry phone system. He squinted at the clock: 06.30. No point trying to get back to sleep, although his eyes felt sandy with the lack of it.

During the night his phone had rung – according to his phone log – at 12.01, 12.56 and 1.30, at which point he'd admitted defeat and turned it off. The evening before, a pizza boy had been very hacked off when Justin had refused delivery of four double-topped extra large pizzas that he hadn't ordered. After that had come a shipping order of Thai food and his entry phone had almost melted from the vocal fury of the thwarted delivery guy.

He trudged off to the shower, totally, absolutely and dreadfully pissed off at the lunatic ex-tenants who were, evidently, making good their threat to 'get' him. Yesterday, he'd seen the long face of the man glaring across the road and up at his windows.

He wasn't scared of such a loser, he thought, standing under the water, as hot as he could stand it – but he was kind of worried about what the loser would do next.

It wasn't hard to get to work on time when he was awake an hour early. Armed with a giant cup of coffee, he pressed the button to set the big monitor of the Apple Macintosh computer humming into life and opened the file he'd been working with on Friday afternoon.

Yet another ladies' razor; yet another set of packaging. The customer's name had to appear in Pantone 185. Everyone went for Pantone 185, widely accepted as the standard 'I'm bright red – look at me!' colour. He yawned and began to mess around with the background blue to make it greyer … better. Then added turquoise around the image of the razor to fizz it up a bit …

His desk phone rang. 'Studio,' he answered, economically.

'It's Neil, can I see you, please, Justin?'

'On way.' Justin groaned inwardly as he replaced the handset. That was all he needed the moment he got down to work. Neil wasn't a bad bloke, OK for a manager, and a better manager than he'd been a graphic artist; but every 'Can I see you, please?' call was a potential elephant trap. Neil was only a couple of years older than Justin, but seemed to have embraced middle age with thinning hair, a thickening waistline and a diminishing sense of humour. Especially Justin's brand of humour.

Neil's office was designed to give customers a funky impression of Rockley: pearl carpet, inviting squashy grey leather chairs, ultra-blue window blinds and a desk of glass and tubular steel. From habit, Justin glanced at the pink-framed Rockley artwork dotting the walls as he lounged in. The cover of a brochure launching a line of dietary supplements was spotlit on the wall above Neil's bulky left shoulder, a pastiche of sexy lime and calming pale blue overlaid with happy healthy faces in soft focus – a design of Justin's.

The leather chairs weren't as comfortable as they looked. Justin took a minute to get settled.

Neil puffed out his cheeks and laid down his pen. His chin and a half wobbled. 'You'd better shut the door.'

Justin heaved himself back out of the chair, shut the door, and broached the chair again with a suppressed sigh.

Neil slid a letter across to Justin's side of the desk. 'What do you make of this?'

The letter was printed on plain white paper.

Dear Sirs,
I feel you ought to know that your employee, Justin
Mullarkey, was arrested on Friday night for attacking
someone in a nightclub.

It was unsigned.

With sweating hands, Justin tossed the letter down. 'This is getting beyond a fucking joke.'

Neil took the page back. 'If one of our employees is arrested, you'll appreciate that we're concerned.' He waited.

Justin massaged his temples. He wouldn't, as he'd hoped, be able to keep it quiet. 'It was a set-up,' he said, flatly. 'All I did was go out and get bladdered with my mates.'

He had no choice but to tell Neil the whole story. 'But,' he concluded, 'when the cops took me for interview, the complainant and witnesses who'd been waiting out the front had mysteriously scarpered. I had to wait while the police checked it all out, then I was released "refused charge". I went through the whole process in reverse. And went home. It was a fucking set-up from start to finish.'

Thoughtfully, Neil smoothed the letter in his hands. 'You're suggesting that a man must've cut his arm purely to incriminate you, then planted the knife?' His credulity was evidently at full stretch.

Justin let his eyes slide to Neil's Rockley artwork collection again. Was it really worth trying to defend himself when he felt so incredibly weary, when his bruised ribs ached every time he took a decent breath? He was sick of pummelling his brain over it, let alone trying to convince Neil. The letter was anonymous, charges had been refused, all that was left was a nasty taste. Rockley could do nothing. He could just shrug it off.

It was, after all, improbable. Even Drew and Martin looked at him sometimes as if he was fantasising, making remarks like, 'Justin's not paranoid, someone really is out to get him!' If he couldn't convince them …

But this bastard, whoever it was – who was he kidding, it had to be the lunatic ex-tenants – had written to his workplace. Could do again.

He shuffled in the chair, winced, and embarked on an account of the whole dreary background. Coming home from Boston to find his tenants still ensconced, his do-it-yourself eviction, Jason Blumfield threatening, 'I'll getchoo!'

The stuff through the letter box, the fire.

He saw Neil's soft jowly face sharpen when he got to that bit, the arson being such common knowledge.

'The police interviewed the ex-tenants but they had alibis. Recently they've become cleverer with their nuisance crusade and set things up that they can organise remotely. I get deliveries I haven't ordered, they ring in the middle of the night, then ring off.'

'Can't you ring 1471?'

He resisted the impulse to demand, 'Do you think I'm too stupid to think of that?' and said, instead, 'The calls are coming from an unregistered prepaid mobile, which means they're untraceable.' He realised he was rubbing his temples again. He did it so much these days he'd end up with fingerprints in his head.

He clasped his hands together. 'I've been sent enough takeaways to feed a stag party, taxis have turned up on the hour, every hour for an entire night, people phone to buy my car, my flat, my bed, and even my garden shed.'

He stifled a yawn. The disturbed nights were really getting to him.

'But you don't have a garden,' Neil objected.

'So I don't have a shed, either.' Justin groaned. 'I'm conceding this round and accepting a new phone number – before they begin advertising my services in phone boxes as a rent boy!'

Neil laughed, Justin didn't. Instead he said, sombrely, 'It's a real hate campaign. Ignoring it hasn't made it go away. I'm going to move out. I don't want to because they'll have won and also some other poor sod might inherit my troubles. But I can't go on like this – I can't even have my daughter to stay.' Shona. His blood ran cold at the thought of her being mixed up in some lunatic's grudge.

Neil locked the anonymous letter in his desk drawer. 'Why don't you go to the police?'

Justin climbed awkwardly to his feet. 'Have done. They're sympathetic but the Blumfields are getting smart. There's no evidence to link them to any of it. They were even on holiday in Ayia Napa when some calls were made – presumably having got some other low life to campaign on their behalf. Police say there's little they can do but advise me to keep an incident log. They're sympathetic, agree a crime has been committed, but ...' He shrugged.

Cleo glanced through the kitchen window when she heard the gate clatter. 'Justin's here,' she told Shona, who immediately made for the front door.

He smiled and swung Shona up when Cleo opened the door, but he didn't look good. Recently he'd been too pale, too tired, his smile too forced to be natural. 'I should've rung, but I was around and wondered if I could spend a bit of time with her.'

Cleo smiled. 'Brilliant. You entertain her, I'll whiz through my jobs.'

She washed up listening to giggles, happy squeals and deep laughs while Justin rolled Shona round the sitting-room floor. It sounded fun.

She crossed the one-step hall to the sitting-room doorway. 'Fancy getting her ready for bed and doing the story routine?'

'Sure.' His eyes seemed big in his face.

Shona was soon fresh in doggy-embroidered pyjamas, and Cleo blitzing her ironing pile instead of it lurking for later, while Justin's voice upstairs rose and fell on the rhythms of the bedtime story. He was great at stories, giving the characters ridiculous voices, making Shona breathless with giggles. When Cleo read, it was to continuous interruptions from Shona of 'Woss zat?' or 'Yook!'

Eventually his footsteps returned softly down the stairs. Cleo, breathing in the pleasant warmth of ironed clothes, heard him go into the sitting room.

By the time she'd put the iron away he was asleep in the chair. But his eyes flipped open as she crossed the room.

'Are you ill?' she asked, gently.

He sighed. 'Just sick of hassle.'

She sat down, legs crossed, on the floor in front of him. 'Tell me.'

He rubbed his forehead. 'I suppose I'd better, in case any of it affects Shona. It's mad, it's incredible – but the nuisance calls and stuff I was getting have got completely out of hand. A funeral director rang today, saying that he understood I had need of his services.' And suddenly he was like a pot boiling over with a froth of horrible deliveries and calls and stuff.

'So, having no wish to be arrested again, I'm leaving the flat,' he concluded. He hesitated, hitched himself forward on the chair. 'Cleo, we get on OK, reconsider about our buying somewhere together! I want to be near Shona. She's mine as much as yours, I love her too. It worked OK before, didn't it?'

Oh no. Hadn't he got this out of his head yet? This crazy idea that would be great in the short term but probably hell in the end? She tried her best to smile. 'Like some old brother and sister left on the shelf together? Why should either of us settle for that? We've talked about this and it won't work.'

'I think it would.'

'Maybe now, you think that. You're exhausted and at your wits' end. You're not yourself. Once you're free of all this shit you'll bounce back, go out on the pull with Martin and Drew, get into all the relationships you deserve. Then sharing a house with me will be a burden. I'll be in the way.'

She got up, flooding the room with yellow light as she switched on the lamp, making him blink and squint. 'And anyway, I've just started seeing someone. I don't need you cluttering the place up.'

Chapter Thirty-Eight

Cleo rarely saw Ratty. He'd been kind in an offhand way, renting her a home when she really needed somewhere. The rent vanished from her account once a month and presumably materialised safely in his. But he did call in occasionally to check his asset wasn't being devalued, stepping in and out of economical conversations without preamble.

'You're cramped here,' he observed, stepping carefully over Shona's new yellow plastic teapot. He had a black spaniel puppy called Button tucked under his arm, wagging its tail and trying to lick his chin. Button's black, curly fur was a lot like Ratty's hair.

Cleo sighed. 'I know. But there's hardly anything up for sale in the proper village, only up in the Bankside bit where they're all too new.'

'Yeah.' He pulled a face. 'I do know an older one that might suit you, though. Elderly bloke called Patrick lives there, but he's going into sheltered accommodation. I can introduce you if you're interested, before he instructs agents.'

Her spirits hopped up a gear. 'Wow, yes!'

'We can stroll up there.' He moved towards the front door and Cleo, suddenly realising that he meant now, had to dart around for jackets and shoes and Shona's buggy while he waited in the garden where he could put Button down to shake his long ears and snuffle at the gateposts.

The house was on the way out of the village, much further up Port Road, on the left. Extended and chopped about in less building-control-conscious times, the add-ons were red brick and not the original russet ironstone. But the modifications were so old that any discord had mellowed.

The roof tiles were speckled with moss. The house was just what Cleo wanted: quirky, not conventionally pretty but with its own charm.

A jungle of a garden surrounded the house and backed onto flat farmland.

Cleo gazed about her as she recovered her breath from the pace of Ratty's 'stroll' and they waited for Patrick to answer the door. A big shambling man leaning on two walking sticks, he apologised for not shaving, clucked at Shona and stick-stepped his way back to his tall armchair.

'Well, now,' he said, after a knees-locked and obviously painful descent to his seat, peering at Cleo carefully through thick glasses. 'Well, now. I think you might just look round, eh? That all right? Because I don't get about like I did. Any questions and I'll be here, watching the TV.'

Cleo tried to stop Shona tugging herself free of her restraining hand. 'If you don't mind.'

He let out a wheezy cough. 'This is the sitting room, you can see that. This door's to the dining room, that to the kitchen. Go through the kitchen and there's another door, that's your scullery. Do people still call them that? Well, now, young Rattenbury, how are your parents, do you know? This is your new dog, then? And how's your new wife?'

Cleo left them to talk. Excitement sent butterflies fluttering inside her chest. The house was lovely. Or could be, in time. Warm and welcoming with just a sniff of comfortable old-house mustiness.

She looked around a sitting room crowded with a large blue seventies-type suite plus Patrick's old-man armchair in a green that didn't go, a hulking sideboard, a coffee table, two footstools and the television in a cabinet. Rainbows of crocheted throws stretched across chair arms and sofa backs. What could be seen of the carpet was a riot of black and orange circles, pristine, as if no one ever set a shoe to it. Cleo hated the furniture, the carpet and the paisley wallpaper, surely put together by a colour-blind decorator.

But it could be a lovely room.

French doors led into the back garden. Beams supported the low ceiling and the fireplace was stone. Answering absently as Ratty called his snuffly black dog and called goodbye, Cleo pushed open a creaky door into a dining room crowded with display cabinets, dusty silk plants on stands, a single bed with a quilted bedspread, and a wardrobe. Evidently, it was Patrick's bedroom these days. She backtracked to the kitchen.

Oh dear! Units that must've been wheeled in around 1950 had been painted in shades of mud around their reeded glass panes. A pot sink big enough to wash a baby hippopotamus hugged the wall under the window. The cooker – a relic – crouched close by and a fat, white microwave perched incongruously on a table by the wall. The scullery contained an even bigger white sink, maybe in case the mother hippo also fancied a swill, and a huge mangle.

A door beside the mangle led to an up-to-date loo, a welcome late modification.

As she crossed back to the hall and stairs, Patrick warned, 'It'll be a bit neglected upstairs, because I don't get about. I live down here.' He switched his attention back to the television as the audience erupted amidst wildly flashing lights. 'There, you see, he's done it!' he cried, as a jubilant on-screen contestant accepted congratulations from the presenter. 'There was one last week, too.' His watery eyes shone with the pleasure of witnessing some stranger's success.

Cleo left him to his game show. The stairs, steep and with no handrail, were heavy going with a toddler collapsing tiredly against her shoulder. But apart from dust, thirty-year-old decor and a collection of lampshades like flying saucers, upstairs wasn't bad. An elderly double bed stood stripped and forlorn in the largest bedroom with a wide oak wardrobe alongside; but the other two rooms were empty. The carpets, in bold colours and sculptured patterns, had obviously been treated as carefully as the downstairs ones. Pity they were so damned ugly.

The bathroom was much in keeping with the rest, as if it had been fitted at the beginning of the seventies and never touched again: a white cast-iron bath with a black panel, black and yellow vinyl floor tiles, a mean quantity of white wall tiles veined in mustard and a basin like a bird bath.

From the bedroom at the back, the smaller of the two doubles, she gazed out over field after field after field across the fens, enjoying the sensation of space.

The main bedroom looked out across the road to a smallholding with a house and orchard. It would be a great view when the blossom was out. The whole house felt … peaceful. This could be a wonderful place to bring her daughter up.

When she reappeared downstairs, Patrick smiled. 'Roof still on, is it?'

She laughed. 'Seems to be.'

'Good. Good. Well, now.'

Cleo sat down with her daughter drowsy and hot against her neck and prepared to find out how much Patrick wanted for his house, hardly daring to hope she could have it.

'Stay here, tonight.'

Justin's droopy eyelids lifted. 'Are you making me a rude offer?'

She could. Perfect opportunity. Could be flip, say, 'OK last time, wasn't it?' Because it had been triple OK for her. Temptation wriggled down her spine. Have to let him sleep first; he looked too knackered to raise an eyebrow –

Stop it, she told herself severely. 'I was thinking about the air bed. You'd at least get eight hours' uninterrupted sleep.'

When he dropped his head back, shut his eyes and groaned like that, it reminded her of when he … 'Eight hours' sleep! Sounds like bliss. Last night, those bastards sent four taxis. Would you truly not mind me crashing here again?'

She picked up the empty coffee mugs. 'Truly. You can crawl in the sleeping bag and I'll tell you all about my new house. You'll be asleep in about a minute.'

In fact, she was amazed that he was even awake when she put her head back around the door. The normally sharp lines of his face almost sagged with fatigue but he was in his makeshift bed, eyes open. 'Ready for my bedtime story,' he joked. 'What about this brilliant new house?'

So she sprawled on the sofa and explained and described and enthused, watching his lids fluttering from time to time and imagining how her sentences must be swimming and breaking up in his ears. Letting her eyes run across his naked upper chest and arms as his closed.

'So, can you afford it?'

She pulled a face. '*Just*, if I can get a mortgage. The only thing I won't have is furniture.'

'So,' he yawned. 'What's the new boyfriend think of it?'

'Clive? He hasn't seen it. He's not officially a boyfriend yet, anyway. He's "someone I'm seeing" – I'm being offish until I make up my mind.'

He yawned again, the helpless, jaw-cracking, eye-watering yawn of the desperate for sleep. 'Nice bloke?'

She thought about Clive who she'd met at a Team Spirit workshop. He was nice. Separated, no kids, big brown eyes, hair in a collar-length 1970s style a bit like a young Barry Gibb. Just an ordinary bloke who worked in insurance and, in his spare time, wrote horror for the smaller subscription-only magazines. He'd hung around after the workshop to talk, shaking his hair out of his eyes and looking bashful, but made surprisingly short work of establishing that she was free to go out with him. 'Very nice bloke,' she agreed, with bright enthusiasm. And went on to describe the views from the windows of her house-to-be.

When Justin's breathing was even and slow, she took herself up to her own bed to worry about how the hell she was going to afford little things like food, shoes and clothing.

Gav waited in the pub. Facing the door, he'd see her when she arrived in her usual whirl because she never seemed to get away from her desk promptly, hair tossed, jacket open. He took his glasses off and tucked them into his top pocket.

And there she was, flying in as if she'd travelled on the wind as a sudden flurry of rain clattered against the windows. He waved.

'Summer can't come soon enough,' she observed, dropping into a seat and grabbing a menu. 'Shall we order?' She glanced at her watch. 'I must be back for a two-fifteen meeting. I think I'll have a hot chicken sandwich and white wine.'

Waiting to give their order at the bar, he turned sideways so that he could watch her but glide his eyes away quickly if she turned and caught him. She looked great. It felt great to be with her again. His heart felt light for the first time in weeks. He missed her and it had been a masterstroke to use an excuse about paperwork of hers he'd found in his things to suggest meeting for lunch on a working day. It was just like old times; he could almost kid himself that there was no Shona and no separation. As if they'd just made time for each other in a busy day, like they used to, and he'd be going home to her tonight.

He returned to the table with two glasses of wine. 'So what's new?' He kind of meant, 'What's new at work?' because that's what she used to tell him about, indignant about all the planning she'd done for XYZ Co. only to have them hum and haver and change the brief. In those days, of course, he already knew just about everything else that happened in her life, except, maybe, what she and Liza found to giggle about. And, it turned out, her lover.

What he didn't want to hear about was her eventful Saturday, deciding to *buy a house* and letting that bastard-bastard *stay over*.

'Hasn't he got a home of his own?' Look at that, he'd drunk half his wine in a slurp.

A frown settled over her eyes. 'You wouldn't believe what's happening to him. He's become the victim of some lunatic's hate campaign! Taxis and pizzas turn up at all times so he can't sleep, people answering adverts he never placed. It's a nightmare.'

What a pity, what an awful list of awful things. 'Couldn't happen to a nicer chap,' he said, mock-pleasantly.

Slowly, she sipped her wine. 'I suppose this is where I ask how Lillian is,' she responded. 'If you want to get into a pissing match?'

'Haven't drunk enough yet.' He grinned. After a moment she grinned back and everything was OK, as long as he didn't mind listening to endless reflections on how quickly she hoped the house sale would go through and how in the world she was going to afford everything. He hoped she wasn't leading up to asking for some of their furniture, which he now looked upon as his, set out in his rented house in Bettsbrough. He wouldn't mind it being theirs again; but he sure as hell didn't want any of it to be hers.

He changed the subject. 'Doing anything interesting this weekend?'

A young barman brought their sandwiches over and Cleo gave him a smile. 'I'm going out with Liza on Friday.'

Liza was a safe topic. She'd talk about Liza until the cows came home. 'How is she?'

A laugh. He missed her laugh. Particularly on Sunday mornings when he lay in bed alone and remembered how they used to mock-squabble over the papers, how he'd tickle her or pretend to beat her up to get the interesting pages first. 'Liza doesn't change much. Except she's in lurve with an astonishingly normal bloke called Adam who's about to move in with her.'

'Sounds like a recipe for disaster.'

She shrugged, cutting her sandwich into smaller pieces. 'Don't see why. He likes drinking and nightclubs so it's a match made in heaven.'

The sandwiches were too hot to eat without a lot of blowing and rapid chewing as if getting the scalding mouthful down the gullet was somehow preferable to having it on the tongue. Between scalding bites, he told her about working at Hillson's and how Keith was having a heavy thing with a married woman. Then, like a bad tooth he was unable to resist probing, he veered back onto the subject of Justin. 'So, Father of the Year doesn't mind babysitting on Friday? Even if there's nothing in it for him?' He couldn't stop the heavily sarcastic emphasis in his last few words.

Her eyes glittered. 'He babysits because Shona's his daughter. Of course there's "nothing in it".' She paused. 'Because I'm seeing someone called Clive.' She tipped her wrist to look at her watch. 'I'll give coffee a miss this time.'

Heart sinking slowly to his gut, he watched her shrug into her jacket.

Not even a peck on the cheek. Not even a friendly clasp of hands. He checked the time. One forty five. Loads of time to toddle up the street to Ntrain for a two-fifteen meeting. She had had time for coffee.

She'd obviously wanted to get away.

He'd leave it a week or two before he suggested lunch again.

In fact, Cleo was seeing Clive that evening. A date that had reached its end in her car where condensation was forming on the windows. Clive's lips, framed by the softness of his beard, snuffled their way up the side of her neck. She tried not to squirm when it tickled, nor be reminded of Ratty's little dog. A change of course and his mouth reached hers, soft, searching. And he kissed her, slowly, deeply.

Mmm. Gentle, rather than demanding, but nice. Nice-ish. Not the kind of kisses that made her back tingle, though.

His arms tightened and he whispered, 'Coffee?' He kissed her ear and his hand burrowed inside her jacket. Cleo wasn't so rusty that she didn't recognise Clive's invitation meant a token cup of coffee and 'this is our fifth date, I'm hoping for a hell of a lot more. I've done the hand-holding, it's about time we had sex.' Clive's house was empty and available, Justin would by now be dossed down on her sitting-room floor ready to attend to Shona, and there was absolutely no reason for her to be home until breakfast.

She thought about sex with Clive as he industriously worked his lips across her forehead and eyes. Clive, whose soft beard and gentle good looks actually hid the mind of a guy who wrote about swinging corpses and mouldy bodies for entertainment. Hmm. Fun for him was sitting in front of his computer, working out the sexual dynamics of an unnatural relationship with a werewolf. Hmm-mm.

Now what kind of a bedmate might a man like that be? Sensitive? Unlikely. Exciting? Possibly. Imaginative? Ought to be. Hopefully not ... y'know, *odd*.

She shivered. 'Sorry. Babysitter.'

Clive found her lips again with his. 'Sure?'

'Sure.'

Kiss. 'OK.' Kiss. 'Will you be all right driving home?'

'I usually am.'

'Sure you can't stay?'

'Not this time.'

He stopped kissing her, his expression rueful. 'You're really not ready to take this relationship further, are you?'

She squeezed his hand and withdrew it from inside her jacket. 'You're very understanding.'

A very long kiss. 'Another time.' His voice was heavy with promise. Still no tingles.

Cleo began the fifteen-minute drive home.

Maybe next time she would go to bed with him. There was nothing to stop her and it might be nice. She'd even got her own supply of condoms for her handbag.

These days, condoms were essential for all new encounters. Just look at how Gav could have avoided trouble – there would have been no suspicion of unwelcome infection if he'd used condoms for his little adventure with Lillian.

Everyone ought to be protected by condoms what with AIDS and other nasties, hence the obligation to carry her own, according to Liza. But what if the ones Cleo had bought were the wrong size or shape …? After all, one size certainly didn't fit all. Imagine the dismay if a lover didn't fill out the condom she supplied to him. Maybe she should have bought a sort of selection box.

'Pretty bloody complicated,' she said aloud, as she swung out of Bettsbrough and onto the road to Middledip. 'Maybe I'll leave it a bit longer.'

Chapter Thirty-Nine

'I was beginning to think you'd forgotten!' She stepped back to let Justin in. 'Shona's been standing on a chair watching for you – now she's lurking in the sitting room, punishing you for being late.' She pushed the sitting-room door open to show Shona, kneeling on the floor, back to the door, studiously hitting a doll with a brush.

Justin's grin wiped a layer of strain from his face. 'I'll have to sort her out.'

Shona shot to her feet. 'No, no!' She giggled, eyes each a separate sparkle in the curves of her face, and began to edge backwards, ready to be chased. Her favourite game.

In the furore of squeals and roars, Cleo stepped into her shoes and slipped into her jacket. During a lull, she managed to be heard. 'I'll be on my mobile. I'm going for a drink with Liza.'

'OK.'

'Sorry everywhere's such a tip, I've been having a spring clean ready to hand the house back. And as quickly as I pack up ready for the move, Shona unpacks it.'

'Don't worry.'

Slowly she put her hand up to unlatch the door. 'I won't be late.'

'Fine.' He pretended to bite at Shona's fingers when she pinched his nose. Shona yipped in delight and did it again.

Cleo rested her hand on the door latch. 'Is everything all right? You seem ...'

He shrugged, as well as he could with Shona on his shoulder, meeting her eyes. 'The usual. You know.'

She let her hand drop. 'What is it this time? A shipping

order of Indian food? A three-piece suite from a catalogue?'

'On the way here I was pulled over by the police.'

She let her head tip to one side. 'That can't be anything to do with malicious person unknown, can it?'

'It can if the police have had information that I'm ferrying drugs.' He tipped Shona slowly off his shoulders and caught her upside down, her rich giggles pouring out like bubbles.

Cleo slowly shook her head. 'They're getting cleverer, aren't they?'

''Fraid so. Now I've got five days to produce my documents at a police station. Just another hassle. I thought once I'd let my flat I'd be able to see an end to it. But if they've got hold of my car registration it gives them another avenue of attack.'

Cleo moved back into the room. 'Can you change your car?'

He turned Shona up the right way, brought her red, giggling face up to his and kissed her little bobble nose. 'What's the point? They'd only get the new registration the same way they got this, wouldn't they?'

'Poor old Justin.' Liza got herself comfortable on the bench seat of the pub and held out a foot to admire her new red ankle boots that were decorated with pompoms and went beautifully with her new black lacy tights. Apart from her white therapy tunic workwear, Liza never wore anything plain or boring, if she could help it. 'And he normally seems one of the most difficult-to-worry people.'

Cleo checked that her phone would pick up a signal. 'I don't know if he's worried, exactly, more fed up. The phone calls at all hours of the night were bad enough, and meals and taxis turning up. But the fight at the club was just plain frightening. He could have been knifed or anything. Then the scumbags had the cheek to send an anonymous letter about it to his employer.'

Liza frowned. 'Can't the police do anything?'

'No evidence. The people he's certain are behind it all have got damned good at it. Very inventive. Now he's changed his phone number, alerted all the takeaways and arranged to let the flat, they've started on his car.'

'Gruesome. I haven't seen him at Muggie's for the last couple of weeks, either. Shall we open the crisps? So what about Gav? Seen him lately?'

Cleo gazed into her crisps. There were so few in a bag these days it was a wonder anyone ever got fat on them. 'I met him for lunch this week.'

Liza snorted. 'What on earth *for*?'

Cleo shrugged defensively. 'Because he asked me. Because he seems a bit lost and I felt sorry for him. You know that I always felt guilty about him.'

'What on earth did you talk about?'

'We sometimes talk about Keith and Ian, Dora and Rhianne. He says things like, "We used to do everything together, three couples, and now we've all broken up. Who'd have thought it?" And he usually can't resist having a dig at Justin.'

Liza balled up her crisp bag and delicately sucked her fingers, one at a time. Her nail art featured dominoes today. 'Have you told him about Clive?'

'Sure, but it seems to pass him by. It's definitely Justin he's got the hate for.'

Liza raised her fair eyebrows. 'And when do I get to give Clive my seal of approval, by the way?'

'You don't need to, he's nice. Kind and gentle.' Somehow it didn't sound like a commendation.

'I'd like you to be happy with someone again, Cleo. Like I am with my fabulous Adam. Do you ever wonder if you'd met Justin after breaking up with Gav, whether you'd have got it together? Then you'd be sitting here boring me about how lovely and kind he is?'

Cleo considered. 'He's not always lovely or kind. But mostly.'

'Was Gav?'

'I would've thought so, once, but he hid a lot, didn't he? Infertility. Suspected clap. Infidelity. Not lovely or kind.'

Cleo let herself into the quiet house. From the sofa, Justin looked up from his book and waved half a pack of biscuits. 'I pinched your biscuits.'

She dropped down beside him, kicked off her shoes and snaffled two. 'You unerringly discover the chocolate digestives.'

He took another. 'I know where you hide them, at the back of the top shelf. At least I didn't pinch the Hobnobs.'

She laughed. 'I'll have to think of somewhere new.'

'Waste of time, I'll find them.' He twisted the top of the biscuit packet over. 'Looking forward to moving into your new house?'

She beamed. 'Absolutely! It'll be difficult, though. The bank wouldn't give me as much as I wanted and the bills are endless. Surveyor, solicitor, you name it. It's a good job Patrick is leaving the carpets because I won't be able to afford any for about two years. I've got my bed and Shona's cot, and that's about it. We'll have to camp until my Christmas bonus. If business has been good enough for Nathan to pay one.'

'I'll lend you a deckchair.' He stretched, hunting around for his shoes, jacket and keys, dropped a careless peck on her hair and let himself out with an equally careless ''Bye!'

She sat on after the sound of his car had faded, staring into the fire and thinking about how these cottage suites might not be very comfortable with their wooden arms but they were, at least, something to sit on. If she didn't get that Christmas bonus, she'd be reduced to furnishing her sitting room with beanbags.

And, with Patrick eager to sell and Cleo eager to buy, the conveyancing formalities swept Cleo through the next couple of weeks. So it was no wonder that her mind was only half on her work when she answered the phone on her desk.

'Hello, stranger!' Clive's voice was light, teasing.

Cleo adjusted the phone between her shoulder and head. 'It's only two days since I saw you, Clive. And … ah. I was supposed to phone you last night.' With her free hand she used the mouse to try various colours on a chart she was creating for a seminar introduction.

He chuckled understandingly. 'I expect your head was in packing boxes and your mind setting out the furniture in your new house.'

'Half right. Unfortunately, setting out my furniture isn't going to be a long job.'

'So, is the packing finished?'

She sighed. ''Fraid not. It's not very easy with Shona around and she doesn't seem to want to go to bed at the moment. I can't believe how much stuff there is of hers alone. But tonight Liza's coming over to entertain her and I might make progress.'

His turn to sigh. 'So you're not coming out? Any chance of a nice long, late-night phone call?'

'Um …' Actually, she craved the pleasure of flaking out after yet another evening sorting possessions into supermarket boxes on top of all her other evening chores. Once Clive began to tell her about what editors had said about his latest zombie mash-up, she could be on the phone for an hour.

'So how about tomorrow night?'

She tried to make her voice matter-of-fact rather than apologetic. 'Justin's coming to see Shona, so I should just about get finished with the packing. But completion's on Monday and my tenancy is officially up, so getting ready to move is my priority.'

His voice went flat. 'OK, I get the picture. You're busy. Moving house, looking after your daughter. And your daughter's father to play Happy Families with. The only good thing about going out with you, Cleo, is that I get a lot of stories written because we never actually go out.'

'We could do something on Sunday,' she suggested guiltily. 'If you don't mind the house being like a tip, I'll cook you dinner –'

'Brilliant!' He agreed so quickly and sounded so pleased that she realised with a sinking feeling, as she replaced the phone, that he thought he might get lucky.

She glanced at the clock in the corner of her computer screen. And then again, in amazement. Good God! How did it get to twelve fifteen? Now she'd be late to meet Gav. Again.

Struggling into her coat, cantering down the stairs rather than hanging on for the lift, scurrying along the pavement, weaving through halted cars, hopping on and off traffic islands.

The pub was on a corner. Tall, white, bay windows jutting into the street: a favourite office-worker lunch venue.

Bowling through the door, she found Gav tucking away his mobile phone. 'Phew!' she laughed. 'I thought I might have missed you.'

He didn't answer her smile. 'I was just ringing your office.' He looked pointedly at his watch. She recognised his expression. Gav was sulking at her bad timekeeping and was waiting to be won round.

She shrugged out of her coat and plonked herself in a chair, swooping on the menu. She called to the barman, 'Could I have a stilton and bacon ciabatta, please? I'm a bit short of time.'

Gav waited until the barman had taken the order. 'I can't bear the smell of stilton.'

Absently, she nodded. In fact, she realised, she'd ordered it specifically to annoy him. Liza was right – she shouldn't let him hang about like a stale smell. Their marriage was well and truly over and there was no point in swapping news over a toasted sandwich and a glass of wine as if they were a couple. They no longer were. End of.

But she put off telling him, because she didn't want to think of him being hurt. Crazy how it was so easy to postpone something so important.

'So,' he said glumly. 'What's new?'

'I had a lovely day out with Clive and Shona at the weekend. A nice lunch and then a long walk along the embankment in Bedford, watching the canoeists bobbing about.'

He grunted. 'I thought you said it wasn't serious?'

She examined her ring finger, now bare. 'We don't need to be serious to have lunch and a walk.'

'Anything more interesting?'

'My packing's driving me mad. Liza's entertaining Shona tonight and Justin's doing the same tomorrow, so I really ought to get finished.'

His expression set. 'How very accommodating of Justin. I don't suppose you're ever going to be free of him, now. You've let him get too fond of the girl.'

Anger flickered through her. '"*The girl*" – you mean my daughter, Shona? Justin's daughter? You think I ought to have deprived Shona of her father?'

He shrugged. His bacon and mushroom baguette arrived

and he snatched it up to bite into it as if it had done him a personal injury.

He'd always been a bad loser, even at Pictionary or Monopoly. Now, of course, Cleo didn't have to put up with it. She could even antagonise him. 'Did I mention?' Her voice sounded unnaturally clear and high. 'We discussed moving in together, me and Justin? Just on a house-share basis. That way Shona would have both her parents –'

Bang! Gav's fist crashed down on the wooden table so hard that the whole bar paused.

Cleo froze, her food halfway to her mouth.

With eyes of stone he hissed, 'You're never going to share a house with that bastard if I've got anything to do with it.'

The following silence seemed even louder than the crashing of his fist.

Steadily, she reached for her coat, tucking her bag and her lunch under her arm. 'But you haven't got anything to do with it.'

She was angry all the way back to the office. Then he sent a text of a sad face and she began to feel sorry for him all over again ...

But then she received a call from her garage to say that her car had failed its MOT and she felt sorrier for herself.

Chapter Forty

It was a pain, having to drive back into Peterborough after picking Shona up from Dora's. But good old Dora had made Shona a soft cheese roll to keep her going while Cleo took care of her bit of business. Business that had to be broached this evening, now, before she lost her bottle.

She found the road, keyed his flat number into the security thingy, waited for the tinned sound of his voice, then pushed in through the door and trod upstairs at Shona's pace. He was waiting for them at his front door.

'Jussin!' squealed Shona, letting go of Cleo's hand and launching into her bouncing run.

'This is handy,' he grinned, swooping her up. 'I've just bought some biscuits.'

Cleo had to wait for Shona to get over the excitement of seeing Justin, being somewhere new and having a biscuit in each hand. Sitting on his sofa, Cleo tried not to be mega-aware of the door to his bedroom. Shona finally settled in front of the big television with her favourite satellite channel, *Nick Junior*, and Justin plumped down beside Cleo.

'It was a pleasant surprise when I heard your voice. I was sure it'd be another delivery or taxi.'

'Bob!' Shona shouted, launching herself to her feet to point at the television.

'Bob the Builder,' Cleo agreed. 'Your favourite.' Shona sank back down to the carpet.

Justin still looked tired, strained. The tiny lines that ran away from his startling eyes seemed more deeply grooved. When he flashed a grin, she could see how those lines had formed over the course of a hundred thousand smiles.

Right, deep breath. Say it. 'I have a proposition for you. I mean a proposal,' she amended quickly to try and forestall the clever-clever remark she saw coming.

Obviously a failure, as he replied, 'I'll say yes to either.'

She tried to frown him down. His eyes shone with silent laughter.

She cleared her throat. 'Right. The thing is ... do you remember saying ...' Why was she making such heavy weather of this? She who'd been specifically trained to be articulate, cogent, concise, to get up in front of any amount of people and engage and maintain their attention? She metaphorically squared her shoulders.

'I'm going to find things tough, financially, with the new house. And it really hasn't been helped by an unexpected car bill of over five hundred pounds.'

He frowned. 'Ought I to be paying more towards Shona's keep?'

She flushed. 'That wasn't what I meant! I've come to tell you that I've made a decision to take in a lodger, preferably one with their own furniture that I can share the use of.'

He looked dubious. 'I suppose that's sensible. So long as it's the right person.' His gaze flicked automatically to Shona.

She dropped her eyes. 'I wondered if you'd be interested.'

He stared. 'But you swore you didn't want to house share with me. What about all the stuff about girlfriends and boyfriends at breakfast?'

'I still don't want to buy a house with you. The offer is for you to be a paying guest and the first six months would be on a trial basis. The rent will be reasonable but I'm not offering to do your washing or pick up your towels. There's a double room each, plus a single for Shona, we'd have to share the other rooms and you might hate it. But it'll get you out of this place, in the short term. And solve some of my financial woes, also in the short term.' There. Concise and cogent.

If she'd anticipated that he'd leap on the suggestion with bellows of joy, she was in for a disappointment. Instead, his frown deepened. So she added, 'Perhaps you'd better think about it.' Was she disappointed? No, of course not. It was just a possible solution, one she'd been toying with and, until Gav had pissed her off so much, hadn't been serious about. But it *was* definitely a solution, even if only for six months.

But she hadn't foreseen such a complete lack of enthusiasm. He was staring at Shona who was bouncing her nappied bottom on the floor in excitement that *Paddington Bear* was beginning. He turned back to Cleo. 'What if all the crap stuff comes with me? Then it'll be your house bombarded with pizzas and dog turds, taxis and fire bombs. It'll be you and Shona, not just me.'

'Oh.' She hadn't even thought about it.

A silence developed as the idea circulated her brain, a silence except for *Nick Junior* and her heartbeat. This very room had been filled with black smoke, the kitchen, the bedroom where they'd had the sex they never talked about now. If Shona had been there the night of the fire ... Panic nipped her throat.

Be sensible. Think. Slowly, she said, 'It's never followed you to my house. You've stayed over, you stayed for weeks and nothing happened.'

He hesitated. 'True. But I'd hate to bring my problems with me.' He sighed and rubbed his eyes with the heels of his hands. 'They're nothing to do with you, after all.'

'We could give it a go.'

Wearily, he smiled. 'Really?'

'Really.'

With a deep sigh, he let his head fall back. 'Cleo, it would be brilliant. I've got to get out of here. If I hear that tosser shout, "I'll getchoo!" again I'll smack him one. Then I'll get arrested again.'

Gav stared at his phone and thought about making a call. A simple call, an everyday occurrence.

He checked his watch.

Looked at the phone.

She'd been so annoyed with him today, left him sitting in the pub like some idiot with a half-eaten lunch and a nasty taste in his mouth. He'd managed things very badly, starting on that bastard Justin. He should've learnt that it always made her edgy.

But why? She insisted there was nothing between them, apart from the child. She insisted it was right to let the child and its father remain close. What was right about it? What claim did bastard Justin have to the bastard child, anyway? Surely any rights ought to be nullified, forfeit, by his stealing another man's wife to grow his child in.

His wife. She'd been his wife. Still was, officially, although she was so far from him now, separated by time, a lover, a child. A child he couldn't give her. It wasn't fair, that. He hadn't asked to be infertile, didn't deserve it, that terrible condition that had robbed him of everything.

His wife. His Cleo. His lover, partner, friend.

The lunches had been a good idea, he knew, because they almost brought that old Cleo back into focus, to when her body had been his, not known by bastard Justin, not a host to a baby. His.

But today he'd let his temper get the better of him. He should have continued to be the good-natured guy he could be for her.

Now he'd screwed up. She'd been so cold, so angry, he couldn't settle until he'd straightened things out. He reached for the phone.

'It's me,' he began, cheerfully. He liked to begin, 'It's me,' not, 'It's Gav.' That would be suggesting she might not recognise his voice. He hurried on before she could speak, letting his voice become boyishly rueful, apologetic, but with undertones of mischief. 'I know you're busy, I won't keep you more than a second – I just wanted to say sorry about today. You're dead right, it's nothing to do with me, I promise in future to keep my opinions to myself. Are we still friends? Puh-leeze?'

Silence. Then a giggle. 'As I presume that nauseating creeping was intended for Cleo, I'll call her.' A rattle as the phone was dropped carelessly. Waves of mortification swept up his body. *Bloody* Liza! He imagined her laughing, repeating what he'd just said. Perhaps making Cleo laugh too.

His mind churned rapidly, choosing words to redeem the situation. So he groaned when Cleo finally reached the phone, made his voice strained, half-anguished, half-laughing at his own misery. 'I'm afraid I've just mistakenly abased myself at your sister's feet! I rang to apologise for being so unforgivably arsey today but now you'll think I'm more of a prick than ever. I'd better put the phone down before things get any worse –'

She didn't let him do that; he'd known she wouldn't. She sighed. 'You shouldn't give me a hard time, Gav.'

Cleo might be a bad lass sometimes, but she had a good heart that wouldn't let him ring off until he seemed reasonably happy. He could spin the process out and get a larger slice of her time. 'I know, but the whole situation's hard on me, Cleo ...' When he finally put the phone down he felt better about everything.

She was meeting him for lunch again next week.

He'd make it up to her.

'Well?' Justin held the door open, looking back expectantly at Martin, Drew and Gez.

They slid lower in their seats, gazing through the windscreen. After a moment Drew said, 'We'll wait here while you check things out.'

Justin shrugged, jumped out of the cab of the box van, took the path to the front door and knocked. He heard a window above his head open and tipped his head back to find Cleo grinning down at him, hair swinging either side of her face. 'I'm here,' he pointed out.

'So you are. The door's unlocked, come and join the madhouse!'

He twisted the black iron doorknob and stepped into his new home to find his daughter climbing rapidly backwards down the stairs to greet him. 'Jussin! House! See, yook, house!'

He hugged her, laid his tough, seasoned cheek against her adorable, soft, new one. 'Come on outside and meet the boys.'

Drew, Martin and Gez climbed down from the van to inspect his daughter.

Martin said, 'Jeez! She's a mini Justin.'

'But she's pretty,' Gez joked.

After a careful inspection, Drew put out his hand and jiggled Shona's fingers. 'Hello, sweetheart.' And then to Justin, 'All right, Jus, she's definitely yours. Pity she comes with mother attached.'

They all glanced up as Cleo appeared at the front door, dishevelled in a T-shirt and jeans but, happily, out of earshot. Martin drew in his breath. 'Oh, I don't know. She fills that T-shirt a treat.'

Drew made a face. 'But Justin doesn't get to have sex with her so what use is that? Husband's still around, too.' He walked round to the rear of the van to throw up the roller door with a loud rattle.

The mission was to get all Justin's gear on the premises. The big sofa, television and stereo were a bit of struggle to coax through the sitting-room door, the stairs were awkward for the bed; but they managed eventually. Justin's room was the smaller double, with Shona's the middle room between that and Cleo's. By the time they'd carried his boxes in, Cleo was offering round tea and Boasters and there was a rush for seats.

Justin sat on the floor surrounded by a litter of boxes. Cleo had put a box of toys in the dining room, bare as neither of them possessed dining furniture, and Shona was busy emptying it as if she'd never seen any of the toys before.

Gez, Martin and Drew claimed the sofa. Gez and Martin thanked Cleo for the coffee. Drew was silent and kept staring at Cleo, who perched on a box of books. Sometimes he removed his gaze to glance around the room, then turned his attention back to her.

Occasionally, Justin noticed, Cleo intercepted the gaze. Mainly, she ignored it. It didn't take her ten seconds to make friends with Gez and Martin, thanking them for their help although it was Justin's gear they'd helped with, pressing more biscuits on them, smiling that wide smile, flicking her hair back from her shoulders. They were blokes and soon responding with smiles of their own, admiring the house, groaning with her about the antique state of the kitchen.

Eventually, she turned her attention to Drew. 'More coffee, Drew?'

Drew shook his head.

'You're very quiet.'

He nodded. Then, just as Cleo was giving up on him, said, 'I don't get what it is that you expect to get out of moving Justin in. Built-in babysitter? Decorator? Money provider?'

Justin opened his mouth to interfere, but Cleo was leagues

279

ahead of him.

'Hasn't he told you?' She opened her eyes very wide. 'Justin's going to be my sexual plaything. It'll save him rent. I'll give him Sundays off but he has to provide a matinee performance on Saturdays.'

Gez and Martin laughed. Drew's eyebrows dived down to meet over his ferocious glare. 'You're avoiding the question,' he snapped.

Cleo's eyebrows lifted. 'Because you've no business asking it.' She collected the coffee mugs and carried them into the kitchen.

Justin smirked at Drew. 'You lost that round, mate.'

Drew launched himself out of the embrace of the sofa. 'This just cannot work. You know this woman's bad news because she's never straight with you. Don't let her get her claws in. She's got a hidden agenda, something to do with the kid. Come and crash with me and Martin until you get sorted out with a new place.'

Justin smiled. 'Thanks, Drew. But I'll take my chances.'

When Gez's works van had rattled off down Port Road, Cleo returned to the kitchen to run cold water into the coffee cups. There would be hot water from a boiler the size of a washing machine in the scullery, later. She'd have to work the system out. Just one of twenty million jobs; she'd get around to it.

As Justin walked into the kitchen she glanced at him from under her lashes. 'Has he put you off the whole scheme? You can leave any time.'

He took his jacket off and hung it on the back of the door. 'What? And miss out on all that sex?'

Chapter Forty-One

Wearily, Justin parked outside his new home, where he'd lived with Cleo and Shona for one month.

He was pretty sure that it wouldn't be his home for much longer. Today had been terrible. Awful. Nothing that went before had been so bad. He felt as if the buffalo had come back and galloped over him all day.

He was scared and he wanted someone to tell him it was all going to come right. But he couldn't see that happening any time soon.

He let himself in the house.

It was beginning to look better, the past weeks' work were beginning to show. Even the circles of the black and orange carpet in the sitting room looked tolerable with his plain furniture. They'd painted the walls a buttery cream and clubbed together for velvet curtains. It looked like some funky retro designer job.

His bedroom he'd decorated in ivory and inky blue, financing it himself and telling Cleo that he'd had the shades specially mixed and could not, therefore, expect her to pay. He'd helped her wallpaper her room with a tiny pattern of palest grey and lilac flowers and they were going to do Shona's room soon.

It was brilliant to be living with Shona. He couldn't get over the absolute privilege of being with her on a daily basis. And then there was Cleo ...

Everything was going pretty well. They'd had the period of getting used to the new situation, when Cleo would laughingly ask permission before sitting on the sofa or he'd wash a single coffee mug rather than leave it for the next mealtime clear-up.

Nowadays he'd find Cleo lounging the length of the sofa as if she owned it, merely lifting her feet so that he could sit down. They talked for hours. He told her what was going on in his life – he wasn't seeing anyone at the moment, he'd settled back in at Rockley, Drew was waiting darkly for Cleo to trick Justin into something. She told him about Nathan giving her more account work, that she was still seeing Clive but hadn't slept with him.

He'd teased gently, 'Back on the celibacy kick?'

She'd flushed. And that was the only reference they made to the sex they'd shared.

But it all could end at any minute, even sharing Shona. Especially sharing Shona. He trudged indoors and flopped down on the sofa, too scared and pissed off to get a drink or turn on the television or climb the stairs; only fit to lie alone. Stewing.

He heard Cleo and Shona come home, Cleo's bright voice, 'Gosh, the house is dark. I wonder where Justin is?' She fumbled her way to the light switch and found him lying silently on the sofa, his arm flung across his eyes. 'Justin!'

Shona grizzled and clung, she only ever wanted her mother when she was tired and hungry. Hung about with her, Cleo discarded her bag and struggled out of her coat. 'What's the matter?'

He grunted without moving his arm, keeping the light out and making his eyeballs feel dull and bruised.

'Are you ill?'

'No.'

'I seem to remember some promise of chicken and chips?'

He groaned. 'Forgot.'

A hesitation. 'I'll do it. Are you hungry?'

'No.' And he lay there like a great selfish pig while she bustled round trying to cook something really quickly with

Shona dangling round her legs and whingeing. After they'd eaten, Cleo washed up and Shona played and then she bathed Shona ready for bed.

In all that time all he managed was, 'I must talk to you as soon as Shona's in bed.' He didn't even kiss Shona goodnight.

He heard Cleo's footsteps coming down the stairs. This was it. Time to tell. No escape. He dragged his arm away from his face, blinked, and hauled himself to his feet. Fetched a glass of water. If he didn't have something to drink his voice might crack.

'What?' she said, dropping onto the sofa, her eyes huge in her face.

Miserably, he cleared his throat. 'More trouble. It's completely out of order.' He had to look away from her. He couldn't meet that calm, direct gaze. Couldn't watch her expression turn to suspicion. Disgust.

He took a drink. 'I didn't get any warning. Neil called me in and I thought it was going to be something to do with my work, because we'd just been arguing about how to make my little line-drawn guy look as if he could happily exist on the crisps he was scoffing.' He'd automatically saved his work in progress and trekked off to Neil's office where Neil was waiting, fidgeting about the room.

Two men in suits waited with him. Short-haired, clean-shaven. Calm. As if it were their business to be in charge at all times.

'And Neil said, "These gentlemen want to speak to you, Justin. They're CID." And I was suddenly plunged into a nightmare. They said –' He had to force the words past stiff lips. 'They said that they'd had information that I'm using my office computer and downloading images from the Internet. That I'm part of a distribution circle.'

He closed his eyes, remembering how he'd felt as if Neil's

283

office had somehow attached itself to the back of a train and was whooshing, bucketing and rocking around him even while the detective sergeant's steady voice filled his ears. 'Can you tell us anything about this, Mr Mullarkey?'

'Images?' he'd repeated, stupidly.

'Pornographic images. Children.'

'Children!' His voice had burst out of him at a ridiculous volume, so loud, so harsh he could almost see the words blaze across the air in orange or red. Pantone 185, perhaps. '*Kiddie porn*? You mean kiddie porn? *Me*?'

He covered his eyes. Could hear his own voice rising, protesting, as he poured it all out to Cleo. 'They're anonymous complaints but CID say they have to establish whether there's any truth in them. This can't be happening. Not to me! I told them that this is like all the rest. The police know someone's doing this stuff. The nuisance calls, the arson at my flat, the set-up to get me arrested at the nightclub. Anonymous again – they must realise this is fabricated. I am absolutely not involved in kiddie porn, it repels me!

'With them and Neil staring at me, I even began to feel guilty! And I agreed to them taking my computer away to have a look. And I had to get my laptop out of the car, too.'

He'd had no choice but to stand there, clammy with fury and humiliation, with his colleagues looking on, while the police rapidly unplugged leads and gave Neil a receipt and lugged the computer down to their vehicle. No doubt Neil was grateful that the artists all used stand-alone computers so his could at least be isolated.

He felt tainted, as if his body was crawling with lice, and was sure rage and disgust would dissolve his heart like fat in a pan.

'So, there you go,' he told Cleo bleakly. 'I'm under suspicion of dealing in kiddie porn.' Silence. 'I expect you'll want me to leave.'

With an effort, he uncovered his eyes and looked at her. Yes, if her look of repugnance was anything to go by – the answer would be yes.

He forced himself to maintain eye contact, desperate not to let this awful unsubstantiated feeling of guilt show in his body language; and desperate not to give way to the dreadful sensation that he'd somehow transmogrified into the repellent beast he was suspected of being.

He was shocked when Cleo's dark eyes suddenly brimmed with tears. 'What kind of people would do this? I thought they were leaving you alone since you moved here.'

'They have, until now. Presumably they've lost track of where I'm living so they're concentrating on where I work.'

'Can't you change jobs?'

'If there's a job to leave! It was horrible. No one would meet my eye, Neil tried to find me another computer but all my work was on my own hard drive. The unnatural silence – I don't suppose the others know what I'm accused of, but CID don't seize your computer for playing FreeCell at lunchtimes, do they? And I've got to go in and face it all again tomorrow.'

Cleo patted his arm.

He couldn't bear her silence. 'I thought you'd want me to go. To get me away from … from Shona.'

She frowned. 'But you haven't done anything. Have you?'

Chapter Forty-Two

Oh great, just what she needed when she was late to meet Gav – Liza lying in wait for her in the busy street outside the Ntrain office. As if things weren't exasperating enough at the moment!

She pretended to rack her brain, tapping her foot and frowning. 'Now, what are you doing here?'

Liza scowled. On such a titchy, fragile-looking person, a scowl was incongruous. 'I want to talk some sense into you.'

'Too late by about thirty years. Anything else?' The sisters stared at each other as people brushed past and the rush of the traffic rumbled by.

Liza folded her arms. 'What good do you think this will do?'

Cleo shrugged. 'It might make him feel better, it might be kind.'

'Kind? It's one of the unkindest things I've heard of. What would be kind would be to tell him, once and for all, that it's over.'

'He knows that.'

Liza snorted. 'Of course he doesn't! You're keeping up these stupid dates, letting him hope. And that's not kind, that's mean. Push him away and let him move on.'

Cleo sighed. 'Gav just wants to stay friends, we're not going on "dates". It's civilised behaviour, that's all. Don't you think the fact that I've got a daughter with someone else might just be enough to put him off?'

'No. You're kidding yourself. Gav was always a bad loser and he can't bear to let Justin get away with you.'

Cleo fastened her coat against the chill in the winter

sunshine and prepared to sidestep her sister. 'Justin hasn't got away with me. Don't be so ridiculous. It's not that kind of relationship.' She moved to the road edge, ready to cross.

Irritatingly, Liza fell in beside her. 'Where are you meeting him?'

Cleo sighed. 'At Myers Hotel – OK? Inquisition over?'

'Myers! Got your gold card handy, have you?'

A blush warmed Cleo's cheeks. Myers was pretty grand, she'd been thinking that herself. 'His treat. To say sorry he upset me, last time.'

Beside her, Liza nodded in exaggerated triumph. 'What upset you? Remind me – something to do with Justin, was it?'

In a few minutes they had reached the two pale-grey marble steps up to the bevelled-glass doors of Myers Hotel. Through them could be seen more marble, glowing chandeliers and huge waxy plants. And Gav. Waiting. In his good suit. Bugger. She turned to Liza. 'Aren't you supposed to be at work, tweaking clients' toes?'

Liza smirked. 'I've got a couple of hours owing.'

Cleo suddenly felt frustrated that she seemed to be trapped into a routine she didn't want of meeting Gav. And now defending him to Liza. With a reflex that had its origins in a lifetime's sibling bickering, she took it out on her sister. 'Piss off and bother someone else, Liza. When I want your help I'll book an appointment for some reflexology, OK?' She snatched at the long brass door handle and swung through the doors into the heavily ornate interior.

Gav rose to meet her from his seat by a spiky cascade of minty green spider plants in a wrought-iron jardinière, face alight and both hands extended. 'Hello, darl— Cleo!'

She shoved hers in her pockets. 'Hello,' she said, shortly. And, aware that Liza was probably still watching through the glass, she started towards the brocade and moulded plasterwork depths of the dining room. 'Shall we go straight in? Time's pressing, as usual.'

Time didn't seem to be pressing very hard on Gav. He spent ages over a menu that was, naturally, miles more involved than their usual pub-grub choice. She skimmed through and chose pasta in the hope that it wouldn't take forever to cook.

But her hopes were groundless because the pasta took an age making an appearance. Or maybe it was Gav's lamb with new potatoes that slowed things up; but Cleo was almost due back at work before the waiter sailed in their direction, steaming plates in either hand. Sod it, she'd have to stay behind tonight and ring Dora to explain why she'd be late. Unless she could get hold of Justin and he'd fetch Shona? She snatched up her fork.

Then she had a funny feeling. Acutely uncomfortable. She almost dropped her fork.

Gav was rubbing one of his calves against hers! She pulled her legs back sharply under her chair. Because it had once been so familiar, she'd been slow to react. She stared at him. He smiled and reached out to cover her hand with one of his, laughing gently. 'Spoilsport.'

Her heart began to slither towards her boots, squelching her appetite on the way. She made an effort to extricate her hand. 'Don't. And don't do the thing with the legs.'

He held on. 'You've always enjoyed it.'

With her free hand, she picked up the water jug from the rose-pink damask cloth. 'Let. Go.'

After a hesitation, he loosed her hand, looking at her with reproachful puppy-dog eyes.

She ate as quickly as was elegant, trying not to stretch out her legs in case he got chummy again. She refused more wine, dessert and coffee.

'Oh come on,' he protested. 'You've time for coffee,

surely? Nathan won't miss you for an hour.'

She shook her head. 'Sorry.' She wanted, hugely, to get away. It had come to this: she felt uncomfortable in Gav's company.

His voice halted her as she searched for her bag beneath her chair. 'Hang on. I need to talk to you.'

She lodged her bag on her lap, waiting, keeping firmly to her side of the table in case he began the touchy-feely stuff again.

His voice dropped to a conspiratorial whisper. 'I've got a room.'

Oh no. He didn't mean what she thought he meant, did he?

He took a hotel key from his jacket pocket and laid it on the table as if he was bestowing jewels upon her. 'I'm tired of always discussing our problems in public with a table between us. We need privacy. Time.' He jiggled the key with his finger. 'I want us to give it another go.'

Oh. Shit. He did mean that.

She stared, at the key, at Gav's hopeful expression. Liza had been right, why hadn't she listened? She tried to make her voice gentle and compassionate. 'Gav, I don't know where you got the idea –' Her hands clutched sweatily at her bag at the thought of sharing a bed with him again. She swallowed. 'I won't meet you like this any more. I didn't think this was a heavy talk about problems, I thought it was just a light friendship between exes. We obviously want different things. I suppose you got a lot of what you wanted, when we were together.' She watched him flinch. 'But that's long, long gone. Even if it weren't for Shona – well, there wouldn't be any chance.' She rose, keen to get away from his accusing silence, his eyes.

Suddenly angry eyes.

His swift hand grabbed for her wrist as she tried for a discreet exit from the grandly curlicued dining room of

Myers. 'It'll work if we make it!' His voice was a harsh hiss. 'I'll put up with the child. We can be wonderful again and you can stop that bastard turning up all the time on the pretext of seeing his kid.'

Heart galloping, aware that forks all over the room had paused in mid-air, Cleo hissed back, 'He doesn't have to "turn up" – he's my lodger.' She snatched her wrist away and made her escape.

He caught up with her halfway across the marble foyer under the central chandelier. His voice was raised, furious. 'You must want your head examining! You've let that bastard into your home? And your bed? Him – a pervert for kids! A man who drools over pictures –'

He hesitated as Liza rose suddenly from a seat between banks of plants. 'Hello, Gav,' she said pleasantly. 'I'll walk with Cleo, I'm going that way. I think that man in the bow tie wants a word with you.' She pointed to the waiter, who was steaming in on an interception course.

So they left Gav stabbing at a credit card machine presented on a scalloped silver salver. And Cleo had to listen to indignant and triumphant 'I told you so!'s all the way back to the office. And it had begun to rain, slanting into their faces and making Liza madder than ever because her pompoms began to wilt.

And then the final straw. When Cleo rushed back to her desk, flustered and apologising to the office in general for being late, Francesca removed her switchboard headset to say, 'But your husband rang ten minutes after you left, and said you wouldn't be back this afternoon because you'd developed a bug.'

'*Ex*-husband!' Cleo snapped. Tricky bastard. Crafty conniver. Who did he think he could manipulate?

She reached for the Yellow Pages. Now, S ... S, for Solicitor.

'I hate to see you like this.'

Justin looked up dully. 'If you tell me to cheer up I'll top myself.'

Shona was in bed. Cleo and Justin sat at opposite ends of the sofa. The television was on to fill the silence while Cleo chewed her pen over a crossword and Justin stared at a book. As far as she could see, he'd been staring at the same page for twenty-five minutes.

'It's weird,' she said. 'You haven't smiled in three days.'

He shrugged, still staring at the book.

'Fancy a beer?'

He shook his head.

'Coffee?'

'No.' After a silence, he added, 'Thanks.'

The day before had been his thirtieth birthday. He'd condemned any suggestion of a celebration. Cards from family and friends had lain in a sorry heap until Cleo stood them around the room. She made a special dinner of duck in plum sauce, new potatoes and baby sweetcorn and Justin had barely eaten a quarter of his portion.

Cleo tossed her paper onto the table. It slid off the other side. She glared at Justin. 'You're letting them win, you realise? They set out to give you a hard time, they've devoted untold hours to it, and now they've got the satisfaction of watching you squirm.'

Slowly, he looked up. For once, his spectacular eyes were dead. 'I couldn't manage a squirm if I had the assistance of two nurses and a zimmer frame. They've destroyed me. My life's black and grey, I feel as if I'm breathing in noxious gas. Each day I have to go into the studio and fart about with trivial projects in an atmosphere thick with suspicion. Everyone knows I've done something unspeakable, no one knows what it is. They speculate behind my back.'

Cleo sat up suddenly. 'You have *not* done something

unspeakable – you've done nothing at all,' she cried. 'And when the police bring your computer back they'll confirm that.'

With his hand he shaded his face from her eyes. 'Will they?'

Something cold and horrible clutched Cleo's insides. 'Won't they?'

His voice was defeated. 'What if they've got to my computer and nobbled it? Got into the studio and downloaded this filth, hidden the files for the police to find? I'll go to prison.'

Her heart began to judder unpleasantly. 'They couldn't. Could they? *Could* they?'

He slammed shut his book. 'I'm beginning to think they could do anything. Just look at the fight, the way they framed me. They've obviously got some very heavy friends.' He shuddered. 'It's a nightmare.'

Cleo hitched up the sofa towards him, taking his hand. 'You've got to battle, Justin. You can't just give in.'

'Can't I?' He lifted her hand, his eyes on their laced fingers. 'They've got me. I can't fight them because I can't see them or where the next blow is coming from, they're invisible, invulnerable. They're more cunning than me. And they know it.'

Cleo gusted a huge sigh. 'They didn't seem particularly ingenious at first, did they?'

He laughed a creaky, bitter laugh, a mockery of the joyful cackle of the old Justin. 'They got better, with practice.'

'But don't let them get the better of you.'

Slowly, as if exhausted, he closed his eyes. 'Cleo, for God's *sake*, they already have. They've won! Sometimes I look in the mirror at this stranger who gets into knife fights and fantasises over kiddie porn, and I want to set fire to myself.'

Chapter Forty-Three

Monday, and a Powerful Listening workshop. The members of the group were too young and heedless to listen to anything more demanding than James Blunt. The client, a leisure industry giant, had allowed itself to be seduced by the workshop's groovy write-up instead of analysing what was useful for their employees, and hadn't been inclined to listen to advice.

Cleo heard her customary bright and interesting tone rattling out the tried and tested theories, got them going in the role playing, then had to watch them fall about laughing at their own uselessness. Listening wasn't their thing and they did it badly. She gritted her teeth and by the time she'd finished with them they did it better; but very evidently didn't see the point and would probably never apply a single thing they'd learnt.

A relief, after such a frustrating day, to leave them behind. Queuing at the roundabout for the Soke Parkway she saw she'd be in good time to fetch Shona from Dora.

Dora and Sean. Sean and Dora; seeming so happy together. Dora was comfortable and content in the ordinary terraced house – in a way she'd never appeared to be in the Posh Pad where Keith now lived alone, except for, according to Gav, a mini harem.

Gav. She'd been trying not to think about his pushiness and how her flesh had shrunk from the contact with his. How things had changed.

It made her wonder whether she'd ever actually been in love with *Gav* – or just what she thought he'd been?

She shook off her introspection the moment her daughter tumbled into her arms, her face alight with the joy of being able to shout, 'Mummee's here!'

Cleo folded her arms around the light, tight-knit little body. 'Hello, sweetie!'

This was love.

It wasn't about possession or point scoring or getting your own way. It was about coming alive when your loved one walked into the room.

Justin was evidently already home. His car stood outside, the kitchen window was spilling light into a garden of bare twigs and mud. A bit like his life at the moment – no colour and nothing nice.

Cleo carried Shona, the familiar trusting weight snuggled into her side as they stepped into the warmth. Instantly, she was aware of the smell of something good cooking.

Then Justin hurtled through the sitting-room door. '*TARRAH*! Tan-tan-*TARRAH*!'

Shona reacted with a fluid 'har-har-har' of toddler chuckles like musical notes, while Cleo gasped. 'You frightened me to death!'

But Justin was beaming, Justin was dancing on the spot, eyes sparkling. 'GOOD NEWS!' He snatched Shona from Cleo's arms and tossed her once, twice, high up in the air. 'BRILLIANT, FABULOUS, FANTASTICO NEWS!'

Cleo laughed, relief at seeing the lighthouse beam of his smile once more surging through her, but arms hovering as if he might make a mistake and let Shona fall. 'Tell me.'

He hoisted Shona up onto his shoulders. 'The CID returned my Mac today – TOTALLY CLEAN! THOSE BASTARDS DIDN'T GET TO IT.' And then, in a more normal voice, 'I'm completely cleared of suspicion. And Neil, wonderful, wonderful Neil, called the whole studio together and explained about me being set up and that if he finds out anyone in the studio is anything to do with this vendetta against me, it'll mean instant dismissal.' He began to twirl round, Shona, from her shoulder-carry perch, squeaking in delighted fear, fastening little hands tightly under his chin so it looked as if he was wearing a Shona hat.

Cleo was struck by such a hot rush of thankfulness and relief that she had to fight her way out of her coat. 'That's wonderful,' she choked. 'I'm so *relieved* for you.' She ventured a brief hug of solidarity.

And then she was clamped against his chest in a one-armed embrace, his voice muffled against her hair. 'I've been so scared –'

She patted his back. 'I know.'

'It's been absolute hell.'

'But it's over.'

He gave her one final squeeze and released her. 'And now we're going to celebrate.' He lifted both of Shona's hands high in the air. 'Yeahhhh!'

Shona instantly echoed him in her squeaky little toy voice. 'Yeahhhh!'

It was a lovely evening.

Justin cooked his speciality, chicken and chips, setting a festive table with wine glasses and kitchen-roll napkins. Even Shona drank her apple juice out of a (very chunky) wine glass – messily – and giggled and gargled and banged her tray every time she ran out of chips.

Justin abandoned the dishes into the sink and herded Cleo away. 'I'll get up early and do them tomorrow.' Then produced chocolate eclairs filled with fresh cream.

Shona piped, 'Oooh, cake!'

Cleo protested, 'I'll never eat one of those.' But did.

Justin devoured his in huge, silly mouthfuls, making yumming noises and rolling his eyes until Shona began to do the same and grew a rhino horn of cream on her nose, nearly choking Cleo with laughter.

Justin played Dire Straits loudly on the stereo and they all danced in a ridiculous, giggling, Men Behaving Badly way, spilling wine all over the orange-and-black carpet when they collided, Shona bouncing and wobbling at their knees.

Finally, Justin put a wilting Shona to bed and Cleo rushed to get the washing-up done but he came stomping into the kitchen to tell her off, pulling her away from the sink with suds up to her elbows and dancing her round in circles as he composed a song that mainly consisted of 'Justin's not a pervert, Justin's not a per-er-er-vert!'

And something clanged in Cleo's head.

It fell into place so heavily that the kitchen executed an extra spin around her.

She pushed him away, slapping both hands to her mouth, her hair standing up on her neck with horror.

'What?' His face was still creased into a great grin, his hair a nest of wild spikes.

Cleo felt her eyes burn as she gazed at his laughing face, his eyes shining with joyful relief. 'It can't be. *Can't* be.' She covered her eyes, pressed the heels of her hands hard against them until she saw stars. 'It must be. Oh no.'

She felt his fingers on her wrists, pulling her hands away, the laughter fading. 'What?'

This was what misery was, chewing you up and spitting you out, washing the bones from your legs. She crashed down into a kitchen chair. 'When I saw Gav ... He called you a pervert. A man who drools over kids.'

Justin stared.

Cleo coughed up sudden tears. 'I hadn't told him anything about it.'

Justin sat down suddenly on the edge of the kitchen table, almost missing. 'So how did he know?'

Cleo groaned and pounded her temples with her fists. 'It must be him.'

Chapter Forty-Four

Cleo banged the brass doorknocker, hard. Then again, harder. Shona had been overtired to be left with Liza, but Cleo hadn't been able to put off this confrontation for an instant. Through the panels of patterned glass she watched a wobbly person shape approaching.

Gav opened the door, shirt collar unbuttoned, tie missing, stocking feet peeping from under his trousers, hair tossed above his eyes. 'Hello,' he beamed. 'This is a great surprise … oh.'

Justin must've stepped into view behind her, judging by the way Gav's face stilled into aversion. Cleo's throat felt stretched and strained, and she was sickened with guilt. Without speaking, she brushed past Gav and trailed across his rented-house brown cord carpet, aware of Justin's following footfalls and Gav blustering, 'What the hell's going on? What do you think you're doing?'

Cleo followed the sound of the television into a small, square sitting room containing the furniture that had been hers and Gav's. And waited to face her ex-husband.

It was difficult. Unthinkable. If she didn't feel so unbelievably, deeply implicated, she'd find it impossible. She swallowed.

A pale Gav swam into view. 'What do you think you're doing, Cleo? And why have you brought this bastard? I'd –'

'Shut up,' Cleo snapped. 'Just shut the fuck up. We know it's you.'

Shock washed over Gav's face and he looked suddenly apprehensive. Cleo looked away. Flipped a glance at Justin. His eyes waited.

Silence.

Huddling into her coat, Cleo glanced about the room. Gav's homecoming routine hadn't altered. Jacket and tie flung over the back of the sofa, his watch, keys, mobile phone and small change parked in the blue willow-pattern bowl that used to be theirs, on top of the television. She went over. A bowl that, instead of fruit, hosted the miscellany of daily living: a credit card statement, a birthday card waiting to be written, keys. But no second mobile phone. Disappointing. She'd more or less convinced herself that that was where she'd find it.

She rifled her fingers gently through the bowl. And there it was, at the bottom, taking her by surprise: a tiny white oblong of plastic with a small, gleaming, gold square that she knew was the brain and heart for a mobile phone. A SIM card.

At least a thousand years older, Cleo extracted it. Held it in the air with distasteful fingertips. 'Spare SIM card?'

She forced herself to watch Gav, the panic of expressions jostling across his face, the sweat beading his pallor, the furtive tongue moistening his lips. 'No law against it, is there?'

From behind her she heard Justin laugh. 'That depends what you use it for.'

Cleo was tired. So extraordinarily, desperately, hopelessly spent, so exhausted that even breathing seemed effortful. She pushed the card slowly into the deep pocket of her coat, closing her fingers round, feeling the corners dig in. She heard her own voice, but as if from a dream. 'What would happen if we took this SIM card to the police?'

Gav's eyes widened.

She waited. Justin fidgeted. Silence lengthened. Abruptly, Cleo flumpfed down onto one of the chairs, her ears ringing unpleasantly. 'Oh Gav! Was it all too easy? I suppose you sat here persuading yourself that all your troubles were down to Justin, then swapped the unregistered, prepaid SIM card into your phone. Then what? Ring Justin at two in the morning? Call out the fire brigade to his address? Order him a pizza? These untraceable calls, did they make you feel clever?'

Despite her angry attempts to stop it, her voice began to shake. Ignominiously, she had to blow her nose before continuing. 'And you even *set fire to his flat*. Gav, you *bastard*. Shona might've been inside. You could've killed my baby!'

Gav's voice was bleak but defensive. 'The fire wasn't down to me. It was when the police began asking questions about it ... well, that's what gave me the idea. The bastard deserves a hard time. If you just think what he's done to me –'

Justin interrupted, sounding somehow satisfied. 'That would explain how the campaign appeared to become cleverer. Presumably, the lunatic tenants began it but were put off by the police enquiries, and you took over? What about the guys who set on me in Muggie's?'

Cleo interrupted her nose blowing to glare at Gav. 'Manny?'

After a moment, Gav nodded.

Cleo explained drearily to Justin. 'Ian Mansfield was at school with Gav. He's a trained bodyguard.'

Justin nodded slowly. 'He could really handle himself, that guy.' He stared meditatively at Gav. 'You've gone to extraordinary lengths to make me miserable. Particularly by involving the CID.'

Gav smiled, thinly. 'When you moved in with Cleo I had to get creative so she wouldn't be hurt. I wrote to the police a couple of times, but nothing seemed to happen. Then I rang Crimestoppers. Efficient service, isn't it? Aren't you impressed?' He took off his glasses. 'Are you sorry yet that you screwed my wife?'

Justin took his hands out of his pockets. 'Not one bit.'

The air almost crackling with the hostility between the two men, Cleo spoke swiftly to claim Gav's attention before he flared up. She let her voice emerge as a hiss. 'You're going to stop now.' Her hand tightened over the SIM card. She watched his eyes.

'I suppose so.' A pause. 'Are you going to the police?'

She glared. 'I should do. But we've got the card so I think you know it's over. Your nasty games and cowardly conniving are useless now we're in the know.' She took a deep breath. 'And *just you try anything else* – I will go straight to the police.'

His lip quivered momentarily. 'I don't know why you spoiled what we had.'

'I don't think we ever had anything.' She mustn't give him even a microcosm of hope to cling to. 'My solicitor will write to you.'

He nodded slowly, miserably.

'Apart from that, I don't want contact.'

A final nod.

She let the silence spin out, before turning to leave.

Gav sank onto the sofa, let his head tip back, and closed his eyes.

His heart, which had been thumping against his ribs, began finally to slow. The worst had happened: he'd been found out. He almost felt relieved. Continuing the vendetta was now impossible. He had his dark moments, like anyone, but sustaining a hate campaign had consumed him. He wasn't a bad bloke. Not really. He'd got carried away. That was all.

He clenched his eyes and thought about Cleo with that bastard, Justin. Deliberated carefully how they'd been together in his house, their body language towards one another. That

Justin had kept his distance, not making even a single gesture towards Cleo when she became angry and upset.

He opened his eyes.

It was for all the world as if their affair was over. In fact, the more he considered it, the more convinced he became. Justin hadn't tried to console Cleo, Cleo hadn't looked to Justin for comfort. They were no longer lovers! Any fool could see that, if they looked in the right way.

He went into the kitchen and reached into the fridge for a beer, cracked it open and took a shaky draught.

If Cleo wasn't with Justin, he didn't feel so bad. Gav might not have won but neither had Justin. Tipping his head back, he let the icy, angry fizz of the beer race into his mouth. So he hadn't really lost.

There seemed little point hanging around now. He'd ask Dad for a couple of Doncaster papers and look for another job in the friendly north. At the interviews they'd want to know why he'd been shuttling about between jobs. He'd smile ruefully and explain about Mum's death, Dad's health, that he felt uneasy about him living alone. They'd appreciate his loyalty. And, he'd add, who wouldn't want to live in Yorkshire, given the choice? They'd grin and nod at one another.

He'd tell Dad he'd tried his best with Cleo.

He was going to miss her.

Cleo was upstairs. Justin could hear her footfalls. Bathroom, landing, Shona's room. Her murmurs falling into the soothing cadences of the bedtime story. Shona's bird-voice replies.

He turned on the television ready for *Frost*. If she took much longer, she'd miss the beginning. He tuned out the irritating adverts and considered events.

That utter shite monster, Gav! Fancy it being him. So

much grief. Everything since the fire down to him. Months of fury over unwanted deliveries, nuisance calls, being roughed up. And worst, of course, the police, the kiddie porn thing. Fancy him doing all that. Bastard.

He jerked suddenly, waking to stare uncomprehendingly at David Jason's face, exasperated under his trilby, on the screen. Had he been asleep? The video clock suggested that half an hour had mysteriously disappeared from his life.

Funny Cleo hadn't come down. But, now that Shona was in a bed rather than a cot, Cleo got so cuddled up and comfy that she occasionally dozed off, too. If he looked in he'd see her fringe sliding across her face, lips slack, arm round their daughter, book fallen across her legs. He trod up the stairs.

But no, Shona was alone in mouth-open sleep, titchy and adorable in the full-size bed.

On the landing he hovered outside Cleo's closed bedroom door, slightly disappointed. They often watched police dramas together, theorising who'd "dunnit" and whether the personal problems of the detective in question were going to have a bearing on the finale. Maybe she needed space, an early night? Funny she hadn't even shouted down that she wasn't bothering with *Frost*.

He turned away.

From behind the old-fashioned, panelled door, he heard Cleo blow her nose.

He turned back, hesitated, then tapped on a panel. 'Fancy a coffee?'

Her reply sounded thick. 'No thanks.'

'You're missing *Frost*.'

'Am I? Oh.' More nose blowing.

He cocked his head, listening hard. 'Are you OK? Can I come in?'

'No! I mean, I'm fine – you go watch telly.' Her voice wavered and caught.

Oh right, he was bound to. He opened the door.

On the far side of the bed Cleo was an instant too late in rolling onto her other side to hide the red blotches around her eyes.

He made his voice gentle. 'You've been crying.'

Shaking her head, she wiped furiously at her face. ''Course not.'

He rested one knee cautiously on the bed. 'Are you upset about losing contact with Gav?' He dropped his hands onto the quilt cover strewn with lilac blossoms and crawled a couple of feet towards her.

She shook her head, snatching three clean tissues from the box beside her and burying her face in them. Her shoulders shook.

Hmm. Well, he couldn't just crouch next to her like some guardian ape. He eased full length then scooted until he was spoon-like behind her, an inch away. Tentatively, he patted her shoulder.

For a moment, she stiffened. Then, abruptly, wriggled round, buried her face against his shoulder and collapsed into big, chest-tucking, head-aching sobs. 'I'm so sorry,' she choked. 'I'm so, so sorry. How could I've not realised? How could I marry a man like that, a cunning, low bastard? All that trouble, because of me, my fault, all the time, my fault!'

Somehow his arms got themselves wrapped around her back. 'It wasn't.'

'But it was! Because of me! It could've driven you round the bend, you could've lost your job or gone to prison.'

He tutted. 'You're not responsible for a sad git who copes with rejection in such a shitty, underhand manner. Also, you didn't sleep with his wife – I did!'

Her sobs became a strangled laugh and she settled into a thoughtful, sniffy silence. He even had the opportunity for a bit of thought. To slowly assimilate that he was lying on

Cleo's bed with Cleo clutched to his chest. The bedclothes were soft and smelled freshly laundered. Her shoulder blade was firm and warm under one of his hands, the nape of her neck soft and downy beneath the other.

His hands were developing a yen to travel, to trail across her back, tiptoe up the ladder of her ribcage, to brush across her breast and feel the nipple harden.

He eased his hips away. Wouldn't want to worry her with a stonking great erection. Mustn't take advantage of a damsel in distress.

But her chest touching his like that was a bit of an attention-grabber. He allowed one hand to drift from her nape to smooth the glossiness of her hair.

And that's when all hell broke loose at the front door, a creative rhythm of knock-knock-ring-ring, ring-ring-knock-knock.

Cleo jerked backwards.

After a moment, he rolled away from her. 'I'll see who it is.'

Thump-thump, the beat in her heavy head pounded with every movement. But after five minutes with a cold flannel, her face no longer looked like uncooked sausage. Cleo combed her hair and trod downstairs.

Justin had taken the visitor into the sitting room and hadn't come back upstairs. Why would he? So she could blub all over him again? Men hated being cried over, he'd probably been delighted that answering the door had provided an excuse to leave.

At the foot of the stairs she halted, recognising Drew's voice over the companionable sound of hissing ring-pulls. Crap. Could she be bothered with Drew tonight? Probably not. She'd tried to get on with him when he called to see Justin, but it was a lost cause.

Whether she kept in the background, ignored him, tried to be friendly or batted his little barbs straight back, he was offish and snippy towards her. But she wanted a glass of water because her throat was raw. And whose house was this, anyway? Was she a woman or a mouse?

She got as far as the partly open door before Drew's scornful tones stopped her. 'So, where's the mother of your child tonight?'

She listened to Justin's laconic, 'Around.'

Drew. 'Thought you might be babysitting. Again.'

Justin, taking a swig before answering. 'Not tonight.'

She was just considering stepping into view when Drew said, 'So, why are you never out with your buddies?'

'What about last Friday?'

'The first time for a month! What's the matter with you, mate? Surely she lets you off the leash sometimes? Off stud duties?'

The leather of the sofa creaked before Justin replied. 'No leash, no stud duty. But it's my business – OK?'

Cleo lifted her hand and wiped away a small bandana of sweat. This wasn't very nice, listening, but she was kind of stuck. Maybe she should back quietly away. Or just stride in with a big smile and get herself that drink. She licked her lips.

Drew's laugh sliced across her thoughts. 'So if I say, "Let's go to the pub", what do you say?'

'Not tonight.'

'Because you haven't got permission?'

She wished she could see Justin's expression. His voice gave nothing away. 'Because Cleo's had some bad news and she's upset. We can go tomorrow night, if you like. Or Friday.'

She heard Drew sigh. 'Jus, it was bad enough that when you found out you'd got a kid you showed dreadful signs of responsibility. But since you moved in here you're a saint. Wake up, mate. She's had to give up the clubbing and bad behaviour, so she's settled for this domestic shit. She's trapped and she's trying to trap you with her.'

'Do you think so?' Justin's voice sharpened.

'This woman's just a heap of baggage and a reasonable body.'

'Oh come on. It's more than reasonable –'

'Justin, she's got a husband and a child!'

Cleo coughed loudly and sailed into the sitting room. Her sitting room. Face hot, which meant her colour was probably high, she stared at Drew. 'Anyone want coffee?'

He didn't even have the grace to look uncomfortable, although he must have known he'd been overheard. He just stared right back.

Chapter Forty-Five

As she'd been awake for much of the night after the evening's tears, her eyes looked like piggy little slits, pink and poisoned. But at least she'd made some decisions about her life in the long dark hours.

Shona trotted round the bedroom clutching a cuddly snowman, her lips stuck out as she chirruped to herself. Cleo watched. Was there anything more gorgeous than Shona in her dressing gown?

Dressed in a dark grey trouser suit with a flaming orange blouse, Cleo dried her hair into a glossy sheet, tossed the fringe about in an 'I just got up and look this fantastic' style, and set about her piggy pink eyes with soft eye-liner and thick mascara.

Much better.

She was in the kitchen, hoping Shona would soon finish her last toast finger, by the time Justin dashed in, looking sheepish. 'I've just seen the cans from last night – mind if I leave clearing them up until tonight? I'm late. Is that my coffee? You're an absolute angel. And you look great, by the way, something special on at work?'

She wiped Shona's fingers, shook her head. 'It's a "first day of the rest of my life" moment.'

He gulped at the coffee, which could only be tepid by now. 'Oh?'

Moving on to Shona's face, she nodded. 'I'm going to stop being mumsy, hiding away in tracksuits. Now Shona's past the baby stage I'm going to get a life.' She lifted Shona out of the high chair and watched her reach her arms up to her father.

Justin put down his coffee to take her. 'You don't wear tracksuits.'

She pulled a face. 'Figuratively, I do. I slob around at home and do nothing. Clive hasn't even rung for a week, he's probably fed up with making all the effort while I hedge in case something better happens.' She laughed, to show she wasn't taking herself too seriously. 'He's a nice, good-looking bloke and I ought to give him a go. It's time we did the bed thing.'

She held out her arms to take Shona back. 'I'm going to rejoin the world. Take a salsa class, maybe, get out with Liza or Dora. Perhaps I'll even go down and see Rhianne for a weekend. These are things I should be doing.'

He moved slightly to block her way. 'Why should you?'

She flicked back her hair. She could hardly say, 'To prove to Drew that I'm not a needy bitch that you feel obliged to keep company.' Instead, she breezed, 'Because I can.'

Justin watched her at the evening meal. She seemed brittle and restless.

She'd had her hair cut during the day, it was all feathery at the bottom. First he'd thought he didn't like it, then as he'd watched it moving round her face he'd decided it was fabulous. 'Nice hair,' he mentioned, casually.

She tossed it back from her eyes as she ran hot water in the sink. 'By the way, can you sit for Shona on Friday? I rang Clive and –'

He shook his head. 'Sorry. I've arranged to go out with Drew on Friday. I can do Saturday.'

She wrinkled her nose as she did when something didn't suit her. 'Clive has something special planned. A friend of his is in a show, on Friday there's a big dinner afterwards. You couldn't swap to Saturday?'

He didn't even pretend to consider. 'Sorry.'

Bedtime duty, his turn. When he went downstairs Cleo was just putting the phone down. 'Liza says she'll have Shona overnight at her place on Friday, so we can both go out.'

'I must remember to tell her how grateful I am.' Not.

Much as she loved her darling daughter, it was bliss to drive her over to her Auntie Liza and then come home and get ready without Shona dabbling her fingers in the face powder or trying to stick her face between the hairdryer and Cleo's hair. To be able to play around with her new haircut and get it exactly as she wanted it.

She'd even time to paint her nails, sad little ovals compared with the tailored talons of pre-Shona days, but still worth a coat of blood red. Her eyes were sexy, smudgy works of art, her lips a kissable invitation, her breasts more than a hint at the neckline of her short, black dress. Step into ridiculous shoes that no one in their right mind would wear for more than ten minutes, and there! Cleo, ready for action. Clean knickers and toothbrush in handbag, irresistible and up for it.

OK, not quite as up for it as she could be, perhaps not dancing with big-date, knicker-wetting anticipation at the thought of letting Clive seduce her. But it should be quite a pleasant evening. A show. Dinner. Sex.

Presumably, once she embarked on The Act she'd garner a little more enthusiasm.

In her ridiculous shoes she stalked downstairs for a steadying glass of wine. Justin, who hadn't yet left for his own evening of jollies, was flicking at his hair in front of the mirror. He stopped. He looked.

Nervously, she grinned. 'Do I look OK?'

After a second he nodded. 'Totally fuck-off fabulous.'

'Oh.' She cleared her throat. 'Wine?'

He took the glass she offered. 'Dutch courage?'

She felt herself flush. 'No! Yes. Not really.'

He nodded slowly. He seemed to be in one of his non-smiling moods. 'Is tonight still "the night"?'

She grimaced. 'Yes. Probably. I think so. It's time –'

'Probably – because it's time?' He laughed suddenly, looking, as he always did, nine hundred per cent nicer. 'Not because you're burning for him or you think it's going to be a fabulous fantastic experience? Not even because you expect to be drunk and it'll seem a good idea?' He moved nearer.

She swallowed.

His eyes locked with hers. She felt as if she'd become super-sensitive, could feel the heat from his body, even the chill from his glass across the stride that separated them.

She swallowed again. 'Well, I'm going now. Have a nice evening –'

'But you owe me that sex.'

Chapter Forty-Six

His words snapped out like a whip to grab her round the heart. She laughed, incredulously. 'That's preposterous. "But you owe me that sex", as if it was twenty quid I'd borrowed!'

He smiled. 'Sex can't be equated with money.'

She waited vainly for some explanation, cheeks on fire, throat constricted. Then she launched into stumbling speech herself, voice squeaky with outrage. 'You think you did me a favour, do you? But we *had* s-s-sex,' she could hardly say the word. '*We*. Reciprocal situation. No favours involved.' She clenched her fists, felt palms clammy with fury.

He allowed her to stutter to a halt. '*We* had sex because *you* weren't getting any – I was sorted.'

'You stopped me going home with Brad!'

He shook his head. 'Just like when we met, I offered an option. I didn't "stop" you doing a thing.' Apparently impassive, he sipped his wine, the only hint that he might be anything but calm lying in the glitter of his eyes. She imagined this was how he'd be during a workplace disagreement, calm, thoughtful, putting forward awkward little arguments to wrong-foot his opponent.

Whereas she, infuriatingly, felt as if she were being tossed about by a fairground ride; throat drying, heart chugging, face hectic. She heard her own nervous laugh. 'I ought to be really angry with you, this is scandalous. You can't hold me to ransom, for sex. We made no bargain, you never said you expected the "favour" returned.'

His glass was almost empty. 'There was no bargain. But maybe a moral obligation.'

Her temper began to blossom; she could feel her control sliding. 'Moral! How you, you manipulating arse, have the absolute face to even say the word! This is the most immoral thing I've heard, you can't insist on the return of sex! It's not nice!'

His eyes were so bright she could almost count the golden flecks. 'Sometimes I'm not nice.'

Something seemed to have happened to her throat to trip up her breath and make her words emerge in gasps. 'So ... so you're saying you want sex? I ought to ring Clive, perhaps, and stand him up? And we'll —' Words failed her.

Justin smiled.

Boiling, shaking, Cleo snatched up her bag and coat, fished out her car keys. 'And when I refuse?'

He shrugged. 'I won't insist.'

'You won't ...?' And suddenly she was yelling. 'You absurd, arrogant bastard! Go play with yourself!' On that satisfactorily juvenile note she flung herself from the room, slam through one door, bang through the next.

She was trembling, could hardly find the ignition, let alone drive. Bastard! Awful, treacherous, unreasonable bastard. How dare he suggest that she owed him? As if she should've expected that, at some unspecified time, he'd call the favour in and want to go to bed with her.

Want to go to bed with her? As if!

Palms damp, she wiped them down her dress. 'Get a grip.' Why on earth was she getting so excited? A minor disagreement with Justin, a difference of opinion, that's all it was. No reason for constant gulps of fresh air, sweaty hands, trembling legs. It's not as if he'd tried to force her into anything, all he'd said, if she was analytical, was that he wanted her.

And she'd got all excited.

So that had gone atrociously. He poured himself another glass of wine, hearing the bottle chatter slightly against the glass. A total balls-up. Words he hadn't meant to say had burbled out on their own, he'd grinned when he should've apologised and, basically, acted like a prick.

So.

Cleo had dashed off, furious, to spend the night with yukky Clive. Predictable. He knew well enough that Cleo liked to confound people. Perhaps he should've insisted she vault between Clive's sheets immediately, then she would have refused to go to bed with Clive even if he was wrapped in a gold-spangled certificate of merit. Cleo made her own decisions.

Then he heard the front door reopen. He flicked his eyes to the doorway. And smiled.

Hair wind-tossed, cheeks flushed, chest heaving as if she'd run all the way from Peterborough, her dress clung to places he'd like to cling himself. She looked edible. He poured her another glass of wine and tried to sound calm. 'What about Clive?'

She shrugged. 'Maybe I'm better with the devil I know.' Then she smiled back, a naughty, knowing, sexy smile.

She rang Clive, because she didn't want him waiting around all night, and Justin didn't want him turning up. But she only got as far as, 'Sorry, I can't make it tonight, something's come up.' That's when Justin took her phone and snapped it shut, turning her face up to his as his hands slid her coat from her shoulders, as he brushed the cords of her neck with his fingertips, making her dizzy with desire.

He steered her from the room, covering her face with kisses as he backed her one step at a time up the staircase, laughing because it made her shriek every time she stumbled and he fell on top of her.

And they kicked off their shoes and fell onto her duvet, struggling with zips and buttons, enmeshed in a porridge of half-removed garments and inquisitive hands as Justin groaned, 'Hell, you're pretty. All over.'

Perfect, it was a perfect night. Everything was perfect. Even the condoms behaved impeccably.

Chapter Forty-Seven

Cleo lay awake and watched the light brighten around the curtain edges and ripple in a fan shape across her ceiling. The cold light of day.

A stark contrast to the hot darkness of night.

It had been pretty wonderful, again, annoyingly enough. Absolutely wonderful, hot, sweaty, delicious sex. And if there was a next time, it would probably be astonishingly wonderful. But would there be a next time?

Better not. Anyone could see it was crazy. Sex with Justin had been the catalyst to change her life. An episode that should've ended when she went home and might well have done if she hadn't, inconveniently, been so pregnant.

She watched the fan of light brighten. But she wouldn't want to still be married to Gav, not knowing that they had lived a lie, that he was a consummate underhand dealer. So the pregnancy had been a good thing and Shona was a fantastic, marvellous thing. But also the thing that made Justin part of her life again.

Reluctantly, he'd said. No future and only a grubby past.

He seemed to have ended up liking her despite himself, but he didn't trust her. And it was no good to keep swallowing that information afterwards, like another form of morning-after pill. They shouldn't have done it again.

And this living together thing wasn't going to work because there was always going to be the danger of it happening.

A single tear seeped from the corner of her eye. She brushed it away.

No good feeling sorry for herself! She must fetch her

daughter from Liza's flat. She must apologise to Clive. What she didn't want was for Justin to wake and reach for her. That would just make everything more difficult.

Stealthily, she lifted the covers to swing her legs from the bed. But came to an abrupt halt. 'Ouch!' She rubbed at the burning part of her scalp and tried to reach behind her head to free her hair where it was caught under Justin. Then a hand looped fingers with hers.

His voice was early morning grumbly. 'Why have you been glaring ferociously at the ceiling?'

She rolled back down. Sighed. 'We shouldn't have done it.'

When he frowned his spikes of hair quivered. 'No good?'

'Of course it was –' She halted, laughed unwillingly. 'You know how good.'

'So what's the problem?' His thumb stroked her knuckles.

She took a deep breath. 'Because it's never going to go any further, but it stops either of us getting it on with someone else.' Another breath, still deeper. 'I think you ought to move out. I know you've loved living with Shona and I'm sorry if leaving her is painful, but you can see her as much as you want. I don't want you to be bound by some misplaced responsibility to me. You ought to be thinking of the rest of your life now, not babysitting, helping with my decorating and being couply.

'For a while it gave you somewhere to get over all the shit Gav caused and me a chance to get on my feet. But the nuisance campaign's over. And if this is going to keep happening –' She jerked away and scurried for the bathroom.

A nice hot shower, a few private tears, Justin would have time to vacate her room. She'd be bright and breezy again by the time she next saw him.

But when she re-entered her room he hadn't moved an inch. In fact, as soon as she appeared, he carried on as if she'd never left. 'So you'd like me to live somewhere else?'

She nodded, tugging her towelling dressing-gown belt and searching for her brush.

'If you want me to, I'll go. Just explain why.'

She sat on the bottom of the bed, scraping her hairbrush moodily on the duvet cover. 'I don't like the idea of being friends who share a daughter and, occasionally, a bed. It's a compromise. Half-hearted.'

Through the silence that followed, the lilac blossom on the quilt cover melted and blurred as her eyes filled. She concentrated very hard on not letting the tears fall. When Justin snatched back the covers and lurched to his feet, walking naked across the bed before jumping down to land beside her, she looked away and concentrated harder. She would not cry!

The gentleness of his arms around her almost tempted her to sag against the comfort of his chest, the bed-warm, man smell of his skin, but she would not cry. His voice was a deep, sympathetic rumble. 'Suppose I want to be couply?'

The tears began to fall. 'You shouldn't say things like that!' The sleeve of her dressing gown had to do to wipe her eyes. 'It's all wrong. Drew said I had a husband and a child –'

'Ex-husband. And my child.'

'Exactly. You're here out of some misplaced sense of responsibility, and because you're mad about Shona. Not me! I'm bad for you.'

He pulled her round to face him. 'What misplaced responsibility?'

She scrubbed her eyes with her other sleeve and sniffed unattractively. 'Because of Shona. But your responsibility's to her, not me.'

'I know I'm responsible for her. Why are you bad for me?'

She sniffed again, digging in her pocket for a tissue. 'All

317

that stuff. You know, you said it. And Drew says it.'

'What stuff? When? What does Drew say?'

She risked a glance through lashes spiky with tears. 'You said I wasn't straight with you, we had too much bad history. And Drew thinks I'm after someone to look after me. And, anyway,' she added, turning to face him properly, inspired by a flash of insight. 'You only kept in touch once you found out about Shona.'

His eyes flashed. She noticed that, if he frowned horribly enough, one eyebrow did a little curl above the bridge of his nose.

'Listen,' he said very clearly, as if talking to some drunken imbecile. He grasped her hands and squeezed them too hard. 'I did say some of that stuff when I first found out about Shona. My brain was all to hell in a handcart. Suddenly there was this little person on the planet that I'd helped put there – you'd had ages to get your head round it but I'd had a few hours. I was jet-lagged, I'd had to throw those jokers out of the flat. I wasn't at my best.

'I had some jumbled idea of giving myself space while I got back on an even keel. Truthfully, it was just an awful lot of bollocks.' His lips pressed momentarily on her hair. 'Look at me.'

Slowly, she peeped.

He smiled.

Her heart did that funny, blossomy thing, making the back of her neck prickle.

He murmured, 'When I came to see you – I didn't know Shona existed.' He kissed her nose. 'I came back to see you.' Another kiss. 'Because mad and bad as I thought you were, I couldn't forget you. And I thought it was worth a little drive to Middledip to find out what your husband situation was.'

'Really?' She tipped her head back.

'Truly.' He nibbled her throat.

'Positive?' She sniffed.

He blew gently between her breasts. 'Why do you think I've been hanging around like some loser with a crush? I do love Shona, but Cleo ...' He raised his mouth to hover over hers. 'I've loved you since you climbed off that jet-ski, fully dressed, soaked to the skin, and laughing.'

Epilogue

She was home before him, letting Shona run in first, following on with the mother's burden of toys, jacket and backpack as well as her own bag of pens, badges and handouts that she'd need for work the next day. The house was warm and welcoming in the sunshine and much fresher now she'd gone through almost every room with the magnolia paint.

She'd been dying to come home all day. It had been a real Monday kind of long day, the weekend still fresh in her mind and the working week repellent. Probably because she'd spent the weekend in a cloud of happiness. So much happiness her legs felt weak. So much sex her life had gone funny.

Briskly, she dumped her burdens in the kitchen and began putting the finishing touches to the evening meal, answering Shona's stream of words and nearly-words until she heard the front door open. Instantly, she was deserted as Shona trundled energetically into the hall. 'Jussin!'

'Sho-naaaaa!'

A fit of giggles and a happy shriek, then Shona reappeared upside down over Justin's shoulder.

Cleo's heart missed a beat as Justin yanked Cleo to him for a kiss, his lips hot and hard on hers, while Shona continued to squeal with pleasure from behind his back. 'Do you know I've got to adopt Shona if I want normal parental rights?'

Wrong-footed by his plunging into such an unexpected conversation, Cleo broke away to shuffle the cutlery onto the table. 'I think I did know that. I'd forgotten. But you can do that, can't you? It's only sensible.'

'It's not sensible, it's stupid because she's my daughter. I thought it might be good if we all had the same name and when I looked into it I found out all this other legal stuff. It's unreal!' He swivelled Shona right side up.

Cleo stared at him. A flush of shock began to creep up her body. She said, faintly, 'But we don't have the same name.'

'Ah.' He put Shona down. Very slowly he leaned forward and kissed Cleo's eyelids. 'I think it'll be better if we're all Mullarkey, for Shona's sake. What do you think?'

She turned to stir the sauce, letting her hair slide down and cover her face. 'I'll tell you when I know what you're actually asking.' She turned to drain the carrots, hoping that he'd think that it was the steam that was making her face so red.

Silence.

She flicked a glance behind her as she returned the carrots to the hob. And then stopped dead! 'Oh *Justin*!' she wailed, almost dropping the pan. 'That wall's only just been painted.'

Guiltily, he examined the pen in his hand. 'It's one of those for a whiteboard, isn't it? It'll wipe off?'

She began to laugh. 'It's for a flip chart! It's called a *marker*.'

'Oh.'

On the wall, black on the fresh cream wall, it said: *I love you. I want to marry you. Love Justin.*

Slowly, he picked up a cloth and wiped at the corner of the final 'n'. It didn't come off.

He grinned. 'That's fine. It's permanent.'

About the Author

Sue Moorcroft is an accomplished writer of novels and short stories, as well as a creative writing tutor.

Her previous novels include *Starting Over*, *Uphill All the Way* and *A Place to Call Home*.

She is also the commissioning editor and a contributor to *Loves Me, Loves Me Not*, an anthology of short stories celebrating the Romantic Novelists' Association's 50th anniversary.

www.suemoorcroft.com
www.suemoorcroft.wordpress.com
www.twitter.com/suemoorcroft

More Choc Lit

Why not try something else from the Choc Lit selection?

**New home, new friends, new love.
Can starting over be that simple?**

Tess Riddell reckons her beloved Freelander is more
reliable than any man – especially her ex-fiancé, Olly Gray.
She's moving on from her old life and into the perfect
cottage in the country.

Miles Rattenbury's passions? Old cars and new women!
Romance? He's into fun rather than commitment. When
Tess crashes the Freelander into his breakdown truck, they
find that they're nearly neighbours – yet worlds apart.
Despite her overprotective parents and a suddenly attentive
Olly, she discovers the joys of village life and even forms
an unlikely friendship with Miles. Then, just as their
relationship develops into something deeper, an old flame
comes looking for him...

Is their love strong enough to overcome the past? Or will
it take more than either of them is prepared to give?

ISBN: 978-1-906931-22-3

Juliet Archer

The Importance of Being *Emma*

A modern retelling of Jane Austen's *Emma*.

Mark Knightley – handsome, clever, rich – is used to women falling at his feet. Except Emma Woodhouse, who's like part of the family – and the furniture. When their relationship changes dramatically, is it an ending or a new beginning?

Emma's grown into a stunningly attractive young woman, full of ideas for modernising her family business.
Then Mark gets involved and the sparks begin to fly. It's just like the old days, except that now he's seeing her through totally new eyes.

While Mark struggles to keep his feelings in check, Emma remains immune to the Knightley charm. She's never forgotten that embarrassing moment when he discovered her teenage crush on him. He's still pouring scorn on all her projects, especially her beautifully orchestrated campaign to find Mr Right for her ditzy PA. And finally, when the mysterious Flynn Churchill – the man of her dreams – turns up, how could she have eyes for anyone else?

The Importance of Being Emma was shortlisted for the 2009 Melissa Nathan Award for Comedy Romance.

ISBN: 978-1-906931-20-9

30 June 2010:

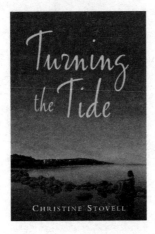

All's fair in love and war?
Depends on who's making the rules.

Harry Watling has spent the past five years keeping
her father's boat yard afloat, despite its dying clientele.
Now all she wants to do is enjoy the peace and quiet of
her sleepy backwater.

So when property developer Matthew Corrigan wants
to turn the boat yard into an upmarket housing complex for
his exotic new restaurant, it's like declaring war.

And the odds seem to be stacked in Matthew's favour.
He's got the colourful locals on board, his hard-to-please
girlfriend is warming to the idea and he has the means to
force Harry's hand. Meanwhile, Harry has to fight not just
his plans but also her feelings for the man himself.

Then a family secret from the past creates heartbreak
for Harry, and neither of them is prepared for
what happens next …

ISBN: 978-1-906931-25-4

September 2010:

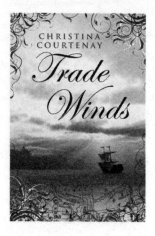

Marriage of convenience – or a love for life?

It's 1732 in Gothenburg, Sweden, and strong-willed
Jess van Sandt knows only too well that it's a man's world.
She believes she's being swindled out of her inheritance by
her stepfather – and she's determined to stop it.

When help appears in the unlikely form of handsome
Scotsman Killian Kinross, himself disinherited by his
grandfather, Jess finds herself both intrigued and infuriated
by him. In an attempt to recover her fortune, she proposes
a marriage of convenience. Then Killian is offered the
chance of a lifetime with the Swedish East India Company's
Expedition and he's determined that nothing will stand in
his way, not even his new bride.

He sets sail on a daring voyage to the Far East, believing
he's put his feelings and past behind him. But the journey
doesn't quite work out as he expects....

ISBN: 978-1-906931-23-0

Introducing the Choc Lit Club

Join us at the Choc Lit Club where we're
creating a delicious selection of romantic fiction
for today's independent woman.
Where heroes are like chocolate – irresistible!

Join our authors in Author's Corner, read author interviews
and see our featured books that have been recommended
and rated by our readers and the Choc Lit Tasting Panel.

If you have a favourite novel with an irresistible hero,
then let us know.

We'd also love to hear how you enjoyed
All That Mullarkey. Just visit www.choc-lit.co.uk
and give your feedback. Describe Justin in
terms of chocolate and you could be our
Flavour of the Month Winner!